"You wer⋯⋯⋯ ⋯⋯⋯⋯ champion this night."

He took her hand, long fingers closing around hers . . . and hesitated. Amanda looked into his eyes. Then he bowed and released her.

"Hells like Mellors are no place for you, but I fancy you've realized that." He reached into his pocket and drew out a silver card case. He extracted a card and offered it between two fingers. "So you know where to send for the mare. Leave a message and one of my grooms will bring her around. Good-bye, Miss Cynster."

She brightly reiterated her thanks. As he turned away, she glanced at the card. "Good God!"

The exclamation escaped her despite years of training. She couldn't, at first, drag her eyes from the it—a simple, expensive rectangle of white with a gold crest. Beneath the crest was stamped one word: *Dexter*. It was a name that turned her world upside down.

"You're Dexter?"

He raised one brow, cynical, yes, but world-weary as well. "Who else?"

STEPHANIE LAURENS

On A Wild Night

AVON BOOKS
An Imprint of HarperCollinsPublishers

HarperCollins*Publishers*
77-85 Fulham Palace Road
Hammersmith
London W6 8JB

Copyright © 2002 by Savdek Management Proprietory Ltd.

ISBN: 0 00 773968 0
www.avonromance.com

This edition published 2005
First Avon Books paperback printing: April 2002

Avon Trademark Reg. U.S. Pat. Off. and in Other Countries, Marca Registrada, Hecho en U.S.A.
HarperCollins® is a registered trademark of HarperCollins Publishers Inc.

Printed and bound in Great Britain by Clays Ltd, St Ives plc

On A Wild Night

The Bar Cynster Family Tree

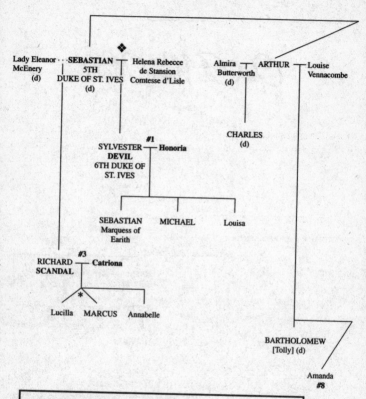

Lady Eleanor McEnery (d) ··· **SEBASTIAN 5TH DUKE OF ST. IVES** (d) ❖ — Helena Rebecce de Stansion Comtesse d'Lisle

Almira Butterworth (d) — **ARTHUR** — Louise Vennacombe

SYLVESTER DEVIL 6TH DUKE OF ST. IVES — **#1** Honoria

CHARLES (d)

SEBASTIAN Marquess of Earith   MICHAEL   Louisa

RICHARD SCANDAL — **#3** Catriona

*

Lucilla   MARCUS   Annabelle

BARTHOLOMEW [Tolly] (d)

Amanda **#8**

THE CYNSTER NOVELS

#1 *Devil's Bride*
#2 *A Rake's Vow*
#3 *Scandal's Bride*
#4 *A Rogue's Proposal*
#5 *A Secret Love*

#6 *All About Love*
#7 *All About Passion*
#8 *This Volume*
#9 *On a Wicked Dawn*
  (May 2002 from Avon)

❖ *Special—The Promise in a Kiss*

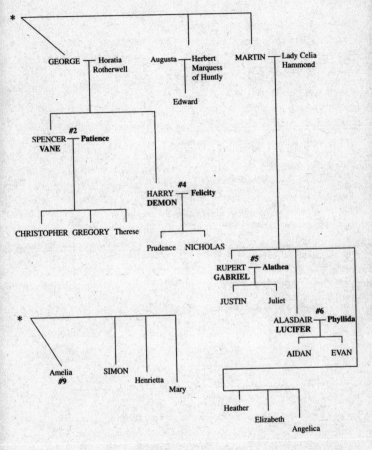

MALE CYNSTERS in capitals   * denotes twins

Chapter 1

Upper Brook Street, London
February 20, 1825

"It's *hopeless!*" Amanda Cynster flopped on her back on her twin sister's bed. "There is simply no gentleman in the ton worth considering—not at present."

"There hasn't been for the last five years—well, not gentlemen interested in taking a wife." Stretched beside Amanda, Amelia stared up at the canopy. "We've searched and searched—"

"Turned every stone."

"And the only ones even vaguely interesting are . . . not interested."

"It's ludicrous!"

"It's depressing."

Alike in both feature and figure, blessed with blond ringlets, cornflower blue eyes and porcelain complexions, the twins could easily have posed for *La Belle Assemblée* as the epitome of well-bred fashionable young ladies, except for their expressions. Amelia looked disgusted, Amanda mutinous. "I refuse to lower my standards."

They'd discussed their requirements in a husband *ad infinitum* over the years. Their standards did not materially differ from those espoused by their mentors—their mother and aunts, their cousins' wives. They were surrounded by strong women, ladies all, who had, one and all, found happiness in their marriages. The twins had little doubt as to the qualities they sought.

A gentleman who loved them, who would set them and the family they would raise above all other considerations. A protector, a helpmate, with a reliable, strong arm who would always be there to keep them safe. A man who valued their skills, intelligence and opinions, who would accept them as an equal however much he wished to be lord and master of his world. A gentleman of sufficient substance to render their not-inconsiderable dowries by-the-by; a man of their world well connected enough to take the powerful Cynster clan in his stride.

A man of passion and family feeling—lover, protector, partner. Husband.

Amanda humphed. "There have to be *some* out there who measure up to our cousins"—the Bar Cynster, that notorious group of six who had for so long lorded it over the ton, leaving uncounted ladies languishing in their wake until, one by one, fate had snared their hearts. "They can't be unique."

"They're not. Think of Chillingworth."

"True—but when I do, I think of Lady Francesca, so that's not much help. He's already taken."

"He's too old, anyway. We need someone nearer our age."

"But not too near—I've had my fill of earnest young men." It had been a road-to-Damascus revelation when they'd realized that their cousins—those arrogant, dictatorial males they had for so long fought to be free of—were in fact the embodiment of their ideals. The realization had thrown the shortcomings of the current candidates for their hands into even more dismal relief. "If we're ever to find husbands, we're going to have to *do* something!"

"We need a plan."

"One different to last year's, or the year before that's!" Amanda glanced at Amelia; her twin's expression was abstracted, eyes fixed on some vision only she could see. "You look as if you have one."

Amelia glanced her way. "No, not a plan. Not yet. But

there *are* suitable gentlemen, only they aren't on the lookout for a wife. I can think of at least one, and there must be others. I was thinking . . . maybe we should stop waiting and take matters into our own hands."

"I couldn't agree more, but what are you proposing?"

Amelia's jaw firmed. "I'm sick of waiting—we're *twenty-three*! I want to be married by June. Once the Season starts, I'm going to reassess and make a new list of candidates, regardless of whether they're thinking of marriage or not. Then I intend picking the one that suits *me* best, and taking steps to ensure he accompanies me to the altar."

That last phrase rang with determination. Amanda studied Amelia's profile. Many thought she was the stubborn one, the stronger, more overtly confident one. Amelia appeared so much quieter, yet in reality, once Amelia set her sights on a goal it was well nigh impossible to turn her from it.

All of which begged the point.

"You sly minx—you've got your eye on someone."

Amelia wrinkled her nose. "I do, but I'm not sure. He may not be the best choice—if you disregard the caveat that they should be looking for a bride, then there are a lot more to chose from."

"True." Amanda flopped onto her back. "But not for me. I've looked." A moment passed. "Are you going to tell me who he is, or should I guess?"

"Neither." Amelia glanced at her. "I don't know for certain that he's the one, and you might inadvertently give away my interest if you know."

Weighing the likelihood, Amanda had to admit it was real; dissembling wasn't her strong suit. "Very well, but how do you intend ensuring he accompanies you to the altar?"

"I don't know, but I'll do whatever is necessary to get him there."

The grimly determined vow sent a shiver down Amanda's spine. She knew perfectly well what "whatever is necessary" encompassed. It was a risky strategy, yet she had little doubt Amelia, with her core of steel, could follow it to victory.

Amelia glanced at her. "What about you? What of your plan? You needn't bother telling me you don't have one."

Amanda grinned. That was the best of being twins—they followed each other's thoughts instinctively. "I've already looked through the ton, and not just among those who've deigned to worship at our dainty feet. I've concluded that, as I can't find a gentleman within the ton, then I need to search *outside* it."

"Where will you find marriageable gentlemen *outside* the ton?"

"Where did our cousins spend most of their evenings before they married?"

"They used to attend some of the balls and parties."

"Ah, but think back and you'll recall they attended on sufferance, danced twice, then left. They only appeared because our aunts insisted. Not all suitable gentlemen—gentlemen *we* would consider eligible *partis*—have female relatives capable of compelling their attendance within the ton."

"So . . ." Amelia refocused on Amanda's face. "You'll search for eligible partis in the private clubs and gaming hells—gentlemen we haven't yet met because they don't, or don't often, appear in our circle."

"Precisely—in the clubs and hells, and at the private parties held in various ladies' salons."

"Mmm . . . It seems a good plan."

"I believe it has great potential." Amanda considered Amelia's face. "Do you want to search with me? There's sure to be more than one eligible *parti* hiding in the shadows."

Amelia met her gaze, then looked past her; after a moment, her twin shook her head. "No. If I wasn't determined . . . but I am."

Their gazes locked, thoughts in perfect communion, then Amanda nodded. "It's time to part ways." She grinned and gestured dramatically. "You to wield your wiles under the light of the chandeliers . . ."

"While you?"

"While I seek my destiny in the shadows."

There were shadows aplenty in the main room of Mellors, the newest, most dangerously fashionable gaming hell; resisting an urge to peer into them, Amanda paused on the threshold and coolly surveyed the company.

While they, not so coolly, surveyed her.

Four of six round tables were circled by gentlemen, hard-eyed and heavy-lidded, glasses by their elbows, cards in their hands. Their gazes swept insolently over her; Amanda ignored them. A larger table hosted a game of faro; two ladies clung, sirenlike, to two of the players. The banker looked directly at Amanda, froze as if he'd just remembered something, then looked down and turned the next card.

Beside Amanda, Reggie Carmarthen, childhood friend and exceedingly reluctant escort, surreptitiously tweaked her sleeve. "Nothing here, really. If we leave now, we can make it to the Henrys' before supper's over."

Completing her survey, Amanda met Reggie's gaze. "How can you tell there's nothing here? We've barely arrived and the corners are dark."

The owners had decorated the rooms off Duke Street with dark brown flocked wallpaper, matching leather chairs and wooden tables. Lit only by well-spaced wall sconces, the result was a shadowy, distinctly masculine den. Amanda glanced around. A sense of danger swept her, a skittery sensation washing over her skin. She lifted her chin. "Let me do the rounds. If there's truly *nothing* of interest, then we can leave." Reggie knew what particular *thing* she was searching for, even if he definitely didn't approve. Linking her arm in his, she smiled. "You can't sound the retreat quite so soon."

"Meaning you won't listen even if I do."

They were conversing in muted tones in deference to the concentration of those playing. Amanda steered Reggie toward the tables, doing nothing to shatter the assumption anyone seeing them would make—that Reggie was her cavalier and she'd talked him into bringing her here for a dare. She had talked him into it, but her purpose was a great deal more scandalous than a dare.

Being new, the hell had attracted the most dangerous bucks and blades searching for the latest in dissipation. If she'd found any *thing* to her taste in the more established venues, she would never have considered coming here. But she'd been doing the rounds of the established hells and salons for the past fortnight; her presence here tonight, in a room where the only familiar faces besides Reggie's were ones she would prefer not to acknowledge, was a measure of her desperation.

Parading on Reggie's arm, pretending an innocent, wholly spurious interest in the games, she cast her jaded eye over the players, and rejected every one.

Where, she inwardly wailed, was the gentleman for her?

They reached the last table and paused. The room was deep, stretching double the length they'd already traversed. Unrelieved gloom enveloped the area before them, the glow cast by two wall lamps the only illumination. Large armchairs were grouped here and there, their occupants barely discernible. Small tables stood between the armchairs; Amanda saw a long-fingered white hand languidly toss a card onto one polished top. It was patently clear that this end of the room hosted the truly serious play.

The truly dangerous players.

Before she could decide whether she was game to enter what loomed as a lair, one of the groups they'd passed ended their game. Cards slapped the table, jests mingled with curses; chairs scraped.

With Reggie, Amanda turned—and found herself the object of four pairs of male eyes, all hard, overbright. All fixed, intently, on her.

The nearest of the four men rose. To his full height, a head taller than Reggie. One of his companions joined him on his feet. And smiled.

Wolfishly.

The first gentleman didn't even smile. He took one insolently swaggering step forward—then his gaze went past them and he hesitated.

"Well, well—if it isn't little Miss Cynster. Come to see how the other half enjoys itself, have you?"

Amanda swiveled regally; despite the fact the speaker was taller than she, she looked down her nose at him. When she saw who it was, she lifted her chin higher. "Lord Connor." She curtsied—he was an earl, after all—but she made the deference a triviality; her social standing was higher than his.

The earl was a reprobate cut to a pattern for which they'd thankfully lost the card. His reputation painted him as lecherous, steeped in vice, disreputable in the extreme; the liquid gleam in his pale eyes, the lid of one of which, courtesy of some ancient duel, was permanently at half-mast, suggested that in his case rumor understated the fact. Corpulent—indeed, wider than he was tall—Connor had a plodding gait, pallid skin and heavy jowls, making him appear old enough to be her father, except that his hair was a solid dark brown.

"Well? Are you here to gawk, or are you game to play?" Connor's fleshy lips curved in a taunting smile; the lines years of dissipation had etched in his face deepened. "Surely, now you've braved the doors of Mellors, you won't leave without chancing your dainty hand? Without trying your Cynster luck? I hear you've been quite successful in your forays on the town."

Reggie locked his fingers about her wrist. "Actually, we were just—"

"Looking for the right challenge? Let's see if I can accommodate you. Shall we say a rubber of whist?"

Amanda didn't look at Reggie—she knew what he was thinking, but she'd be damned if she'd turn tail and run just because a man of Connor's ilk approached her. She allowed amused haughtiness to infuse her expression. "I cannot conceive, my lord, that triumphing over a novice such as myself would afford you any great amusement."

"On the contrary"—Connor's voice hardened—"I'm expecting to be amused come what may." He smiled, an evil eel fixing on his prey. "I've heard you're a dab hand with the cards—surely you won't pass up this chance to test your skills against mine?"

"No!" Reggie hissed *sotto voce*.

Amanda knew she should coolly dismiss Connor and let Reggie lead her away, but she couldn't—simply could not—stomach the thought that Connor and every gentleman present would smirk knowingly at her departing back, and laugh about her once she was gone.

"Whist?" she heard herself say. Beside her, Reggie groaned.

She was well versed in the game and was indeed lucky with cards, but she wasn't fool enough to think herself in Connor's league. She pretended to consider his proposal, conscious that all eyes had turned their way, then she shook her head, a dismissive smile on her lips. "I think—"

"I've a pretty little mare, pure Arab—bought her for breeding, but she's proving deuced picky, altogether un-amenable. She should suit you well." The comment was just glib enough not to rate as an insult. Connor smiled, very definitely too knowing. "Beat your cousin to her, as a matter of fact."

That last comment, thrown in no doubt to pique her interest, pricked her pride instead.

"*No!*" Reggie insisted, his whisper despairing.

Amanda locked gazes with Connor and raised a haughty brow; her smile had disappeared. "A mare, you say?"

Connor nodded, somewhat distracted. "Worth a small fortune." His tone suggested he was having second thoughts about the wisdom of his wager.

For one instant, Amanda teetered on the brink of accepting his challenge, then caution reared its head. If she rejected Connor, playing a rubber with some of the blades watching would be sufficient to prevent her being labelled a silly chit out of her depth, a dilettante. She couldn't afford to be contemptuously dismissed by the crowd she suspected harbored her future husband. But how to slide out of Connor's trap?

The answer was blindingly obvious. Letting her lips curve, she murmured, "How intriguing. Unfortunately, I have nothing I'd care to wager against such a valuable stake."

Turning away, she let her gaze meet those of the two blades who had started to approach. Blatantly considered them. They straightened.

Connor growled, "Not even three hours of your time?"

She swung back to face him. "Three hours?"

"Three hours, to be spent by my side"—Connor waved magnanimously—"in whatever surroundings you choose." The last phrase was delivered with an intense leer.

He was laughing at her. If she ran away, everyone would laugh at her.

She'd laugh derisively at herself.

Amanda lifted her chin. "My time is exceedingly valuable."

Connor's lip curled. "You don't say?"

"But I daresay this mare of yours is valuable, too." Her heart was thumping. She smiled condescendingly. "Well, she must be if Demon was interested." She brightened. "If I win, I'll give her to him."

He'd wring her neck.

Reggie's groan was audible. Amanda smiled into Connor's pale eyes. "A rubber of whist, I believe you said?"

She'd finally stepped over the line into real danger. Even as she said the words, even as she registered the hardening in Connor's eyes, Amanda felt a thrill beyond anything she'd ever known. Anticipation laced with dread flowed through her; exhilaration drove her. "Your partner?" She looked inquiringly at Connor.

Expressionless, he waved back into the gloom. "Meredith."

A thin gentleman rose from an armchair and stiffly bowed.

"He says little but has an excellent head for cards." Connor's gaze traveled to Reggie. "And who will partner you, Miss Cynster? Carmarthen, here?"

"No." Reggie's tone declared he'd drawn a line and would not be tempted over it. He shook Amanda's arm. "This is madness! Come away *now!* What do you care what such hellions think of you?"

She did care—therein lay the rub. She couldn't explain it, yet she couldn't imagine any of her cousins walking away from Connor's thinly veiled insults. Not before they'd exacted retribution.

His Arab mare sounded like just the right amount of retribution. And if she lost, she'd take great delight in stipulating just *where* she would spend her three hours at his side. Retribution indeed. That would teach him to make game of Cynster ladies, however young.

But first she had to find a partner, preferably one who would help her win. She didn't waste a second persuading Reggie—he could barely remember the suits. Smiling reassuringly, trying to ease his concern, she turned to survey the tables at which all activity had ceased.

There had to be some gentleman willing to come to her aid . . .

Her heart plummeted. There was no lighthearted interest, none of the game-to-be-part-of-any-lark expressions she'd expected to see. Calculation, raw and undisguised, filled every man's eyes. The equation they were weighing was easy to grasp: How much would she give to be rescued from Connor?

One glance was enough. To them she was a succulent, innocent pigeon ripe for a plucking. Exhilaration deserted her; a deadening, sinking feeling dragged at her.

Given the precise words of their wager, she was confident she had Connor's measure, but if, in order to satisfy her pride, she took one of these men as her partner, where would that leave her at the end of the game?

Triumphant regardless of the outcome, but with another, possibly more dangerous debt hanging over her head.

She met eye after eye; her heart sank to her slippers. Surely there was *one* gentleman honorable enough to partner her purely for the hell of it?

Smiles slowly dawned; chairs scraped. A number of gentlemen stood . . .

It would have to be Reggie, no matter how much she had to plead.

As she turned to him, the attention of the gentlemen facing them was deflected, caught by some sight in the shadows behind them, deeper in the room.

Both she and Reggie turned.

Something large stirred in the gloom.

A dark shape rose from a chair at the end of the room—a man, broad-shouldered and tall. With a languid grace all the more compelling, given his size, he walked unhurriedly toward them.

The shadows fell from him as he neared; light reached him and illuminated details. A coat that could only have come from one of the ton's foremost tailors topped trousers that skimmed muscled thighs before sweeping down long legs; an ivory cravat intricately tied and a rich satin waistcoat completed the picture, one of expensive elegance. His carriage, effortless and aloof, exuded confidence and more—an absolute belief in his ability to succeed, regardless of the challenge.

His hair was thick, brown, falling in fashionable disarray about his head, shading his broad brow, brushing his collar. Candlelight reflected from lighter strands, turning the whole into a tawny mane.

He neared, his approach in no way threatening, yet there was a sense of force distilled and harnessed in each long, prowling stride.

At the last, the shadows gave up their hold and revealed his face.

Amanda caught her breath.

Sharp bones rode high above the austere sweep of his cheeks, lean, lightly shadowed where they met his jaw, uncompromisingly square. His nose was straight, definite, a clear indication of his antecedents; his eyes were large, heavy lidded, set beneath sweeping brows. As for his lips, the upper was straight, the lower full and frankly sensual. His was a face she recognized instantly, not in specific but in general. A face as elegantly aristocratic as his clothes, as powerful and definite as his carriage.

Eyes the color of moss agates met hers, held her gaze as he halted before her.

Not a hint of the predatory reached her; she searched but could find no trace of disguised intent in his changeable eyes. Understanding was what she saw, what she sensed—that, and self-deprecatory amusement.

"If you're in need of a partner, I would be honored to assist you."

The voice suited the body—deep, slightly gravelly—rusty, as if underused. Amanda felt his words as much as heard them, felt her senses leap. His gaze didn't shift from her face, although his eyes left hers to travel quickly over her features before returning, once more, to her eyes. Although he hadn't looked at Reggie, Amanda knew he was aware of her friend tugging at her sleeve, hissing disjointed injunctions.

"Thank you." She trusted him—trusted those moss agate eyes. Even if she was wrong, she didn't care. "Miss Amanda Cynster." She extended her hand. "And you are?"

He took her hand; his lips curved as he bowed. "Martin."

She sincerely doubted he was Mr. Martin—Lord Martin, then. She vaguely recalled hearing of a Lord Martin.

Releasing her hand, Martin turned to Connor. "I assume you have no objection?"

Following his gaze, Amanda realized that Connor did indeed have an objection. A serious one, if the scowl in his eyes spoke true. Perfect! Perhaps Connor would now draw back . . .

Even as the thought formed, she realized how unlikely that would be. Men and their ridiculous rules!

Sure enough, Connor brusquely nodded in assent. He would have liked to protest, but felt he couldn't.

Amanda glanced at Reggie. His expression was utterly defeated, utterly aghast. He opened his mouth—his gaze flicked past her, then slowly he shut his lips tight. "I hope you know what you're doing."

His mutter reached her as she turned to her new partner.

Martin was looking at Connor. "Perhaps we should get started." He waved into the shadows.

"Indeed." Turning, Connor stumped into the gloom. "The night hours are winging."

Considering the shadows, Amanda suppressed a grimace. She looked up to find Martin's gaze on her face, then he looked over her head toward the main door. "Two fresh packs, Mellors." Martin glanced down at her again. "And two lighted candelabras."

He hesitated, then offered her his arm. "Shall we?"

She smiled and placed her hand on his sleeve, instantly aware of the steely strength beneath it. He guided her toward the corner where Connor and Meredith stood waiting.

"Are you a good player, sir?"

Lips quirking, he glanced down at her. "I'm considered to play a tolerable hand."

"Good, because Connor's an expert, and I'm not. And I think he plays often with Meredith."

After an instant, Martin asked, "How well do you play?"

"Reasonably well, but I'm not in Connor's class."

"In that case, we shall do." He lowered his voice as they neared the others. "Play straight—don't try to be clever. Leave that to me."

Those were all the instructions he had time for, but they were clear enough. Amanda adhered to them as the first game got under way. They had the corner to themselves. Reggie slouched in an armchair some yards away, broodingly watching. Connor sat on her left, Meredith to her right. When Mellors arrived with the candelabras, both Connor and Meredith flinched.

Unperturbed, Martin instructed Mellors to place the candlesticks on small tables on either side of her chair. Connor shot Martin a venomous look but said nothing; Martin, it seemed, wielded the sort of authority few dared question. Bathed in golden light, she felt a great deal more comfortable; relaxing, she found it easier to concentrate.

The first game was a series of trials, Connor testing her strength and Martin's, too, while Martin assessed both Connor and Meredith, at the same time watching her play closely. As often happened, the cards fell her way, but capitalizing against an opponent of Connor's caliber was no easy task. Nevertheless, with Martin's guidance, they triumphed and took the first game.

With the rubber decided on the best of three games, Amanda was delighted. Sitting back, she stretched her arms, smiling at Mellors when he served her a glass of champagne. Glasses were dispensed all around; she took a gulp, then sipped. The men finished theirs in two mouthfuls; Mellors topped up the glasses, including hers.

Martin cut, Connor dealt and the second game began.

As hand followed hand, Martin was, for the first time in a long time, unsure whether he would win. Even more surprisingly, he cared, not for himself, but for the angel who sat across from him, candlelight laying a tracery of gold over her fair hair. It was lush, thick, lustrous. His fingers itched to touch, to stroke, and not only her hair. Her complexion was flawless, that milky perfection found only among certain English damsels. Many struggled to attain the same effect with potions and creams, but in Amanda Cynster's case, her skin was natural, unblemished alabaster.

As for her eyes, they were cornflower blue, the same shade as the most expensive sapphires. Jewels by any name, those eyes were curiously innocent, aware yet . . . she was not naive, but was as yet untouched by worldly cynicism. The dross of life had yet to tarnish her. She was a virgin, he had not a doubt.

For a connoisseur of his highly developed, distinctly exotic tastes, she was the perfect English rose.

Just waiting to be plucked.

She very likely would have been as an outcome of this night if he hadn't stepped in. What the devil she was doing here, swanning through the latest hell like a lure in a pond full of hungry trout, he couldn't conceive.

In truth, he didn't want to think too much of her, of her thoughts, her actions, her desires. His only motive in hauling her out of the hole she'd fallen into was purely altruistic. He'd seen her trying to avoid old Connor while still retaining her pride; he'd understood why she'd dug in her heels, made a stand, then flown in the face of all wisdom and accepted Connor's wager.

He knew very well what it meant to lose one's pride.

But once they won and she was safe, he'd walk away, return to the shadows where he belonged.

Regretfully, admittedly, but he'd do it nonetheless.

She was not for him and never would be. He'd left her world long ago.

The last trick fell to Connor. Martin scanned the tally Connor was keeping on the table between them. One more hand, and unless the gods intervened, Connor and Meredith would take the current game, evening the score.

Time to change tactics.

The next hand went as he expected. Connor crowed and called for more champagne as he shuffled for the first hand of the deciding game. Noting the faint flush in his partner's fair cheeks, Martin beckoned Mellors closer as the man bent to fill his glass, and murmured his own instructions.

Mellors had a nice appreciation of who was who among his wealthier patrons; passing back by Amanda's chair, he clipped the candelabra, grabbed to steady it and instead knocked her glass—the glass he'd just filled with fine French champagne—to the floor. With copious apologies, Mellors retrieved the glass and promised to bring another.

He did, sometime later, as they were nearing the end of the first hand.

Amanda studied her cards and waited for Connor to lead. Neither she nor any of the others had yet played a false card—they'd done the best possible with the hands they'd been dealt. Luck, to date, had been the deciding factor.

Not a comforting thought. Especially as Connor had proved to be even more expert than she'd suspected. If it hadn't been for the large, reassuring figure seated opposite her, languidly tossing cards across Connor's, she'd have panicked long ago. Not that spending three hours in Connor's company was all that worrisome, but how to do so safely without her family hearing of it . . . that aspect had only occurred to her once they'd started the second game.

Now it exercised her greatly. Losing to Connor would not help her search for a husband at all. Damn the man. Why had he had to challenge her, especially as he had, triggering her temper and her pride?

Still, that challenge had brought Martin out of the shadows . . .

She concentrated on her cards, steadfastly keeping her senses from stealing across the table. That she couldn't afford, not at present; once they won, she could indulge said senses all she wished. That promise, dangling before her, kept her wits focused. The cards fell; the temperature increased. She reached for her glass, sipped.

Frowned, and sipped again. Frown easing, she gulped gratefully.

Water.

"Your play, my dear."

She smiled at Connor; setting aside her glass, she considered briefly, then trumped his ace. A smile flickered over Martin's lips; she refused to stare and carefully led another trump.

They won the hand, but the points were sparse. Connor was not inclined to grant them any favors. Hand followed hand, fought tooth and nail. Martin was playing more aggressively, but so, too, was Connor.

By the fourth hand, Martin could with absolute confidence state that the Earl of Connor was the finest player he'd ever had the pleasure of opposing. Unfortunately, that pleasure was muted by the wager hanging on the game's outcome. Both he and Connor were pressing every advantage in a duel of feints and misleads. Thus far, Amanda had adhered to his injunction; he prayed she wouldn't get distracted by his or Connor's tactics.

Time and again, she would glance at him, worrying her full lower lip between small white teeth. He'd meet her gaze, hold it . . . as if gaining strength from that fragile contact, she'd draw breath, then play her card—straight and true, as he'd asked. For a female, she was proving surprisingly good at holding to a difficult line. His respect for her grew as the cards continued to fall.

The candles burned down. Mellors came to replace them. All four players sat back and waited, grasping the moment to rest eyes and minds.

They'd been playing for hours.

Martin, Connor and Meredith were used to all-night games. Amanda was not. Tiredness dulled her eyes even though she fought to keep it at bay. When she stifled a yawn, Martin felt Connor glance—surprisingly—at him.

He met the old reprobate's gaze. Sharp as a lance, it rested heavily on him, as if Connor was trying to see into his soul. Martin raised his brows. Connor hesitated, then turned back to the cards. They were neck and neck, two points each, but the hands continued to turn without adding to either result, so evenly were they matched.

He dealt the next hand and they continued.

It was experience, in the end, that handed them the game. Even so, when the habitual counter in Martin's head alerted him to the revoke, he didn't immediately call it.

Why Connor would make such a mistake was difficult to see. Even had he been wilting, which he wasn't. Anyone could make a mistake, true enough—Martin was sure Connor would offer precisely those words if asked.

He waited until the last trick was played. He and Amanda had gained one point on the hand. Before Connor could sweep up the cards, Martin murmured, "If you'll turn up the last four tricks . . . ?"

Connor glanced at him, then did. The revoke was instantly apparent. Connor stared at the cards, then blew out a breath. "Damn! My apologies."

Amanda blinked at the cards, then raised her eyes to Martin's face, a question in the blue.

He felt his lips curve. "We've won."

Her lips formed an O. She looked down at the cards with greater interest. With increasing delight.

The crowd watching from afar had dwindled, but all present now woke up, leaving the tables to learn of the outcome. Within minutes, an excited hum of conversation and exclamation lapped around them.

Against it, Connor, in quite gentlemanly vein, considering the circumstances, explained his fault to Amanda, and how the penalty had handed them the game and thus the rubber. Then, with an almost comical switch in his tone, he pushed back his chair and stood. "Well! That's that, then!"

He scowled down at Amanda.

Amanda blinked, wary of the mischievous, malicious light that gleamed in Connor's eyes.

"I'll send the mare around first thing tomorrow morning—Upper Brook Street, ain't it? Enjoy her in good health."

That last was said with unholy glee.

Reality crashed down on her. "No! Wait—" Where the devil was she to stable this horse? How could she explain how she'd come by such an animal? And it was odds on that Demon, currently in town, would drop by the instant he heard, recognize the beast, know to whom it had belonged—and start asking all manner of awkward questions.

"Let me think . . ." She glanced at Reggie, blinking owlishly, half asleep. No help there; Reggie resided with his parents and his mother was her mother's bosom-bow. "Perhaps . . ." She glanced at Connor, still standing over her. Could she refuse the horse? Or, given the incomprehensible slew of rules surrounding male wagers, was even suggesting such a thing a base insult?

"I daresay—" Martin's deep voice, cool and calm, cut across her whirling thoughts.

She and Connor turned to him, a conquering hero elegantly at ease in the large chair, a glass of champagne in one long-fingered hand.

"—that Miss Cynster might not have room in her stables at present for the mare." His changeable green gaze fixed on her face. "My stables are large and only half full. If you wish, Connor can send the mare to my establishment and you may send word whenever you wish to ride her, or to move her, once you've had time to make the necessary arrangements."

Relief swept her. The man was a godsend in more ways than one. She beamed. "Thank you. That would suit admirably." She glanced up at Connor. "If you would be so good, my lord, as to deliver the mare to Lord Martin's house?"

Connor stared down at her, his expression inscrutable. "Lord Martin's house, heh?" Then he nodded. "Very well. Consider it done." He hesitated, then reached down, took her hand and bowed. "You play remarkably well for a female,

my dear, but you're not in my class—or his." With his head
he indicated Martin. "In your future forays into the hells,
you'd be wise to remember that."

Amanda smiled sweetly. Thanks to Connor's wager, the
need for further forays into the hells had evaporated, and she
had no intention of forgetting Martin.

Releasing her hand, Connor stumped off. Meredith, who
had said not a word throughout, rose stiffly, bowed, and
murmured, "It was a pleasure, Miss Cynster."

With that, he followed Connor through the gloom and
away.

Amanda turned to Martin and favored him with her best
smile. "Thank you for your offer, my lord—I would indeed
find it difficult to accommodate the mare on such short notice."

He regarded her steadily, that gentle, somewhat wistful
amusement very evident, at least to her. "So I would imagine." He raised his glass to her, then drained it and set it
down. He rose; she did, too.

"I must thank you, too, for your assistance throughout."
She smiled again, her mind skating over his offer to partner
her, his replacement of her champagne with water, his arranging for the candlelight, the many moments during the play
when his steady, moss-green, gold-flecked gaze had kept her
from panicking. She let the thoughts light her eyes, and held
out her hand. "You were indeed my champion this night."

His lips kicked up at the ends; he took her hand, long fingers closing strongly about hers . . . and hesitated. Amanda
looked into his eyes and realized they'd changed again,
grown darker. Then he bowed and released her.

"Connor was right—hells like Mellors are no place for
you, but I fancy you've realized that." His gaze roamed her
face, then he reached into his pocket and drew out a silver
card case. He extracted a card and offered it between two
fingers. "So you know where to send for the mare. Send a
message and one of my grooms will bring her around." His
gaze touched her face again, then he inclined his head.
"Good-bye, Miss Cynster."

She brightly reiterated her thanks. As he turned away, she glanced at his card. *"Good God!"*

The exclamation escaped her despite her years of training. Without thinking, eyes fixed on the card, she caught the sleeve of the man who had been her partner through the night. Obediently, he halted.

She couldn't, at first, drag her eyes from the card—a simple, expensive rectangle of white with a gold crest upon it. Beneath the crest was stamped one word: Dexter. Beneath that was an address in Park Lane, one she knew had to belong to one of the huge old mansions fronting the park. But it was the name that turned her world upside down.

Hauling her gaze from it, she looked up at him. It took a moment to get enough breath to even gasp, "You're *Dexter?*"

The rakish, rumored-to-be-profligate, elusively mysterious Martin Fulbridge, fifth Earl of Dexter. She certainly knew of him, of his reputation, but tonight was the first time she'd set eyes on him. She realized she was clutching his sleeve and released him.

That self-deprecatory amusement was back in his eyes. When, stunned, she continued to stare, he raised one brow, cynical, yes, but world-weary as well. "Who else?"

His gaze held hers, then moved unhurriedly over her face, returned to her eyes. Then he inclined his head, and, as always unhurriedly, left her.

Chapter 2

Exiting Mellors, Martin sauntered out into Duke Street. He walked along, senses honed in a more dangerous world instinctively noting that there were no miscreants lurking in the ink-black shadows.

A projecting store front cast its own front door into stygian gloom. He stopped, cloaked in the darkness, and waited.

Three minutes later, a footman hauled open the door of Mellors, peered out, then whistled and beckoned; a small black carriage that had been waiting down the street rumbled forward. Martin inwardly nodded in approval. Mellors appeared, escorting Amanda Cynster and Reggie Carmarthen to the carriage. They entered, the door was shut, then the driver shook his reins and the carriage lumbered off.

A statue in the dark, Martin watched it roll past—caught a fleeting glimpse of honey gold hair, saw Carmarthen leaning forward, lecturing determinedly. Martin grinned; quitting the shadows, he continued on his way.

The night enveloped him. He felt completely at home walking the London streets in the small hours, completely at peace. Why that should be so was a mystery, but he'd long ago learned the futility of questioning fate. Peculiar indeed that here, surrounded by the society into which he'd been born, the society he now eschewed, was one of the few places on earth he felt at one with all about him, even though all those who would rush to recognize him were snoring in their beds, oblivious as he walked past their doors.

Turning into Piccadilly, he lengthened his stride, his mind sliding back to the fascinating question of what game had been played out that night.

His initial interpretation had been that Connor, the lecherous old toad, had set his sights on Amanda Cynster, but as the challenge had played out, he'd grown increasingly unsure. Connor's wording of the wager had left her, win or lose, in no danger, but playing a rubber with Connor had prevented her from interacting with Mellors' other patrons. What Connor hadn't foreseen was that Carmarthen wouldn't—presumably couldn't—partner her, landing her in an invidious position that Connor hadn't, he felt sure, intended at all.

He'd watched her, those huge blue eyes scanning the room, looking for a savior . . .

Inwardly he shook his head, wondering at his unexpected susceptibility. When had he become so ridiculously chivalrous, prey to a pair of admittedly fine eyes? There were many in London and far beyond who would laugh at the very idea, yet when faced with the sight of Amanda Cynster struggling to hang on to her pride, to his immense surprise he'd found himself on his feet, offering to be her champion.

Even more surprising, he'd enjoyed it. The game had been more challenging, more riveting than any he'd enjoyed since returning to England, doubly amazing given his partner had been female. Not only had she demonstrated uncommon wit and intelligence, she'd also had the sense not to gush, not to be excessive in her thanks. He thought again of her reactions, and smiled. To some extent, she'd taken his support as her natural due, even though she hadn't, then, known who he was. She was in some degree a princess—it was only right she have a knight as her champion.

Connor's contribution intrigued him. His suspicions of the other man's benevolent intentions had been all conjecture, until that revoke. Not in a month of Sundays would he believe Connor had made the mistake. Sometime during the course of the game, Connor had decided that losing and leaving Amanda Cynster in debt to him was an acceptable risk.

Martin was not at all sure what he should make of that. Perhaps nothing beyond the fact that Connor was inordinately shrewd. For he was perfectly correct—Amanda Cynster stood in no danger from the raffish Earl of Dexter. He harbored no designs on her at all. He knew precisely who he was, who she was, and she wasn't for him. He'd enjoyed the past hours in her company, but he wasn't about to let a pair of jewel eyes and rosebud lips—not even a skin like satin and hair like silk—change his careful ways.

Ladies such as Amanda Cynster had no place in his life. Not now, not ever again. Ignoring the regret that whispered, a faint, suppressed echo through his mind, he turned into Park Lane and strode for his house.

"I've found him!" Eyes alight, Amanda dragged Amelia into her bedchamber and shut the door. "He's perfect. Simply *magnificent*—I couldn't wish for more."

Amelia squeezed her hands. "Tell me."

Amanda did. When she finished, Amelia looked as stunned as Amanda had. *"Dexter?"*

"The mysterious, elusive, rumor-cloaked Earl of Dexter."

"And he's handsome?"

"Dev-astatingly. He's . . ." Amanda struggled for words, then waved. "Simply better than any other I've seen."

"What else do you know of him?"

"He's intelligent, astute—he actually thought enough to get Mellors to change my wine for water *and* to do it so no one knew." Amanda flopped back on her pillows; they'd taken refuge on her bed. "In short, on a physical and intellectual level, Dexter's perfect. Add to that he's as rich as Croesus—far too rich, anyway, to be after my dowry—and that, if half the rumors are true, he's led the most amazingly exciting life, far, far wilder than anything I would even think of doing, and his perfection takes on an even brighter gloss."

"Hmm, but there is that old scandal, don't forget."

Amanda waved the caveat aside. "If none of the matrons

nor any of the *grandes dames* consider it worth remembering, who am I to argue?" She frowned. "Did you ever hear what it was about?"

"Only that it involved some girl whom he *supposedly* seduced who then took her own life, but it was all years ago when he first came on the town. Whatever the truth, he was banished by his own father—"

"And only returned to England last year, a year after he'd succeeded to the title—that much I know."

"How old is he?"

Amanda raised her brows. "Thirty? About that. I think he appears older than he is. He's . . . serious."

Amelia stared. *"Serious?"*

"Not that sort of serious. I mean . . . deep. Reserved—no!—*controlled.* That always makes men seem older."

Amelia nodded. "Very well—I'll allow he seems just perfect for you, but how are you going to tackle the big problem? Every hostess in the ton has been trying to lure him back into society, but he refuses every invitation."

"Let's be perfectly frank—he *ignores* every invitation."

"Precisely. So how are you going to meet him often enough to convince him . . ." Amelia's words trailed away. She studied her twin's face. "You're not going to try to draw him into our world—you're going to go into *his* world instead."

Amanda grinned. "That's my plan, at least until he's well enough snared so he'll follow me anywhere."

Amelia giggled. "You make him sound like a dog."

"Hardly a dog—a lion, perhaps. A huge tawny beast who delights in lazing in his lair and who hunts at night." Amanda nodded, her expression determined. "That's exactly what I need to do—snare and tame my lion."

She wasn't fool enough to think it would be easy. Amanda spent the day evaluating various approaches. The horse was one, but she didn't want to appear too eager, and besides, if she played that card too early, he might do exactly as he'd said and send a groom with the mount, preserving a cool, sensible distance.

Cool, sensible distance was not what she needed.

But she couldn't go back to Mellors, not when he'd warned her away. Aside from being supremely foolish, that would show her hand far too clearly. *And* he wouldn't approve . . .

That thought triggered another, and another in quick succession; suddenly she knew *exactly* how to bring her lion to heel.

"Last night, Mellors—tonight, Lady Hennessy's. Have you taken leave of your senses?" Through the gloom in the carriage, Reggie glared at her. "If m'mother finds out I've accompanied you to such a place, she'll disinherit me!"

"Don't be silly." Amanda patted his knee. "Both she and my mother think we're joining the Montagues at Chelsea. Why would they imagine we're anywhere else?"

As the years had rolled by, she and Reggie, often accompanied by Amelia, had taken to making their own selection among the ton's proffered entertainments. As their choices did not always match those of their parents, they consequently and increasingly went their own way. Not a gossipmonger in the ton would make anything of it; it was common knowledge Reggie Carmarthen had known the Cynster twins from childhood.

The arrangement provided benefits to all concerned. The twins gained an acceptable escort who they could twist around their little fingers, Reggie gained a reprieve from the mamas who would otherwise pressure his mother to have him escort their simpering daughters, and both sets of parents rested comfortable in the knowledge their offspring were safe.

Reasonably safe.

"And you needn't carry on as if visiting Lady Hennessy's will ruin me."

"You're not *married* yet!" Reggie's tone suggested that event could not occur too soon for his liking. "Every other lady there will be."

"That's by the by. I'm twenty-three. I've been out for six years. No one could imagine I'm an innocent miss."

Reggie uttered a strangled sound, slammed his arms across his chest and slumped back against the seat. He said nothing more as the carriage joined the line leading to the discreetly lit door of Number 19, Gloucester Street.

The carriage stopped; tight-lipped, Reggie descended and helped her down. Amanda shook out her skirts and looked up at the door. A liveried footman stood beside it. Reggie gave her his arm. "Say the word and we'll leave."

"Onward, Horatio!"

Reggie grumbled but complied, leading her up the steps. He gave the footman their names; instantly, the door swung open and the footman bowed them through. In the marble-floored hall, Reggie looked about as Amanda surrendered her cloak to a very correct-looking butler.

"Always wanted to know what this place looked like inside," Reggie confided as Amanda rejoined him.

"See." Taking his arm, she turned him toward the drawing room. "You were just waiting for me to give you a valid excuse to come."

"Humph!"

They entered the drawing room, stopped and looked about.

Lady Hennessy's was a world apart from Mellors—here a lady's touch reigned supreme. The walls were hung with cream silk bearing a delicately worked turquoise pattern. The cream, gold and turquoise theme was reflected in the satin-striped upholstery of chaises and chairs, in the heavy curtains screening long windows. Expensive Chinese rugs covered the floor, muting the click of fashionable heels.

The wealthy relict of a Scottish peer, Lady Hennessy had decided to enliven her life and that of a good portion of the ton by creating a salon in the tradition of the previous century. Her rooms were furnished with an eye to luxurious comfort and fashionable elegance; her ladyship's refreshments were always of the best. As for the play, on the few nights on which gaming was permitted, the wagers were rumored to be astronomical.

For the most part, however, Lady Hennessy concentrated on providing entertainment guaranteed to attract the most blue-blooded rakes in town. This in turn ensured the attendance of the cream of the married ladies looking for distraction, which in turn guaranteed that every rake worthy of the name invariably returned to Gloucester Street. Her ladyship's genius lay in perceiving the connection between her two principal groups of guests, and promoting it; there was an excellent string quartet playing softly in one corner, and the lighting, provided by lamps large and small, wall sconces and candelabra, created patches of soft light and shadow more conducive to the discreet pursuit of passion than the harsh light of a chandelier.

There were whispers of other rooms which were occasionally given over to private parties. Although curious, Amanda was certain she wouldn't need to experience such functions. Lady Hennessy's public rooms should be more than sufficient for her purpose.

Reggie frowned. "Rather quiet, ain't it? Not what I expected at all."

Amanda hid a smile; Reggie had expected a cross between a bordello and a public house. Yet while the elegant crowd conversed in quiet, well-modulated tones, while the murmurs, chuckles and laughter were distinctly well bred, the tenor of the comments, the tension that passed between couples in close converse was anything but mild. As for the glances exchanged, some could have set flame to coal.

Almack's was the ton's marriage mart; Lady Hennessy's was a market of a different stamp, frequented by the same class of both sellers and buyers. It was said that on any given evening during the Season, more aristocratic male blood was to be discovered in Gloucester Street than at any other venue in the capital.

Completing an exhaustive survey, Amanda was relieved to see no one she would rather not—like one of her father's cronies. Or one of her mother's circle. Or any of her cousins' friends. That had been her only fear in embarking on this strategy. Reassured, she relaxed, and gave her mind to her immediate next step.

"I'm parched. Do you think you could get me a glass of champagne?"

"Right-o. I think the refreshments are laid out in there."
Reggie nodded to the connecting salon, and headed in that
direction.

Amanda waited until he was out of sight, screened by
shoulders and broad backs. Then she stepped into the crowd,
and let her eye roam.

It took her five minutes to gather three admirers of precisely the right stamp. Gentlemen well favored, attractive,
elegantly turned out, who were witty, charming in a bantering way, and who were all extremely interested in discovering the reason for her appearance in Lady Hennessy's salon.

Amanda had attended too many balls and parties, too
many houseparties, to feel challanged by the task of crossing
verbal swords with the three—Mr. Fitzgibbon, Lord Walter
and Lord Cranbourne—while concealing her intentions. Indeed, the very fact she was so glib in shielding her purpose
only fired the gentlemen's imaginations and anchored them
within her circle.

By the time Reggie found her, she was creditably beseiged.

Greeting him with a smile, she accepted the glass he'd
brought for her and made him known to her three admirers.
His expression bland, Reggie acknowledged the introductions. Ignoring his severe look when he turned back to her,
she smiled at Mr. Fitzgibbon. "You were describing boating
on the Thames by night, sir. Is the experience truly worth the
inconvenience?"

Mr. Fitzgibbon was quick to assure her it was. She took
mental notes as he waxed lyrical on the sight of the stars reflected in the black waters. She had no idea how many nights
she would have to spend here, keeping her trap baited with
men like Fitzgibbon, Walter and Cranbourne—men only too
ready to help her take her first steps into the less virtuous
world they inhabited.

She had no intention of accepting their aid, but she hid
that well. Logic suggested that Dexter would visit Lady Hennessy's salons; she was betting she had his real measure.

If he didn't appear, she would waste a few nights, a drop
in the ocean of time she'd already spent searching for a husband. If he appeared but failed to react as predicted, she

would gain an immensely valuable insight, enough to conclude that despite all she believed, Dexter was not in fact for her.

But if all went as planned . . . she stood to win all she desired.

She thought her plan quite splendid. With a glorious smile, shamelessly deploying her eyes and her charms, she threw herself into its execution.

Martin saw Amanda the instant he entered Helen Hennessy's drawing room. She was standing to one side of the hearth; the light from a candelabra on the mantelpiece fell full on her, bathing her in golden light.

The effect of seeing her surprised him—the sudden clench of possessiveness, the unexpected visceral tug. He shook the sensations aside; his cynically amused mask in place, he strolled forward to greet his hostess.

Helen was delighted to see him. She chatted, drawing his attention to three separate experienced ladies who were attending that night. "They'd each and every one be delighted to make your acquaintance."

She glanced at him, one brow raised. Martin barely glanced at the ladies in question. "Not tonight."

Helen sighed. "I don't know whether to applaud or pout—your reticence only heightens their interest, as you well know, but continued refusals to engage . . . well, it does call into question my ability to deliver."

"You always deliver in the end, my dear, as I'm quite sure your ladies know. But tonight they'll have to make do with someone else's talents. I . . ."—Martin considered Amanda, a golden angel dispensing smiles and laughter upon her captives—"have other fish to fry."

He looked at Helen before, intrigued, she could follow his gaze. "And no, you needn't wonder. I suspect the role I'm scripted to play is that of knight-protector, not demon lover."

"How fascinating." Helen opened her eyes wide, then smiled. "Very well. You have my permission to dispense your favors as you wish—not that you'd listen to any edicts otherwise. But beware!" She slanted him an arch glance as she turned to greet another guest. "You know what they say of rakehells visited by a sudden urge to reform."

He didn't know and didn't need to. The warning faded from his mind as he ambled through the crowd, ostensibly looking the ladies over, in truth watching just one.

She hadn't seen him, or so it appeared; he'd yet to see her gaze turn his way and she'd given no sign of recognition. She continued to engage the three others and Carmarthen, although he was looking more worried than entranced.

Martin had to admit she was a dab hand at entrancing. Her smiles, her laughter—which he couldn't hear but wished he could—the lively chatter, the gaiety dancing in her eyes, all served to project the persona of a confident young lady brimming with sparkling, bubbling charm. Indeed, she reminded him of the very best champagne, fine wine subtly effervescent, deepened by just the right touch of age to the point where it promised liquid gold on the tongue and glory to the senses.

He couldn't tell if she knew he was present. Couldn't tell if his suspicion that her current situation had been staged with him specifically in mind owed more to his arrogance than reality.

His prowl carried him beyond her line of sight. The crowd between them thinned; he could see her clearly, yet she didn't turn his way. Instead, she laughed—light, airy, a sound both joyous and earthy, it carried to him. Caressed him, enticed him, as it did the other men before her.

It didn't matter if she'd schemed to capture his attention. She had it.

Amanda felt him approach; like a storm sweeping in, his very nearness had her tensing. The sensation unnerved her; she fought not to whirl and face what her senses screamed was danger—if she did, she'd give her game away. Then he halted beside her, his towering figure excuse enough for her to break off her tale and glance his way.

She let recognition flow across her face, let pleasure light her eyes. No difficulty there—he looked even more sinfully handsome in full light, in more formal attire than he'd worn the previous night. She smiled and held out her hand. "My lord."

Brazenly, she left it at that—let him, and the others, make of it what they would. He took her hand and she curtsied. He raised her; eyes on hers, he inclined his head. "Miss Cynster."

Her smile ingenuous, she struggled to keep her fingers from fluttering in his, too wise to attempt to retrieve her hand until he deigned to let her go.

He released her; she drew in a quick breath and launched into the introductions. "And I believe you'll remember Mr. Carmarthen."

"Indeed."

Reggie favored him with a wary look and a polite nod. Dexter's gaze lingered on Reggie's face, then he turned it, smoothly, on her. "I admit to surprise at encountering you here. I thought, after your most recent foray into such realms, caution would . . . how does that saying go? . . . overcome valor?"

He's here! He's here! And he took the bait! Her eyes locked on his, Amanda ruthlessly cut off the delirious litany; he might be here, but he wasn't yet snared. And if she wasn't careful, *she* might be the one in a coil.

As if pleased he'd remembered their last meeting, she smiled. "I did toy with the notion of attending Lady Sutcliffe's ball, yet"—she swept her smile over her three now earnest would-be cavaliers—"formal engagements do pall when one has spent so many years in the ballrooms." She glanced again at Dexter. "It seems a waste not to avail oneself of the more varied *divertissements* offered by such as her ladyship. So much more entertaining. I daresay you find it so yourself?"

Martin held her gaze and debated whether to call her bluff. "My tastes, admittedly, lie somewhat beyond the diversions provided by the ton's hostesses. However, I wouldn't have imagined such esoteric distractions would hold much allure for a young lady such as you."

Her chin lifted, her eyes sparkled, with challenge, with

humor. "On the contrary, my lord. I've a definite taste for wilder pastimes." Her smile confiding, she briefly touched his sleeve. "I daresay you haven't heard, living retired as you do."

"Wilder pastimes, heh?" Cranbourne grabbed the opening. "Heard a tale of wild doings at Mrs. Croxton's last night."

"Indeed?" Amanda turned to Cranbourne.

Martin watched as she encouraged all three gentlemen to dazzle her with their wildest suggestions. He might live "retired" but he knew what he was seeing. Carmarthen was growing increasingly nervous. Yet if he, Dexter, bowed and walked away, would she continue on this path? If he declined to be her protector, would she go on without one? What sort of net was she weaving—how much was true, how much for his confusion?

Not that it mattered; he was more than capable of dealing with her whatever tack she took. And she clearly needed someone to watch over her, someone with more muscle than dear Reggie.

Cranbourne, Fitzgibbon and Walter were intent; given how long she'd spent allowing them to entertain her, they'd expect her shortly to choose from among them. And contrary to what she was expecting, accustomed as she was to the rules pertaining in ballroom and drawing room, a charming dismissal would not be well received.

Reaching out, he took her hand; surprised, she glanced his way, throwing Walter, concluding some tale, off his stride. "My dear, I promised Helen—Lady Hennessey—that, given this is your first visit, I would make sure you became acquainted with all she has to offer." He looked into Amanda's blue eyes as he placed her hand on his sleeve. "It's time we strolled on, or you'll never see all before dawn." He glanced at Walter, Cranbourne and Fitzgibbon. "I'm sure these gentlemen will excuse you."

They had little choice; none was game to challenge one of Helen's edicts, a fact Martin had counted on. The three made their adieus, then withdrew. Martin considered Reggie. "I believe Miss Cynster would like another glass of champagne."

Reggie looked at Amanda.

Who nodded, ringlets dancing. "Yes, I would."

Frowning, Reggie flicked a glance at Martin. "Just as long as you don't do a bunk while I'm gone."

Martin suppressed a grin; perhaps Reggie was not as spineless as he'd thought. "She'll be in this room, but we'll be strolling." He paused, eyes on Reggie's. "It's not wise to remain stationary for too long."

He saw horrified comprehension dawn, then Reggie nodded. "Right. I'll find you." With a disapproving glance at Amanda, he headed for the secondary salon.

Martin scanned the room, then lowered his arm and waved Amanda on before him. Keeping her hand on his arm—keeping her that close—would be unwise. He wanted it seen that she was under his protection in the social sense; the last thing he wanted was for her ladyship's guests to imagine that protection extended to a more personal state.

As she walked ahead of him, tacking slowly through the crowd, she glanced back at him. "Are you really friends with Lady Hennessy?"

"Yes." Helen was another who had the entree to the ton but had chosen to turn her back on it.

Amanda slowed. "What did I do wrong?"

He caught her eye, realized she meant the question to be as simple as it sounded. "If you spend much more than fifteen minutes conversing with one man, it will be inferred that you're interested in pursuing some of those wilder pastimes you mentioned with him."

Her beautiful face blanked. "Oh." Facing forward, she continued their slow amble. "That's not what I intended."

She paused to acknowledge a greeting; he performed three introductions before they moved on. Closing the distance between them, he bent his head and murmured, "What did you intend?"

She stopped; he nearly walked into her. Halted with a bare inch between her shoulders and his chest, her silk-clad bottom and his thighs. She looked back and up at him, met his eyes.

He fought an urge to slide his arms about her and draw her back against him.

"I want to live a little before I grow old." She searched his eyes. "Is that a crime?"

"If it is, half the world's guilty."

She looked forward and started strolling again. He took a firmer grip on his impulses, then followed. She glanced back. "I understand you've had a great deal of experience in 'living.'"

"Not all of it pleasant."

She waved airily. "I'm only interested in the pleasurable aspects."

Her tone was straightforward, not facetious. She intended to seek out the pleasures of life while avoiding the pitfalls.

If only life was that simple.

They continued their peregrination, stopping to spend a few minutes in this circle or that before moving on again, she a foot before him, he prowling, relaxed but watchful, in her wake. He doubted she'd encountered many pitfalls to date; her faith in life, in its ultimate joy, remained undimmed. The light in her eyes, the exuberance of her smiles, all spoke of innocence intact.

It was not his place to shatter it.

Reaching an empty space by the side of the room, Amanda turned. "Actually, speaking of life's pleasures . . ."

He halted before her, broad shoulders blocking her view of the room. He met her gaze, and raised a too-knowing, distinctly suspicious, odiously superior brow.

She smiled up at him. "I was thinking I might ride the mare tomorrow morning. Early. In the park. Do you think your groom could oblige me?"

He blinked, once; she smiled more brightly.

And prayed it wasn't too soon to play that card. Elusive as he was, if she didn't set up another meeting, he might, after tonight, simply fade back into the shadows—and she would have tonight's work to do again.

His face was unreadable. Eventually, he said, "Connor mentioned Upper Brook Street."

"My parents' house is Number 12."

He nodded. "I'll have my groom wait for you with the horses at the corner of Park Lane. After your ride, he'll return the mare to my stables."

"Thank you." She smiled gratefully, too wise to suggest that she would much prefer his company to that of his groom's.

"What time?"

She wrinkled her nose. "Six o'clock."

"Six?" Martin stared. It was nearly twelve now, and at six in the morning, the park would be deserted.

"I'll need to return home before the regulars get about." She glanced up at him. "I don't want my cousins to see the horse and ask where I got her."

"Your cousins?"

"My male Cynster cousins. They're older than me. They're all married and have turned dreadfully stuffy."

Martin inwardly kicked himself for not making the connection sooner. Admittedly, there were a lot of Cynsters, and he'd never heard of any girls. All the family members he'd previously encountered had been male.

The Bar Cynster—that's what they'd been called. When he'd first come on the town they'd been little short of gods, lording it over the ton's ladies. But now they'd all married . . . he hadn't met a single one in the past year while he'd been creating his own fiefdom in the world in which they'd previously reigned supreme.

He frowned. "You're first cousin to St. Ives?"

She nodded, her gaze open, direct.

If any of her cousins had been about, he would have handed her into their care forthwith, cutting short her adventures. Infinitely safer all around. However, she was here now and they weren't.

They both turned as Reggie neared, a champagne flute in one hand.

Lips compressed, Martin nodded. "Very well. Six o'clock at the corner of Park Lane."

At six o'clock the next morning, it was dull, gray and cold. Amanda's heart soared as, perched on the exceedingly frisky mare, she trotted toward Mount Gate—and the figure perched atop a huge horse waiting impatiently under a tree just inside the gates.

Clad in her riding habit, she'd slipped out of her parents' side door and hurried up the street. Reaching the corner, she'd found the groom waiting as arranged. Hopes dashed, she'd lectured herself against expecting too much too soon. Dexter knew she was out riding—one day he'd be tempted to join her.

She'd apparently tempted him enough. Mounted on a magnificent roan gelding, Dexter held the fractious horse effortlessly, long, muscular thighs clamped to the beast's sides. He was wearing a conventional riding coat over buckskin breeches and boots; cantering up, she thought he looked wilder, definitely more dangerous than he had in evening clothes.

His hair was rakishly disheveled, his gaze disconcertingly acute. He wasn't frowning, but looked distinctly grim. Joining him, she got the definite impression he wasn't pleased to be there.

"Good morning, my lord. I didn't expect to have the pleasure of your company." She smiled sunnily, delighted to be able to make the comment truthfully. "Are you game for a gallop?"

Martin eyed her impassively. "You'll find that I'm game for almost anything."

Her smile brightened before she looked away. "Let's head down to the Row."

Martin flicked a glance at his groom. "Wait here."

They set out in unison, trotting across the lawns beneath the trees. She busied herself trying out the mare's paces. Martin watched, relieved to note she was a competent horsewoman—not that he'd seriously expected less from a Cynster, female or not.

"From what Connor said, I take it your cousin—I can't remember which one—still has an active interest in horses."

"Demon." She experimented with the mare's reins. "He's got a stud outside Newmarket, now. He breeds racehorses, and Flick rides them."

"Flick?"

"His wife, Felicity. She's a wonder with horses—she helps train them."

Martin couldn't settle that image in his mind. The Demon Cynster he'd known would never have let a mere woman near his mounts. He shook that conundrum aside and refocused on the one at hand. "So if Demon sees the mare, he'll recognize her."

"Even if someone else sees her and describes her. *Nothing* is more certain." Amanda glanced at him. "That's why I can only ride this early, when there's no one else about."

Martin hid a grimace; he couldn't fault her reasoning. However, the knowledge that she would be riding in the deserted park had been enough to wake him even before the ungodly hour had arrived; the mental images evoked had made falling asleep again impossible. So here he was, despite the fact he'd had no intention of dancing attendance on her.

He didn't delude himself that the next morning she rode would be any different.

If the ton learned she was riding with him alone, so early in the morning, there would be whispers and raised brows aplenty, but she was an experienced, sensible, well-bred twenty-three-year-old; her reputation would be examined, but would not, by the fact of their riding alone in a public place, actually be blemished. Her family—her cousins— would not be pleased, but she and he would have to transgress more direfully to invite intervention.

On the other hand, if her cousins learned that he'd known she was riding alone in the deserted park, and had done nothing beyond roll over and fall asleep, *then,* he was sure, he'd be the recipient of remarkably speedy intervention.

He couldn't decide if it was a lucky circumstance that the latter scenario would never take place. The only fact that lightened his grim mood was the certainty that she hadn't realized what his position was. Her delight at finding him waiting for her had been transparently genuine; she hadn't counted on seeing him. At least he had that much rein to work with.

He glanced at her as she made the mare prance, then dance, then drew the horse back into line.

"She's wonderfully responsive."

He looked at the sky—it was the color of black pearls, night softening its hold before the approaching dawn. "If we're going to gallop, we'd better get on."

She set the mare for the tan track specially prepared for galloping. Turning onto it, she shot him a glance as he brought the roan alongside, then sprang the mare. She surprised him, but the roan went with her; the mare was fast but the roan's longer strides quickly closed the distance until they were riding neck and neck. The park was empty, silent and still as they thundered down the track. The roan would have outdistanced the mare but he held the horse back. So he could see her face, see the unfettered joy that lit her features, sense the exhilaration that gripped her.

The heavy pounding of the hooves swept up and over them until it echoed in their blood. The air whipped past them, slicing through their hair, leaving skin tingling, eyes bright.

She slowed; ahead the tan ended. They eased from gallop to canter, finally dropping to a walk; their mounts blew horsey breaths in the quiet stillness. Harness jingled as the roan shook his head; Martin turned back toward Mount Gate, running an expert eye over the mare as he did.

She'd pulled up well. So had her rider.

He'd seen too much feminine beauty to be easily susceptible, yet luxurious colors and even more textures never failed to catch his eye. Her velvet habit was the color of her eyes; he hadn't been able to appreciate the shade earlier but the light was strengthening—as she turned to him, smiling, dizzy with delight, he saw her clearly.

Under a jaunty cap the same color as the habit, her hair caught the first light of dawn and reflected it in shades of pure gold. Last night, when the curls had been piled high, he'd imagined her hair to be shoulder-length. Now he could see it had to be longer—mid-back, at least. A display of sheening, lustrous curls, the mass was caught up, anchored under her cap, loose ends brushing her throat, wisps curling lovingly about her small ears.

Her hair made his palms tingle.

Her skin made him ache.

The ride had tinged the flawless alabaster a delicate rose. He knew if he touched his lips to her throat, if he skated his fingers over her bare shoulder, he would be able to feel the heat of her blood coursing beneath that sumptuous skin. Knew desire would evoke the same effect. As for her lips, parted, rosy red . . .

He dragged his eyes from her, looked across the park. "We'd better get back. The regulars will soon be arriving."

Still catching her breath, she nodded and brought the mare in beside the roan. They walked, then trotted. They were within sight of the groom, waiting by the gates, when she murmured, "Lady Cavendish is hosting a dinner tonight—one of those affairs one *has* to attend."

Martin told himself he was relieved. No need to feel obliged to play knight-protector tonight.

"But later, I'd thought to look in on the *soirée* at the Corsican Consulate. It's just around the corner from Cavendish House, I believe."

He fixed her with a stony look. "Who sent you an invitation?" The Corsican Consulate's *"soirées"* were by invitation only. For a very good reason.

She glanced at him. "Leopold Korsinsky."

The Corsican Consul. And when had she met Leopold? Doubtless during her travels through the underside of the ton. Martin looked ahead, jettisoning any thought of dissuading her. The woman was intent on tasting the wilder side of life; attending Leopold's *soirée* unquestionably fitted her bill.

"I'll leave you here." Gentlemen were emerging, ambling down the streets of Mayfair heading for their morning ride. He reined in. "The groom will ride with you to Upper Brook Street, then bring away the horse."

She smiled. "Then I will thank you for your company, my lord."

A polite nod and she turned away, with not a hint, not a wink, not the slightest indication that she expected to meet him that night.

Martin narrowed his eyes on her departing back. Once she'd joined his groom and, without a single glance back, quit the park, he trotted back down to the Stanhope Gate, crossed Park Lane and rode in between the pair of huge gates that guarded the drive to Fulbridge House.

He entered through the kitchens and headed into the huge house. Ignoring the furniture draped in holland covers, the many closed doors and the sense of pervasive gloom, he strode for the library.

Other than the small dining parlor, of the many rooms on the ground floor, the library was the only one he used. He flung open the door and entered, into a den of decadent luxury.

Like any library, the walls were covered with bookshelves packed with books. Here, the display, by its diversity and order, demonstrated wealth, pride and scholarship, a deep respect for accumulated wisdom. In all other respects, the library was unique.

Velvet curtains were still drawn over the long windows. Martin crossed the parquet decorated with exquisite inlays partly concealed by deep-toned rugs and flung the curtains wide. Beyond the windows lay a walled courtyard, a fountain rising from a circular pool at its center, stone walls hidden by the rampant growth of ivys and creepers.

Martin turned, his gaze skating over the satin-covered chaise and the daybed draped with brightly colored silk shawls, over the jewel-hued cushions piled here and there, over the ornately carved tables standing amidst the glory. Everywhere his eye touched, there was some delight of color and texture, some simple, sensual gratification.

It was a room that filled his senses, compensation for the bleak emptiness of his life.

His gaze came to rest on the pile of invitations stacked on the end of the marble mantelpiece. Crossing the room, he grabbed them, swiftly sorted through the pile. Selected the one he sought.

Stared at it.

Returning the others to the mantelpiece, he propped the selected card on a mahogany side table, dropped onto the daybed, propped his feet on an embossed leather ottoman—and scowled at Leopold Korsinsky's invitation.

Chapter 3

If the minx was setting her cap at him, she was going about it in a damned unusual way.

From a corner of the Consulate ballroom, one shoulder propped against the wall, Martin watched Amanda Cynster as she stood on the threshold, looking about. No hint of expectation colored her fair face; she projected the image of a lady calmly considering her options.

Leopold swiftly came forward. She smiled charmingly and held out her hand; Leopold grasped it eagerly, and favored her with a too-elegant, too-delighted bow.

Martin's jaw set. Leopold talked, gestured, clearly attempting to dazzle. Martin watched, wondered . . .

He'd been the target for too many ladies with matrimonial intentions not to have developed a sixth sense for being stalked. Yet with Amanda Cynster . . . he wasn't sure. She was different from other ladies he'd dealt with—younger, less experienced, yet not so young he could dismiss her as a girl, not so inexperienced he was daft enough to think her, or her machinations, of no account.

He hadn't amassed a huge fortune in trade by underestimating the opposition. In this case, however, he wasn't even sure the damned female had him in her sights.

Two other gentlemen approached her, bucks of the most dangerous sort on the lookout for risky titillation. Leopold sized them up in a glance; he introduced them to Amanda, but gave no indication of leaving her side, far less of relinquishing her attention. The bucks bowed and moved on.

Martin relaxed, only then realizing he'd tensed. He fixed his gaze on the cause, taking in her tumbling curls, glossy gold in the strong light, let his gaze linger on the lissome figure draped in soft silk the color of ripe peach. Wondered how succulent the flesh beneath the silk would be . . .

He caught himself up, wiped the developing image from his mind.

Focused on the reality, on the conundrum before him.

Thus far, every time he'd appeared, she'd clearly been pleased to see him, willing—even glad—to accept the protection he offered. However, he'd yet to see any sign that she was *specifically* interested in him. She was used to protective males—like her cousins; the possibility existed—lowering thought—that she would with equal ease accept the protection of some other, similar gentleman. He couldn't offhand think of any other who might appear to squire her platonically, but the prospect remained. Her transparent liking for and encouragement of his company might simply reflect a natural gravitation toward the sort of male in whose company she felt comfortable.

She wasn't stalking him—she was haunting him. An entirely different circumstance, for as of that moment, he had no idea if she intended to or not.

That, he decided, was the issue he had to deal with—the point he needed to clarify.

He pushed away from the wall. Leopold had monopolized her for long enough, and the bucks who'd approached earlier hadn't gone far.

Her attention on Leopold, she didn't see him approach. Nor did Leopold, a willing captive, his dark gaze locked on her face. Only when he loomed beside her did she break off and look up—then she smiled gloriously and held out her hand.

"My lord."

He closed his fingers about hers. She curtsied. He raised her and bowed. "Miss Cynster."

Her lips remained curved, her eyes alight with a delight that had not been there before. The frown growing in Leopold's eyes as they flicked from him to her suggested that the last was not a fabrication of his imagination.

"Dexter." Leopold's nod was curt. "You are acquainted with Miss Cynster."

Not a question—at least, not the obvious one; Martin met Leopold's gaze. "We're . . . friends."

Leopold's frown grew more definite; "friends" uttered in that way could mean just about anything. Leopold, however, knew Martin quite well.

If the object of their discussion had any inkling of the communication passing over her head, she gave no sign, but glanced from one to the other, the expectation of entertainment in her eyes. Her gaze came to rest on Martin.

Looking down, he smiled easily. "Would you care to stroll and see who else is present? You've been here for a while— I'm sure Leopold has other claims on his time."

He'd meant the last sentence as a warning; a sudden gleam in her eye, the deepening of her smile had him rapidly replaying his words. As she prettily took her leave of Leopold, Martin inwardly kicked himself. He'd just told her he'd been watching her—for a while.

As host, Leopold couldn't scowl, but the look he cast Martin as they parted stated he'd be back—back to pry Amanda from Martin's side. Leopold liked nothing better than to cross swords, metaphorically, with a peer.

Martin offered his arm; Amanda laid her hand on his sleeve.

"Do you know Mr. Korsinsky well?"

"Yes. I have business interests in Corsica." And Leopold's family were the biggest bandits on the island.

"Is he . . ."—she gestured—"trustworthy? Or should I view him in the same light as the other two he introduced?"

Martin went to answer, caught himself, then inwardly shrugged. She knew he'd been watching. "Leopold has his own brand of honor, but it isn't English. I'm not even sure it falls within the realms of 'civilized.' It would be wiser to treat him as you would the other two." He paused, then added in tones rather less drawled, "In other words, avoid them."

Her lips quirked; she glanced up. "I'm more than seven, you know."

He caught her gaze. "They, however, are more than eight."

"And you?"

They'd slowed. Ahead, a lady waved to attract their attention. Martin saw, but didn't respond, absorbed in studying the face turned up to his—it could be that of an angel except it held too much vitality. He drew breath, glanced up. "I, my dear, am beyond your ken."

She followed his gaze; the hiatus that had held them dissolved. Smoothly, they made the transition to social discourse, stopping to chat with a group they'd met at Lady Hennessy's.

Martin was content to stand beside Amanda and let her animation carry the day. She was assured, confident, and quick-witted, glibly turning aside an arch query as to their friendship. The ladies in the group were intrigued; the gentlemen simply enjoyed her company, watching her face, her eyes, listening to her musical laugh.

He did the same, but with a different intent, trying to see past her facade. He'd felt the tensing of her breathing, the tightening of her fingers on his sleeve during that one, taut moment. He'd tried, again, to warn her; only once he'd uttered the words, heard them, glimpsed—so fleetingly he wasn't sure he'd seen aright—a steely stubbornness behind her delicate features, had he considered that she might interpret those words differently.

Might see them as a challenge.

She was, after all, looking for excitement.

Watching the flow of expression across her features, through the blue of her eyes, he couldn't tell what her reaction was. Would be.

Worse—he was no longer sure how he wanted her to react. Whether he wanted her to run from him, or to him.

Inwardly, he frowned; the surrounding conversation slid from his mind. Logically, he knew what he wanted. She was not for him; he didn't want to become involved with her. Logically, all was clear.

Why, then, this sense of confusion?

A screech from a violin hauled him from his thoughts. Everyone turned, looked, confirmed that a waltz was about to begin. He glanced down, met Amanda's blue eyes. She arched a brow.

He gestured to the dance floor. "Shall we?"

She smiled and gave him her hand. He led her to the floor, determined to find answers to his questions.

Waltzes at the Corsican Consulate had never conformed to the style approved by the patronesses of Almack's. Martin drew Amanda into his arms, drew her closer still as couples crowded onto the floor.

They started to revolve; Amanda looked about them as she struggled to master her breathing, to give no sign of the breathlessness that had assailed her the moment Dexter's hand had come to rest on her back. It was large, strong— effortlessly he steered her through the throng. But the heat, not just from his hand, burning through silk, but the pervasive heat of his large body so close, a bare inch from hers . . . little wonder that ladies swooned on crowded dance floors.

Not that she'd ever been in danger of joining their ranks before, and she'd danced on crowded floors aplenty.

Out of her ken. She focused on those words, on all they promised—all she intended to have. From him. Serve him right. He was as arrogantly superior as her cousins; truth be known, she didn't mind at all. It would make his conquest all the sweeter.

She glanced at his face, smiled lightly. "You waltz well, my lord."

"You're an expert, I take it."

"After six years in the ton? Indeed I am."

He hesitated; she couldn't read anything in his changeable green eyes. "You're not, however, an expert in this arena, as Connor rightly stated."

"Connor told me I was out of my depth in gaming with such as he, and in that I agree." She glanced at the dancers surrounding them. "In other respects, I see little here I would feel challenged managing."

When he said nothing, she glanced at his face. He was waiting—he trapped her gaze. "What are you after?"

You. "I told you. I want to live a little—I want to experience entertainments more exciting than can be found within the ton." She met his gaze boldly. "As you agreed, that's no crime."

"No crime, perhaps, but it's dangerous. Especially for such as you."

She glanced about. "A little danger adds spice to the excitement."

Martin couldn't believe the battery of emotions she so effortlessly evoked. "And if the danger is more than just 'a little'?"

She looked back at him; again he glimpsed steel. "If that was the case, then I wouldn't be interested. I've been out for six years—I know where the lines are drawn. I'm not interested in stepping over them."

Again she looked away.

Deliberately, he drew her closer, held her to him as they went through the turns so his thighs parted and brushed hers, so their hips met, slid apart, met again, so her gown shifted, shushing, against his coat, his thighs. He felt the hitch in her breathing, felt the tremor that raced down her spine. She glanced briefly at his face, but remained supple, gloriously light in his arms.

He waited until they were precessing up the long room. "These entertainments you wish to experience. I take it you have some specific event in mind."

"Events."

She said nothing further; he was forced to prompt, "And they are?"

His tone brought her gaze to his face, then, her decision to oblige him clear, she recited, "To drive—or more correctly to be driven—around Richmond Park by moonlight. To go boating to see the stars reflected in the Thames. To attend Vauxhall in a private party organized by someone my parents don't know. To attend one of the masquerades at Covent Garden."

She fell silent; he tersely inquired, "Nothing else?"

Amanda ignored his tone. "For the present, that's the limit of my ambition."

His lips thinned. "If you're discovered doing any of those things—if it becomes known you have—you'll be—"

"Exclaimed over, dubbed foolish beyond permission, lectured until my ears ache, then closely watched for the duration of the Season." She let her gaze rest on his face, noting the hard, uncompromising lines. "That prospect is hardly likely to sway me. At my age, nothing short of a proven indiscretion is going to harm my standing."

He made a derisive sound. She smiled and let her gaze wander. "If you must know, my list is so short precisely because of society's demands." The waltz concluded; they swirled to a halt. "I have only so many weeks before the Season gets into full swing. Once it does, my calendar will fill with socially obligatory events, and I won't have time to seek excitement."

She stepped back, out of his arms; he let her draw her fingers from his, but slowly. As if, at any moment, he might change his mind and seize them, and her. Freed, she turned, feeling his hand fall from her. Missed its heat. She looked at the gentlemen about them. "I wonder who would be willing to squire me to Richmond."

Eyes narrowing, Martin reached for her hand to yank her back and tell her what he thought of that idea—*and* that he didn't appreciate being baited—when Agnes Korsinsky, Leopold's sister, materialized before them.

"Dexter, *mon cher!*"

Agnes launched herself into his arms; he had no choice but to catch her. She planted two noisy kisses, one on each cheek—then for good measure, went back and repeated the greeting.

He gripped her waist and set her away from him. "Agnes." He kept his gaze on her face. She was all but indecently dressed, her voluptuous charms very much on display. That she harbored designs on him, on his title, his wealth and his person, he was well aware; she had for years and was as dangerous as her brother. Amanda was watching, assessing; he said the first thing that came into his head. "You've had an excellent turnout—you must be delighted."

"Ah, them!" Agnes dismissed the crowd with a wave that included Amanda. "They are as nothing compared to you, *mon cher*. But how wicked to slip in without paying your respects—I didn't even know you were here."

Precisely. He reached for Amanda an instant before Agnes reached for his arm. "Permit me to introduce . . . Miss Wallace."

Agnes's black eyes flashed with the temper that was never far from her surface. She drew herself up, turned haughtily to Amanda. "Miss Wallace?"

Martin glanced at Amanda, and saw her smile. She held out her hand. "Miss Korsinsky. Your *soirée* has been quite delightful. I spent some moments talking to your brother . . ."

It took effort to smother his grin. He stood and watched Agnes get bowled over by an effortless tide of ballroom patter. She was no match for one who'd spent six years in the ton. In the end, Agnes recalled someone she had to see. With a mere nod for him, but polite words to Amanda, she left them.

Only then could he allow his lips to curve. "Thank you." Lifting Amanda's hand to his lips, he brushed her fingertips—just as their eyes met.

He felt the shiver that raced through her to his toes. Felt arousal surge through him in response, saw her eyes widen.

She drew breath, smiled, slid her fingers from his. "Was there some reason for my change of identity?" She turned away, scanning the crowd.

His gaze locked on the golden curls before his face, he murmured, "Agnes is not one to trust. She can be . . . vindictive."

Amanda glanced briefly his way. "Especially over things she wants but hasn't succeeded in getting?"

"Especially then."

She started to stroll; he fell in in her wake. The crowd had grown; it was difficult to walk abreast.

Her voice drifted back to him. "Now that I've saved you

from Miss Korsinsky, perhaps I can prevail upon you to assist me."

This was where she would ask him to drive her around Richmond at midnight. "In what matter do you require assistance?"

She glanced back, smiling easily. "In the matter of selecting which gentlemen I should ask to squire me on my quests for excitement."

She faced forward again; again he was left staring at her golden curls. Left, once again, wondering what it was about her that evoked such a maelstrom of impulses in him—impulses stronger, wilder, infinitely more dangerous than anything she was imagining experiencing.

And she was the focus of those impulses.

Jaw locked, he prowled in her wake, grateful she couldn't see his face, his eyes. They tacked through the crowd; he kept close, unwilling to let her get more than six inches away while he wrestled his demons into some semblance of subjection. She wasn't intending to ask any other gentleman to squire her. She was baiting him, he was sure.

Amanda stopped here and there, exchanging greetings, very conscious of Dexter at her back, aware that, although he exchanged nods and names, he said nothing more. She could feel his heat, his strength like a hot storm threatening. Smiling confidently, she continued searching for the right provocation to make the storm break.

Then she spied Lord Cranbourne. His lordship was elegant of manner, assured, glibly pleasant. Perfect.

She stopped walking, steeled herself not to react when Dexter walked into her. As he stepped back, without looking at him, she put a hand on his arm. "Lord Cranbourne," she murmured. She sensed rather than saw Dexter follow her gaze. "I should think he'd be perfect to drive me to Richmond. His conversation is superior, and his greys are magnificent."

Plastering on her best smile, she released Dexter's arm and stepped out, her gaze fixed on Lord Cranbourne.

She'd managed all of two steps before hard fingers wrapped, manaclelike, about her wrist.

"No."

The low growl that had preceded the word nearly made her grin. She turned back to Dexter, eyes wide. "No?"

His jaw was clenched. His eyes bored into hers, searching . . .

Then he looked up, over her head, over the crowd. His fingers shifted; he changed his hold on her hand, locking it in his. "Come with me."

She hid her grin as he towed her to the side of the room. She expected him to stop there; instead, he pushed open a door left ajar and stepped through, drawing her into a long gallery that marched down one side of the ballroom. The gallery was narrow; the wall it shared with the ballroom was punctuated by three sets of doors. The other wall contained a succession of windows that looked out over the Consulate gardens.

Other couples strolled in the light shed by wall sconces set between the ballroom doors. The windows were uncurtained, letting moonlight stream in, adding its silvery tint to the scene. The gallery was considerably less stuffy than the ballroom; gratefully, she drew a deep breath.

Dexter set her hand on his sleeve and covered it with his. Face grim, he steered her down the room. "This entire start of yours is madness."

She didn't deign to reply. The last window, just out from the room's corner, drew near; it looked down on a small courtyard. "How pretty."

They halted before the window; drawing her hand from beneath his hard fingers, she leaned on the windowsill and looked down.

"You're not seriously considering doing any of those things on your so-called list."

She said nothing, merely smiled. Kept her gaze on the courtyard.

"You know very well how your cousins will react."

"They won't know, so they won't react."

"Your parents, then—you can't expect me to believe you can slip out night after night and they won't notice."

"You're right. I can't manage night after night. But . . ."—
she shrugged—"occasionally is not so hard. I've already
spent two nights this week outside the ton. There's really no
impediment to my plans."

She wondered if the sound she heard was his teeth grind-
ing. She glanced at him—and noticed the other couples returning to the ballroom. Music drifted out to them, muted by
the doors. Dexter watched as the last stragglers departed,
leaving them alone in the quiet gallery, then he looked back
at her.

The silvery light threw the planes of his face into sharp relief, leaving the whole much harsher, more intimidating. He
was the descendant of Norman warriors; in this light, he
looked it, every angle stripped of its assumed softness, the
elegance he wore like a cloak.

She lifted her chin. "I'm determined to experience at least
a little excitement—I intend to ask Lord Cranbourne to
squire me to Richmond on the next fine night."

Already hard, his face turned to stone. "I can't allow that."

Haughtily, she raised both brows. "Why?"

Not the response he'd expected; a frown gathered in his
eyes. "Why?"

"Why do you imagine you have anything to say in the
matter? My behavior, my actions, are no concern of yours."
She paused before adding, deliberately provocative, "Earl or
not."

She shifted to slide past him and head for the ballroom.
One hard arm rose; his hand locked on the window frame,
caging her. She eyed it, then returned her gaze to his face.
Raised an even more haughty brow.

His eyes held hers. Then he raised his hand; fingers
curved, he brushed the backs, featherlight, down her cheek.

She quelled the resulting shiver before it showed, yet knew
he sensed it. His lips, long, thin, set until then in a straight
line, eased. His gaze sharpened. "If you want excitement,
you can find it here. There's no need to travel to Richmond."

His voice had deepened; he seemed much closer, although
he hadn't moved. His strength and heat were palpable

things, beating against her. His eyes held hers; she didn't dare look away. Barely dared to blink.

He leaned closer still, lowered his head. She lost sight of his eyes, fixed her gaze on his lips.

Behind her, she felt the side of the window frame, was grateful for its immovable support.

His head ducked and his lips brushed hers, cruised gently as if testing their resilience, then, not with a swoop but with the confidence of one sure of his welcome, he settled them over hers.

She felt that first kiss all the way to her toes. In response, sweet heat swept up from her soles to her heart. Her breathing locked. She swayed—raised a hand, locked it on the steely arm beside her.

Felt his other hand firm about her jaw, tipping her face up to his.

Alarm bells were ringing in Martin's head with the wild abandon of banshees. He blocked them out; he knew what he was doing, knew that, in this arena, he wielded absolute control. Instead of retreating, he turned his considerable talents to savoring her luscious lips, then teasing them apart.

Within seconds, he realized that although she'd been kissed, she'd never yielded her mouth to any man. He wanted it. Ruthless but still gentle, he shifted his fingers about her chin, pressed—her lips parted. He surged in— sensed her gasp, felt the sudden tensing of her spine.

Lowering his arm, he locked that hand at her waist, steadying her, fingers pressing to her spine, then soothingly shifting along the slender muscles framing it, distracting her, quieting her. Easing her into the caress.

Until she was kissing him back, luring him in, inexpertly but definitely returning each caress. Growing bolder by the minute.

He angled his head and deepened the kiss.

She tasted sweet. Delicate. Vulnerable.

He wanted more—couldn't get enough to appease his sudden need.

Every muscle strained to draw her to him, against him. He resisted, reminding himself just what he was doing—demonstrating to her the dangers in her plan to seek excitement. Drawing her to him would be tempting fate.

No matter how desirable that fate might be.

He took her mouth again, glorying in the softness, the subtle beckoning that, innocent though she was, seemed to have come to her instinctively. He let them both sink into the kiss, let the pleasure seep to their bones.

Kept his hand locked at her waist, refused to let it shift up, or down.

Ending the kiss, lifting his head, letting his hand fall from her face, took more effort than he'd expected. It left him slightly dizzy, blinking down into her wide eyes.

"Excitement enough?" He heard the gravelly tone in his voice and wondered to whom the question was addressed.

She blinked dazedly, then awareness flowed into her eyes.

Amanda dropped her gaze to his lips, felt her own tingle. Still felt the thrill of the invasion of his tongue, and all the sensations that had followed. Felt, recognized, her hunger for more. Knew she couldn't have it—yet.

"For the moment." She wondered at her tone—a beguiling, still confident purr she couldn't have bettered if she'd tried.

She glanced up, met his gaze. Saw a frown in the darkened green. Looking away to hide her satisfaction, she slid her hand down his arm to the hand at her waist, eased it away.

He straightened as she stepped out of his shadow. The waltz in the ballroom had just ended; no one else had yet joined them in the gallery.

She started toward the doors. "Incidentally, you were wrong."

"About what?"

She slowed, glanced back; he'd swung to watch her but hadn't moved from the window. "I do need to travel to Richmond." She held his gaze for a moment, then turned and continued to the nearest doors.

"Amanda."

She halted, then faced him. Across the room, she met his gaze.

Silence stretched.

"When?"

She considered his tone—flat, unforgiving. "We can discuss when tomorrow morning. In the park."

Turning, she opened the door, then looked back. "Will you send your groom as before?"

He watched her. When her nerves had stretched taut, he nodded. "As before."

With a graceful nod, she escaped into the ballroom. Within a minute, she felt his gaze on her back. Moving too determinedly for any to waylay her, she left the ballroom, made her way to the stairs and descended without a backward glance. A footman hurried to get her cloak, another rushed to summon a hackney. All the while, she knew Dexter watched her.

Not until the hackney turned into Upper Brook Street did she relax enough to gloat.

In the pre-dawn chill, Martin sat his roan under the tree in the park and watched her ride toward him. The great houses of Mayfair formed a backdrop, emphasizing the fact she was leaving their regimented world for the less structured, more dangerous and exciting world waiting for her beneath the trees.

He watched as she clattered across Park Lane. Felt a familiar quickening in his veins. The roan shifted; he tightened the reins, settled the huge beast.

She'd won their last round comprehensively. He was trapped, yet he doubted she knew it, let alone understood why. He wasn't sure *he* understood, not completely. He definitely didn't understand how he'd come to this pass.

Advised of her purpose, it was impossible to let her swan off and seek excitement with other men, knowing as he did that following such a path would likely lead to her ruin. Impossible because of the type of man he was, because of the absolute, ingrained conviction that, given he had the power to protect her and keep her safe, it was his duty to do so.

All that was clear enough. He'd long been aware of his

protective streak and accepted it, accepted himself, as he was. What he didn't understand was how she had come to invoke his protectiveness, to hold him hostage courtesy of his own convictions, without, apparently, trying.

He scanned her features as she neared, saw nothing beyond cheery good humor and her customary delight on meeting him. She didn't appear to be considering demanding anything more from him, didn't appear calculating in any way. She seemed to be revelling in the prospect of their ride.

Bringing the mare alongside, she tilted her head, blue eyes searching his face. Her smile was lightly teasing. "Are you always this grim in the morning, or is there something other than our ride on your mind?"

Narrowing his eyes, he locked them on hers, then brusquely gestured down the park. "I suggest we get on."

Her smile deepened, but she acquiesced with a nod. They set off at a trot, heading for the tan track.

He watched her as they rode, conscious of a need to simply let his gaze rest on her, uncertain from where such a need sprang. She rode well, hands and posture assured, apparently unconscious of his gaze.

As before, the park was deserted; as before, they sprang their horses the instant they gained the tan. Side by side, they thundered through the morning, the air sharp, biting as they flew through it, drawing color into her cheeks and eyes. When they slowed, the mare danced, eager for more; Amanda steadied her and brought the horse alongside his.

They turned back up the park to where the groom waited under the tree. Martin watched her still, aware to his fingertips of how alive she was, with the dawn just bringing the gold to her hair, deepening the blue of her eyes. Feminine vitality incarnate—he was conscious of the tug, the visceral attraction.

She glanced his way. He met her gaze, brimming with life and a still innocent joy in all life's pleasures, no matter how small, no matter how unsophisticated. No matter how private.

He looked ahead. "Richmond. It'll be fine tonight." He glanced at her. "Can you steal away again?"

"Tonight?" She worried her lower lip, clearly running down her list of engagements. "My parents are attending the Devonshires' dinner, but Amelia and I cried off."

"Amelia?"

"My sister. We often go to our own engagements these days, so tonight, indeed, I can easily be free."

Martin reined in. "Very well. Tonight. But I have a stipulation."

She considered him. "What stipulation?"

"That you tell no one where or with whom you're spending your evening. Furthermore"—he locked his gaze with hers—"I will agree to escort you to your four selected entertainments on condition that you will not, this Season, add to that list, and that you will not at any time tell anyone of those entertainments or of your association with me."

Amanda didn't reply immediately, too busy evaluating the proposition, too busy keeping a too-delighted, too-victorious smile from her lips. When she was sure she could manage both, she met his gaze. "Very well. I agree."

The roan shifted; he steadied the horse. "I'll meet you at the corner of North Audley and Upper Brook Streets. A black carriage will be waiting."

"A closed carriage?"

"Most definitely. We'll switch to my curricle once away from fashionable eyes."

She smiled, let her gaze dwell on him, then confidingly stated, "Such a relief to be in the hands of one who knows."

His eyes narrowed; she smiled more brightly and saluted. "Until tonight, then. What time?"

"Nine. Everyone else will be at the dinner table then."

She allowed her smile to widen, laughed at him with her eyes, then shook the reins and headed for the gates—before she became too flown on success and gave herself away.

"It's working perfectly! Absolutely *perfectly*—he can't help himself."

"How so?" Amelia climbed onto Amanda's bed and

slumped beside her. It was late afternoon, a time when they often spent an hour alone.

"He's so like our cousins, just as I suspected. He can't stop himself from protecting me."

Amelia frowned. "From what? You're not doing anything too dangerous, are you?"

"Of course not." Amanda flopped back on the bed so she didn't have to meet Amelia's eyes. Attending the Corsican Consul's *soirée* had been the most risky thing she'd ever done; she'd been very much aware of that as she'd chatted to Leopold Korsinsky and prayed Dexter would come to her side. Reggie had refused to escort her there, but she'd had to go. Amelia had explained her disappearance from Lady Cavendish's drawing room on the grounds of a headache, and, thanks to Dexter, to the accuracy of her perceptions of him, all had gone well. As long as he was in the same room, she would never be in danger. "It's more a case of creating the *potential* for danger, at least in his mind. For him, that's more than enough."

"So tell me—what exactly are you doing?"

"I can't tell—he made it a condition that I tell no one what we're about. Not even that it's him escorting me, but you already know that."

Amelia's frown deepened, but then eased. "Well, after all these years, you should know what you're doing." She settled deeper into the bed.

"How's your plan progressing?" Amanda asked.

"Slowly. I hadn't realized how many possible husbands exist in the ton once you disregard the matter of them actually wanting a wife."

"I thought you already had a gentleman in your sights." Amanda had a suspicion she knew who it was.

Amelia blew out a breath. "I do, but it's not going to be easy."

Amanda said nothing; if it was who she suspected, that was an understatement.

"I've decided I have to be sure, beyond all doubt, that he's the one above all others I want, given snaring him is going to take so much effort." Amelia paused, then added, "And given I might not succeed."

Amanda glanced at her twin, but could think of nothing to suggest.

Minutes ticked by and they simply lay, content in each others' company, their minds flitting over their hopes, their plans—all the things they never spoke of except to each other. Amanda was deep in imagining what might come of her jaunt to Richmond when Amelia asked, "Are you really sure it's safe to *encourage* Dexter's protectiveness?"

"Safe?" Amanda blinked. "What do you mean?"

"I mean that if you remember all we've heard from Honoria and Patience and the others, then that protectiveness you're playing with goes hand in hand with *possessiveness*. And not just common or garden possessiveness, either. At least, not with our cousins."

Amanda considered. "But that's what I want, isn't it?"

Amelia's voice reached her. "Are you absolutely sure?"

Chapter 4

Amanda slipped through the side gate of her parents' house into a narrow lane. Closing the gate, wrapping her cloak about her, she walked quickly to the end of the lane and peeped out.

A black carriage stood waiting at the corner of North Audley Street.

He was watching for her; the carriage door swung open as she neared.

"Come. Quickly."

His hand appeared; large, long-fingered, it beckoned imperiously. Hiding a smile, she placed her fingers in his and let him help her in. She sat and he leaned past her, closing the door, then he tapped on the carriage ceiling; the carriage lurched and rumbled off.

Only then did his fingers slide slowly from hers. In the light from a street flare, she saw him looking down at her. She smiled delightedly, then glanced at the passing streets.

Excitement skittered along her veins, flickered over her skin. The sensation owed more to his presence, his nearness in the dark, than to their intended destination. She felt his gaze leave her face, sweep down; she was acutely aware of him, of his heat, his sheer maleness, aware she was confined in the cocoon of the carriage with all that, and the consequent possibilities.

"At least you had the sense to wear a pelisse."

She glanced at him. "I doubt I would enjoy the drive while shivering with cold." She was prepared to shiver from another cause, but not cold.

The carriage slowed, then turned in through tall gateposts topped with . . . were they eagles? They'd driven around a large block and down Park Lane. A mansion appeared; the drive wended past it and on.

"My curricle's waiting."

The carriage rocked to a stop on the words. Dexter opened his door and alighted, then helped her down.

The yard was heavily shadowed. Dexter led her to a curricle and handed her up to the seat. Two grooms were leading the coach horses away; another held the prancing pair harnessed to the curricle. Taking the reins, Dexter sat beside her. He glanced at her, then reached around and rummaged. "Here." He dropped a thick, soft wrap on her lap. "It'll be colder driving." Looking forward, he nodded to the groom. "Let them go."

Releasing the horses, the boy dashed for the back of the curricle as Dexter flicked the reins. Amanda grabbed the rail as gravel crunched and the curricle rocketed forward. As they rounded the house, she scanned the massive edifice but it was shrouded in darkness and shadows. They swept on and the gates loomed ahead. Once Dexter took the turn and the wheels were rolling evenly, she released the rail and settled back.

Shaking out the wrap, she found it beyond luxurious—silk with a sumptuous weight. And the colors—deep, rich, even in the weak light. It had long fringes at both ends. She swung it over her shoulders, then tucked it about her. Dexter glanced at her, confirmed she was suitably swathed, then looked to his horses.

His house stood near the south end of Park Lane, the southeast corner of the fashionable area. Safe enough for her to ride openly beside him through the night as he steered the curricle further south and onto the Kings Road.

The horses were fresh, other carriages few and far between. Amanda sat back and enjoyed the cool air, the quiet of the night. They made good time, crossing the river at Putney, then rolling on through villages and hamlets. During the journey, the clouds dispersed, leaving the moon to shine freely. Eventually, they came to the village of Richmond, sleeping beneath a star-spangled, black-velvet sky. Beyond the last house, running from the village to the river, lay the dark expanse of the Deer Park.

She straightened as the first huge tree, bare branches spread wide, drew near. She'd been here often over the years, recognized the area, yet all seemed different in the dark. More evocative, the promise of excitement infinitely more acute. Cool tingles prickled over her skin and she shivered.

Instantly she felt Dexter's gaze, but made no move to meet it. He was forced to look to his horses as they rolled deeper into the shadowy park.

Silence engulfed them, pervasive and profound, disturbed only by the hoot of an owl, the scurrying of some nocturnal creature and the dull clop of the horses' hooves. The moonlight was faint, enough to see shapes but not colors. The breeze was faint, too, wafting the scent of trees, grass and leaf mold. The deer were asleep, round lumps beneath the trees. Some were standing, but evinced no interest in the interlopers into their moonlit world.

They were deep in the park, out of sight of all things human, when Dexter drew the horses to a halt. The silence, the eerie quality of the night, intensified and closed about them. He tied off the reins and turned to her. Eyes wide, she drank in the sight of the parkland rolling away from the carriage drive, edged by trees and copses, empty of all save the moonlight.

"Exciting enough?"

The words reached her on a whisper; no cynicism came with them—he seemed as appreciative as she.

She drew in a breath—the air was cooler, sweeter than any she'd ever tasted. "It's . . . strange." She glanced at him. "Come—let's walk a little way."

His brows rose but he stood, stepped past her and jumped down. He gave her his hands, helped her down the steps, then, enclosing one of her hands in a firm grasp, he surveyed the silvered sward. "Which way?"

"There." She pointed across the expanse before them to a pinetum.

Dexter called a command to the groom, then, her hand still locked in his, they set out.

It had been years since she'd walked hand-in-hand. She found it unexpectedly enjoyable, leaving her freer than if she'd taken his arm. Yet when her boot slipped in a dip, he pulled her up, steadied her easily. She laughed and smiled her thanks, resettled the luxurious wrap, then let him take her hand and they walked on.

Behind them, the carriage drive dwindled. The sense of being alone, the sole living beings in the quiet landscape, grew with every step. The consciousness of being isolated, one male, one female, burgeoned; there was no other living creature to distract or deflect their senses.

The magic that hung in the moonlit air was a drug. Amanda felt giddy by the time they were nearing the pines. She was aware Dexter was watching her; his thoughts were impossible to guess.

How did he see her? As an obligation, a young lady he felt honor-bound to protect? Or as a lady with whom he was happy to be walking handfasted through the moonlight?

She didn't know which, but she was determined to find out.

The pines were grouped to create a grove with a path winding through it; she glanced at Dexter. "Can we go in?"

His eyes met hers. "If you wish."

She led the way, gazing about her as they moved into the trees' shadows. The path led to a clearing where the interested could pause and admire the individual trees. She did so. The trees hid the moon; the clearing was lit only by diffused light, even softer, less substantial, than moonlight.

Sliding her fingers from Dexter's, she adjusted the silken wrap. She paused, eyes on the trees, senses alive to the subtle promise, the elusive whisper on the night air. She turned to him. His gaze shifted from the trees to her. She hesitated for only a heartbeat, then stepped closer. Lifted one hand to his shoulder, stretched up and set her lips to his.

He didn't immediately react, then he stirred; his hands locked about her waist and anchored her in the same instant his lips firmed. He returned her caress, then his tongue touched her lips and she parted them. He surged in.

Their lips clung, their tongues twined, caressed, made artful promises. His fingers flexed against her spine, sinking deeper, as if to hold her where she was, her feet firmly on the ground. Preserving the small but definite distance between their bodies, when all she wanted was to close it.

He drew back from the kiss, lifted his head, but seemed incapable of lifting it far. His eyes searched hers. "What are you seeking?"

She slid her fingers to his nape. "I told you—excitement. You told me I could find it here." *In your arms*. With her eyes, she dared him to misunderstand as, ignoring the pressure of his hands at her waist, she stepped closer. Her pelisse brushed his coat. She held his gaze, darkly shadowed, and prayed she struck the right note—one of blatant challenge. "Show me, then." Her gaze fell to his lips. "I want to know—I want to feel it."

Stretching up, she kissed him again; this time he met her from the start. Their lips melded, tongues tangled . . . then, as if she'd succeeded in getting him to open some door, the muscles of his arms unlocked. His fingers eased from her waist; his hands slid over, then under the slipping silk wrap. Slowly, deliberately, he drew her to him.

The contact, body to body, was a shock—a delicious one. The sheer strength now caging her would have had her resisting had it been any other man. Instead, she sank against him, inwardly smiled as his arms tightened and his hands shifted over her back. Gloried in the contrasts—her slenderness against his large body, the fineness of her bones against the heaviness of his. Her body reacted; she felt his react to her—felt her pulses leap. Sensed his need to seize. Was grateful that he didn't.

He felt like iron beneath his clothes—hot, resilient—male. Her breasts, flush against his coat, started to ache; her palms itched. Sliding her hand into his hair, she tumbled the thick locks, as heavy and silken as the wrap, over and through her fingers. Her other hand rested on his chest; she would have sent it wandering but he distracted her.

Drew her deep into the kiss, caught her wits, captured her senses with a sudden flare of sensual heat. With the sudden unmasking of desire, his and hers, the temptation of an unfamiliar need.

Martin angled his head and took the kiss still further, drawing her with him, holding her captive—where he needed to keep her. Where his brain had been when he'd followed her into the grove, heaven only knew. He hadn't been thinking clearly since they'd entered the deserted landscape. Which was how she'd trapped him, how she'd been able to draw him into this exchange, one he knew very well was unwise. Yet how to refuse, how to deny her . . . an impossible task in his present frame of mind.

Her lips were luscious, her mouth pure temptation, the soft, supple body trapped against his quintessentially feminine. He focused on the kiss, on exploring further, on extracting every last ounce of pleasure from the next caress, and the next . . .

Better that than allow his rakish senses time to evaluate, to consider the possibilities inherent in the lissome body filling his arms.

She murmured and pressed nearer, delicately shivered; his arms tightened reflexively, molding her to him, seeking her pleasure, and his. He took her mouth in a searing kiss, let her feel, sense, more of the fire with which she seemed so keen to play.

That lick of heat enthralled her—he sensed it in the faint tensing of her spine, the focusing of her attention, of her desire. That last was elusive, sweet when he could evoke it but veiled, cautious . . .

The welling need to lure her desire into the open shook him. An unfamiliar wish—he'd never coveted a woman's wanting before. All his life, the shoe had been on the other foot; they had always wanted him to want them. Yet now . . .

He tried to rein back—found he couldn't. The temptation was simply too great.

She met his next, more demanding kiss readily, but he still sensed a barrier, insubstantial but real, limiting how much she would show him, reveal to him—how much of herself she was prepared to give him.

Even as he took her mouth again, felt her cling, sensed her gasp, even as desire insidiously infused his frame, the realization that he couldn't press for more, not yet—if he was wise, not ever—rang through his brain.

He broke the kiss, tipped her head back, set his lips to skate her jaw, then dip lower. The slender column of her throat lured him, the skin covering it like peach-satin. His fingers drifted, senses caught, mesmerized; his lips explored, tasted, found her heartbeat thudding wildly at the base of her throat.

Her fingers were in his hair, tangling, trailing. When he finally found the strength to lift his head, she brushed back the fall of hair across his brow and looked into his face, studied his eyes. Then her fingers touched his cheek, traced down, fleetingly brushed his lips.

She smiled—pleased, satisfied. Just a little rattled—the breath she drew was shaky. It shook even more as her breasts pressed against his chest.

"Thank you." Her eyes shone brilliantly even in the weak light. She eased back—he had to order his muscles to unlock, force his arms to loosen.

She tilted her head, her eyes still on his. "We'd better get back to the carriage. It'll be late by the time we return to town."

That should have been his line, not hers. He resisted the urge to shake his head—shake his laggard wits into place. His expression was set, impassive; impossible to project any thought through the etched mask of desire.

She stepped back and he let her, but felt his reluctance to his bones.

Her hand slid down his arm—he caught it, held it. Eyes on hers, he raised it to his lips, pressed a kiss to her trapped fingers.

"Come." He kept hold of her hand. "The carriage awaits."

The return journey was as uneventful as their outward leg, but differed in one notable respect. Amanda prattled. All but continually; despite the fact she constantly made sense—a feat, considering the distance—Martin was not deceived.

She'd gained more than she'd expected; the degree of excitement she'd experienced had shaken her.

Leaving his carriage and horses to his grooms, he strode into his house. Serve her right if she was shaken—just look what she'd done to him.

Carrying the silk wrap, still warm from her body, he entered the house and headed for his library. Only when he was ensconced in its luxurious embrace, slumped on the daybed, the silk wrap flung beside him, a glass of brandy in his hand, did he allow his thoughts to drift back over the night.

The embers glowing in the grate slowly died as he revisited their earlier meetings, comparing, analyzing. Two things seemed certain: she was following some plan. And that plan now involved him.

Two aspects remained hidden, unknown. Had she from the first intended him to be the one to assist her in her quest for excitement, or did she only settle on him later as the best choice available? A supremely pertinent point, given the other aspect of her plan of which he remained in ignorance.

Where was she heading? What was her ultimate goal?

Was she simply pursuing a final fling before settling to marriage with some socially acceptable peer? Her citing of the start of the Season proper as the limit for her adventures suggested that might be the case.

But what if it wasn't? What if, behind her artlessness, which he accepted not at all, she was focused on achieving rather more?

What if her goal was marriage . . . to him?

He frowned, waited, took a long sip of brandy, savored it—and still his expected reaction didn't show. The determination to cut her off, keep her at a distance . . . where was his instinctive, never-before-in-abeyance response?

"Good God!" He took another swig of brandy. That's what she'd done to him—tempted that part of him he'd thought buried long ago.

He shied from thinking too far along that line, but the sensation of his mind clearing, thoughts settling, told him he was right. He waited, sipping, eyes on the nearly dead embers, until he could, with some degree of impassivity, view the question of where he—they—now were.

They were playing some game, one of her choosing, in which, despite all, he was now a committed player. Stepping back, quitting the game, was not an option he wished to pursue. So much for that. As for where they were headed, he didn't know, couldn't see—he would have to follow her lead. That was part of the game. She'd managed to take the reins into her small hands, and he could see no way of getting them back just yet.

Which meant he was being driven, managed, manipulated by a woman.

Again he waited for his inevitable reaction; again, it didn't materialize. For the first time in his life, he wasn't totally averse to running in a woman's harness. At least, for a time.

With a self-deprecatory grimace, he drained his glass.

Given the field on which their game was to be played, given his expertise in that sphere, ultimate control—the ability to stop, redirect the play, even rescript the rules—lay in his hands. And always would.

He wondered if she'd realized that.

After strolling in Richmond Park by moonlight, Amanda found it hard to pretend to any great interest in such a mundane event as a ball.

"I wish I could escape," she whispered to Amelia as they promenaded down Lady Carmichael's ballroom in their mother's wake.

Amelia shot her a worried glance. "You can't have another headache. I only just stopped Mama from sending for Doctor Graham last time."

Amanda eyed the flower of the ton with a jaundiced eye. "It'll have to be another party, then. Aren't the Farthingales entertaining tonight?"

"Yes, but you'll have to do the pretty for another hour before you can leave. *And* you'll have to find Reggie."

"True." Amanda scanned the crowd in earnest. "Have you seen him?"

Amelia shook her head. Louise settled on a chaise with Lady Osbaldestone and their aunt, the Dowager Duchess of St. Ives. After curtsying and exchanging greetings, the twins strolled on through the gathering crowd.

"There's Emily and Anne."

Amanda followed Amelia's gaze to where two girls, patently nervous, stood by one wall. Emily and Anne Ashford were to make their come-outs that Season. The twins had known the Ashfords all their lives. With identical, reassuring smiles, they made their way to the younger girls' sides.

Emily's and Anne's faces lit.

"This is your first ball, isn't it?" Amelia asked as they joined them.

The girls nodded, brown ringlets dancing.

"Don't worry," Amanda said. "I know it's hard to believe, but you will survive the night without doing anything to sink yourselves."

Emily smiled, nervous but grateful. "It's just so . . . overwhelming." She gestured at the throng filling the room.

"At first," Amelia said. "But after a few weeks, you'll be as used to it as we are."

Together with Amelia, Amanda chatted of inconsequential matters, skillfully encouraging the younger girls to relax.

She was looking about for some suitable young gentlemen to snare for Emily and Anne when Edward Ashford, one of their brothers, emerged from the crowd. Tall, well built, soberly dressed, Edward bowed to the twins, then, taking up a stance beside his sisters, considered the crowd. "A relatively small gathering. Once the Season proper starts, it'll be much worse than this."

Emily shot Amanda a startled glance.

She suppressed an urge to kick Edward. "One hundred or five hundred, there's not much difference. You can only ever see twenty bodies at a time."

"And by the time the larger balls start, you'll be feeling much more at home," Amelia put in.

Edward glanced at his sisters assessingly, censoriously. "This Season is your chance to make a good match. It might be wise to make a greater effort to attract the right notice. Hiding by the wall—"

"Edward." Amanda smiled daggers at him when he looked at her. "Can you see Reggie Carmarthen?"

"Carmarthen?" Edward lifted his head, looked about. "I wouldn't have thought he'd be much use."

More use than Edward. At twenty-seven, he was a certified bore, pompous and prideful. Amelia seized the moment to draw the girls' attention; Amanda shifted to keep Edward's gaze from his sisters.

"I can't see . . . oh."

A familiar blankness infused Edward's features. Following his gaze, Amanda was unsurprised to see his older brother, Lucien Ashford, Viscount Calverton, step from the crowd, his customary taunting, oddly crooked smile lifting his long lips.

"There you are."

Amanda knew Luc was perfectly aware of Amelia and herself, yet his hooded gaze was all for his sisters. They blossomed—unfurled like buds in the sun—under its impact. Rakishly elegant, he bowed, then raised them from their answering curtsies, twirling first Emily, then Anne, his razor-sharp gaze taking stock of their new dresses, approval writ large in his face.

"I suspect you'll do very well, *mes enfants,* so I'd better get in quick. I'll dance the first dance with you"—he solemnly inclined his dark head to Emily—"and the second dance with you." He smiled at Anne.

Both girls were delighted; their glowing expressions transformed them from pretty to bewitching. Amanda bit back the caustic observation that Luc would now have to remain in a ballroom for at least two dances, something he rarely did. The fact he'd committed to do so contrasted strongly with Edward's contribution to his sisters' success.

Although the brothers were similar in height and build, Luc was blessed with a frankly sensual beauty, and the character and aptitude to match. That fact had for years placed the brothers at odds, forming the touchstone of Edward's frequent carping over his older brother's rakehell ways.

Glancing at Edward, Amanda noted the ill-concealed sullenness in his eyes as they rested on Luc. There was anger there, too, as if Edward resented the affection that flowed so easily Luc's way. Amanda suppressed a humph; there was an easy solution if only Edward would take a page from Luc's book. Luc could be supercilious and odiously patronizing and he had a fiendishly sharp tongue, but he never pontificated, sermonized or lectured—Edward's favorite pastimes. Moreover, Luc also possessed a genuine kindliness any female worthy of the name recognized, appreciated and responded to.

Amanda watched as Amelia joined forces with Luc, bantering, bolstering the younger girls' confidence. Her twin was a good foil for Luc's dark, Byronic beauty. Her gaze lingered on his profile. It was familiar; she'd known Luc for years . . . she blinked, glanced at Edward, also presently presenting her with his profile. Both were exceedingly like one even more familiar.

She swung her gaze back to Luc. *Are you related to Dexter?* She only just bit back the words. The certain response had she been fool enough to utter them flashed across her brain; Luc would slowly turn, an intense, unnervingly acute look in his eye, and softly ask, *How do you know Dexter?*

She couldn't ask, but now she thought of it, she'd heard of a connection between the Ashfords and the Fulbridges. She studied Luc afresh, then looked again at Edward; compared to Luc, he cut a less visually compelling figure. Luc was a fraction more lean, more rangy, and had black hair and dark blue eyes. Brown haired, hazel eyed, Edward more closely resembled Dexter, yet with his disdainful, pompous hauteur and that underlying sullenness, he seemed somehow less than—less than either Dexter or Luc. In features and form, they'd all been struck from the same mold, but in Edward's case, something had gone awry and flaws had crept in, rendering him less attractive, physically and otherwise.

"And now, my dears, I must leave you." Luc's voice cut across her thoughts. "Nevertheless, at the first screech, I'll be back."

He tugged one of Emily's ringlets, bent a fond smile on

Anne, then bowed to Amelia, and with an inclination of his head extended the courtesy to Amanda. Then he straightened and looked at his brother. "Edward, if I might have a word . . ." With a crooking of one long finger, Luc strolled away, forcing Edward to stalk after him.

Leaving his sisters in peace. Amanda inwardly nodded approvingly, and saw her approbation mirrored in Amelia's eyes. She looked around. "Now . . ."

Five minutes later, she viewed the circle of admirers she and Amelia had gathered about Emily and Anne. Most gratifying. In its own way, satisfying. She caught Amelia's eye. "I'm going to look for Reggie. If I'm not here when you leave, will you tell Mama?"

Smiling, Amelia nodded; her gaze was more somber. "Take care."

Amanda smiled reassuringly. "I always do."

She slipped into the crowd. The first dance could not be far off. Reggie would be somewhere in the room; her mother had been expecting to meet his here, and Reggie would attend in her train given they'd made no other arrangements.

She hadn't made any because she hadn't been sure. Not over what she wanted; *that* was engraved on her heart. Her uncertainty stemmed from something more nebulous. Something about that kiss in the moonlight—perhaps the ease with which Dexter had drawn her into the heat, made her yearn for more. Or was it simply some lingering missish reaction? Whatever, caution had unexpectedly reared its head. A wary sort of caution she'd never felt before—a playing-with-fire, tempting-a-wild-beast-unwisely sort of edginess, purely instinctive.

But wariness, edginess and caution could not stand against that other emotion born in the moonlight.

Impatience.

It was an itch under her skin, a need insisting on fulfillment as its only cure. Every time she recalled the sensations she'd felt while locked in Dexter's arms, feeling his strength surrounding her, his lips on hers, his tongue—

"Well, my dear Miss Cynster—well met, indeed!"

She blinked twice before she managed to focus on the

gentleman bowing before her. Hiding her frown behind a weak smile, she bobbed a curtsy and gave him her hand. "Mr. Lytton-Smythe."

Blond, brown eyed, Percival Lytton-Symthe clasped her fingers and smiled his usual superior smile. "Lady Carmichael assured me you'd be attending tonight. I had wondered whether I could be bothered with such gadding thus early in the Season, but the thought of you drifting alone through the crowd, starved of suitable companionship, stiffened my spine. So here I am, come once more to lend you my arm."

He offered it with a flourish.

She resisted the urge to roll her eyes. Knowing there would be no easy escape, she laid her hand on the proffered sleeve. "I've just left some friends."

"Indeed, indeed."

He didn't believe her. Amanda gritted her teeth, a frequent reaction in Percival's presence. She scanned the crowd. Percival was a half-head taller but good manners forbade her asking him to find Reggie so she could escape him.

Good manners, let alone wisdom, did not raise their heads when Percival, considering her gown with a growing frown, cleared his throat. "Ahem! Miss Cynster—I fear I must comment, given the understanding between us, that your gown strikes me as somewhat . . . well, fast."

Understanding? *Fast?*

Amanda halted. Taking her hand from Percival's sleeve, she faced him. There was nothing wrong with her apricot silk gown with its heart-shaped neckline and tiny sleeves. Percival had been dropping hints ever since he'd stumbled on her during the last Season that he considered they would make a good match. From his perspective, maybe; not from hers. "Mr. Lytton-Smythe, I fear I must comment on your presumption. There is no understanding between us, no connection whatsoever that would excuse your making such unflattering and inaccurate statements regarding my appearance." She looked down her nose at him, grabbed the opportunity he'd presented with both hands. "I am insulted, and would appreciate it if you refrained from approaching me in future."

With a glacial nod, she swept around—

He grabbed her hand. "No, no, my dear. Forgive my foolishness, cowhanded as I am. I seek nothing more than your approbation. Indeed—"

He went on and on until she feared she'd scream. She tried to tug her fingers free, but he wouldn't let go; there was nothing she could do but let him pour out his apologies. Grovel for her forgiveness.

Disgusted, she let him get on with it. Goodness only knew how she was going to disabuse his mind of the erroneous assumption now clearly fixed in it. She'd tried to ignore him in the hope he'd realize but the sensitivity required to recognize a subtle dismissal was clearly beyond him.

Which left the unsubtle, but she hadn't reached that stage yet.

A violin screeched; Percival paused. She seized the moment. "Very well. You may stand up with me in the cotillion."

The smug smile that creased his face made her want to scream again—the fool thought her irritation had been feigned! Perilously close to real fury, she blocked off all thought of him and concentrated on her real objective. Reggie. He loved to dance; if he was here, he'd take to the floor.

She scanned the dancers as the sets formed. Two sets away, Luc led Emily, proud as punch and totally at ease, into formation. And in the set beyond that, Reggie was partnering a large young lady, one Muriel Brownley.

Amanda grinned. As the music commenced, she looked at Percival; his expression stated he thought she was grinning at him. Erasing all bar the most distant hauteur from her face and eyes, she gave her attention to the dance.

The instant the last chord sounded, she bobbed a quick curtsy. "I fear you must excuse me—there's someone I must catch."

She left Percival standing staring after her. If her mother had witnessed such unladylike behavior, she'd have been called to account; luckily, her mother, her aunt and Lady Osbaldestone were at the other end of the room.

She reached Reggie and his partner before they quit the floor. She exchanged the usual greetings, noting the possessive hold Miss Brownley kept on Reggie's sleeve, and the trapped-rabbit expression in his eyes.

Miss Brownley was a relative newcomer to the ton, no match for her. Amanda chatted brightly, engaging both Reggie and Miss Brownley in an animated discussion of upcoming events.

Miss Brownley didn't notice the time passing.

Not until the violins started up and she realized she couldn't dance the next dance with Reggie. Two dances in a row would cause comment. Having established herself as an old family friend, Amanda suggested Reggie partner her in the dance. Reluctantly, Miss Brownley agreed, and let him go.

"Thank heavens! Thought I was going to be stuck for the rest of the night. Latched on to me the instant I set foot in the ballroom. Mama waltzed off with her mother—and there I was. Snared!"

"Yes, well—" Her arm through Reggie's, Amanda hurried him down the line of dancers. "Let's make sure we fetch up by the door at the end." She bustled them into the position experience told her would achieve that aim.

Reggie stared at her. "Why?" The possibility he might have jumped from the frying pan into the fire was clearly rising in his mind.

"I want to visit Lady Hennessy's."

"Again?"

The dance commenced and they parted momentarily; when they came together, she hissed, "Given what I've just rescued you from, I would have thought you'd be grateful, and only too ready to play least-in-sight."

She let Reggie ponder that for two movements, then added, "She'll find you again if you don't."

Which was true. When they next met, Reggie nodded grimly. "You're right—Lady Hennessy's it is. Much safer, all things considered."

They slipped out immediately the dance ended without encountering Miss Brownley or any other likely to impede their escape. They did, however, encounter another escapee; while waiting in the hall for Amanda's cloak to be unearthed and a hackney to be summoned, they were joined by Luc

Ashford. Sauntering down the stairs, he nodded to Reggie; his gaze sharpened as he considered Amanda. "And where are you off to?"

Amanda smiled innocently, ruthlessly quashing a nearly overwhelming urge to tell him it was none of his business. This was Luc; any such response would have the worst possible effect—he'd become more intent, more determined to learn all. He was a rake with four sisters; she knew his type well. "We're off to the Farthingales'."

Reggie had, as usual, adopted his vaguest expression and left the answers to her; now he nodded. "Cavendish Square."

Luc looked at him. Just looked.

"And where are *you* off to?" Amanda asked. She didn't care what Luc suspected—he'd never suspect the truth—but she saw no reason to stand by and let him bolster Reggie's resistance to her schemes.

Luc didn't immediately turn her way, but when he did, his dark blue gaze was acute. "I plan to spend the rest of the evening in"—his long lashes veiled his eyes as he straightened a cuff—"rather more private surrounds."

A footman approached. "Your carriage is waiting, my lord."

"Thank you." Luc turned to the door, glancing again at Amanda. "Can I offer you two a lift?"

Amanda smiled sweetly. "I doubt Cavendish Square is on your way."

Luc held her gaze, then nodded. "As you say." With a nod to Reggie, he strolled to the door.

Leaving Reggie looking uncomfortable; Amanda looped her arm in his and chatted to distract him.

She managed well enough; by the time they were admitted to Lady Hennessy's, Reggie's usual amenable temper was restored. After greeting their hostess, Amanda pressed his arm. "I want to check who's here. Why don't you fetch some champagne?"

"Right-o."

Five minutes later, she'd verified that Dexter was not gracing any of her ladyship's rooms—at least, not the public ones. She didn't want to think that he might be gracing one of the private rooms. Determinedly, she envisioned him at Mellors, or one of the other exclusive hells.

Hiding in the shadows. Out of her reach.

Damn him—he was clearly not going to make his conquest easy.

She found Reggie loitering by a well-stocked table. Munching on a pastry, he handed her a glass of champagne. She took one sip, then set the glass aside. "There's no one here I want to meet. We may as well go home."

"Home?" Reggie stared. "But we've only just arrived."

"Without the right company, any place is boring. And I've just remembered I have an appointment tomorrow morning at six o'clock."

"*Six?* No one has appointments that early, not even with modistes."

"I do." She tugged at his sleeve. "Come on. I need to get home." In time to send a footman with a note to Fulbridge House.

Looking over the table, Reggie sighed. "Dashed fine salmon patties."

She let him take another, then dragged him away.

Chapter 5

When she saw the dark figure atop the pawing roan waiting under the tree the next morning, Amanda knew a moment of abject relief. That much, at least, she could count on. Trotting up, she smiled sunnily. "Good morning."

It was damp, cold and grey, a light drizzle turning all about them fuzzy, indistinct. His expression impassive, Dexter inclined his head and turned his horse toward the distant track.

She'd half-expected a grunt. Falling in beside him, she set the mare pacing alongside the roan.

How to prod him into arranging for the rest of her adventures? Into spending more time with her, alone.

She glanced at him, waited to catch his eye.

He didn't look her way. He rode straight to the start of the tan, then, with barely a glance at her, sprang the roan.

Jaw setting, she went with him. That he was determined to be difficult could not have been clearer. Through the thunder and rush of the ride, it occurred to her that he knew perfectly well what she wanted to ask.

It irked her that she felt too wary to demand openly, as she would with any other man. Dexter was hard enough, untamed enough, simply to refuse. And then where would she be? Dealing with him was like a game of snakes and ladders—one foot wrong and she'd be back at the start.

The end of the track neared; they slowed, then turned aside onto the turf. He drew rein and halted; she did the same. They were both breathing hard, the exhilaration of the ride still streaking through their veins. She lifted her head, looked into his face. Fell into his moss-agatey eyes.

Green, gold flecked, they held her gaze; in the cool of the morning, she again felt the heat, the rush of sweet warmth she'd experienced in his arms. The fire still burned, embers now, perhaps, but the heat and the promise of flame were still there.

Still exerted their tug, a powerful fascination that made her want to go to him, to plunge into the heart of the fire, bathe in the flames.

Give herself up to them and burn.

She blinked, refocused. What he had read in her face she had no idea, but he looked away over the park.

"You said you wished to attend a party at Vauxhall, one hosted by someone your parents don't know. I plan to host a private party at the Gardens two nights from now. Will you be able to attend?"

She forced herself to wait, to pretend to consider before inclining her head. "Yes." He was untamed, ruthless, difficult to manage; she was determined to snare him.

His gaze returned to her face; she met it, cool challenge in her eyes.

"Very well. My carriage will be waiting as before, at nine o'clock at the corner." He hesitated, then added, "Wear a cloak with a hood."

As before, the black carriage was waiting; as before, his hand reached for hers and he helped her in. Amanda suppressed a shiver of anticipation as the carriage rumbled off, wending south through the streets to the river and Vauxhall Gardens.

He travelled in silence; she could feel his gaze on her face, on her figure, concealed by her long velvet cloak, the hood up to cover her hair. She'd spent hours deciding what to wear beneath the cloak—whether to dazzle or entice. She'd settled on enticement; he was too experienced to dazzle.

The horses' hooves clopped hollowly as they turned onto

the bridge. Ahead, the lights of the pleasure gardens bobbed through the trees, their reflections dancing on the water.

"How many others are in your party?" A question that had intrigued her ever since his invitation.

She glanced his way. Shrouded in shadows, he studied her, then said, "You'll see in a few moments."

She doubted she'd misjudged him. Nevertheless, the knowledge that she'd placed herself and her reputation in his hands set an edge to nerves already taut, further heightened senses set alive simply by his nearness.

Confirming her judgment, the carriage halted, not at the main entrance, but at an exclusive side entrance. Infinitely more discreet. Dexter descended, looked briefly around before handing her down, his gaze passing approvingly over her hood, pulled forward, shadowing her face. Thus attired, unless someone came close and peered at her face, she was unidentifiable.

An attendant greeted them, bowing low as Dexter ushered her through the gate. "Your booth is prepared, my lord."

Dexter nodded. The attendant turned and led them down a heavily shaded path.

She'd been to Vauxhall often, yet had never ventured into this part of the gardens. The rotunda, well lit, the source of plentiful music, lay some way ahead, screened by trees. The path curved under spreading branches, the thick shrubs bordering it interrupted now and then by the square shape of a booth. Each booth was well spaced from its neighbors, shuttered and private. Stopping before one such dark outline, the attendant opened a door, spilling soft candlelight onto the path; he bowed them in.

Amanda stepped over the threshold, uncertain what she would find—eager to see. The booth was smaller than those in the public part of the gardens, but was furnished in considerably better style. A rug covered the floor; the table was set with a damask cloth, sparkling glasses, white dishes and cutlery for two. Two upholstered chairs stood ready. A single candle burned in a holder at the table's center; a two-armed candelabra shed light from a sidetable set beside a comfortable chaise. By the table, an ornate stand supported an ice-bucket containing a bottle of champagne.

The answer to her question was none. Reassured, she set back her hood.

"You may bring our meal." Martin closed the door on the attendant. He hesitated, then strolled to where temptation stood. He lifted the cloak from her shoulders as she slid the strings free; she glanced back, smiled her thanks.

He used the moment taken in laying her cloak on the chaise, in adding his to it, to steel himself. Then he turned back to her.

And saw her clearly for the first time that evening, knowing she was here, alone with him in a completely private setting.

Limned by the candlelight, she was half turned his way, the fingers of one hand resting on the back of the nearer chair. The weak light deepened the gold of her hair but did nothing to conceal its luster, to hide her flawless complexion or the intensely feminine curves of breast, hip and thigh, all draped in cornflower silk the exact shade of her eyes.

The gown made the most of her charms. Severely simple, it led the eye to see, showcased the bounty it concealed.

All that, he'd foreseen. What he hadn't expected was the aura of anticipation, blatantly sensual, that filled the space between them, that invested her expression, widened her eyes, lingered in the curve of her lips.

The effect was worse—far worse—than he'd expected.

He couldn't recall taking the steps, but he was suddenly beside her. She'd lifted her head to keep her eyes on his; raising one hand, he trailed the backs of his fingers up the exposed line of her throat, then turned his hand, cupped her jaw and bent his head to hers.

Her lips met his confidently. Not overeagerly, but she was ready and willing to follow wherever he led.

It was her control that gave him his, gave him the strength to raise his head without taking the caress any further. Hearing a sound outside the door, he reached around her and drew out her chair. Her eyes met his briefly, then she turned

and sat, settling her skirts as the attendant entered pushing
the trolley carrying their meal.

Once the trolley was positioned and the dishes displayed,
Martin dismissed the man and took his seat. Amanda helped
herself to the various delicacies; he reached for the bottle
and filled her glass, then his.

"You've been here before."

Across the table, her eyes quizzed him.

"On occasion." He had no intention of letting her imagine
he was any less dangerous than society had painted him.

Her lips curved; a dimple winked. She raised her glass.
Obligingly, he lifted his and clinked the edge to hers.

"To my adventures," she declared, and drank.

To sanity. He took a fortifying swallow.

"Can we go out and about the gardens?"

He took another gulp. "After we've eaten."

She applied herself to the food with unfeigned appreciation. However, other than commenting on the culinary skills
of the unknown cook, she did not speak. Prattle. Fill his ears
with the usual babble, as women were wont to do.

He found her reticence disconcerting. Disorienting.

As he tended to keep silent, having long ago discovered
the advantage that conferred, the ladies he escorted usually
felt obliged to fill the vacuum. Consequently, he was never
consumed by any wish to know what was going on in their
heads; if they were talking, they weren't thinking.

Now, however, Amanda's silence focused his attention as
no feminine discourse ever would. What was going on under
her golden locks? What plot was she hatching? And why?

That last nagging question rang warning bells. Why did
he want to know? He mentally shrugged the quibble aside—
he definitely wanted to know *why* she'd selected him as her
partner in adventure.

On a sigh of pleasant repletion, she laid down her knife
and fork. He drained the last of the champagne into his glass
and sat back, sipping.

Across the table, she met his gaze. "It's odd—although
we're in the gardens, you can't hear the crowd."

"The bushes absorb the sound." Including any sound from the isolated booths. Pushing back his chair, he stood. "Come. Let's take the air."

Amanda was very ready to do so; the strain of not giving way to nervous babble was wearing her down. Outside among the crowd there would be plenty of distraction, and ease for her overstretched nerves. Sharing an enclosed space with a large, intensely predatory male, one who looked like sin personified, was not a calming experience; she knew she was safe, yet her senses insisted on screaming she was not.

In her cloak with the hood up, shielding her face, she left the booth on Dexter's arm. They retraced the path, then took another turning. It opened into one of the main walks. Immediately, they were surrounded by couples and groups all flown with good cheer. As they walked toward the rotunda, the center of the garden's entertainments, the crowd steadily increased.

It was not a Gala Night, so when they reached the area where couples were waltzing, there was space enough for Dexter to draw her into his arms and steer them into the swirling throng.

She glanced at his face; he was watching her. He studied her eyes, her expression, then had to look up as they turned. The lanterns bobbing overhead sent light, then shadow, dancing across his features. Illuminating the strong patrician lines, then veiling them.

Following his lead without thought, she let her mind drift, allowed her senses to appreciate as they would. She was aware of his strength, of the ease with which he steered her, of the sudden tensing of his arm, drawing her protectively closer when more couples joined in and limited their space.

Those about them were of all walks, all types, including others of their ilk, ladies and gentlemen enjoying an evening in the gardens, others even more like them with the lady cloaked and in some cases veiled. A *frisson* of daring tickled her spine; for the first time in her life, she was flirting with the illicit.

Dexter's gaze returned to her face. She met it boldly, her lips curved, awareness naked in her eyes. They continued to twirl, neither willing to look away, to risk missing the next moment. Breathing became a secondary concern; absorption in the moment was all.

Magic shimmered in the shifting light, touching them fleetingly, teasing their senses. It was as mesmerizing an experience as she'd hoped for, twirling through the shadows with him. They were surrounded, but they might as well have been alone, so intent on each other were they.

The music ended and they slowed; she broke the contact, mentally reaffirmed her plan. She'd lured him this far; now she had to tempt him to take the next step.

Martin noted the faint crease between her brows. "Would you care for some punch?" What was she plotting?

"Please." She flashed him a brilliant smile, banishing the frown. "I haven't been here for years."

"I doubt the punch has changed." He took two cups from a passing waiter, handed her one, watched her sip. Watched red liquid stain her lips, watched her tongue slide across the lower.

He raised his cup and drained it in one gulp.

"Dexter!"

Martin turned and saw Leopold Korsinsky pushing through the crowd. Mentally cursing, he tossed his empty cup to a passing attendant and reached for Amanda's hand. "Careful," was all he had time to growl before Leopold reached them, a cloaked lady on his arm.

Barely nodding to Martin, Leopold bowed elaborately before Amanda. "*Madame*—have we met?"

Using the cup to shield her lower face, Amanda looked out from the shadow of her hood, noting the sharpness of the Corsican's gaze as he scanned all he could see. She lowered her voice to a deeper key. "I believe we have met, sir, although you might not recall."

Dexter squeezed her fingers. Amanda grinned behind the cup.

Korsinsky's eyes narrowed. "My memory is often at fault, yet were I so remiss as to forget such an attractive *parti*, I would be a lost cause indeed."

The other lady was eyeing Dexter as if he were a meal.

Keeping her voice low, Amanda laughed. "How do you know I'm attractive, covered as I am?"

Leopold shot a glance at Dexter and she had her answer.

"I would not suppose it otherwise, *ma belle,*" Leopold returned. "But perhaps I can persuade you—"

"Leopold."

Just one word, loaded with warning; Leopold looked at Dexter, brows rising. "But *mon ami,* there is plenty of distraction for you here. Agnes, she is attending. She will be delighted to know you are present."

"I daresay. However, *Madame* is keen to see the gardens. If you and your lady will excuse us?" With a bow for the lady, a brusque nod for Leopold, Martin gripped Amanda's hand and stepped back. He barely gave her time to nod in farewell before he led her away.

Into the gardens, down the long, shadowed walks; Amanda saw no reason to remonstrate. "Who was the lady?"

"Not one of your circle." He took her empty glass and handed it to an attendant. Then he stopped, contemplated the poorly lit walk before them, then turned and led the way back to a cross path. "The fireworks will start soon."

They headed toward the grassy area where the fireworks would be set, meeting more and more people similarly inclined. When they stepped onto the lawn, there was a gaggle of couples milling and shifting. Dexter scanned the field. He grasped her elbow. "Up there."

"There" was a small hill affording a good view of the display. The slope was crowded, but he found them a place near the top.

"Stand in front of me." He wasn't the sort of man people crowded; he positioned her before him, protected by his body from the crowd behind and to some extent from the sides as well.

Almost immediately, the first rocket streaked upward and exploded. Accompanied by rapt "ooohs" and "aaahs," the exhibition progressed, a man-made tapestry of white fire hung against the ink-black sky.

The crowd was transfixed by a depiction of a horse, when

Amanda sensed movement behind her, then heard, "Martin? I thought it was you."

Luc Ashford!

She felt the loss of Dexter's protective presence, the loss of his heat down her back, felt suddenly vulnerable, exposed. He'd stepped back to avoid any suggestion of a connection between them. Luc was sharp-eyed and sharp-witted. Neither she nor Dexter wanted to direct Luc's gaze her way.

"Luc. Are you here for the *ambiance,* or are you with a party?"

After an instant's hesitation, Luc responded, "I'm with friends. They're down there, but I thought I glimpsed you through the crowd."

"Ah."

"And what of you? According to the gossips, you avoid social gatherings like the plague."

"One should never listen to gossips. I found little else of interest tonight, so thought to take the air here." After a pause, Dexter added, "I'd forgotten what it was like."

Another pause; Luc's voice was softer when he said, "Do you remember the first time we came? A girl each, a cheap booth and we thought we were kings."

"That"—Dexter spoke quietly but his tone was hard—"was a long time ago."

Luc shifted. "Indeed." After an instant's awkward silence, he said, "I'll leave you to enjoy the night, then."

Amanda could imagine their stiff nods; they were alike in more ways than the purely physical.

Minutes ticked past; she didn't move—had stopped seeing the fireworks long before. Then Martin stepped nearer; through her cloak, his fingers closed about her elbow. "Come with me."

The words were a whisper drifting past her ear. Without hesitation, she turned and let him lead her down the hill, into the empty walks.

Behind them, white fire lit the sky. A breeze stirred the leaves, setting the shadows shifting, sighing through the boughs like some watchful ghost. They turned from the main cross walk into an even darker avenue. Martin slowed, Amanda looked about and recognized where they were.

The Dark Walk.

The one Walk no young lady was ever supposed to let herself be lured into. She'd never heard of any verified drama associated with breaking that rule, but she'd never known any young lady who'd travelled the Dark Walk.

Especially with a man like Martin Fulbridge at her side.

She shot him a glance; he was waiting to capture it. Shadowed, unreadable, his eyes held hers. "I assumed a promenade down the Dark Walk would feature in your scheme for excitement."

"Indeed." In her scheme for excitement, and more; she knew opportunity when she saw it, when fate offered it to her on a plate. Tucking her hand in Martin's arm, she moved nearer. "Can we walk the whole way?"

He hesitated, then replied, "That was my intention."

It was a narrow, winding walk. The bushes that bordered it were dense, crowding in, rendering it secretive and gothic. Dotted along its length, tucked around bends, were benches and structures designed for dalliance. With the crowd distracted by the fireworks, the Dark Walk was deserted.

Save for them.

Amanda considered each bench, each gazebo as it appeared; none was quite right for her purpose. Then she saw what she needed—a small Grecian temple set back a little way from the walk and hemmed in by thick shrubs.

"Look!" She towed Dexter toward it. "Can we go in?"

She felt his sharp glance, but he took her hand and led her up the steps.

Inside was a tiny circular room; in the dark, with the bushes so close, it seemed enclosed. In the center stood a pedestal supporting the bust of some god; she couldn't tell which. There was nothing else—just empty darkness.

In which she stood with her own particular god.

He was looking at the bust. She'd slipped her fingers from

his when they'd entered; now she joined him, slippers silent on the marble floor.

Martin's senses alerted him to her nearness—too late. He'd been distracted by the bust—Apollo, the gods' messenger. He'd been wondering what message there was in this for him. Now he knew.

He was too late to stop her from pressing close, from laying her hand on his chest. From leaning into him, reaching up and drawing his face to hers.

Too late to stop his body from reacting, to stop himself from bending his head, meeting her lips, taking what she offered. He tried—for one instant fought against her spell. But she'd captured him; despite all his logical arguments, there was too much of him that simply wanted her.

And it was only a kiss. That was what he told himself as he sank into her mouth, let his arms slide around her and gathered her to him.

One kiss. What harm could one kiss do? It wasn't as if he wasn't in control, of himself as well as her.

The kiss lengthened, deepened. She wound her arms about his neck and stretched upward against him.

He let her. Gloried in the feel of her lithe body pressed to his, the feminine curves, the tempting contrast of softness and resilience that beckoned, promised and teased.

She wanted more; he knew it. All sense of time, of place, of safety, fled from his reckoning. He knew nothing beyond her innocent hunger, and the powerful need to be the one to slake it.

Innocent though she was, Amanda recognized that need. She tasted it in his kiss, felt it in the arms that caged her, cradled her. Coveted it, wanted it—wanted him.

Wanted him to be hers, linked to her and her alone with a chain strong enough to withstand whatever pressures life brought to bear.

Knew in her heart what she would give to forge that chain.

Realized it would have to be created link by link. Episode by episode; interlude by interlude. Kiss by kiss.

Desire was a drug, its addiction potent. He stole her

breath, held her mind and senses captive. His slow, achingly thorough exploration, the lazy, compelling conquest left her mentally reeling, emotionally bound.

She'd been right—this was what she wanted, what she needed to be all she'd been created to be.

If she told him, she'd lose him. If her actions became overt, he'd pull back, leave her and slide back into the shadows. The occasional sharp glance he'd thrown her were warnings; she had to walk a line between naive encouragement and deliberate sensual beckoning without a single stumble. She had to tempt him further while keeping her intentions veiled so he couldn't be sure she was luring him on.

The ultimate game given his experience, given his steadfast reticence.

She kissed him back boldly but briefly, enough to evoke a reaction, to tug him an iota deeper into the game. Desire flared, heated and sultry, contained behind the wall of his will.

Crack by crack, she would demolish that wall.

She let her lips soften, tempted his to harden, tempted him to take just a fraction more. Clung, fingers sinking in reaction when he did. He was sensuality incarnate, each languid caress an invocation of pleasure. Her fingers threaded through his silky hair as inside she felt herself melt.

His hands tensed, flexed on her back; she sensed the war he waged to keep them from wandering. She considered trying to tip the scales—realized her inexperience would give her game away.

He won his inner battle too easily for her liking. Time to try another tack.

She drew away, gently broke the kiss—hid her triumph at the brief instant that passed before his arms eased and let her do so. As her senses returned, she heard voices outside. They both turned, listening, then she stepped back, out of his arms.

She cast about for some quip to cover her retreat, to disguise her hope that it would evoke his desire for something denied.

"Excitement enough?"

The deep words and their underlying challenge had her lifting her head. He was no more than a shadow looming close in the dark. She let her lips curve with a haughty confidence she hoped he could see. "The night's young."

Her tone struck the perfect note, low, warm yet even.

It was the tilt of her head that ruffled Martin's surface, an elementally feminine gesture of defiance that sparked an instanteous reaction. One he ruthlessly quelled.

She looked toward the Walk. "Shall we return to the booth?"

He reached for her hand. "We won't be returning." When she glanced at him, surprised, he murmured, "The night's young."

And he'd been a fool for thinking that cramming two of her adventures into one night would be a good idea. More of her "excitement" was not going to be easy to withstand. Yet he would. Leading her down the temple steps, he glanced at her. "You said you wished to see the stars in the Thames."

The anticipation that lit her face was a joy to behold. "A boat? From here?"

It had been a long time since he'd been with a woman who could conjure such innocent delight. His lips curved in a genuine, entirely spontaneous smile. "The Water Gate's this way."

He led her further up the Dark Walk, then across to the gate opening onto the riverbank, steadfastly refusing to dwell on the difficulties that doubtless lay before him. During his years in India, he'd survived his fair share of life-and-death encounters; one hour floating down the Thames with Amanda Cynster could hardly be that dangerous.

From the Water Gate to the stone quays where a plethora of river craft waited was but a few steps. The pleasure craft he'd hired waited, bobbing gently, a pair of brawny oarsmen slumped over the oars, the owner standing by the tiller. The latter spotted him, straightened and saluted. The oarsmen stirred, nodding respectfully as Martin stepped down to the deck. He held out a hand to Amanda; eyes huge, she eagerly descended.

"M'lady." The owner bowed low.

Amanda inclined her head, then glanced at Dexter. He gestured to the curtain cutting off the front two-thirds of the deck. The owner hurried to lift one side. She walked through. And stopped. Looked around. Offered mute thanks to fate for her assistance.

Dexter ducked through the curtain behind her; the heavy material fell closed, shutting them off from the watermen, leaving them in a private world.

A world composed of a narrow path leading around the railings. Fixed in the prow, a wickerwork basket held a platter of fruit, a bowl of nuts, two glasses and an open bottle of wine. The rest of the space was taken up by a thick pallet on a wooden base, covered by a plain black cloth. Piled atop was a mound of cushions encased in brightly colored Indian silk.

The deck of the pleasure craft looked exactly as she'd always imagined such a notorious venue would look—a setting for seduction. Lowering her hood, she glanced back at Dexter.

He looked down at her face, studied her eyes. The deck rocked as the vessel pushed off from the quay; his fingers closed about her elbow. "Come. Sit down."

He handed her to the couch; she sat and found it as comfortable as it looked. He sat beside her, angling against the cushions. "Does it live up to expectations?"

She smiled. "Thus far." Sliding back, she let herself sink against the silk-sheathed mound. She looked up at the stars. And said nothing more.

She kept her eyes on the heavens, on the pinpricks of light bright against the darkness, aware that Dexter's gaze never shifted, never left her.

The boat swung into the current, then the oarsmen rested and the craft drifted south with the tide.

Martin eventually stirred, then rose and crossed to the basket. Ignoring the wine, he plucked a grape from the platter, tasted it, then picked up the platter and returned to offer it to her.

Smiling, she chose a sprig of grapes and murmured her thanks. He hesitated, then sat once again beside her, placing the platter between them.

Amanda eyed it, then lifted her gaze to his face, to his profile as he looked out over the water. Popping a grape into her mouth, she looked in the same direction. "You spent many years in India."

His gaze touched her face briefly. "Yes."

She waited, then prompted, "In one place, or"—she gestured with a grape—"all over?"

He hesitated, then replied, "All over."

Pulling teeth would be easier. She looked directly at him, and inquired, sweetly determined, "All over where?" He met her gaze; she sensed the frown in his eyes. Frowned back. "Your travels can hardly be state secrets."

Unexpectedly, his lips kicked up at the ends. "Actually"—he leaned back against the cushions—"some of them were."

Shifting, she faced him. "You worked for the government?"

"And the Company."

"The East India Company?"

He nodded; after a fractional pause he answered the question forming in her mind, "There were precious few Etonites in Delhi, and the maharajahs preferred to deal with those they considered their peers."

"So where did you go?"

"Mostly along the trade routes through the north, occasionally south to Bangalore, Calcutta or Madras."

"What was it like? Tell me."

It was the light in her eyes, Martin later told himself, that and the genuine interest in her face that had him complying— and, of course, the knowledge that while she was listening wide-eyed to his tales, she wasn't plotting his downfall. She peppered him with questions; he found himself telling her things, recounting the years as he had to no one else. No one else had asked.

The end of her questions coincided with the last of the grapes. With a satisfied sigh, she picked up the platter and rose.

He watched as she crossed the few steps to the basket and set the platter in its niche. She stood in the prow, looking out over the black waters, presumably studying the reflections of the stars. She'd flipped her hood up; from where he sat she appeared the very essence of mysterious—a cloaked and silent female, mind and body shielded, hidden from his knowledge.

The urge to know, in every way, completely, waxed strong; he quelled it, restlessly shook aside the impulse to go to her, take her in his arms . . . he looked away, to the shore, indistinct in the dark. Between them and the banks, other craft slid through the waters, some, like theirs, idling, others pressing on.

Recollection of their unexpected meeting with Luc had him glancing at Amanda. "Sit down." Another craft was coming up swiftly on their right. Leaning forward, he grasped her wrist. "Someone might recognize you."

She turned at the same instant he tugged, the same instant the swell from the other vessel lifted the deck. She lost her balance. Before she could fall, he yanked—she fell across him.

Wriggled and ended up alongside him, breathless, tangled in her cloak, laughing up at him, her free hand trailing down his chest.

He couldn't breathe.

Their gazes met—she stopped breathing, too.

The laughter faded from her eyes; awakening desire replaced it. Her gaze lowered from his eyes to his lips. Her lips parted, softened; the tip of her tongue skated over the lower.

When he didn't move, she lifted her gaze to his eyes. Studied them. Then, with a deliberation he could feel, she slid her hand up, around his nape and drew his lips to hers.

No, no, no, no . . . despite the clarion warning in his mind, he permitted it, let her draw him down so he could feast on her lips, sink into the warm haven of her mouth and devour. She welcomed him in, offered herself up to him, and he knew very well what she did.

Knew she was trying to snare him, knew he would be wise to refuse her lures.

Simply couldn't.

Especially not when his logical mind pointed out her inexperience; she could have no weapon, no plan he had not already escaped, that women more experienced had not already used to try to capture him. She was no threat to him. So there was no reason he couldn't savor her, and give her a taste of the excitement she craved. She was safe with him, and, logically, he was safe from her.

He kissed her again, took her breath, drew her to him. He sensed her inner gasp, felt her yearning rise. Her hand drifted to his cheek, touched, stroked, a featherlight caress. Tantalizing. Taunting. He deepened the kiss and she shivered. He felt it to his marrow.

Before he knew it, he'd shifted, angling over her to take the kiss further, the better to touch her—

No. Caution caught his reins. Mentally hauled him back. He wasn't that foolish. She lay beside him, cocooned in her cloak, her svelte form shielded from him—temptation under velvet wraps.

Infinitely safer than temptation under his hands, no matter how his palms itched. But the impulse wouldn't leave him. He pressed his palms to the silk cushions in a vain attempt to ease their burning.

Amanda knew all about that burgeoning heat; she was far too hot swathed in her cloak. Each kiss, slow, deep and languorous, poured liquid fire down her veins, yet focusing her mind enough to free herself . . . every time she tried, he stole her wits, caught her senses with some shifting nuance in the steadily deepening intimacy of their kiss.

A shared delight—she didn't need experience to tell her he enjoyed the heated exchange as much as she. She was a novice, he an expert, yet his every exploration spoke of desire, each invasion of building passion.

Passion severely restrained. The fact gradually dawned. Despite the tale told by his lips and tongue, by the tension thrumming through the large body so tantalizingly close to hers, iron will kept his muscles locked, kept his chest fixed two inches from hers.

The realization gave her strength—stubbornness enough— to focus her wayward wits. She wanted him to touch her, caress her—to lay hands on her. At the thought, her breasts ached, and kept aching.

He'd set wards, limits, boundaries—the challenge was: how to break them. How to make *him* break them; even if she grabbed and yanked, she doubted she could move him. How—*how?*

With every minute that passed, her inner ache intensified. She managed to raise her hands to her throat and tug the ties of her cloak loose, managed to push back her hood. Instantly, he shifted, spearing the fingers of one hand through her curls, gripping, holding her head steady as he plundered, deeper, hotter, stronger—

She'd been burning before—now she was aflame.

On a gasp, she pulled back, tipping her head back against the cushions, desperate for air. For ease. His head dipped, lips tracing the line of her jaw, then skating down her taut throat to press heat to the pulse point at its base.

Her body reacted, her spine arched. The need to be closer, much closer to him flooded her. "Please." She couldn't think, couldn't form a thought, but she knew what she wanted. "Touch me. I hurt. So much. Just . . . touch me."

The fractured plea fell into silence. His voice gravelly, he replied, "You'll hurt even more if I do."

She forced her lids up. From beneath her lashes, she looked into his face, into his mossy green eyes. "I'll risk it."

But would he? Should he? Martin fought to distance himself from her, to hold his clamorous impulses at bay.

Her gaze dropped to his lips; lifting one hand, she traced his cheek. *"Please."*

The fleeting touch even more than the whispered word shattered his good intentions. He drank the last syllable from her lips, then took her mouth again. Sliding his fingers from her golden locks, feeling them fall like silk from his skin, he reached for the edge of her cloak.

Slipped his hand beneath. Told himself that if he left her fully covered, fully clothed, all would be well—

Knew the instant he touched her he'd been wrong.

His fingers skated over silk, then he cupped her breast. And something shattered. Whether in him or in her he couldn't tell. Her walls or his—one at least had cracked. She clung to their kiss as did he, but their attention had shifted, coalesced, focused completely on his fingers, on the firm flesh, hot and swollen, about which they curved, then gently kneaded.

The tension in her spine transmuted, eased by his touch, appeased by each caress. He continued to fondle and she moaned softly; without thought, his fingers shifted, circled her tightly budded nipple, then firmed, squeezed.

Until she gasped with pleasure. He drank the exhalation from her lips, continued to stroke, to fondle, to ease her hurt, to soothe her with pleasure.

Lifting his head, he watched her face, and wished he could draw back from her fire. Knew he couldn't. He couldn't recall when a woman's neediness had had the power to so arouse him. Worse, to arouse him to such a painful state.

Worse yet, a state for which there would be no relief.

Regardless . . . he flipped back her cloak, pushed the folds from her shoulders. Bent his head to pay homage to the alabaster skin sheathing her collarbone, trailing kisses along every curve. Her neckline was cut low; easy enough to hook a thumb beneath and ease gown and chemise down enough to free one rosy nipple so he could taste.

Amanda thought she would die when he did.

The touch of his lips there was excruciatingly right—*exactly* what she needed, wanted, even though she hadn't known, not until the instant when the hot wetness of his mouth had so briefly engulfed her sensitive flesh. Her gasp shivered in the night; her fingers threaded through his hair and clenched, holding him to her. He licked, lapped, then took the peak of her breast into his mouth again.

Oh, yes! The words whispered through her mind, escaped on her sigh.

He continued to caress her, lifting his head every now and then to press brief appeasing kisses to her hungry lips. Desire rose, spread about them, lapping gently, lazily, until she felt afloat on its gentle tide, quite unlike the rushing, pummeling, compelling stream she'd expected. It was as if their desire, strong and forceful though it was, had been diverted into a wider landscape so its power was dissipated in the vastness.

So she could know and enjoy without losing her mind, while in full possession of her senses.

The tide slowly ebbed, little by little, touch by touch. She made no demur, made no effort to encourage him further; in truth, she doubted she could. Throughout, his resistance had stood firm as a fortress wall, but she'd managed one crack, and with that she was content.

With that and the knowledge she'd gained, the sensations she'd felt—the experience. She felt a little shocked by how *un*shocked she was as she watched him ease her gown back into place.

She gazed at his face, at the harsh planes so set, so rigid. At the evidence of desire ruthlessly controlled. She wasn't ignorant of his state; she could feel his erection against her thigh. While she might wish to experience a great deal more, the time was not right—she was too wise to press him further.

Too wise to challenge his control overtly.

When he flicked her cloak back over her arms, she stayed him. Lifted one hand to his cheek, drawing his dark eyes to hers. Coming up on her elbow, she lifted her face and pressed her lips to his in a long, lingering, simple kiss, as sweet as she could make it.

"Thank you." She murmured the words as their lips parted. Lifting her gaze, she looked into his eyes, no more than two inches from hers. Let him search her eyes, let her sincerity show.

His gaze drifted from hers; he hesitated, then bent his head and touched his lips, not to her mouth but to the corner of her lips.

"It was entirely my pleasure."

When he stalked into his house two hours later, Martin recalled those words with a certain savage irony. He'd succumbed to her plea with the sole intention of pleasuring her, of easing the ache his kisses had caused.

He'd ended lost, fascinated, enthralled to his bones by the simple act of touching her. Caressing her. Savoring the different textures, the incredibly fine skin of her breasts, her tightly ruched nipples, the silken fall of her hair.

He'd enjoyed her far too much. He'd wanted to enjoy her a great deal more. And that way lay madness.

More specifically, that way led beyond the narrow confines of the world in which he'd chosen to live.

She'd already made him want, made him start to yearn for things he couldn't have. The longer he let her remain in his life, the more she'd undermine his defenses.

Slumping onto the daybed in the library, he took a long sip of brandy and stared into the fire. Her presence lingered, imprinted on his hands, on his senses; her taste was addictive, remembered and desired.

He directed his mind to the problem of how—how to sever all contact.

Chapter 6

Two mornings later, Amanda tiptoed around her bedchamber, wriggling into her chemise and petticoats, then donning her riding habit. She performed the actions by rote, her mind engrossed with thoughts of Dexter, or more correctly, Martin Fulbridge, the man behind the wall. Their last interlude had confirmed that her instincts had been right; the man within was precisely as she'd guessed, and more. There were deeper currents there, deeper wants, deeper needs. A character more complex than she'd expected.

A conquest more challenging than any man she'd met.

Contentment warmed her. She now knew she could succeed; she'd sighted her true quarry—the elusive man. On the boat, he'd revealed himself more clearly than at any time previously. He'd dropped his guard long enough for her to recognize the difference, to feel it in his kiss, sense it in his touch.

A wish, a need, a wonderment that was only partly sensual, although his overt sensuality provided a distracting screen. She had something the elusive lion wanted, something with which she could lure him out of his lair.

That evening had confirmed that all she dreamed of could truly be.

His control, absolute and unwavering, was the next hurdle she needed to overcome; twisting up her hair, she considered how that might best be done, how she might strengthen her hold on him. Rewarding though their dual adventures had proved, she now had only one more outing to which he was committed, one more chance to work her wiles. What possibilities might a Covent Garden masquerade throw her way?

She continued to think, to plot, to plan as she slipped through the silent house and out through the side door. How far would she need to go to trap him, to snare his senses and overthrow his will? What actions on her part were most likely to evoke the desired reaction on his? Protectiveness. Pride. Ultimately, possessiveness, as Amelia had warned. Strong emotions all. Which was it safe to prod, which wiser to let be?

Which did she dare provoke? Where would she draw her line?

Ten minutes later, she rode into the park.

There was no one waiting under the oak by the gates—no roan, no large, dangerous rider.

She felt his absence like a slap. A shock. A sudden emptiness.

She didn't know what to think. After a minute of simply sitting the mare, staring at the empty space, she gathered the reins and set off down the park. Dexter's groom trailed after her.

Her heart, so light mere minutes ago, buoyed by the expectation of seeing him again, had plummeted. A constriction tightened about her chest; inside, she felt hollow. Skittering from one recollection to the next, her mind again and again returned to one question: how much had he guessed?

She reached the tan track; without thought, she sprang the mare. The groom stopped under the trees and watched.

Halfway along with the mare in full stride, the wind whipping her cheeks and tangling her curls, desolation swept her as realization struck. She did not enjoy the moment—the excitement, the thrill—half as much alone.

On the thought, she heard thunder. The thudding of heavy hooves closing rapidly. She flung a glance behind; the roan with its familiar rider was quickly making up lost ground. Facing forward, she smiled ecstatically, knowing he couldn't yet see.

Seconds later, he ranged alongside; she met his eyes, smiled in easy welcome, and prayed no hint of the triumph she felt showed in her face.

He might be here, but he was far from tame. And she wasn't fool enough to think he didn't, at least in part, have her measure.

The end of the track neared; Martin slowed, then they turned aside onto the sward. He drew rein, noting the color the wind had brought to her cheeks. They were both breathing rapidly, courtesy of the ride; he fought not to let his mind focus on the rise and fall of her breasts.

The same breasts that had filled his dreams, not just with sensual images but with sensual longings, with the simple need to experience the sensations again, to sate his tactile senses with a feast more sumptuous, more enthralling than any before.

Signalling the groom back to the gate, he gathered his reins and nodded to a path wending through the trees. "Let's return this way."

He'd meant to stay away, to cut the connection, to withdraw from her game. The fact he was here, riding beside her, didn't please him at all.

He glanced at her face, found it studiously serene, her gaze fixed on the trees. As if she thought he'd simply been a little late rolling from his bed. He wasn't fool enough to swallow it, but reluctantly acknowledged her strategy. Her subtlety. In this arena, she was a more worthy opponent than any who had gone before.

They were deep in the trees, screened from any early riders, when he again drew rein. She halted, considered him, then raised a questioning brow.

"Your wish to attend a Covent Garden masquerade—I fear I'll be unable to accommodate you."

"Oh?" Her gaze remained steady on his face. "And why is that?"

Because after their interlude on the Thames, he was too

wise to give her another chance to tempt him. "Because such an outing is entirely out of bounds for a lady of your station." He returned her regard and deliberately added, "Especially with me as your escort."

Her cornflower blue gaze didn't waver, but he couldn't read her eyes; her expression said only that she was considering his words.

Then she nodded and picked up the mare's reins. "Very well."

With that, she set the mare ambling on.

Martin stared, then urged the roan along in her wake. *Very well?* "So you accept that you won't be attending one of the masquerades?"

She glanced back. "Of course not." She faced forward again. "I'll just have to find another escort."

What had he expected? She was damned well turning him into another "dear Reggie."

He could call her bluff. He would, if he could be certain it was indeed a bluff.

Amanda bit her tongue, kept her expression fixed as if pondering her male acquaintances, trying to decide which to ask to escort her to a Covent Garden masquerade.

They were within sight of the gate, his groom waiting beside it, before she heard the words she'd been praying she'd hear.

"All right, all right!"

She glanced at Martin; he fixed her with a stony look. "I promised I'd take you to the blasted masquerade—so I will."

Swallowing her whoop of delight was not easy, but she managed it, smiled evenly instead. "Thank you. It would make life easier." Letting her lips curve a touch further, she murmured, "Better the devil one knows, after all."

His expression grew stonier. He nodded curtly. "I'll make the arrangements."

He swung the roan's head, clearly intending to ride deeper into the park. With a graceful salute, Amanda set the mare for the gate.

She didn't look back, didn't need to look to know that after a moment of watching her, he turned away. As the mare's hooves clopped on the cobbles, all confidence faded from her eyes.

"He's going to pull back—escape! I *know* it!" Pacing across her bedchamber, Amanda flung the comment at Amelia, perched on the bed.

"Isn't there some way you can . . . well, tie him up?"

She snorted. "He's too careful—too wide awake, no matter how lazily he moves." Swinging around, she paced back. "You see, he knows we're playing some game. I've made him interested enough to indulge me by playing, but he knows—and he knows I know he knows, too. What he *doesn't* know is that I mean the game to end at the altar. I could simply be after a taste of excitement before succumbing to a boring marriage."

"A *boring marriage?* He can't believe that."

"He doesn't go about in the ton. He doesn't know the family. So he can't guess where I'm heading, which is part of the attraction, part of what makes him willing to be my guide."

"Ah." Leaning on her elbows, Amelia considered. "But what about the other part—the rest of the reason he's spending time with you?"

Amanda grimaced. "Did I tell you he's hard to read—elusive? I don't truly know what that 'rest' is. In fact, I'm not sure he knows, either. But whatever it is, it's too . . ."—she waved her hands—"amorphous to pin down and use. Besides, I don't want him focusing on that yet. If there's anything there, it needs time to grow *before* he recognizes it."

Amelia nodded. "So you need another tack—another prod."

"Yes. But what?" Amanda paced on. After some minutes, her twin's voice broke through her tortured thoughts.

"You know, I think you're looking at this from the wrong angle."

Turning, she met Amelia's eyes.

"You're thinking of him specifically, and that's difficult because you simply can't know. But he's still a man—a man like our cousins. Isn't he?"

Amanda stared, then her face cleared. Smiling brilliantly,

she flung herself on the bed and hugged her sister. "Melly, you're a genius."

Four mornings later, Martin sat his roan under the tree in the park, and watched Amanda Cynster ride toward him. The smile on her face was mildly sunny—not a hint of a smirk, not the faintest glimmer of triumph showed.

He stifled a disaffected grunt, but couldn't keep his gaze from drinking in the sight of her, golden curls bright against the early morning sky, figure supple and trim in her velvet habit.

The clash of his emotions left him feeling like gnashing his teeth. He hadn't felt so *exercised* in years. Irritation was nearest his surface, roused by the perception that fate was, once again, not treating him fairly. He was trying to do the right and honorable thing, trying to keep faith and give her the adventures they'd agreed on, then cut the connection he sensed growing between them and slide into the shadows once more, yet fate—and she—were conspiring to tease him.

After making the necessary arrangements for her evening at Covent Garden, he'd waited for her to send for the mare again. And waited. It had finally dawned on him that she was spending her mornings sleeping in.

She was either supremely sure of him, or she didn't truly care.

The rub was, he couldn't decide which.

Regardless, because of her new tack, instead of adhering to his sworn oath not to encourage her in any way, he'd had to send a note asking her to meet him. Irked was not the half of what he felt.

She reined to a halt; the mare pranced. Patting its glossy neck, she smiled fondly. "You were right—she does need to be ridden." Lifting her head, she regarded him evenly, then raised a brow.

He studied her blue eyes, face hardening as his mind recited her words. Tightening his reins, he jerked his head toward the track. "Let's go."

They did; despite his frequent glances, he detected not the slightest smugness. Indeed, her demeanor suggested her adventures with him were merely by-the-by, that they didn't figure highly in her life. That she wasn't, at that very moment, wondering if he'd made the arrangements she'd earlier been so keen for him to make.

Reaching the track, they turned as one, then thundered down its length. As usual, the exhilaration claimed him; he was aware it claimed her, too. For those minutes as they raced side by side, neck and neck, there was just them and the birds and the sky. No expectations. No obligations. Just simple excitement and delight.

They had that in common—an ability to give themselves up to the moment without reservation. The realization dawned as they slowed and turned onto the lawns.

His irritation had eased, leaving behind it . . . something he'd thought never to feel.

With a brusque nod, he directed her onto the screened path they'd taken previously. The sun was rising earlier; other gentlemen were already sleepily plodding toward the park.

"I have a box at Covent Garden for the masquerade next Tuesday."

She smiled gloriously at him. "Wonderful."

He fought against a scowl. "If the date suits, I'll wait in the carriage as before."

Her smile didn't falter. "Tuesday evening will suit admirably. There are major balls on Monday and Wednesday nights, so if I cry off on Tuesday, no one will be surprised."

He studied her face. She bore the scrutiny calmly; her expression gave nothing away. Yet she had to know that he could have sent the details in the summons he'd sent her. He hadn't; the last thing he wanted to think about was why.

Perhaps she hadn't realized—perhaps she thought horses were what he preferred to ride at this hour.

He hauled his mind off that tack, away from the ache in his loins. "Tuesday night, then." After that, he'd be free.

Still smiling, she inclined her head. Barely waiting for him to acknowledge the gesture, she flicked her reins and left him.

He watched her ride away, calmly assured, then turned and rode home, even more determined to end her game.

The pit of Covent Garden, cleared and crammed with revelers, was a scene lifted from Amanda's wildest imaginings. When Dexter escorted her into their box in the first tier, she didn't know where to look first.

Everyone wore masks, but many ladies had already dispensed with their black cloaks, revealing gowns the likes of which Amanda had never seen. Eyes round, she drank in the sights—and corrected her thoughts. Not ladies. No lady would ever wear such provocative attire. Sinking into a chair at the front of the box, she viewed this one, then that, with voyeuristic fascination; these were the demimonde in all their glory. The Cyprians, the ladybirds, the opera dancers who more frequently appeared on the stage of the huge hall, presently hosting an orchestra laboring to be heard over the din. Ribald comments, raucous laughter, rose from all quarters. Arch glances, teasing titters captured men's senses and tempted them nearer.

The gentlemen were unremarkable, the same crowd she saw every night in the ton. What enthralled her was their behavior, their open worship of the bold and brazen who flaunted their charms directly beneath their noses.

The flagrant play—the inciting of desire and the subsequent negotiation over its satisfaction—intrigued her. Although aware of Dexter's frowning gaze, she continued to sit and stare. After a time, he sprawled in a chair beside her, large, watchful—intensely lionlike.

Once she'd drunk her fill and confirmed that, as far as she could tell, there were no familiar faces hidden among the throng, she turned and regarded him through the slits in her halfmask. "Can we go down?"

He wanted to say "No." She could see it in his eyes—he hadn't worn a mask. Little point; he was easily recognizable—there was no other with hair of his particular shade, so richly burnished. The gold overlaying the brown was doubtless one of the changes his years in India had wrought.

Indolently, he stirred; his gaze drifted to the crowd. "If you wish."

He stood; she gave him her hand and let him raise her. His gaze returned, slid down, over her, taking in her gown of apricot silk revealed as her domino parted. She'd chosen the gown carefully; its hue made her skin glow and turned her hair a deeper gold.

For one instant, he stared, then, reaching out, twitched the cloak closed. "It would be wise to remain incognito. One look at that gown and the cogniscenti will be rabid to learn who you are."

An angel slumming in hell. Her hand anchored on his sleeve, Martin escorted her down the stairs to the vestibule. As they reached the pit and the noise engulfed them, he reminded himself it wasn't truly hell; if it had been, he'd never have brought her here.

Here, however, was a place she didn't need to be, didn't need to see—she didn't need to be exposed to this kind of company. At least in his opinion.

He knew better than to argue. Jaw set, he guided her into the throng, intent on ensuring that what she did see was, if not acceptable, then at least not shocking. He was counting on the fact he had a woman on his arm to ward off any approaches; nevertheless, numerous arch glances, come-hither pouts and knowing winks were directed his way. A fact his partner didn't miss.

She stiffened; her fingertips sank into his arm. But as they penetrated further into the crowd, her tension gradually eased.

He glanced at her face, but with her mask on and her gaze on the crowd, he couldn't see her expression, couldn't guess her thoughts.

Didn't forsee her direction.

Amanda's openmindedness over the women parading the pit ended the instant she realized they were as aware of her escort's potential as she. Fifteen feet of slow progress, however, demonstrated that he had no interest in them—his attention remained firmly rivetted precisely where she wanted it.

On her.

Which left her free to take in all she would, to catalogue the flourishes, the teasing glances, the flirting whisk of a fan, to glean all she could from experts in the field. Yet the fact he seemed immune suggested that she would need more subtle weapons.

She'd turned her mind to evaluating exactly what subtle weapons she possessed when a jocularly jostling couple bumped her, sent her careening—

Dexter hauled her to him—she fetched up against his chest, breathlessly locked against him. Protectively shielded.

She glanced up. His face was a stony warrior's mask, his gaze fixed beyond her. She could hear some gentleman gabbling his apologies. Beneath her hands, in the arms around her, she felt tension swell, muscles flex. Dragging in a breath, she fought to turn—but only succeeded in turning her head. "That's quite all right." She glanced up as Dexter looked down.

He looked ready to argue.

She smiled. Patted his chest. "No harm done."

The couple took advantage of his distraction to melt into the crowd; Martin looked up and they were gone—he felt as if he'd been deprived of his rightful prey. It took an instant more to shackle his instincts. To quell his reaction enough so he could ease his arms from . . .

Damn! He refused to meet her gaze as he forced his arms from her. Closing one hand about hers, he twined her arm with his and anchored her hand on his sleeve. "What now?"

The growled words were barely polite, but . . . she was the one who had wanted to come here.

He felt the glance she threw him, declined to meet it.

"Let's amble. I want to see all there is to be seen."

There was not a chance of him permitting that. He steered her through sections of the crowd that he'd first ascertained were safe, avoiding any group whose behavior he considered too lewd for her angelic blue eyes.

And reminded himself why he was here.

Because he'd agreed to bring her here, because he'd extracted a promise that if he did, she'd return to the ballrooms where she belonged. The years had taught him wisdom; he knew she'd keep her word. She had her own brand of honor, as did he. His demanded that once this night was over, he retire from her life. And he would. Regardless. All he had to do was survive tonight, and all would be well.

The shrill shrieks, the high-pitched gibber of excitement that always seemed to occur beyond her view, informed Amanda that she was missing a good deal of what she had ostensibly come to see.

She no longer cared. The game she and Dexter were engaged in demanded her entire attention. Tonight would be her last chance to breach his walls. While he might be a superior card player, in this particular game they were more evenly matched. All she had to do was tip the scales her way.

As the crowd grew more unruly, she considered every opportunity, ready to seize any advantage. Before the stage, they came upon an area filled with waltzing couples. Abruptly stopping, she turned. Into Dexter's arms.

"Can we dance?" Suppressing her reaction at the sudden contact, breast to chest, hip to thigh, she ignored the tension locking his frame, the possessive grip of his hand at her waist. Eyes wide, she looked up at him.

He glanced at her, then at the dancers. His jaw hardened. "If you wish."

Smiling, she lifted her hand to his shoulder. He gathered her close and steered her into the twirling couples. Here, the waltz was a different dance to that performed in the ballrooms. Slower, more intimate. Infinitely more useful.

He'd used the dance for seduction before—the moves came too easily, second nature to him. Even now, when she knew he wished it otherwise. They slowly revolved; the floor was too crowded for him to hold her at any distance. The domino he'd brought for her shifted constantly against his coat, against her silk gown, making it hard for him to hold her firmly. Then she misread his direction and was jostled again. Jaw set, he flicked the domino open and slid his hand beneath, to rest at the back of her waist, firm against her gown. He drew her to him—not close so that their bodies shifted against each other, teasing and tantalizing—but all the way, so she was locked flush against him, held, trapped. His.

For one instant, she couldn't breathe, then she leaned closer, rested her temple against his shoulder. Lips curving, she relaxed into his tight embrace, let her body flow with the suddenly intense tide. He felt like hot rock against her; they slowly whirled, hips and thighs caressing, pressing close.

Excitement, a hot streak of sensation, raced through her, then pooled, liquid heat, deep inside. Barely able to breathe, she raised her head, looked up—fell into his mesmerizing eyes. Soft, deep green flecked with gold, they burned with the promise of limitless passion, limitless but restrained. She couldn't look away, wondered what he could read in her eyes.

That he wanted her was plain; the desire she'd sought to evoke was there, and even more potent than she'd guessed. The knowledge thrilled her—unexpectedly scared her. This was what she'd plotted to get; now she'd got it . . . the thought of what came next set her heart pounding.

Shifting her hand, she grazed her fingertips through his silky locks, then, wonderingly, ran the backs of her fingers along his jaw. With his habitual languor, he bent his head; her heart stood still, her lips throbbed, parted.

As he had once before, he touched his lips to the very corner of hers. "Don't worry." His voice was deep, a rumbling purr. "I won't eat you."

Damn! She rapidly reassessed, read again the tension holding him, the strength of his restraint. He was going to spare her. Noble of him, but not what she had in mind. How to explain—

"Oh! You *dreadful man!*"

The words and the slap that followed had them glancing to their right. Raucous laughter engulfed a group surrounding the protesting woman. She was smiling and laughing, too— she'd merely slapped a gentleman's straying hand away.

Amanda's eyes nearly started from her head. The woman's gown . . . the bodice was transparent. Her breasts, nipples erect, were displayed for all to see. A number of gentlemen were looking.

Her faint "Good God!" was overridden by Dexter's much more decisive "Come on."

He whisked her around; holding her close, he steered her in the opposite direction.

Scanning the crowd, Martin mentally cursed. The waltz had distracted him; he'd missed the moment he'd been watching for—the moment when, by general consensus, the tenor of the evening changed. From the licentious to the determinedly bawdy. From what he could see as he glanced about, matters would soon descend to the outright lewd.

The change had happened early tonight, as it sometimes did. Normally, he would retire to his box with whichever lady he had on his arm, there to indulge as they would in privacy; over the past year he might have eschewed the ton, but he hadn't lived the life of a monk.

Tonight, however, celibacy was definitely his fate. As he bundled Amanda up the stairs to their box, the idea of spending any length of time with her there, alone, his behavior rigidly correct when what he wanted to do—

He cut off the thought with another mental curse.

She stepped into the box. Before he could stop her, she went straight to the front and looked out. "Great *heavens!*" After scanning the throng, her gaze fixed on one spot. Her jaw fell. "Good Lord—look at that!"

He didn't need to; she didn't, either. Martin grasped her elbow—

A muffled shriek jerked their attention to the next box. Other sounds followed—panting, incoherent exclamations, garbled directions. Martin gave thanks that the occupants had had the foresight to draw the curtains. Tightening his grip, he drew Amanda back. "Come on—we're leaving."

"Leaving? But—"

"No."

On that uncompromising syllable, Amanda found herself drawn irresistibly to the door. One part of her wanted to dig in her heels; this was her last night with him, her last chance at him, and he was cutting it short. On the other hand, the venue had not proven as amenable as she'd hoped—not romantic, not subtly seductive—not subtle at all. Subtle was what she needed, she was sure of that.

The behavior of the revellers they passed as Dexter grimly escorted her out of the building reinforced the notion that Covent Garden was the wrong place for her purposes. Fighting her blushes, disguising her shock, was too distracting; she needed her wits about her.

She was actually relieved when Dexter handed her into his carriage, but she had no time to relax, although she pretended to do so when the door shut and he sat beside her. The carriage rocked, rolled forward. She glanced at the street and racked her brains for inspiration. She'd got him where she'd hoped to get him—burning with desire for her. But how to capitalize when he was so determined to resist? How to snatch victory from his jaws?

The horses clopped along Pall Mall as she frantically searched for some way to prolong her time with him. Tried to think what she could do to further weaken his defenses; if he escaped her now in the mood in which he presently was, she would not, she felt sure, see him again. The carriage passed St. James; the dark shadows of Green Park lay ahead. Amanda glimpsed them, and suddenly knew what to do. A sense of calm descended; she waited until the carriage had turned into the street bordering the park before glancing at Dexter. "It's still early, the night's mild. Can we walk in Green Park for a while?"

Martin looked at the park, designed for strolling, gravel walks spread beneath tall trees. During the day, it was the preferred venue of governesses and nursemaids with young children; by night, it was deserted. It was free space, not fenced; safe enough given it was all lawns and trees, no bushes or anywhere any miscreant could hide.

"I *did* expect a whole evening at Covent Garden. However . . ." Amanda shrugged as he glanced at her. "In the circumstances, let's stroll under the trees and I'll be satisfied."

He smothered a "humph," yet it was a reasonable suggestion. That he was acutely conscious that this would otherwise be his last moments with her—that strolling in the park would put off the instant when he would bid her good-bye for the last time—he steadfastly ignored, along with the unwelcome yearning that he could instead keep her, take her to his house and shut her in his library, his to enjoy for all time.

Jaw setting, he shook aside the thought. "Very well."

At his direction, the carriage pulled up by the verge; he descended, handed Amanda down, then helped her change the domino for her velvet cloak. Knotting the ties at her throat, she left the cloak partly open, revealing the warm hue of her gown. Even more to his silent approval, she left the hood down, so her lustrous curls sheened in the weak light.

His fingers itched to touch. Instead, he reached for her hand, twined her arm with his, and they set off down the nearest path.

Amanda accepted his silence without comment; she'd realized he used the tactic to keep people at a distance, but she knew how to slip through his guard. They strolled under the trees, in and out of the shadows. She waited until they were deep within the park, out of sight of his coachman.

Then she drew her hand from his arm and stepped across him. Let him walk into her, let him catch her to him, his hands on her gown beneath her cloak. Smiling, she laid her palm to his cheek, stretched up and set her lips to his.

It wasn't a "thank you" kiss, but she hoped he might think so long enough to give her the opening she needed. Whether he was fooled or simply surprised, she gained the breach she wanted—his lips met hers easily, readily.

She seized the moment, seized control of the kiss.

He'd kissed her often enough for her to understand how to be brazen and bold. Their lips merged; her tongue sought his, found, stroked, tangled. Winding her arms about his neck, she stretched up, pressed herself to him.

His hands tightened about her waist, fingers gripping as if to put her from him. She angled her lips, pressed the kiss deeper, fanned the flames licking between them . . . and the moment passed. His hands eased, then, hesitantly, as if he'd lost direction, they slid over her back, his touch gentle, wondering.

The advantage was hers. She wasn't about to let it slide,

not before she made it clear just where they stood, just what she was offering.

Herself.

She let the fact infuse her kiss, let that truth ring clearly as she sank against him. He didn't seize, but gathered her to him as if she were delicate porcelain, something he feared to break. She pressed closer yet, as if to prove him wrong.

Suddenly, the kiss changed.

Shifted to a plane different from any she'd previously been on, a place of whirling pleasures, a kaleidoscope of sensual delight. He drew her deeper, then returned the pleasure she'd been lavishing on him, with interest. Yet something had changed. He wanted her, but it wasn't ravenous desire that drove him. The restraint that had earlier held him back was gone, yet some barrier still stood between them—between her needs and his, barring their mutual fulfillment.

It was his needs that had changed, or rather, clarified. She could taste it in the way his lips took hers, in the languid, unhurried, wondrous depths of their kiss. In the gentle way he held her, in the subtle coaxing that had her head spinning, in the hesitant, reluctant acknowledgment of the possibility that lay between them.

Deep in the kiss, wrapped in his arms, she suddenly saw—suddenly understood. He wanted her not just sexually, but with a deeper, richer, infinitely more alluring need. No simple desire but something profound, the sleeping heart of her lion.

She saw, and wanted—reached with both hands . . .

Only to sense his retreat.

Gradual, as reluctant as he'd been to be lured forth in the first place, yet step by step he eased back from the kiss, backed out of the trap she'd set. The trap she'd baited with herself.

"No." Martin whispered the word as he ended the kiss. His head was spinning, his body one massive ache. An ache so profound, one that went so much deeper than muscle and bone.

He hadn't believed she could do it, or even that she would try. Her wordless plea—one he couldn't pretend he didn't comprehend—had struck straight through every barrier he'd erected over the last ten years. He'd seen the pit yawning at his feet on the first night they'd met, but he'd thought himself safe, his defenses too seasoned and sound for her to dent seriously.

Instead, she'd laid them waste, and left him feeling more exposed than he'd ever felt before. Mentally groping in the dark for some remnants of his shields behind which to hide.

He looked down at her face, into her eyes. She'd chosen her spot so they weren't in shadow; by the weak light of the stars, he could read the confusion, the disbelief, the incipient hurt he knew he had to cause.

That last moved him to state, "You are what I can never have."

He had no idea what she could read in his face; her eyes raced over his features, then returned to his eyes.

"Why?"

Not a demand, not the beginning of a tantrum, but a simple request born of a need to understand.

He'd never answered that question, not for any of the ladies with whom, over the last year, he had on occasion shared a bed. They'd had no right to know, no claim on the knowledge; they had never offered him half as much as she. Even if he hadn't taken. "I killed a man. Or so society believes."

She didn't blink, simply studied his eyes; not a single muscle in the body cradled in his arms tensed. "And did you?"

His lips twisted with the bitterness he found he couldn't hide. "No."

She considered him for a moment more, then eased back until she was standing within the circle of his arms. "Tell me."

It was his turn to consider, then he drew a deep breath. Behind her, a wrought-iron seat caught his eye. "Let's sit."

They did, she sitting forward so she could see his face as he leaned his forearms on his thighs, clasped his hands. And looked back.

When, sucked into his darkest memories, he said nothing, she prompted, "I heard you seduced some girl."

He hesitated, then said, "That's was part of the story, but equally untrue." After a moment, he continued, "There was a girl in the village near my home. We grew up together—I was an only child and saw her as a younger sister. One day, she killed herself, driven to it by her father—a righteous old sod—because she was with child. I was nineteen at the time, and spent most of my days in London. I learned of her death on a visit home. Swearing vengeance, I went in search of her father. I found him. He'd been pushed off a cliff, then his head had been bashed with a rock. I picked up the rock—I wasn't sure . . . that's how the villagers found me, standing there with the rock in my hand."

"They thought you'd killed him?"

"The blacksmith had seen a gentleman he took for me struggling with the old man at the top of the bluff—saw me, as he thought, pitch the old man over."

"But it wasn't you."

No question. Her hand came to rest, warm and alive, on his sleeve.

"No, and of course I denied it." He drew in a long breath. "No one believed me." That, of it all, despite all the years, still hurt unbearably. "My father"—he paused to make sure his voice remained steady—"accepted all that was said as the truth. He wanted to disown me, but because of the title and the family line, he banished me instead. As his heir, I was bundled off abroad instead of being allowed to face any investigation."

She was silent for a long time; he didn't have the strength, couldn't find the words, to end the moment and bring on the time when they would part.

"Did you never try to set the record straight?"

"My father's edict was that I should not set foot in England as long as he lived. I honored that to the letter."

"And more, so I heard."

"Ten years have elapsed since he passed judgment on me. Any chance of proving the truth died long ago." Along with any chance of him being considered an eligible *parti* for such as she; until now, that hadn't bothered him in the least.

The thought propelled him to his feet. He glanced down at her, held out a hand. "Come. I'll take you home."

Amanda looked up at him, considered, not him, but how best to proceed. She knew better than to brush aside his reasoning; she was too much of his world, understood too well the situation as he saw it.

She understood, too, that he saw this moment as a final parting. She didn't agree, but she couldn't argue, not until she'd marshaled more support for her cause. Placing her fingers in his, she rose; arm in arm, they strolled back along the path.

They were almost to the carriage when she halted in the shadows, waited until he stopped and faced her. One hand in his, she stepped closer, with her other hand drew his lips to hers. He was wary, but permitted it—she kissed him sweetly, lingeringly, the merest echo of what had passed between them before.

"Thank you for telling me."

She whispered the words as their lips parted, then stepped back. For a long moment, he stood looking down at her, his face and eyes too deeply shadowed for her to read. His grip on her hand tightened, then abruptly eased.

With the merest inclination of his head, he led her to the waiting carriage.

Chapter 7

She'd snared her lion only to find him wounded. For the moment, he could return to his lair, but she hadn't given up her dream. Indeed, after their stroll in Green Park, giving up was the furthest notion from her mind.

"I need to learn more." Standing with Amelia by the side of Lady Moffat's ballroom, Amanda scanned the crowd. "I need to know if it is as he says, and people believe he's a murderer."

Amelia slanted her a glance. "You're sure he isn't?"

"One needs only to meet him to know the idea's ludicrous, but with him refusing to allow anyone a chance to reassess, society's unlikely to change its collective mind."

"True. But I've never heard a whisper about murder before. It's always been something about his amorous propensities."

"Indeed, but given those are real enough, it's possible the murder was always there, but those warning us declined to sully our delicate ears with the tale."

"That, unfortunately, is perfectly likely."

"So I need to learn the truth as society sees it. I can't pretend I'm willing to throw my cap over the windmill regardless of his status—he won't accept that." Amanda looked around. "The question is: who to ask?"

"Aunt Helena?"

"She'll see straight through me, and might warn Mama."

"I should think Honoria would be difficult for the same reason."

"And it *was* ten years ago—I don't think Honoria would know."

Amelia joined Amanda in assessing the company. "Not so easy. You need someone who would know the details of such an old scandal—"

"Details that would have been at least partly suppressed."

"And they need to remember accurately."

"Indeed . . ." Amanda stopped, her gaze resting on the one person who might well be the perfect source.

Amelia followed her gaze, nodded decisively. "Yes. If anyone can help, she's the one."

"And she's far less likely to thrust a spoke in my wheel." Amanda set off across the ballroom, evading all those who wanted to chat. She had to wait, hovering beside the chaise, until a matron who'd been seeking support for her daughter's come-out departed.

Quickly, Amanda took her place, skirts swishing as she sat.

Lady Osbaldestone bent her obsidian gaze upon her, regarding her with considerably greater interest than she had the earnest matron. "Well, gel? You ain't pregnant, are you?"

Amanda stared, then stated, commendably evenly, "No."

"Ah, well—daresay there's hope yet."

Amanda grabbed her courage with both hands. "As to that . . . I wanted to ask if you recalled the details of an old scandal."

The black eyes fixed on her face with unnerving intensity. "How old?"

"Ten years."

Lady Osbaldestone's eyes narrowed. "Dexter," she pronounced.

Amanda jumped.

"Good God, gel! Don't tell me you've succeeded where all others have failed?"

She was torn between claiming the crown and denying all knowledge. "Possibly," she temporized. "But I was wondering about the scandal. All we ever heard was he seduced some girl who then killed herself, but I've learned there was a murder involved."

"Learned that, have you? From whom, I wonder? There wouldn't be many ready to bandy that fact about."

"Oh?" She made her expression as innocently inquiring as she could.

Lady Osbaldestone snorted. "Very well—the real tale, then, as you seem to have a need to know. What the ton heard was that Dexter seduced a local girl—the family estate is in the Peak district. The gel fell pregnant, but rather than send to Dexter, she told her father, a religious sort. The father hounded her—she ended taking her own life. Dexter heard of it on his next visit home. He set out to look for the gel's father, and, so we heard, murdered him, then stupidly stood around until the villagers found him.

"Old Dexter—the present one's father—was horrifed. He would have disowned his son, but the title and estate would have reverted to the crown. Add to that, the countess doted on her son—her one and only chick—and Dexter doted on his countess. Letting the lad stand his trial was out of the question, at least, it was in those days. So he was banished while his father lived. That was what we in London heard." Lady Osbaldestone folded her hands over her ample waist. "What we believed . . . that's another matter."

"The ton didn't believe he—the present earl—was the murderer?"

Lady Osbaldestone frowned. "More accurate to say that judgment was reserved. Dexter, the present one, might have been a hothead, a wild and tempestuous youth, but he'd never struck any of us as a bad apple."

Her ladyship looked at Amanda; her tone was softer when she said, "There's often one bad apple among a good crop, and no one's the wiser until it comes to the crunch—the point of seeing what each apple is made of. While Dexter might be capable of killing, what didn't sit well with many of us was that he didn't have the black heart for murder. He was a colorful young lordling, forceful and alive, devil-may-care and the doubters be damned. He'd only been on the town for some months, but we'd seen enough to judge."

Lady Osbaldestone paused, then continued, "And there was the undeniable fact that his father was a martinet. A good man, but righteously so and very stiff about it. The idea that his son had committed murder, let alone the other, would have scored his pride as well as his soul. Decisions were made and acted on in a matter of hours. In such circumstances, with emotions running high, mistakes could have been made."

Amanda struggled to take it all in. Eventually, she asked, "So the ton's present view of Dexter is . . . ?"

Her ladyship snorted. "With his fortune? Let alone his looks, or so I've heard. Naturally, there are any number of mamas who would marry their daughters to him in a blink, murderer or no." Her eyes bored into Amanda's. "Your mother isn't one of them."

Amanda forced herself not to react.

Lady Osbaldestone sat back, gaze shrewd. "The present situation could best be described as undecided. When Dexter comes to his senses and re-enters the ton, he won't be ostracized—there are enough of us who remember to ensure that. However, unless the matter of that old murder is settled, there will always be a question mark over his name."

Amanda nodded. "Thank you." She went to rise, then stopped. "I meant to ask—what's the connection between Dexter and the Ashfords?"

"A blood tie—Luc Ashford is Martin Fulbridge's first cousin. Their mothers were sisters." Lady Osbaldestone paused, then added, "They were inseparable as boys, as I recall. They look alike, don't they?"

Amanda nodded.

Lady Osbaldestone crowed. "Aha! So you *have* met the elusive earl. Well, my gel, let me give you a piece of advice." Closing a clawlike hand on Amanda's wrist, her ladyship leaned near. "If you want something badly and you're convinced it's the right thing for you, if it takes a fight to get it—fight!"

Releasing Amanda, she watched her stand. "Remember

what I said. If it's the right thing, don't give up, no matter the resistance."

Amanda met her ladyship's eyes, so dark, so old, so wise. She bobbed a curtsy. "I'll remember."

It took her two full days to convince Reggie that it was vital she return to Lady Hennessy's. Three nights after she'd walked in Green Park, she once again entered Number 19, Gloucester Street. Again, the drawing room was fashionably full; Lady Hennessy arched a brow but made them welcome.

Amanda patted Reggie's arm. "Remember what you promised."

Reggie was scanning the throng. "I don't like it. What if some other gentleman approaches you?"

"I'll come scurrying back to your side." As she stepped away, she caught his eye. "Just don't disappear altogether."

Reggie snorted. "As if I would."

Mindful of her instructions, he ambled away, heading for the side of the room. Amanda looked about her, but could see no shapely head sporting locks burnished by the sun. Praying Dexter would appear soon, she put on her smile and started strolling the room.

This time, she was careful not to encourage any gentleman to pay court to her; she joined this group, then that, using the skills honed by her years in the ton to flit without giving offence. All the while she was conscious of steadily increasing tension, of her nerves, notch by notch, drawing tight.

She had no idea how Dexter would react to seeing her once more gracing such a venue. It had been his principal condition in fulfilling her desired adventures—that she would not seek further excitement in this sphere for the rest of this Season. He'd delivered on their bargain—now here she was, apparently reneging on her vow. He wouldn't be impressed, but she was ready to defend her actions. What worried her more was that he would view her presence as a stupidly defiant gesture, a deliberate courting of trouble, and decide she and her actions were beneath his notice.

If, instead of reacting hotly—possessively and protectively—

he viewed her coldly and turned his back . . . she wasn't sure what she would do then.

She needn't have worried—he appeared like an avenging angel, all black frown and narrowed eyes, tight lips and burning gaze. In evening black, he stepped directly in front of her, cutting her off, towering over her. "What the *devil* are you doing back here?"

"Oh!" She'd jumped; her hand had instinctively risen to her breast—beneath it, her heart thumped. Then relief flooded her. "Good—you're here."

His eyes narrowed even more.

She stepped closer, clutching his lapel, hoping no one noticed. "We can't meet in the park anymore—the sun's rising so early there are others out by six. And I'm having to attend multiple balls every night, so earlier than six is impossible." Searching his face, she detected no softening in his stony expression. "I need to speak with you."

A wary frown appeared in his eyes, dispelling the thunderclouds. "You are speaking with me."

"Yes." She glanced about. "But I can't discuss the matter I wish to speak of *here*." *In public* was her clear message. "Is there somewhere . . . ?"

After a pregnant pause, she thought she heard him sigh.

"Where's Carmarthen?" Lifting his head, he looked around. "I assume he escorted you here?"

"He's waiting by the wall. He knows I came here to speak with you."

Martin looked into her eager, trusting face, into cornflower blue eyes that held none of the defiance he'd expected to see. Every instinct he possessed was screaming that whatever it was she wished to say to him, he would be better off not hearing. Yet, if he didn't, he'd always wonder . . .

Just the sight of her had been enough to make him forget all the rational, logical arguments for staying away from her.

"Very well." Lips compressing, he took her arm. "This way."

He steered her past the fireplace to a pair of French doors curtained with lace. Reaching between the curtains, he set one door swinging wide. Without hesitation, Amanda slipped through and out; he followed, closing the door, leaving them isolated on a narrow balcony overlooking the garden. Totally private, yet not private enough to cause a scandal.

"What did you wish to discuss?"

She glanced at him; he could almost see her girding her loins as she faced him. "You told me of your past. You made it clear it—or rather its consequences—stand between us. I've quietly investigated how people view what happened, how the ton views you now." Her eyes searched his. "There are many who do not and never have accepted your guilt as a given."

He let his brows rise fractionally; he'd never really considered what the ton at large thought. The ton had never, of itself, been important to him. "How . . ." How what? Heartening? Hardly that. Interesting? The last thing he wished was to encourage her. He shrugged. "It matters little."

Her head rose. "On the contrary—it matters a great deal."

Her tone, the determined light in her eyes, the defiant tilt of her chin, alerted him to her direction. If he were resurrected in the ton's eyes . . .

The vision she was seeing, the impossible dream she was determined to pursue, broke across his mind. Acceptance, his true position . . . her. All that and so much more, all he'd blocked from his mind for the past ten years—

Wrenching his mind away, cutting off the thoughts, drowning the vision, took an effort that left his gut knotted, his lungs tight. "No."

She frowned, opened her lips—

"It won't work." He had to stop her from raising the spectre, stop it from gaining further flesh. "It's not that I haven't considered clearing my name." All too frequently during the past week. "But it happened ten years ago, and even at the time there was not a whisper of proof to support my tale—no one able to bear me witness."

Her frown deepened. After a moment, she said, "You do see, don't you, what could be . . . all that you could have?"

He held her gaze, succinctly replied, "Yes." He saw all too well. Knew how much he longed to seize, to possess. Knew that in this case, trying and failing would be infinitely worse than not trying at all.

If he—they—attempted to clear his name and failed . . .

That was one scenario he didn't ever want to face. To raise the spectre of having a life he'd accepted as denied him long ago, only to see that hope dashed irretrievably. To know she would be tainted by the association; impossible for her interest to go unremarked.

And, despite all, one point had never, over all the years, escaped him—if he hadn't murdered old Buxton, who had?

Since his return to London, he'd grown even more equivocal about learning the answer to that question. Yet uncovering and publishing that answer might well be what it took to clear his name.

Dragging in a breath, he forced his gaze from her, looked out over the garden and tried to drag his senses in, tried to erect some barrier between himself and the woman he was with—usually an easy task.

He'd never managed it with her. And the balcony was so damned small. "There's no point pursuing it. There's nothing I, or even we, can do." He added, his tone harsh, "I didn't tell you the tale to gain your support—I told you so you'd understand why I have no future in the ton." He paused, then added, "The past is dead and buried."

Silence, then she spoke softly, "Buried, perhaps—but not dead."

He didn't glance her way, didn't want to see her face, her eyes.

After a moment, she went on, her tone hardening, "I find it difficult to believe that you're deliberately turning your back on your life—on what your life would be if your name was cleared."

Would be, he noted, not could; she had a singlemindedness he found disarming.

When he didn't respond, she exploded. *"Why?"* The word rang with frustration. "I know you well enough to know you have a reason."

He had a plethora of reasons, none of which she needed to know. He could readily imagine her opinion, her demolition of his concern for her. He forced himself to look into her brilliant eyes, saw emotion glittering in the blue, and knew

in that instant that he had to make her believe she'd misjudged him, that all she'd learned of him over the past weeks
she'd misread.

Refusing to let himself consider the ramifications—her
pain or his—he slowly and clearly stated, his gaze steady on
her eyes, "There is no compelling reason that I can see to
mount such a desperate action, to rake over coals long dead.
Returning to the ton, being restored to the *grandes dames'*
good graces, is *not important to me.*"

The emphasis he placed on those last four words was bru-
tal; she drew back—he felt it physically, a sudden chill, a
loss of warmth. Her expression turned neutral; her eyes, suddenly shuttered, searched his. Then she softly repeated, "Not
important. I see."

She looked toward the long windows spilling light upon
them. Then she drew in a tight breath. "My apologies.
Clearly, I've mistaken your . . . desire to reclaim the life
you were raised to live." Stiffly inclining her head, she
reached for the doors. "I'll leave you to the life you prefer.
Good-bye."

Not "Good night." Martin watched her open the door and
step through the lace curtains; one fist clenched on the railing, he watched her, head high, walk into the room, watched
the crowd swallow her. He trusted that Carmarthen would
escort her home. Turning his back on the lighted room, he
leaned on the railing and looked over the darkened garden,
into the night his life had become.

"He said, 'No.' *Refused!* Absolutely." Amanda kicked her
skirts and swung around. "He said it—me, us!—*wasn't important!*"

Amelia watched Amanda pace distractedly across her
bedchamber. "Are you sure he understood all you were alluding to?"

"Oh, he understood, all right! There's nothing wrong with
his *understanding!* But as for the rest of him!" With a muted
shriek, Amanda whirled and paced on.

Perturbed, Amelia waited. Her sister had a greater flair for
the histrionic than she, but in all their lives, she'd never seen

Amanda more sincerely overset. Overset, however, was unlikely to help her twin's cause.

After a time, she ventured, "So—are you giving up?"

"Giving up?" Amanda halted and stared at her. "Of course not."

Amelia relaxed on the bed. "What are you going to do?"

Amanda met her gaze, then came and flopped on the bed alongside her. She stared up at the canopy. Her chin was set, her expression mulish. "I don't know." An instant later she added, "But I'll think of something."

Three nights later, Martin returned to Gloucester Street, summoned by Helen Hennessy. He'd had no intention of attending, but Helen's note had been succinct and to the point—she wanted him there. They were friends enough that, given he had nothing better to do, he'd felt obliged to humor her.

She greeted him warmly, as always smoothly sophisticated.

"Cut line," he informed her. "I'm here—why?"

She raised both brows at him. "Your manners are deteriorating—always a telling sign."

He frowned. Before he could ask what his deterioration signified, Helen waved to a corner of the room. "But as to why you're here, I suspect you need to be aware of your lady friend's activities."

Martin met her gaze. "Which lady friend?"

"Miss Cynster, of course. And pray don't waste your breath telling me she's not your friend." Helen prodded his arm. "Carmarthen didn't accompany her tonight—she came alone. And rather than glower at me, I suggest such expressions might better serve us all over there." Her nod indicated the corner; her mask fell and she was serious. "Truly, I think you'd better take a look. Whatever you do after that is entirely up to you."

Martin held her gaze, then nodded. "I'll look."

Helen's brows rose; he ignored the sign and turned to the corner she'd indicated. If she thought he'd thank her for summoning him to Amanda Cynster's aid, she would need to think again.

It didn't occur to him to leave without seeing whatever Helen had wanted him to see, not until, skirting the walls, he caught sight of the group in the corner. *Then* he swore under his breath, and wished he'd left. But it was too late then.

He wasn't fool enough to charge in without assessing the situation. He could see why Helen was concerned; the group before him was without precedent, a volatile and likely explosive mix.

Amanda had assembled an extraordinary number of the most eligible but lecherous rakes in town, thus attracting the attention of the well-bred madams who cruised Helen's rooms. Few could hold a candle to Amanda—they would have seen her as an upstart competitor. *Should* have seen her as such, but something had got twisted. And Martin knew who'd done the twisting.

Instead of hissing and showing their claws, the other, more mature ladies and *Miss Cynster* had come to some mutual understanding. Martin could guess what such an understanding might entail, but from the enthralled looks on the gentlemen's faces, the fact that Amanda herself was not about to play their game tonight had not yet sunk in.

Then again . . .

He watched her flirt with an elegant roué, and wondered whether he should be so cocksure. She was a prize at any price but in this arena, she promised an experience well beyond the norm. She was not only beautiful, sensually attractive, untarnished and intelligent, she was also quick-witted, independent—defiantly feminine. There were connoisseurs enough in the circle around her who would appreciate that.

Not, however, tonight. Regardless of her plans.

After a narrow-eyed assessment, he rejected a frontal assault. Turning away, he beckoned a footman.

Laughing up at Lord Rawley, Amanda lifted the note from the salver, flicked it open—and nearly dropped it. She hadn't known Dexter was present; she'd been so intent, so on edge, she hadn't felt his gaze . . . hadn't seen him.

"I say—what is it? Bad news?"

She glanced up to find Lord Rawley and all the other gentlemen looking seriously concerned. "Ah . . . no." The instant brightening of their expressions told her why they'd been concerned. "That is . . ." She crumpled the note, suppressed an urge to rub her forehead. "I'm not sure."

This was what she'd wanted, schemed to get. But why was he waiting in the front hall?

She smiled at her admirers. "There's a messenger in the hall I must speak with. If you'll excuse me for a moment?"

Lady Elrood led the chorus. "Of course, my dear."

Amanda slipped away before any gentleman could offer to accompany her.

Stepping from the crowded drawing room into the front hall, she looked toward the front door, and saw no one bar two footmen. Before she could turn and look toward the stairs, her cloak fell over her shoulders.

Before she could react, the hood was yanked down over her face. Arms like steel wrapped about her and lifted her from the floor.

"The door, you dolts—open it!"

Any doubt she might have harbored over the identity of her attacker fled. She wriggled, tried to kick—all to no avail. By the time she thought of screaming, Dexter had carried her over the threshold and started down the steps. She quieted, waiting to be put down.

He reached the pavement, took two strides, hefted her—and tossed her unceremoniously onto a carriage seat.

Fury erupting, she fought to free herself from the folds of her cloak.

The carriage door slammed; she heard a shout. The carriage shot forward as if fleeing from the devil himself. She struggled free of the cloak—and saw the facades along Belgrave Road flashing past. Absolutely stunned, she slumped back against the seat.

How dared he?

She was so shocked, then so incensed, she couldn't form a coherent thought. The carriage rocketed along, barely slowing to take corners; she had to hang onto the strap to keep upright. Not until the carriage slowed, then rocked to a stop, could she collect her scattered wits.

Gathering her cloak and reticule, she opened the door and stepped down, unsurprised to find herself at the corner of North Audley and Upper Brook Streets, a few steps from home. Turning, she opened her reticule.

The jarvey coughed. "Y'r pardon, ma'am, but the g'ntleman paid h'ndsomely."

Of course he had. Amanda looked up, and smiled. Unsweetly. "In that case, I suggest you leave."

The jarvey didn't argue. She waited until the hackney rounded a corner, then hitched her cloak over her shoulders and trudged home.

"At least it shows he cares."

"It shows he's a *dolt*—an overbearing, conceited, arrogant *ass!* An entirely typical Cynsterlike male."

"So now what?"

"I start on plan B."

Her nemesis next caught up with her at Mrs. Fawcett's *soirée*. Mrs. Fawcett was a widow of not entirely unblemished reputation whose evening entertainments were highly considered amongst the demimonde.

"What the *devil* do you imagine you're doing?"

The deep-throated growl was music to Amanda's ears. Without turning from the game of silver-loo she was supposedly watching, she glanced back at Dexter, just behind her. "I'm enjoying myself."

A smile on her lips, she looked back at the play.

After a moment's brooding silence came: "If you won't think of your reputation, think of Carmarthen—you're placing him in an invidious position."

In this venue, she'd brought Reggie as escort; he was deep in discussion with another gentleman of much the same age. "I don't think he's in any danger." Cocking a brow, she looked up and back to meet Dexter's aggravated gaze. "Would you rather I came without him?"

"I'd rather you didn't come here at all. Or anywhere like it."

Looking away, she shrugged. "I can't conceive why you imagine your opinion is likely to sway me."

"You *promised* if I gave you the adventures you requested—all of them—you'd stay away from venues such as this for the rest of the Season."

He was speaking through clenched teeth.

She turned; they were so close, her breasts brushed his chest. Reaching up, she traced a finger down one lean cheek. And smiled, directly into his eyes. "I lied." Then she widened her eyes at him. "But why should you care?" With a mock salute, she stepped around him. "Now, if you'll excuse me, there're gentlemen present I've yet to meet."

She left him, idly ambling away. But she hadn't missed the jolt of tension that had locked his large frame. Nor the gaze that burned between her shoulder blades for the rest of the night.

Martin wrapped his fingers about Amanda's wrist as she paused on the threshold of Mrs. Swayne's drawing room. He'd seen her slip away to the withdrawing room, and had lain in wait for her; that was what she'd reduced him to.

He drew her out of the flow of guests. "So tell me, just what is your plan?"

He stopped by the wall; she opened her eyes wide. "Plan?"

"Your objective in turning the better part of the ton's rakes into slavering slaves just waiting for you to take your pick."

"Ah—that plan." She looked across the sea of raffish rogues and rakes filling the small drawing room.

Martin grimly held onto his temper. He deeply regretted giving way to it at Helen's—satisfying though it had been at the time, just look where it had landed him. He'd spent the last week attending every blasted function throughout the demimonde, searching for Amanda through the salons and parties. Keeping an eye on her. People were beginning to notice. And the very last thing he wished was to focus attention on his interest in Amanda Cynster.

"There's no need to concern yourself. I fully accept that there's no understanding between us. No connection—you made that plain. I therefore fail to see why you're so intent

on preserving such a dog-in-the-manger attitude toward me.
You can't seriously imagine that I will accept that."

He locked his jaw, bit his tongue against the impulse to
respond to the taunt in her eyes. She had him—his emotions—pegged to a tee.

When he remained silent, her brows rose, then she resur-
veyed the room. "If you'll excuse me, there are others I wish
to speak with."

She started to move away; his hold on her wrist prevented
it. She looked down at his fingers, manacling her wrist. And
waited. He had to force them to open. Her smile serene, she
inclined her head and stepped out.

"Where are you going?" He couldn't hold the question
back, knew she'd understand what he was asking—where
was she headed with this game.

She glanced at him. "To hell and back again." As she
turned away, she added, "If I so choose."

She was walking a tightrope over a pit of ravening wolves; at
some point, she'd put a foot wrong—nothing was more certain. The wolves were counting on it; that was why they
were patiently waiting, willing to be played on a string like
the puppies they most assuredly were not.

Martin gritted his teeth and watched as night followed
night, as *soirée* followed party followed rout. In the ton, the
Season proper had commenced; among the demimonde, the
same frenetic burst of social activity held sway.

Every night, he located Amanda; even if she had tonnish
obligations, at some point, escorted by an increasingly unhappy Carmarthen, she'd appear in his world. And every
night, she seemed a touch wilder, a touch less predictable.

She laughed and charmed; it appeared almost an addiction the way she added conquests to her string. Face grim,
arms folded, he would prop the wall and watch; the most
dangerous had noted their earlier association, and had sufficiently well-honed self-preservatory instincts to be wary. No
one could fathom what lay between them, but few were
game to risk stepping on his toes. It was the only weapon he

had left with which to protect her; the fact it had worked so far was his only success in their game.

Supporting the wall at Mrs. Emerson's rout party, he studied the circle of which Amanda was the focus. Some argument was brewing, yet its tone seemed intellectual rather than sexual—odd, considering the company, not so odd given Amanda was leading one side of the debate.

Then Reggie Carmarthen stepped back from the group; he scanned the crowd, the expression on his face one of incipient panic. He spotted Martin.

To Martin's surprise, Reggie made a beeline for him. Fetching up beside him, Reggie dispensed with all formality. "You've got to do something. She's"—he waved at Amanda—"about to step seriously out of her depth!"

Martin returned Reggie's earnest look impassively. "So stop her."

Reggie's expression turned impatient. "If I could stop her doing anything, she wouldn't be here in the first place! That's obvious. I've never been able to turn her a damn once she gets the bit between her teeth." He met Martin's gaze belligerently. "And she's had the bit between her teeth from the moment you offered to partner her at whist."

The accusation was clear, but Martin needed no prod in that respect. He already felt responsible—certainly morally accountable—for Amanda's increasingly brazen behavior, her restless, dissatisfied state. He doubted Reggie had any idea why and how completely the blame rested with him.

To feel so might be illogical—it was her own choice, after all—yet it was how he felt.

He stirred under Reggie's righteous gaze; straightening, he glanced at the increasingly rowdy group. "What's the subject under discussion?"

"Etchings."

Martin looked at Reggie. *"Etchings?"*

Disgusted, Reggie nodded. "Precisely—*those* sort of etchings. Only Amanda has no idea, and some of the men have realized. Any minute, she's going to accept some carefully worded challenge"—he glanced at the group anxiously—"if she hasn't already."

Martin swore and followed his gaze, relieved to see the argument still in full spate. Amanda was holding forth. "They'll let her tie herself up in her own arguments first, if they've any sense."

"Curtin is there, and McLintock, too."

Which answered that. "Damn." Martin watched the drama unfold, considered how best to intervene. He'd been toying with the notion of alerting her cousins to her extracurricular activities, but he hadn't seen even one of them while tracking Amanda through the salons; going into the ton to find them was not an option—not for him.

He looked at Reggie. "If I get her out of this, might I suggest you tip the wink to one of her cousins. Devil or Vane, or one of the others?"

Reggie stared at him as if he—Martin—had misunderstood something crucial. "I can't do that." When he frowned, Reggie offered, "I'm her friend."

Martin studied Reggie's open countenance, then grimaced and looked back at Amanda. Inwardly sighed. "It seems it's up to me, then."

Amanda had all but given up hope—completely and utterly—when Dexter suddenly loomed beside her. For the past week, she'd played an increasingly desperate hand, her smile night by night growing more brittle, her behavior more outrageous. She was now skirting the unforgivable, and part of her didn't care.

It had been frightening to discover just how little she cared for what was left on her plate if Martin Fulbridge was not to be a part of her life. Frightening to realize what her future would hold—a dull and virtuous marriage. Despite her professed interest in the excitement of the demimonde, she was already weary of their entertainments, a poor imitation of those of the ton, the company less erudite, less honestly engaging; she did not approve of the cold eyes of the gentlemen or the brassy insincerity of the women.

Tonight, she'd passed beyond desperation to a state where flirting with a potentially destructive situation seemed acceptable. In her heart, she knew it wasn't so, but her heart was too heavy to save her.

Dexter's reappearance should have sent that organ soaring, but one look at the stony cast of his features was enough to douse her reaction. "Well, my lord." She met his eyes as boldly as any woman present, and a great deal more challengingly. "Which way would you argue—yes, or no?"

He held her gaze. "Yes or no to what?"

"Why, to the thesis that the most noble specimens of the art of etching are guaranteed to inflame a lady's passions." She returned his regard evenly, hiding her contempt for the subject, as she'd done throughout. When, coming upon a conversation on the irresistible lure of a recently acquired etching, she'd given her opinion that such artworks were greatly overrated as to their effect on women, every gentleman within hearing had converged to patronizingly dismiss her view.

That had been all she'd needed, in her present mood, to make her dig in her heels and stick to her theory. The fact that every gentlemen involved assumed it was indeed a theory, and that if suitably encouraged she'd talk herself into an experiment, formed the wellspring of her contempt.

Just how naive did they think she was?

Of course she knew what sort of etchings they meant— she was *twenty-three!* She'd viewed a few firsthand, had heard of others, and had been exposed to the works of artists such as Fragonard from her earliest years. Her opinion was no theory but established fact—artwork, no matter the subject, had never done anything to her passions.

That was a point she'd yet to make clear; starved of entertainment, she'd perhaps unwisely fanned the argument. Her current tack was to discover how long it would take for the assembled gentlemen to realize she was not about to volunteer to test her thesis by viewing one of their collections.

That, of course, was before Dexter appeared. Now he had . . .

She raised a brow. "Surely you have an opinion, my lord? One would suppose you to be quite knowledgeable on the subject."

His eyes held hers, then his lips curved in a smile that sent a shiver down her spine. "I've rarely found them ineffective, although, of course, the sensitivity of the lady in question has a signal bearing on the outcome."

The drawled yet perfectly articulated words fell into a sudden hush.

Amanda stared, trapped in his eyes. She'd assumed he'd glower and try to douse the discussion, not ruthlessly throw down the very gauntlet every other gentleman had been trying to find an opportunity to toss. Behind her polite mask, she was honestly aghast.

"Quite right," Mr. Curtin purred. "That's been my experience, too."

"Indeed," Lord McLintock chimed in. "Which means, my dear, that you'll have to view a set of suitable etchings to prove your point. I'd be happy to offer my collection for your assessment."

"No, no. My collection is more extensive—"

"Ah, but I fancy mine would be preferable—"

A cacophony of offers assailed her ears. Within seconds, an altercation threatened over whose collection was most suitable to test her mettle.

Dexter's deep voice cut across the din. "As it was my observation that sensitivity is key, and as my library contains an extensive collection of such works, including rare volumes from the East, I suggest Miss Cynster should test her thesis by viewing a selection from my collection."

Amanda drew in a slow breath. Not one of the assembled rakes dared protest; they waited, ready to leap in should she refuse Dexter's offer.

She looked up at him, let him alone see her narrowed eyes. He'd deliberately cut short her evening's entertainment, doubtless on the grounds it was for her own good. Well and good—*he* could provide compensation.

Lifting her chin, she smiled. "What a splendid idea." The wariness that flashed into his eyes was a pleasure to behold; she beamed at their audience. "I will, of course, report back to you all on my findings."

A few grumbled; others accepted the loss with good

grace, doubtless anticipating she would return with a heightened appetite they could offer to slake. Amanda inwardly humphed, fully intending to curtail her forays into the demimonde. The only reason she'd ventured there in the first place was to find the man currently by her side. She gave him her hand; he tucked it in his arm. With a nod to the others, Dexter led her away. Straight for the door.

"You don't think," she murmured, "that you're going to get away without showing me a book from your collection—one of those 'rare volumes from the East'?"

He glanced down at her, his expression hard. "You don't need to look at such a book."

She opened her eyes wide, went to draw her hand from his sleeve—his fingers locked hard about hers. She looked down at her trapped hand, then lifted her gaze to his eyes. "If you deem their company too risky for me, then you must provide an alternative. You offered to show me your etchings—I accepted. They all heard you."

"Are you seriously holding me to that?" His tone suggested she was daft.

She held his agatey gaze. "Yes."

Martin swore beneath his breath. He looked away, over the sea of heads, then released her hand and reached into his coat pocket. Drawing out a tablet, he scribbled a note to Reggie Carmarthen, merely stating that in rescuing his friend, he'd had to take her home. The brusque tone of the missive would be entirely comprehensible to Reggie. After dispatching a footman with the folded note, he reclaimed Amanda's hand.

"Come on."

Chapter 8

"I don't suppose," Martin inquired acerbically, as his carriage turned into Park Lane, "that you'll let me set you down by your parents' house and call this evening ended?"

Amanda glanced at him through the shadows. "No."

So much for that. He'd had no choice, yet he'd regretted hijacking her evening from the moment of quitting Mrs. Emerson's door. Why he was so jumpy, he didn't know—he'd take her to his library, show her one of the damned books, then bundle her back out and take her home. And that would be that. For tonight.

The carriage turned into his drive; as per his customary orders, it headed around to the rear yard. Martin inwardly swore, then remembered the front door hadn't been opened for years. The carriage halted. He descended and handed Amanda down, telling himself his nerves were twitchy simply because she was the first member of his ex-circle he'd allowed into this house since it had become his. Yet as he escorted her in via the dark kitchen and on through the dim corridors, his nerves tightened further.

Amanda was glad of the lack of light; other than a candle Dexter had picked up from the kitchen table, the house was in darkness. Not, however, pitch dark—she could see furniture swathed in holland covers, sense the brooding atmosphere of an empty house. The wavering light of the candle didn't reach her face, so she could gawk as much as she liked.

This was his lair.

A shiver snaked down her spine. It was horridly cold, just one notch from chilled, and she suspected that one notch was due to the kitchen hearth. But he couldn't possibly spend his days there. The immense staircase that rose on their right as they entered the mausoleumlike hall was of classical design, its steps leading up to a gallery shrouded in impenetrable shadows. Glancing around, she suppressed another shiver; most doors stood open—not one room showed any evidence of being used.

This was no home. He might be unmarried and live alone, yet this house had had all life sucked out of it. There was nothing left, no human warmth or gentleness, no comfort for a restless spirit.

Without pause, Dexter led her down a second corridor, wider than the first, but equally neglected.

Bleak. The word echoed in Amanda's mind. How could he live here?

Then he opened a door. Light spilled out, a startlingly welcome sight. He waved her in; she stepped forward—and stopped on the threshold.

This was where he lived.

She looked this way, then that, eyes darting, trying to take it all in at a glance—impossible. Trying to reconcile this wonder with the desolate emptiness she'd traversed in the last minutes. Mesmerized, she walked in, only to stop again, unabashedly swivelling to stare about her.

The huge room—massive in proportion, possibly an early ballroom, for the house was old—was now a library. The term didn't do it justice. Yes, every wall was covered with bookshelves, wood glowing all the way to the ceiling; yes, the shelves were packed with tome upon leatherbound tome, many spines heavy with gold or silver. There was a hearth big enough to roast the proverbial ox in the middle of the long inner wall. The opposite wall hosted a regimented row of long windows giving onto a courtyard in which moonlight played on lush greenery surrounding a square lawn and a fountain. The courtyard's high stone walls were covered in vines.

Her gaze drifted to the ceiling; she sucked in a reverent breath and stared. It was a work of art, each segment of the dome depicting a constellation with various deities, animals, fish and fowl. One could stare, spellbound, for hours; she dragged her gaze away, noting the row of crystal chandeliers, all presently unlit.

Glancing around, she felt like she was drowning in sumptuous splendor. Everywhere she looked, there was some object or item, some unexpected sight to engage the senses. His years in the Orient were evident in the delicate ivory ornaments, in the jade figurines that stood on wooden pedestals, the silk runners that covered the tops of heavily carved sideboards. Across the polished floor, bright carpets stretched, sheening in the candlelight, their jewel hues vibrant even in the relative gloom.

Facing each other across the hearth in which a fire blazed, confirming this was the room to which he habitually retired, stood a chaise and a daybed, the latter piled with gold-embroidered silk cushions and draped in a veritable rainbow of silk shawls, their bright, knotted fringes winking in the candlelight.

Dragging in a breath, she looked down the room to gain perspective.

It wasn't just the scale that stunned—it was the color. The richness. The sheer sensory delight.

The house was like him. The thought burst into her mind with the clarity of truth, the conviction of accuracy. The outside was classical yet forbidding, the entrance bleak, but at the heart lay a place of unfettered warmth where beauty, knowledge and sensual pleasures held sway.

She turned and saw Dexter crouched by the fire, building it high. Strolling to the nearest bookcase, she let her gaze roam the spines. Art, the Classics, poetry—all were represented. Essays, philosophies, diaries in Latin, Greek, German and French—the collection was extensive.

Picking up a jewelled egg from one shelf, she examined the intricate work. Replacing it, she turned—to find Dexter standing, watching her, an unreadable expression on his face.

"Well." She waved at the shelves. "Which is the tome I need to peruse?"

His features hardened. He started toward her with his usual prowling gait, the firelight behind him gilding his hair. Steeling her senses, she held her ground. Tilted her chin.

He stopped in front of her, met her gaze. "You don't need to peruse any book."

She tried to read his eyes. Failed. "But I do. It's the least entertainment you can offer me, considering that little scene earlier." Intimidation poured from him; helpfully she added, "And don't forget—one of your volumes from the East."

His jaw set. Through eyes harder than stone, he considered her, then reached up, high above her head, and slid a brown leather-covered tome free. He placed the heavy book in her hands—the spine was more than three inches wide—then waved her to the fire. "Pray be seated."

He'd lighted a candelabra and set it on the low table at the end of the chaise. Amanda headed for the daybed, irresistibly drawn by the silks. She settled among the cushions; they shushed as she wriggled. The daybed was wide, unusually large; the perch was unbelievably comfortable. She looked at the low table, then at Dexter.

Stony-faced, he moved the table and candelabra to the end of the daybed beside her. Setting the book on her lap, she trailed her fingers over the cover, heavily encrusted with gold leaf. "Did you get this on your travels?"

He hesitated, then replied, "It was given to me by a maharanee."

When he remained standing, she looked up at him, let challenge fill her eyes. He stared down at her, then surrendered and sat on the daybed's other end, leaning back amid the cushions, arms wide. He looked so much at home, she suspected the daybed was his favorite resting place. Most un-English, yet the liking of luxurious comforts was definitely a leonine attribute.

Satisfied, she gave her attention to the book. Opening it, she turned to the first page to find it covered with wildly curling characters.

"Sanskrit."

"Can you read it?"

"Yes, but the text is immaterial to your purpose. Go on to the illustrations."

She could think of no way to force him to translate. She turned the page. And came to the first etching. Her first intimation that, no matter that she had not led a truly sheltered life, in comparison with him, assuming this book to be no revelation, she'd spent her entire life in a cloister.

Oddly, she didn't feel the least bit shocked. No telltale blush rose to her cheeks. She did, however, feel as if her eyes couldn't open wide enough, as if she hardly dared breathe.

Not shocked. She was fascinated. Enthralled.

Amazed.

Martin watched the firelight play across her face, watched the change in her expression as she turned the page. Tried not to recall what she was looking at. Then, to his consternation, discovered that he couldn't.

He studied her face. She seemed absorbed. Intrigued. Then she tilted her head, angling her gaze . . . unable to bear it, he stealthily shifted sideways so he could see her more clearly.

Hell! Eyes glued to the page, he realized he'd forgotten how lifelike the illustrations in that particular book were, how detailed. She flipped a page, fell to studying the next image avidly. He stared at the work, then glanced at her face, imagined what must be going through her mind.

His mouth went dry; his whole body reacted.

He looked back at the book, fought to ease the vice slowly tightening, notch by notch, about his lower chest.

She turned the next page—to a picture of a couple, on a daybed very like the one they were on, engaged in flagrant intercourse.

Arousal rushed through him; he couldn't stop his gaze going to her face, couldn't not watch, his breath shallow, as she examined the finely drawn work.

She felt his gaze. She glanced at him; her eyes met his, locked on them. Then she stilled.

A wash of color spread across her collarbones, swept into her porcelain cheeks. Her lips softened; she glanced down at the book, considered the picture again.

The pulse at the base of her throat leapt; her fingers fluttered at the edge of the page. He sensed the change in her breathing, could, through the tension suddenly binding them, feel the rise of her desire.

Hesitantly, she looked at him. Her eyes were dark, pupils dilated, ringed with an intense sapphire blue.

"So you see," he ground out, the words gravelly, deep, "the pictures do affect you." He reached for the book—knew he had to take it from her, bring the moment to an end. Quickly.

"No. You're wrong." She shifted the book away from his hand. Lost her grip. The book slithered from her silk-covered lap, thudded onto the floor.

They both reached for it.

He slid forward—the movement brought him close to her. His weight sinking into the bed pitched her into him.

In a slither of silk, Amanda squirmed around, spread her hands across his chest and stayed him. "No—leave it." She struggled to breathe, to think, to keep her eyes on his rather than on his lips. "It's proved my point."

The muscles under her hands were rigid; she felt his control quake. It held, but only just. The heat of his body washed about her, engulfed her; something primitive prowled just behind his mask. She glanced at his lips. Saw him moisten them, saw them form the words, "How so?"

She looked into his eyes; he continued, "The pictures aroused you."

"No." Triumph warmed her, but it was getting harder and harder to think. "It wasn't the pictures. They were . . . interesting. Revealing. Nothing more." Boldly, she trailed a finger down his lean cheek, her gaze locked on the path she traced until her fingertip touched the corner of his lips. Her wits were slowly spinning away, as if speech, as if thought, no longer mattered.

She looked up; his eyes were a dark, mesmerizing deep

green. "It was you—watching *you* look at the picture. Imagining you imagining me . . ." She slid her hand back, curled her fingers about his nape, drew his lips to hers. "Watching you imagining us . . . like that."

Their lips touched, and they were lost.

She didn't know it, but every instinct reacted. To the fact that she had her lion in thrall, that she'd finally breached his walls and captured the sensualist at his core. Gloried in the fact that he was hers, here and now, without reserve.

And she was his.

The realization streaked through her, not a thought but pure feeling, something she felt in her skin, in her blood, a knowledge that sank to her marrow.

She was with him from the instant that kiss set spark to tinder, followed eagerly as the conflagration grew, as the caress evolved into an explicit exchange. He eased back into the cushions; she went with him, sinking against him, luxuriating in the feel of his hard body beneath hers. Her arms about his neck, she locked him to her as the kiss went on and on.

As they fell deeper under the sensual spell fate had woven about them.

Later, she realized it was that that had driven them, overwhelmed them; at the time all she knew was an inchoate need to be his—female to his male, woman to his man. A need so elementally simple, so emotionally at one with her desires, she had no reason to think, to question.

It felt so right.

His hands speared into her hair and sent her pins flying. The mass tumbled down but he closed his hand in it, held it, savored the feel of the heavy locks sliding through his fingers, then filling his hand again. And again.

Eventually leaving her hair in tumbled disarray, his hands trailed down, fingers skimming the sensitive skin of her throat. Then his lips left hers to follow the trail. She felt a tug, then her cloak slid away, sliding off the bed to pool on the floor. He laid a hand on her breast; she pressed her flesh to his palm, sighing with content, with an anticipation he swiftly fulfilled. His lips returned to hers, appeasing their hunger while between them his hands closed, kneading gently at first, then more deliberately, until her breasts were swollen, aching, pulsating. But he didn't touch her as she wished to be touched. Instead, his fingers went to her laces, swiftly undoing them—then she could breathe again, albeit shallowly.

He stripped the gown from her, freeing first one shoulder, then the other, murmuring instructions which she obeyed. She glanced at his face, marveled at the sharp edges desire had lent features already austere. Then he jerked the ribbon ties of her chemise undone, and pushed gown and chemise down, baring her to the waist.

The look on his face sent sheer joy winging through her— he looked stunned, mesmerized, utterly enthralled. Cool air washed over her skin, yet she didn't feel cold, not with his eyes feasting upon her. His hands rose, closed almost worshipfully about each breast, then his fingers firmed. She gasped, closed her eyes, head rising, concentrating, caught by a rush of seductive delight. He'd touched her breasts before, but not like this, not with her above him. It was different— freer—so clear that this was her choice, that she was participating by her own act, rather than accepting a caress he pressed on her.

She moved restlessly against him, felt his erection rigid against her stomach. He shifted and caught her lips with his, drew her senses once more into the heated depths of a kiss.

Then his fingers shifted, tightened about her throbbing nipples—and delight flashed through her, sharp as a lance. He repeated the torture, drank her gasp as her lungs seized. Then his touch eased, drifted, fingers stroking languidly, soothingly. Each touch was reverent, as if he were stroking the richest velvet, the most costly satin.

Heat blossomed, spread.

He slid his lips from hers, nudged her head back so he could trace the line of her throat down to where her pulse throbbed. He closed his mouth over the spot; heat flared beneath her skin as he sucked lightly, subsided when he drew back and licked, laved.

Then his head dipped lower, lips skating over the upper

curve of one breast. Her nerves leapt, tensed, sparked—she caught her breath, knowing, wanting . . .

He urged her up and she eagerly complied, gasped when his mouth closed hotly about the ruched peak of one breast, melted when he sucked lightly, licked—then he suckled and her breathing shattered.

He didn't let her catch her breath, didn't let her senses stop spinning. Supported by the cushions, fingers splayed on his skull, she held him to her, urging him to take as he wished, to feast, to devour to his heart's—and her senses'—content.

Every nerve was alive, every sense she possessed focused on his touch when he finally eased back, lay back on the cushions and reached for her, spearing his hands once more through her hair and drawing her lips to his.

Martin revelled in her eagerness, in her unfettered sensuality, a sensuality that spoke so directly to his. She met him at every turn, at every touch, every beat of their hearts. They were already one—one in intent, one in anticipation. Long habit made him draw the moments out, savoring each step along a road he knew well, caught in the wonder that with her, the way had changed, the scenery altered.

He was as fascinated as she.

So much was different—*she* was different—but more than that, the entire landscape had transformed. He was enthralled, intrigued; they were novices together, learning together, experienced in some ways yet so much was new.

He would never get tired of touching her—simply stroking his fingers, his palms, over her lush curves, over her rose petal skin. But the heat building through their kiss, tended, fed, steadily stoked with each flagrantly evocative caress, was escalating, step by step into urgency. He needed to sate his increasingly clamorous senses, to touch more, explore further. He ravaged her mouth and she gasped, then met him, pressing her demands as boldly as he.

More—he had to have more. Sliding his palms down her sleek sides, he caught her gown and chemise and pressed them further down. The material slipped easily along her skin, down over the curves of her hips, over the lush swell of her derriere. Breaking from their kiss, he shifted, half rising, one hand splaying over her bare waist, locking her to him; with the other, he grasped the crushed fabric and drew it down her legs, all the way down, then tossed the garments to the floor.

She looked down, caught her breath, then toed off her satin slippers, with a small kick sending one, then the other, to join her gown.

His gaze fixed on her silk-stockinged toes, he drew in a long, deep breath, conscious of the expansion of his chest, of the softness of her breast pressed to him. Every nerve he possessed had stilled. Slowly, he swept his gaze up the curves of her legs, from her small, delicately arched feet, past trim ankles and slender calves to her knees, all screened by fine silk, ultimately to where her blue silk garters circled her thighs.

Above them, her skin was bare, glowing like ivory pearl in the soft light. His gaze traced the gentle swells of her thighs, rested on the thatch of blond curls at their apex. Chest tight, he sent his gaze roaming higher, over her taut stomach, over the indentation of her waist to her breasts, swollen and rosy-peaked from his attentions. Lifting his eyes, he took all of her in, drank in the sight. She lay stretched alongside him, within the circle of one arm, totally naked but for her silk stockings, a creation designed to overwhelm his senses, resilient female curves encased in alabaster satin, her golden locks lustrous in the candlelight.

At her back, all around her, the jewelled tones of his silk shawls and cushions created a fitting bed on which she was displayed—a gem, a pearl beyond price.

His.

One part of him wanted to seize, to devour, to slake the lust that rode him. Another part noted the dreamy wonder in her eyes as from under heavy lids she watched him examining her, noted her shallow breathing, and wanted, more than anything, to open her eyes to delight, to steep her in pleasure.

The latter was more to his taste.

He bent his head, found her lips, took her mouth in a slow, drowning kiss, tightened his arm and drew her to him. Her breath hitched as her sensitized skin came into contact with his clothes; he inwardly smiled, and drew her closer yet, let her sense the vulnerability of being naked in his arms while he, conquerorlike, remained fully clothed.

She quivered, then surrendered, opened her mouth to a long, extravagant brazen exploration, an invasion designed to spread heat through her veins, to draw her deeper into the furnace of their mutual need.

Amanda went without hesitation, without even pausing to try to gather her wits. They'd flown long ago; she was operating wholly on instinct, an instinct that insisted heaven lay this way, that together they could scale some fabulous peak and be forever changed. Forever bound.

Fused by fire, bound to each other by golden strands of feeling, by silver threads of shimmering emotion.

His blatantly sexual perusal, gaze burning under lids weighted by reined desire and a passion she could feel, had wound her nerves tight, so taut they ached with every long, slow sweep of his hands over her skin. Over her back, over her bottom; one hand explored in leisurely appraisal, the touch of a pasha learning a new slave. That wandering hand caressed her bottom, tantalizingly tracing, leaving damp heat in its wake, then drifted lower to close, cupping the back of one thigh.

He lifted her to him, held her against him and shifted his hips, letting her feel the insistent pressure of his erection against her lower stomach. Heat bloomed deep inside, flared into flame as he deliberately rocked against her.

She couldn't breathe but took her breath from him, raised her hands and framed his face, spoke to him through their kiss and urged him on. She wanted him inside her—knew it without thought, surrendered without question to the need. Yet . . .

He understood; he shifted again, tipping her back into the silk-strewn softness of the bed. It was incredibly accommodating, designed for the act. As he rose over her, she smiled blissfully; arms freed, she reached for his coat. Pressed the halves wide, temporarily trapped his arms. He frowned slightly, but acquiesced, drawing back to strip off the coat and fling it aside.

Half sitting, she moved onto the studs securing the front of his shirt. Nimble-fingered, driven by a sense of racing urgency, she disposed of them and wrenched the linen open, then stared in open-mouthed fascination at the vista she'd uncovered.

She felt her mouth go dry. Eyes wide, she raised both hands and placed all ten fingers, splayed, over the heavy muscle band crossing his chest. Pressed her fingers in, felt his muscles shift, tense. Enthralled, she trailed her hands down, revelling in the springy hairs that wound about her fingertips. She traced through the indentation at the center of his chest, down over the ridges of his abdomen, rock-hard and rigid.

He was so hard, so hot. Heat rolled off him in waves, intensifying as, eyes dark, almost black, he reached for her.

In the instant before his lips came down on hers, she marveled at the passion blank, desire driven set of his features. Always harshly angular, in the grip of passion they seemed hewn from granite—implacable, unresistible.

Not that she thought of resisting.

She gave herself to him, wrapped her arms about his neck and kissed him back with a fervor to match his, to incite his demands, to drive him on, to bind him to her. Satisfaction rushed through her as he gathered her to him, closed his arms about her and urged her back down.

Until she lay beneath him, thighs spread with him between, his hand on her breast. He drew his lips from hers and ducked his head. She lifted her arms over her head, let them fall on the silk, sighed as his lips teased her breast. Then he drew her nipple into his mouth and suckled sharply; she caught her breath on a gasp, felt her spine arch.

Felt her body react, felt an ache blossom between her thighs.

He repeated the subtle torture, soothing one breast with a knowing hand while with his mouth he teased the other, until she was gripped by a roiling unnameable need, hot, yearning, compulsive.

His lips left her breast and drifted lower, over her midriff.

She caught her breath, glanced down. Tangled her fingers in his hair and tugged.

"Your trousers. Take them off." She had to pause to moisten her lips, met his eyes when he glanced up. Smiled like a cat. "I want to see all of you."

His hands had strayed to her hips. For one instant, his fingers flexed, pressed in, then his grip eased. Bending his head, he returned to tracing kisses about her navel, but his hands drifted down to his waistband.

She lay back, let her lids fall, seized the moment to catch her breath, very conscious of the warmth, the building heat, the rising, rushing tide of desire. His and hers—theirs—to be shared. Totally.

He shifted and she opened her eyes, watched him rear back and strip his trousers and stockings off; he'd already kicked off his shoes. Then he was as naked as she; as he turned back to her she wished there was a mirror usefully hung, so she could see his back, the long planes narrowing to his waist and hips, the long length of his muscled legs.

He was gorgeous—all she could see met with her complete approval, but she still hadn't seen all she wished to see.

She tried to push back from him, tried to glance down, but he followed her too closely, pressing her deep into the silken cushions as he lowered his body to hers, lowered his head and took her lips in a suddenly searing kiss.

A kiss that left little doubt the time had come, that the lion had played enough and now would have his due. A tide of desire seemed to rise at his command—he sent it rushing through her and it swept her away.

Martin couldn't control the force that had claimed him, that had driven him from the moment she'd told him just what had so aroused her. He knew he should think, but couldn't, couldn't free his rational mind from the overwhelming tide of desire, stronger this time than it had ever been before, fueled by a deeper passion, swollen by a whirlpool of emotions he didn't recognize, much less understand.

All he knew was that she was as committed as he to their joining, to the satisfaction of merging their bodies, to the soul-deep pleasure they would share. All he could feel was the driving need to be inside her, buried deeply within her luscious body, savoring the incredible sensation of her surrounding him, pleasuring his senses with the ultimate caress. With instincts trained by long experience, he'd managed to slow the tide, hold it back long enough to ease her way. But his reins had snapped in the instant he'd felt her bare thighs caress his naked flanks.

He caught her up in the kiss, pressed her back into the cushions, anchored one hand in her hair. With his hips, he pressed her thighs wide, then reached down between their bodies. His questing fingers stroked through the soft tufts of her curls; ravenous desire growled through him at the realization they were already damp.

Reaching further, he touched her, shackled his need long enough to trace the swollen folds, seized just one moment to learn her by a lover's touch, intimate and evocative. Hot wetness met his fingertips; sinking into her mouth, boldly probing with his tongue, he equally boldly opened her, then slid one long finger slowly, steadily into her soft sheath.

Her body arched lightly under his; she gasped through their kiss, then he took her mouth again, played havoc with her senses as he stroked once, twice—she clamped tight about his finger. He stroked again, then withdrew, then pressed another finger in alongside the first.

Her hips lifted, tilted; he inwardly smiled—ravenously. Overwhelmed by the kiss, senses dizzily fractured, she responded instinctively to the intimate caress, opening to his penetration, hips and thighs easing, relaxing.

He shifted, rising over her, pressing his hips deep between her thighs. Withdrawing his fingers to her entrance, he used them to guide the throbbing head of his erection into the soft, surrendering flesh. He pressed in and her slickness welcomed him. He rested there, just inside her body, and gave his attention to her mouth, demanding, commanding all her attention, enmeshing her senses . . . then he eased fractionally back and flexed his hips sharply.

Drove deep into her body with a single powerful thrust, felt the fleeting resistance of her maidenhead give way, felt the slick, sleek heat of her enclose him, then clamp tight about his rigid length.

Her cry was more a yelp, a sudden sound of pain. Then she stilled, completely, beneath him. Laboring for breath, in a state close to agony, he forced himself to remain still, held back the need to plunder her warmth, to conquer, claim her and make her his. One hand still anchored in her hair, the other braced beside her, he lifted his head and looked down at her face.

She drew in a huge, long-drawn breath, her breasts swelling against his chest. The ache in his loins increased another notch. Before he could summon wit enough to speak, her lids fluttered, lifted enough for him to see her eyes, the sapphire blue all but drowned, her gaze unfocused.

Then she exhaled, slowly. "Good God!"

She blinked, blinked again. Then her gaze slowly sharpened; she focused on his face. Blinked. Tried to shift—

"No!" He bent his head, touched his lips to hers, made them cling. "Just . . . wait a minute."

She let out another shuddering breath. "It feels like—"

He sealed her lips, kissed her long, hard and deep, and felt every last ounce of resistance melt away, felt her body soften under his.

Surrender.

No moment had ever been so sweet, filled with a heady sense of rightness, of this being his due, his right, his privilege.

As if to have her had been a lifelong ambition at long last realized.

He didn't even need to think to move, to start the slow, steady undulation of the dance that was, in truth, especially here and now, especially with her, second nature to him.

Their lips melded, parted, came together again; their bodies mirrored the movement. Their rhythm was not something he consciously set, so attuned to her needs, so sunk in her splendor, that he moderated the demands of his body instinctively, matching them to hers.

Until she writhed, sobbed, clung, until her hands sought

his shoulders, fingers clutching, sinking deep, clinging frantically as ecstasy beckoned. Her knees rose, clamping about his hips; her hips tilted, taking him deeper, urging him to take, to claim.

He eased back only to spread her thighs wider, lift her knees higher until they gripped his waist, then he drove deeper into her core, deeper into her heat.

She drew back from their kiss, sobbed his name—and it had never sounded so evocative. He braced his arms, lifted his chest from her breasts, then bent his head, claimed her lips, and changed the tenor of their joining.

Changed gliding slide for forceful thrust, changed shallow angle for deeper, more powerful penetration. The strong, repetitive need washed over him; beneath him, she flowered and took him in. Then she seemed to catch her breath, as if her passion welled higher, reached a new level of desire. She boldly met him and matched him, her body caressing his, brazenly intimate.

Her softness drew him in and he was caught, the splendor of her body offering a sumptuous net into which he willingly fell. And then there was no longer her and him, separate entities, but one all-consuming need.

To be one. Utterly, completely—forever.

The wave swept in, broadsided him, lifted them both high on its crest.

Then she shattered, his name on her lips, her body clamping hard about his. Drawing him inexorably with her, into the white heat of the void.

Amanda clung, eyes closed, mind awash with bliss, knowing nothing beyond the incredible pleasure he'd given her, the joy they'd shared—and that he was still with her.

She could feel him, hard and hot at her core, buried so deep he'd touched her heart. She held tight as his body shuddered, convulsed, felt the rush of warmth deep within. Felt the intimacy strongly, powerfully, as with a muted groan he slowly collapsed onto her, their bodies slick, their lungs laboring, their hearts thundering in their ears. The physicality of the deed swept over her, her vulnerability, surrender implicit as she lay trapped beneath him, impaled to her heart.

And she knew she'd committed much more than the act.

Triumph filled her, but not the sort she'd expected to feel. This was a glow, a deeper, richer satisfaction, a tenderness that no girlish delight that he'd wanted her, desired her, and had been driven to have her despite and against his will could ever match.

She was a woman who had found her mate—her one true male—her destiny. Her future, and his.

Drifting on a tide of glory, she reached for him, found his face, trailed her fingers to his lips, then lifted her head and blindly pressed her lips to his.

He returned the caress; their lips clung, then parted.

With a soft sigh, she sank back, and let blissful exhaustion claim her.

He couldn't think.

It was a frightening realization. No matter how hard he tried to focus his mind, it remained blank, overwhelmed.

Martin had no idea how long he'd lain, stretched naked beside Amanda, equally naked, their limbs entwined, before he managed that much rationality. He knew the fact should scare him witless. Instead . . .

He was all too ready to ignore his mental vacuity, to indulge his senses rather than his wits.

His ever-greedy senses were very ready to be indulged. After all she'd given him, all he'd blindly taken, said senses should have been sated, yet ever since he'd attained some semblance of wakefulness, they'd been clamoring for more.

His gaze drifted possessively over her, slumped naked on his chest, his arms about her. Just where she should be, just as he would have her.

He was accustomed to the afterglow of sensual satiation, yet the depth of contentment that weighted his limbs, that sealed his mind against all thought, enmeshed it in soul-deep satisfaction, was beyond all previous experience. Different in intangible ways, ways he couldn't express.

It was simply more. Much more. Deeper, more profound. Infinitely more compelling.

More dangerous. More addictive.

Precisely what he needed. Wanted. Even if he hadn't known that before.

He knew he needed to think—knew he and she had stepped beyond the bounds of their world and would have to find their way back. Yet no matter how hard he tried to prod his laggard wits to action, to face the situation . . .

His mind remained a blank. A blank filled with a sense of wonder that left him feeling both vulnerable and blessed.

In the end, he surrendered—to the moment, to that feeling—and lay there, drinking in the sensations of her body snuggly fitted to his, the feminine softness, the silkiness of her skin, the gentle huff of her breath across his chest. The fingers of one hand idly played with her tumbled curls.

The fire died to embers and the room grew chill. She stirred restlessly, but then settled again, boneless once more.

He didn't want her to wake, not yet.

He wanted her in his bed first, before she could argue.

The impulse was so powerful, even though he was incapable of fathoming the whys or wherefores, he acted on it; carefully, he eased from under her, letting her snuggle down on the warm silks where he'd lain.

He rose, then draped the ends of the silk shawls over her, cocooning her. Gathering her scattered belongings—his own he left where they lay—he opened the door, then returned to the daybed. Piling her dress, chemise and slippers in her cloak, he tucked the soft bundle beside her, then scooped her up, belongings, silk shawls and all, and headed for the door.

Chapter 9

The house was silent and still; his arms full of Amanda's warmth, Martin didn't feel its chill. Reaching his room, he had to juggle her to open the door, but she didn't wake.

Entering, he leaned against the door until the latch clicked, then crossed the room, bare feet silent on silk rugs and polished boards. A fire burned low in the ornately carved fireplace, its glow lighting the scene—one of decadent luxury.

This and the adjoining dressing room and the room beyond that he'd had converted to a bathing chamber were the only rooms he used abovestairs. On the ground floor, he'd taken possession of the library and a small dining parlor; the rest of the huge mansion he'd left as, returning to England, he'd found it. Closed up. Devoid of life.

Not so this room, but then he'd always had a taste for the exotic. The wild, passionate and sensual.

Firelight caressed richly polished woods, glimmered on brass and gold fittings, cast shadows in intricate carvings. Colors took on a darker, mysterious hue, emphasizing the sumptuousness of velvets, satin brocades and silks, the subtle sheen of fine leather.

His bed, a massive four-poster intricately carved, curtained with heavy brocades, was the focal point of the room. Silk sheets and coverlets, thick feather mattress and pillows, created a couch fit for an emperor.

And his temptress.

As he laid Amanda down, pushing the warming pan aside and sliding her between his sheets, he couldn't tear his gaze, let alone his mind, from her sirenlike qualities. For him, they were manifold—he'd recognized that from the first, but had fought to keep his mind from noticing. Now, he could sate his senses to the hilt, could drink in the sight of her lustrous hair spread across his pillows, note the warm tint their love-making had left beneath her skin, the marks of possession his fingers and mouth had left on the alabaster satin. Even though she was swathed in silk shawls, they were too fine to obstruct his view. To hide her luscious body. To mute its effect on him.

He suddenly realized he was giddy, too aroused for comfort. Placing her clothes on the floor, he lifted the warming pan and carried it to the hearth.

He was returning when she stirred, stretched languidly . . . then relaxed once more into slumber. One shapely leg lay bent, the other extended. The shawls had pulled tight across her hips, parted slightly, teasing his senses, taunting, testing . . .

Jaw clenched, he reached for the coverlet. She was new to the game and presumably exhausted—then he glimpsed a scrap of ruched blue silk circling her thigh. Her garters.

He debated for a full minute, then released the coverlet, gritted his teeth and tugged one of the shawls free, exposing one garter and the thigh it encircled. Easing a finger between her skin and the silk confirmed the garter was too tight to leave on.

Her skin felt like flame; he jerked back his hand.

And inwardly cursed. He should have taken her stockings off earlier, but leaving them on had been too tempting. A sensually decadent motif, to sink into a lady totally naked but for her silk stockings.

And her garters.

"Damn!" Rubbing his nape, he tried to ignore the building tension. His mind was still refusing to cooperate in any meaningful way; he couldn't see how to remove her garters without touching her again. He didn't need to think, didn't even need to glance down to know that in his present state, touching her would not be wise.

But it was dangerous to sleep with such tight constrictions around her limbs. He'd be damned if he'd allow her to be in danger in his bed.

That thought—such as it was—was enough.

Steeling his senses to withstand the torture, he reached for the silk band. Holding his breath, he eased it down her leg and over the arch of her foot. Removing the loosened stocking proved more of a trial than he'd bargained for, the silk wisping against her skin, smooth, soft, warm. Impossible not to touch, to stroke, to savor.

The stocking whispered free. Dropping it, he looked at her other leg, the bent one, and mentally girded his loins even more.

He had to draw aside two shawls to expose the second garter, simultaneously exposing more of her than he needed to see. Struggling to blank his mind, he gripped the garter and eased it down; straightening her leg, he slid it free.

He'd shuffled the stocking down past her knee, just smoothed his palm through the sweet hollow behind it and on, over her calf, pushing the soft silk before it—when the ankle he was supporting lifted from his hand.

Her slender leg raised fractionally, encouragingly, presenting itself for his attentions. He looked up—into languorous blue eyes.

Eyes hazed with desire.

His gaze dropped to her lips, then to her breasts; he noted her shallow breathing, could sense anticipation rising like perfume around them. His gaze lowered further, to the sleek, slender form tantalizingly arrayed in translucent silks. To the hips and thighs that had cradled him a short time before.

Irresistibly, his eyes were drawn to the golden triangle of curls imperfectly concealed by the silks.

She shifted; her thighs parted—

He jerked upright, unable to breathe. Dazed, mentally lost, he went to step back—

Her eyes locked on his. Held him captured, mind-blank,

paralyzed, while she fluidly rolled up to her knees, up on the bed before him. Smiling into his eyes, she shuffled closer and laid her hands, palms flat, on the planes of his upper chest.

And purred, "My turn now."

Every muscle in his body locked. His mind reeled as he stared into her eyes, saw flagrant sensuality shimmering in the blue.

Then she looked at her hands. Ran them down his body. Slowly. Following every inch with her eyes.

She stopped when she reached his hips—when his mouth was dry and his heart thundering. Raising her hands, she set them to his shoulders, and fell to tracing every muscle band, each curve of shoulder and rib. Every inch of his skin.

He could only breathe enough to exist, not resist. He closed his eyes as her hands wandered, only to find sensation abruptly heightened. Small hands, delicate caresses. Her touch possessed a power that held him in thrall. He'd never been prized like this, never had a woman pander to his senses—and hers—in such a way.

He was powerless. Her captive.

Regardless of any will he might once have possessed.

Amanda knew it, and gloried. Delighted in the discovery that her lion loved to be stroked. He'd spent what had seemed like hours stroking her; she'd enjoyed his every touch, revelled in his attentions. Now it was her turn to return the pleasure, and reap the consequent reward.

Eager, she explored, searching for those areas on his large body that responded most avidly to her touch. Then she lavished attention on them, brazenly brought her mouth into play, licking, lightly sucking, boldly grazing one hard nipple with her teeth.

He shook, not with weakness but strength, with the sheer power of the reaction he held back—the reaction she evoked. The knowledge thrilled her, sent excitement and heat arcing through her.

The memory of what could be drove her on.

Drove her to close one hand about the rigid length jutting so provocatively against her stomach. Close her fingers and stroke—feel his control quake. With her other hand she drew his head down to hers and kissed him ardently. Took him into her mouth, drew him in, drove him wild with her tongue—and her touch.

A powerful combination. Within minutes, they were both aflame, both burning with the same need, the same aching yearning. The oneness closed in—the same mutually compulsive state they'd experienced earlier; she recognized it, opened her heart and wildly embraced it.

One desire drove them. As one, they moved to assuage it.

When she urged him to join her on the bed, he took her down to the silk sheets, easing her body beneath his, one large hand cradling her bottom.

She tilted her hips, encouraging, inviting—he joined with her in one slow, gliding thrust. Arching beneath him, she marveled at the ease with which he sank in, with which she received him, even though she still felt every inch, still felt her body open and give way, then ease around him.

After that, she felt nothing but the warmth, the heat, the building urgency. The beat of their hearts rising in a crescendo, sweeping them on. Spiralling passion swirled around them, then tightened, degree by degree, notch by notch, until they were breathless and gasping.

Until she writhed beneath him, holding him to her in mindless entreaty as their bodies merged. Again and again.

Until he reared back and drove her on, over the precipice and into blind glory. And still it wasn't enough.

She clung, nails sinking into his arms, her body all his, as his was hers.

Until he was there, too, lost in the wonder of completeness—the unfathomable glory, the incredible joy of two souls touching. Merging.

Being one.

A log popping in the grate jerked Martin awake. The sensation of a warm, naked, feminine-soft body pressed to his was not immediately disturbing. He lay slumped on his stomach; she lay half beneath him, facing away, one hip pressed to his loins.

Then he remembered who she was.

The realization washed over him, through him . . . and left him adrift. Disconnected. His world—the frame of reference he'd established for his life—had been shaken loose from its moorings, swept away by the night's glory, leaving him without anchor or direction.

He shifted, not away but toward her, one hand rising to touch her hair, to feel the soft silk under his palm, to feel her shoulder against his chest. One point of reality—she was real, solid. Here and now.

Conscious of his satiation, of the languor that weighted his limbs, of the bone-deep satisfaction that had only grown with the hours, he lay still as understanding flooded him. This state was not attainable by mere sensual gratification; content this deep sprang from some more profound source, one he hadn't previously tapped.

A wellspring no other woman had previously reached.

He stroked her hair, felt her firm curves against him . . . lifting his hand, he turned onto his back.

His mind was functioning again, yet when he tried to define what had happened, what it meant—where they now were—nothing but a surge of emotions answered him. Emotions he had little experience in handling; many he didn't recognize, could put no name to.

One, however, he felt so intensely there was no disputing it. Possessiveness. She was his.

As for the rest . . . he glanced at her, then turned to her once more, lifted his hand to her hair. Felt her warmth once again against his body. Tried to sort through the unfamiliar emotions.

He'd made little headway when she stirred, when she realized and turned to him, blue eyes blinking wide, swollen lips parting. Her sleep-dazed expression rapidly cleared. He could see the memories rolling across her mind—small wonder she looked shocked.

Even less wonder given his immediate reaction to that tousled, tumbled, wide-eyed look, a reaction which, with her hip pressed to him, she had to be able to feel.

Rolling onto his back, he didn't succeed in stifling his groan, one of pure torment. He literally ached. Dropping his arm over his eyes to block out the sight of her, he stated with commendable calm, "I'll have to marry you."

That much seemed blatantly obvious.

Silence greeted his pronouncement.

Then, quite definitely, she said, "No."

He replayed the word in his mind, then lifted his arm and looked at her. *"No?"*

Her eyes were wide; he couldn't comprehend her stunned, almost horrified expression. Then her lips thinned; her chin took on that mulish cast he'd seen all too often in recent weeks.

"No." This time her tone was firm.

"What the devil do you mean, *'No'?"* He came up on his elbow. Tension of quite a different sort shot through him—it felt perilously close to panic. He pointed a finger at her nose. "No more games. This"—he indicated the pair of them, naked beneath his exceedingly jumbled sheets—"is real."

Her eyes narrowed. "Quite."

With that, she turned and slid from the bed. He dived after her, grabbing—all he ended with was a mass of silk sheets. "Amanda!"

She paid not the slightest heed. Swiping up her clothes, she tossed them on a chair, pulled her chemise free.

Full-blown panic collided with total confusion. Cursing, Martin tossed back the covers and leaped from the bed. He stalked around it, getting between her and the door. She'd shrugged into her gown, was fumbling with the laces; he halted a foot away, towering over her. He didn't offer to help. Fists on hips, he growled through clenched teeth, "Where do you think you're going?"

She flicked him a glance; if she found his naked nearness at all intimidating, she hid it well. "Home."

He bit back the information that she *was* home—where she belonged; that might, perhaps, sound too dictatorial. Too expressive of exactly how he felt. "Before you leave, we have a matter of considerable moment to discuss."

"What?" She reached for her cloak.

"Our marriage."

Balling up her stockings and garters, she stuffed them in her cloak pocket. "We're not getting married because of last night."

He clenched his fists against the urge to shake some sense into her. "No—we're getting married because of the events that occurred *during* the past night." His voice had risen to just short of a roar. "You're a damned lady—you're a Cynster, for God's sake!—and you spent the entire night in my house, in various beds. I realize I've been absent from the ton for a decade, but some things never change. Of course we're getting married!"

She stepped into her slippers. "No."

"No?"

She looked up at him. Unshakeable feminine defiance blazed in her eyes. "If just one thought can penetrate that incredibly thick skull of yours, let it be this: we are not getting married because of some social stricture that decrees we should."

"It doesn't decree we should—it decrees we *must!*"

"Hah!" Amanda hung on to her temper. "*You* won't tell anyone. *I* won't tell anyone. Why should the ton—or anyone else—be concerned?"

He looked magnificent in firelight. Squelching the thought, shackling her fury, using it as a shield to hide the whirlpool of her feelings, she glared at him. "Good night."

She sidestepped quickly and rushed to the door.

"Amanda!"

Did he seriously think she'd stop? Flinging the door wide, she sailed through—into stygian gloom.

She paused, and heard his footsteps following hard on her heels. Stepping out, she headed in the direction she hoped led to the front door.

"Come back here, damn it! We have to talk."

"Not on that subject." Through the gloom she spied a railing—the gallery? She picked up her pace.

"You can't get out—the front door doesn't open."

"Huh!" Did he think she'd believe that? Reaching the gallery, she was relieved to see the head of the staircase rising out of the shadows. He cursed, then she heard his footsteps retreating. Refusing to consider what that might mean, she set her jaw and headed for the stairs.

Swearing under his breath, Martin raced back to his room. God only knew what she intended, but he could follow only so far without clothes.

He ransacked his dressing room. Shrugging into a hunting jacket and trousers, he strode into the corridor and set out in her wake. He crossed the gallery and headed down the stairs; gaining the last flight, he heard her—swearing at the locks on the front door. "I told you it didn't open."

"Don't be ridiculous!" She rounded on him. "This is Park Lane, not the backstreets of Bombay! No self-respecting butler would allow a front door to rust shut."

"I don't have a butler, self-respecting or otherwise."

She stared at him. "You can't live here alone!"

"I have a man."

"Just one?"

"He's more than enough."

"Obviously not." She gestured to the door. "I've undone the lower bolts—it's just that one that's stuck." She pointed to the recalcitrant bolt, at head height, then looked at him. "Open it."

Martin exhaled through his teeth. She seemed consumed by, driven by, some brittle, frenetic fluster; he wasn't game yet to tackle her. Best first to humor her. Raising his arm, he slammed his hand to the bolt, intending to demonstrate the futility of the measure.

Instead, the bolt caught, then slid, grating, across.

He nearly overbalanced.

"There!" With a vindicated nod, Amanda grasped the knob and hauled the door wide.

He grabbed the door to slam it shut before she could escape—it caught on the old runner and jammed.

Amanda slipped out into the night.

Cursing, Martin kicked the runner flat, then hurriedly followed her, dragging the untrustworthy door shut.

He caught up with her mere feet from the street, grasped her elbow. "Amanda—"

She twisted her arm free. "Don't you dare!"

He blinked at the sheer fury in her eyes. "Dare?" He'd already . . .

The memories rose up, a tidal wave of feelings urging him to simply seize her and be damned. Just grab her up, toss her over his shoulder and cart her back to his bed . . . closing his eyes, he clenched his jaw, held back the impulse. When he opened his eyes, she was heading through the gate.

"For God's sake!" Hands on his hips, he glared after her. Why the devil was she so furious? He wanted to marry her, had stated it perfectly clearly. Eyes narrowing, he set out in pursuit.

Head down, Amanda bit her lip and walked—stalked— homeward. Tried to ignore the odd twinges, the heavy warmth that even now lay just beneath her skin. Luckily, home wasn't far—a few blocks would bring her to Upper Brook Street. She tried to focus on her goal—on her bedroom, her bed.

Not his. The dolt!

Muttering imprecations, she fed her wrath; she couldn't afford to face the rest of her emotions, not with him hard on her heels. It must be two or three o'clock; London lay sleeping, the pavements empty. She wasn't averse to Martin— Dexter—following her, but she'd be damned if she'd discuss their putative marriage further, not until she'd had time to consider, to recall all that had happened, all she'd heard, to determine what was the best way forward.

To determine what tack she'd need to take to uncomplicate the matter he'd just done an excellent job of complicating.

He drew alongside her; she felt him glance at her face, felt the hardness in his gaze.

"Let me see if I understand this correctly." His tone suggested great restraint. "You've had me in your sights from the first night we met. You've had one goal from the outset— to find your way to my bed. Now you've succeeded—and what? You're running home in a panic?"

They'd reached the corner of Upper Brook Street. She stopped, faced him, met his eyes with a belligerence as great as his. "I never intended to trap you into marriage."

She didn't see him move, wasn't conscious of retreating, but she was suddenly backed against the corner house wall, caged.

A street flare lit his harsh features as he looked down at her.

"If not marriage, what, then?" His gaze raked her face. "What do you want of me?"

Heart thudding, she met his gaze fearlessly. "When I succeed in getting it, I promise you you'll know."

She ducked under his arm, whisked around the corner and stalked to her home.

"I can't believe you've finally . . ." Perched on the end of Amanda's bed, Amelia gestured, round-eyed. "Was it truly a magnificent moment?"

"Yes." Amanda swung on her heel and continued pacing. "At least, *I* thought so. Who knows what *he* thought. Or if he thought at all."

Amelia frowned. "I thought you were sure he'd felt the same way."

"I *was* sure." At the time. Now, she wasn't so certain. Now, she couldn't recall why, sunk in his silken bed, awash on a sea of intense feelings, she'd felt so convinced she'd succeeded in trapping her lion in precisely the way she'd wished—not with any social contraints, but with the many-splendored ties of a true emotion.

She humphed. "Whatever the case, one way or another, he's not going to escape. We've played out the first hand, but we haven't reached the end of the game."

The note wasn't unexpected. When she descended for dinner, their butler, Colthorpe, cleared his throat and discreetly offered his salver on which a folded square of parchment lay. She accepted it with a nod, tucked it into her reticule, then proceeded into the drawing room, into the throes of a family dinner, the prelude to two balls and a rout.

Exercising her willpower to the utmost, she didn't fish out the note until she returned to her bedchamber in the small hours of the morning.

After changing into her nightgown and brushing out her hair, she dismissed her maid, then, retrieving the note, she curled up in the chair by the fire and opened it.

As she'd anticipated, it was a summons to ride that morning. She studied the bold, brash strokes, the sparse words that constituted nothing more than an outright order. She refolded the note. After a moment of staring into space, she glanced at the fire. One flick sent the note spinning into it.

She watched the flames rise and turn his summons to ash, then rose and went to her bed.

When the City's clocks struck five, he was waiting at the corner, no groom in sight. He sat his roan, the horse impatiently shifting, the mare saddled and held alongside.

Amanda watched him from the deserted nursery. The morning was grey, cool; the sun had yet to rise. She watched him wait as the shadows shortened, lightened, saw him turn aside as the sun topped the roofs.

She watched him wheel the horses and ride away.

Then she slipped downstairs to her bed.

She was going to have to be ruthless. She couldn't weaken and give in—couldn't meet with him again in the shadows. Couldn't return to his lair, nor yet to the underworld where he prowled.

If he truly wanted her . . .

If he did, if he felt for her half of what she felt for him, confused and peculiarly emotional though she was on that point, then he would follow her. Into her world, the world he'd turned his back on.

If he did . . .

"Are you ready?"

Pinning on a bright smile, Amanda swivelled on the dressing stool; Amelia stood by the door. "Yes." Laying aside the brush she'd held for countless minutes past, she picked up her parasol. "Is Reggie here yet?"

"He's just arrived."

Martin pulled his front door shut. Pausing on the porch, he looked across to the park. Carriages crowded the Avenue; the ton paraded on the lawns, the ladies' gowns a bouquet of colors shifting across the green, the gentlemen in their more sober attire providing contrast.

To promenade in the park of an afternoon was clearly still obligatory for members of the haut ton. The female members, at least.

It was a female member he wanted to see.

Descending the steps, he strode to his gates, then across Park Lane. Entering through a minor gate, he passed into the park, into the shadows thrown by the trees. Amanda, he felt sure, would be somewhere among the crowd, laughing, talking, smiling.

He wanted to see her—that was all. He didn't want to examine the reasons why. Absurd, that a man of his experience couldn't accept her desertion, couldn't chalk up the episode with mild regret, shrug and move on. Couldn't, despite her steadfast "No," wash his hands of her and forget her.

It was precisely because he couldn't forget that he was here. He couldn't forget the sense of completion they'd shared, couldn't erase the sensual memory even though his factual memory was hazy over the entire interlude. He couldn't understand how it had happened, how the moment had slid so far out of his control. He didn't understand precisely *what* had happened, and he certainly didn't understand why it had ended so abruptly.

Why she'd run.

But she had; her subsequent actions had underscored her decision. She wanted no more of him.

Well and good. Jaw setting, he strode the lawns, circling the fashionable throng. His words echoed in his mind—mockingly. He thrust them aside.

It wasn't good, none of it. He'd felt like he'd found something inestimably precious—that he'd just discovered such a thing could exist—and she'd taken it, all chance of it, and herself, away.

Gritting his teeth, he halted under a tree, waited for his reaction to subside, at least enough to continue. His plan was simple. If he could see her, watch her long enough to convince himself she was happy and content, relieved to have done with him, then he'd accept his congé.

There would be no alternative. If he'd been wrong in his assessment of her—if he could convince himself she'd just been intent on a dangerous liaison purely for the hell of it—then acceptance would come much more easily.

Stepping out, he continued his search. The Season proper was about to begin; the crowd was substantial enough to provide camouflage, yet not so dense he wouldn't be able to spot Amanda. The day was fine; a light breeze flirted with ribbons and curls.

Then he saw her.

She was walking with another girl who had to be her twin. Seen together, they were too much alike for it to be otherwise, yet they were not identical. Reggie Carmarthen was with them; her parasol up, shading her face, Amanda walked in the middle of the trio.

Sliding into the shadows of a nearby tree, Martin watched. The sister and Carmarthen were conversing freely, smiling and gesticulating. Whenever they turned to Amanda, she beamed, nodded, effervescently charming, even more so than her sister. She would throw in a word or two, then pause. As the other two took up the conversational reins, she'd look down.

The effervescent brightness would drain away; her expression haunted, reserved, she would walk quietly along until appealed to again.

Martin watched the transformation three times, then Amanda's sister, clearly aware, linked her arm in Amanda's. The golden heads dipped close; Reggie was nodding, his attention focused on Amanda.

They were trying to cheer her up.

Then Reggie pointed to a group ahead of them. Amanda looked, and shook her head. A discussion took place, then Amanda pointed to an empty bench set under a tree. The others argued, but she was adamant; waving them on to join the group they'd spotted, she retired to the bench and sat.

Amanda deployed her parasol to screen herself, not from the sun but from idle glances. She'd seized the chance for a moment of peace; the last thing she wanted was to be approached by anyone, especially not Percival Lytton-Smythe, who she'd glimpsed earlier.

She needed peace to think; the Season afforded her precious little of that commodity. With the evening round of balls increasing, she had less and less time to herself, too little time to tend her increasingly tortured thoughts.

What if she'd been wrong? What if he wasn't sufficiently interested to pursue her? What if he hadn't felt the moment as she had, hadn't seen it for what it was? What if . . . ? What if . . . ?

Such questions seemed innumerable and equally unanswerable; determinedly, she focused on what she felt she did know. On what her senses and her instincts insisted was true.

He was the right man for her. After all her years of searching, she was absolutely sure; she knew it in her heart, in her soul. And she was the right woman for him. The thought of some less confident lady dealing with him seemed absurd; he'd rule her like the tyrant he was. Yet . . .

She flatly refused to accept a proposal based on social strictures. When he'd stated he'd *have* to marry her, she'd been aghast. She hadn't wanted to believe her ears. Then she had. Yet she didn't know—couldn't tell—whether in fact he felt more for her, but as she could imagine her cousins doing, had used society's rules to conceal his true motive. Or had the fact he felt more for her not yet occurred to him? Who knew what went on in male brains?

A mystery, but in this case, one she couldn't live without unravelling. She had to learn what he truly felt.

So what should her next move in the game be? Presuming they were still playing and he hadn't simply shrugged and already forgotten her.

The thought dragged at her spirits, then she thrust it aside. Reminded herself that lions did not behave like that. They were possessive, and usually quite obsessive about it.

That being so, she couldn't risk returning to his world. If she did, she'd be at his mercy, with him dictating the rules of their game. Handing him such an advantage was out of the question—who knew what he would do with it? Her imagination supplied a number of possibilities, all of which would result in them marrying under the guise of social necessity. No.

Their game would have to proceed as she'd thought—here, in the ton. The problem was, how to lure him from his lair.

Four days had passed since she'd stalked from his house; after that first note, she'd heard no more. After learning his story, hearing it from his lips, she understood that his antipathy to the ton might run deep, accepted that he would not readily step beyond the walls he himself had constructed.

But if she didn't go to him, he would have to come to her. Was there anything she could do to urge him on?

She formulated wild schemes and rejected them. Tried to ignore her incipient dejection; waiting with nothing but hope to warm her was simply not her style.

Long, cool fingers slid around her throat, curving about the sensitive spot where throat and shoulder met.

Reaction streaked through her; her parasol jerked.

"No. Stay where you are."

His voice drifted down to her; his fingers pressed warningly, then eased, drifted across her skin, slid away. Keeping the parasol steady, realizing it largely hid them both, she turned her head and looked up. Met his eyes.

His expression—politely impassive—said nothing; his moss-agate eyes were much more eloquent.

Where have you been? Why are you avoiding me?

She could see those questions, and others, too, crowding his mind, but he asked none of them, and she made no move to answer.

Instead, they simply looked, watched, gauged . . . wanted.

When he slowly bent to her, she didn't think of moving away—couldn't have done so. Her gaze fell to his lips, then her eyes closed.

The kiss started gently, but then his lips firmed; the caress became more definite, more a statement of intent. Her lips parted and he stole her breath, took it and more from her.

When he lifted his head, she was dizzy and dazed. Then she blinked, focused—hissed, "You can't kiss me in the park!"

"I just did." Rather than straighten, he hunkered down. "No one saw."

She glanced around, confirmed she'd kept the parasol in place; her sudden panic subsided.

"Why aren't you chatting with your sister and Carmarthen?"

The inquiry had her turning to face him; his tone was even, but she could no longer read his eyes.

She waved and looked away. "I'm feeling a touch under the weather."

Silence met the comment; she glanced back, met his eyes—knew precisely what he was thinking. She blushed fierily. "Not that. I'm not . . . indisposed." She looked away, lifted her chin. "Just a trifle jaded."

He'd thought she'd meant she was unwell, as ladies frequently were once a month. But she wasn't. Which meant there was a possibility . . . a possibility that hadn't occurred to her before, one that had her eyes widening, her wits whirling, her emotions seesawing.

"We have to talk." His murmur was definite. "But not now, not here."

"Definitely not here, not now." She fought an urge to fan herself. Drawing breath, she faced him.

He was watching her closely; he studied her face, then said, "Meet me tomorrow morning at five o'clock at the end of your street, as before." He hesitated, then smoothly rose.

She looked up at him. "And if I don't?"

He looked down at her. "If you don't, I'll come knocking at your father's door."

Voices reached them. He looked up; Amanda swivelled, peeked around her parasol. Reggie and Amelia were approaching, arguing. She looked back.

Dexter—Martin—had disappeared. Pushing away from the seat, she stood, searching the surrounding lawns, but he'd vanished.

Amelia and Reggie drew near; she turned to greet them.

And wondered if the victory had been Dexter's, or hers.

Chapter 10

Neither, she decided, as she slipped from the house at five o'clock the next morning. True, he'd come into society to seek her out—she considered that hugely encouraging. But even there, he'd insisted on clinging to the shadows; it seemed prudent to meet him halfway.

He stood waiting at the corner, the horses' reins in his hand. Hearing her footsteps, he looked up; his gaze scanned her, then he moved to the mare's side. She went to him, smiling. "Good morning."

He met her eyes, then reached for her; his fingers flexed about her waist and he paused . . . then lifted her to the saddle.

By the time she'd settled her feet in the stirrups, he'd mounted and was waiting. Muting her smile, she turned the mare and they headed for the park.

Once inside, they set the horses cantering; noting the real pleasure lighting her face, Martin held back the words burning his tonuge and led the way to the track. As usual, they raced; as usual, exhilaration dominated the moment—that zest for speed, for power, for indulging in unbridled wildness they shared.

At the end of the track, they slowed, turned aside, caught their breath. Then she set the mare walking, not to the gate, but into the secluded ride they'd used for discussions before. He noted the conciliatory gesture; he didn't imagine that

meant she was ready to listen to reason. He nudged the roan
in the mare's wake, and set his mind to honing his arguments.

Deep in the ride, completely screened, completely private, Amanda drew rein. She glanced at him as he came up
and raised an inquiring brow.

He captured her gaze. "We need to get married."

Both delicately arched brows rose. "Why?"

He hung on to his temper, refused to grit his teeth. "Because we were intimate. Because you're a gentlewoman, one
of a noble house not known to practise *laissez-faire* in such
matters. Because I'm of a noble house and think the same.
Because society demands it. Do you need more reasons than
that?"

She met his gaze directly. "Yes."

An absolute, unshakable yes. Unwavering resolution invested her blue eyes, determination firmed her chin. He recognized the signs, but was at a loss as to their cause.

He glowered at her. He opened his lips—

She silenced him with a shake of her head. "Only you and
I know we were intimate—there's no reason to feel you've
ruined me." She held his gaze. "I was a perfectly willing par-
ticipant, in case you've forgotten."

To his eternal irritation, he had—or rather, he couldn't remember enough to be sure. "Be that as it may, in circles such
as ours—"

She laughed and set the mare ambling. "You've rejected
'our circles,' so you cannot claim their strictures matter to
you now."

He gritted his teeth, spoke through them as he set the roan
after her. "Regardless of my attitudes, *you* haven't rejected
those circles—their strictures *do* matter to you. Your life—
the life you should live—is very much bound by society's
dictates."

She glanced at him; despite her easy smile, her eyes were
watchful, serious.

He caught her gaze, knew his expression was stony, could
feel the hardness in his face. "Regardless of all else, I will
not again be put in the stocks as a gentlemen who *did not do*
the right thing."

Her eyes widened, then she looked away. "Ah—the old scandal. I didn't think of that."

"There are certain parallels."

"Except that you weren't, in that case, responsible at all"—her voice strengthened—"and in this case, I can assure you I have no intention of taking my life."

Amanda censored the statement that she was also not pregnant; she didn't actually know, and he would guess that was so. The last notion she wished to raise within the present discussion was the possibility she might be carrying his child—his heir. Just the thought was enough to distract her utterly—she hurriedly buried it. "Rather than waste our time in fruitless generalities, might I declare my hand?"

He nodded curtly; as the mare ambled on, she declaimed, "My position is simple: I will not marry—not you, not anyone—purely because society, if it knew all, would deem our wedding a required penance for our sins. I do not consider social obligation to be a viable foundation for marriage. Especially not *my* marriage." She met his eyes. "Is that clear?"

Martin searched her eyes, and wondered what she wasn't telling him. What she'd said was the truth—that he accepted—but was it all?

That she, at twenty-three, with her inherent wildness, her liking for excitement and thrills, should harbor a bone-deep antipathy to the social conventions that ruled her life . . . that wasn't hard to see. That she would therefore react badly to the suggestion that social obligation necessitated their marriage was, unfortunately, entirely logical.

Jaw setting, he nodded. "Perfectly."

She blinked; after a fractional pause, she asked, "So you agree we don't need to wed to appease society's sensibilities?"

He forced himself to nod again.

"Good." Her expression easing, she looked ahead.

Through narrowing eyes, he studied the back of her head, the bright curls glossy gold in the strengthening light, studied the slender lines of her figure, swaying gently. Considered his next avenue of attack.

At the end of the ride where it joined the lawns not far from the gate, he murmured, "There's a private party at Lady Chalcombe's house tonight." Amanda glanced back at him; he added, "It's in Chelsea, by the river. Perhaps we could meet there?"

Very blue, her eyes met his, then she looked away. Shook her head. "No—I'm afraid not." Her tone was regretful, but firm. "The Season proper is upon us—it's the Duchess of Richmond's ball tonight. After that, my evenings are crammed with engagements. I always knew the start of the Season would put an end to less formal entertainments."

What was she telling him? Frowning, he glanced at her profile, all he could see of her face. And saw consternation sweep her features.

"Oh, dear—there are others out already. We'd better part. Is that your groom over there?" She pointed to the figure waiting by the gate.

"Yes."

"I'll leave the mare with him." She glanced at him, smiled. "Good-bye." Flicking the reins, she trotted away.

Martin watched her go in disbelief. A smile, a cheery good-bye—and that was it?

In a pig's eye.

"Thank you, Mr. Lytton-Symthe. Now, if you'll excuse me, I really must circulate."

"But my dear Miss Cynster." Despite Amanda's tugging, Percival held onto her hand. "Naturally, you must. I'll be only too delighted to squire you."

"No!" Amanda searched for some way out, then fell back on her standard ploy. "I must visit the withdrawing room."

"Ah." Deflating, Percival released her, then he brightened and smiled superiorly. "But we can't have you wandering Her Grace's rooms on your own. I'll wait for you to return."

Amanda suppressed the urge to roll her eyes. "If you wish."

She escaped, wondering if it would occur to Percival that she must have some illness—he was such a pest she was forever leaving him for the withdrawing room. Then again, he seemed incapable of adding two and two, steadfastly impervious to all her hints that she did not subscribe to his belief that she should allow him to steer her from what he described as her path of regrettable levity onto his puritanical path of the right and proper.

"Hah!" She'd been heading toward Her Grace's front foyer; now she ducked through an arch into a smaller salon. She'd only danced with Percival from a sense of duty. She hadn't enjoyed it; he was becoming uncomfortably irritating. Not that he held her too close or, heaven forbid, let his hand wander, but while she loved to dance, Percival was definitely the wrong partner. She'd felt like pulling out of his arms the whole time.

Exchanging greetings with various guests, stopping to chat here and there, she gradually made her way to the far corner of the salon where a stand of potted palms screened the space before a pair of long windows. The windows stood open; a breeze occasionally wafted their lace curtains.

The perfect spot to skulk and think.

Slipping behind the palm fronds, she inwardly sighed. There were more gentlemen than just Percival who had her in their sights. It was well known that she and Amelia were well dowered; it was equally well known that they were now twenty-three. Almost on the shelf. Certain gentlemen had concluded that this would make them desperate.

Said gentlemen were right, but their responses to desperation were not as those gentlemen supposed.

"Humph!" She peeked through the fronds. Through an archway giving onto the ballroom, she saw Amelia waltz past in Lord Endicott's arms. Her twin had thrown herself into her own plans; she was set on assessing every eligible-to-them gentleman in the ton.

Mentally wishing Amelia luck, fleetingly wondering if Luc Ashford had yet arrived, Amanda turned her thoughts to her own plan. Would Martin come after her, even into the ton? If so, how long would it be—

A steely arm locked about her waist; a hard palm clapped over her lips. In the space of a heartbeat, she was lifted and whisked back—through the lace curtains, over the threshold of the long windows, onto the terrace beyond.

When her assailant set her on her feet and released her, she whirled, already knowing who it was. Even so, her breath caught, her eyes widened.

He was indeed a sight for sore eyes. She'd seen him in evening dress before, but in a drawing room, not on a terrace in the moonlight. The severe black and white, the stark silvery light, emphasized his contrasts—his harshly angular face, the hardness that was an integral part of him, the strength that gave promise of implacability, set against the tawny fire of his elegantly tumbled locks, the heavy-lidded eyes with their soft, mossy shade, the blatantly sensual cast of his lips.

She took it all in in one glance. Then she raised her arms, beckoned with her fingers. "Come. Dance with me."

In a blink, he'd gathered her into his arms, started slowly revolving to the music drifting out through the windows. He held her a great deal closer than Percival had, a great deal more possessively. The hand at her back, riding low, below her waist, burned through the fine silk of her dress. As they revolved, she was aware of the reined strength with which he steered her, knew, as she gazed into his shadowed eyes, that he was a great deal more powerful, more intrinsically dominant, than Percival could ever be.

At the end of the terrace, he turned them, gathering her even closer. Her body brushed his; instead of stiffening missishly, she moved into him, let her body flow into the dance, gave herself into his embrace.

He held her easily, close, yet so comfortably. Lowering her lids, she rested her temple against his shoulder, and let him steer her back up the flags.

"I didn't expect you to be here tonight." She murmured the words as they neared the end of the terrace and the music died.

"Didn't you?" He halted but made no move to release her.

She looked up at his tone, looked into his eyes. "No. I hoped you might appear one night, but I didn't think you'd come here."

Martin studied her eyes, saw simple honesty looking back, and inwardly marvelled. Did she truly have no idea of the attraction—the sheer compulsion—she now exerted over him? Having her in his arms again, he was supremely conscious that he didn't—ever—want to let her go.

He'd been prepared to walk into the ballroom and draw her out, but then he'd seen her through the windows. He'd mentally called to her, had barely believed his luck when she'd obeyed.

She was studying his face, his eyes, her own narrowing. "Tell me, does our hostess know you're here?"

He smiled, the gesture tight with intent. "No." He lowered his head. "No one knows I'm here . . . bar you."

His lips closed over hers; Amanda opened to him, curled her fingers on his lapel and clung tight.

Just as well. He was ravenous—he took her breath and left her dizzy, sent her senses spinning with a too-knowing hand. Held her tight, his hands hard and possessive on her back, his arms a steel cage about her.

And she knew why he was here, why he'd followed her so close to the bright lights he despised. He wanted her, desired her, wanted her to want him. God help her, she did; the rush of pure need he evoked shook her, drove her on. Drove her to return his kisses avidly, hungrily; the exchange quickly turned greedy. They both wanted more, much more.

Raising his head, he looked into her eyes, then bent his head again, brushed her lips until they clung. "Come with me," he whispered. "There's something I want to show you."

One arm fell from about her as he lifted his head. Releasing his coat, she turned, felt his hand, large, hard and hot in the small of her back as he urged her to the terrace's end.

Steps gave access to another terrace which continued past darkened rooms not open for guests. Rounding the mansion's corner, they came to stone steps leading down to a conservatory. It abutted the house, but was not directly connected. They were well away from all the guests.

Martin opened the conservatory door and she ventured into the cool quiet. The moonlight illuminated a winding path leading down the long room, linking a small fountain just a

few steps further in and an alcove at the room's other end.
There, a bow window looked over the lawns; a cushioned
wrought-iron bench faced the conservatory's splendors.

Those splendors glowed softly in the moonlight, held on
green spikes all along the low benches flanking the path and
circling the alcove. Ferns and palms provided a dark backdrop for the multihued wonders that bobbed gently as Martin closed the door.

"Orchids." Eyes wide, she bent to sniff one cascading
bloom. With an appreciative sigh, she released it. "Aren't
they beautiful?"

Straightening, she glanced back.

Martin dragged his gaze up to her face. "Yes." Closing the
distance, he bent his head and ran his lips over her exposed
nape.

She shivered reactively, felt the caress all the way to her
toes.

"Come."

His hand was again at that spot on her back that made her
feel owned. Her skin prickling with anticipation, she allowed
him to steer her on—to the alcove at the end of the room.

The air was heavy with the orchids' scent, warmed and
slightly humid, no chill to account for her shiver as they
halted before the padded bench.

"What did you want to show me?" Brazenly, she stepped
closer, raised her arms, wound them about his neck.

His hands rose to her sides; she felt slender, helpless, held
between them. He looked into her eyes, studied them, then
bent his head. "Just this."

The kiss was incendiary—deliberately so—she felt herself go up in flames. Heat poured through her veins, rushed
beneath her skin, pooled in her loins, then ignited. He was
the same, as unprotected as she as they plunged into the fire
of their mutual need.

Mutual—most definitely that. Their lips merged, mouths
melded, tongues tangled, a prelude to the act every wit they
jointly possessed was suddenly and unwaveringly focused
on. She clung to him, one set of fingers locking in his hair,
the others sinking into his shoulder as she pressed herself to

him. He crushed her closer yet, molded her to him, evocatively and provocatively inciting their desire.

She drew her hand from his shoulder, trailed her fingers down his chest, reached lower—

He caught her wrist, shackled it. Drew back from the kiss. "No."

His eyes clashed with hers, widening in surprise; he seemed to reconsider. "Not yet."

She let her lids droop; they felt inordinately heavy. "What, then?"

He drew away, held her arms out from her sides, circled her, then closed from behind, his hands sliding across her waist. "Tonight . . ."—his voice was deep, rasping; his breath wafted the curls about one ear—"tonight we take the long road."

His hands rose and closed about her breasts; she let her head fall back against his shoulder, let her spine arch. Tried to recall their previous journey—her recollection was that it had been quite long enough.

"How so?" The words were starved of breath.

Silence, then he said, "Don't think. Just feel."

The command only focused her thoughts more, yet to her delight, they didn't distract her senses. Presumably she was growing used to this, to the worshipful way he fondled her breasts, to the real pleasure of knowing he was absorbed, intent . . . on what?

Seducing her seemed the most likely answer as the bodice of her gown slid down to her waist, followed by her chemise. The fabrics lay pooled about her hips as his fingers continued to play, teasing nipples already pebble-tight, drawing heat like flame under her skin with each deliberate stroke.

Why seduce her again—or was it for the first time? Who'd seduced whom in their earlier encounter was moot; while she'd certainly not intended matters to develop as they had, he'd been even more resistant. None of which had saved him. Or her.

So why was he here, intent on orchestrating a repetition of the act?

What had changed?

Her mind lazily circled that point, buoyed on a swell of rapturous pleasure, then he murmured, "Wait."

He balanced her, then stepped away, crossed to a nearby plant. Seconds later, he returned, three sumptuous white blooms in his hands.

Drawing her to face the bench so the moonlight fell full on her, he threaded a stem into the curls behind first one ear, then the other. The perfume immediately wreathed her; she drew it in; her breasts swelled. The last orchid in his hand, he looked down, then slid the stem into the folds of her gown, just below her navel.

Raising his hands, he cupped her face, lowered his head—and ripped her wits away. Her thoughts came to a dead halt; thinking was impossible as he devoured, then reclaimed every inch of her mouth, branding her his with each invasion.

He shifted, lowering—caught in the kiss, she bent from the waist as he sat on the bench. She put her hands on his shoulders for balance; his drifted down from her face and found her breasts again.

She sighed into the kiss. Leaning forward, her breasts suspended before him, his touch was different, even more rapturous, even more worshipfully reverent. She wasn't surprised when he slid his lips from hers, when he traced the line of her throat as he drew her to stand between his widespread thighs. Then his lips grazed the swollen crest of her breast, lapped, nibbled, then finally suckled the tight peak.

Sensations streaked through her; spine arching, she clutched his head, urged him to feast. He did, pleasuring her, pleasing himself.

She was well aware of that last, of the hot avidness of his mouth, of the greedy suckle of his lips, the demanding rasp of his tongue. She gave herself up to appeasing his hunger, in doing so had her own satisfied.

When her breasts were tight and her skin felt afire, Martin let his hands slide over her back, caressing the long, slender muscles framing her spine. With one hand, he swept the back of her gown and chemise down, over the curve of her bottom; with the other, he plucked the white orchid from the folds at her stomach before, with a soft *whoosh*, the material slithered down.

Poised before him, her hands on his shoulders, she looked down—watching as he threaded the stem of the third orchid through the soft curls at the apex of her thighs. He drew back, blatantly admiring his handiwork; he could feel the tension gripping her as she fought to drag in a breath.

Before she could speak, he reached for her hips and drew her closer—sent his lips skating over her midriff, drifting lower over her waist to her navel. As he probed the indentation with his tongue, the perfume of the orchid reached him, entwined with a scent even more primally evocative.

Dragging in a huge breath, he wrapped his arms about her hips and lifted her. She clutched his shoulders, eyes glinting sapphire blue from under weighted lids. Swivelling on the bench, he set her down, tipped her back, urging her to lie on the cushion, then he shifted back, running his hands down the underside of her thighs, lifting and parting them, draping her legs one on either side of the bench.

Leaving her displayed for him like some delectable houri out of his wildest dreams.

Her skin was pearlescent in the moonlight, her eyes shadowed, her lips lightly bruised, parted. Quivering tension held her; she drew in a tight breath, her gaze fixed on him. On his face.

He wished he knew what she could see there; every muscle felt set in stone. Every instinct he possessed screamed with ravenous hunger, with the desire to capture, plunder and take. The grip of his lust was unexpectedly dizzying, leaving him to fend by instinct alone; he'd schemed to get her precisely where she was—luckily, capitalizing on the victory was ingrained.

No logical direction was needed to make his hands reach for her breasts, to have him lean over her, bend his head and set his lips to one tightly ruched peak. To set the fires racing once more beneath her silken skin; to make her gasp, arch, clutch his skull as he pleasured her.

Pleasuring her was a delight, one that sank through him, filled him. With single-minded determination, he progressed toward his reward.

Amanda wished she could think, wished she could gain some surcease from feeling, however brief. Her position, naked but for stockings, garters, and his orchids, left her feeling both vulnerable and powerful. Vulnerable in being so intimately exposed to him; powerful because she could sense the complusion that fact exerted over him. Could sense in the burning, open-mouthed kisses he pressed to her stomach how very hungry he was. For her.

That hunger, the raw need she sensed behind his experience, behind each calculated caress, would have been overwhelming, even frightening, but for the reverence, the care, the constant worship behind every stroke of his fingers, every kiss, every touch.

He treated her as if she was the priestess of his salvation.

Regardless, he wanted more; his mouth slid lower, lower, until his warm breath brushed her curls. Made her shiver. Made her burn.

"Your coat." She pushed at his shoulders, caught the collar.

"Later," he growled.

"No—now."

She tried to sit up; with a low rumbling growl, he pressed her back down. Jerked off his coat, flung it aside and immediately returned to her, grasping her hips, lowering his head—

"Martin!" She saw stars, grabbed handfuls of his hair. Sensation jolted her; every nerve she possessed leapt, scrinched tight as he licked, then again pressed his lips to the soft flesh between her thighs.

She hadn't thought—couldn't think—could barely breathe as he tasted her, then set about sucking, licking, laving until she was sure she'd lost her mind. Until she was afloat on hot flames of delirious pleasure.

Her hips anchored between his hands, her thighs spread wide, he parted her with his tongue, found the entrance to her body, probed.

Fiery tension coiled tight. She gasped, arched, but he held her down. Ruthlessly gentle, thrust in, pressed deeper.

With a keening cry, she shattered—felt her body and senses implode, felt shards of delight fly down her veins, then melt in hot splendor under her skin.

Panting, desperate for breath, from under heavy lids, she watched him slowly straighten. His gaze remained on her, on her parted thighs, on the heated flesh between. Then he raised his eyes, scanning up her body until he reached her face. She had just enough strength left to lift one arm, hold out one hand and beckon. "Come."

The word was a sultry entreaty. He stared at her, the planes of his face had never looked harder, harsher.

And she realized in that instant that he had not intended to join with her again; that had not been part of his plan. She held his gaze, managed a smile. "I want you. Come."

She did want him, wanted him inside her, with her, sharing the delight, the bone-deep pleasure.

He hesitated, then stood. His hands went to his waistband and she gloried. She held her breath, didn't dare instruct him to take off his shirt. He released the buttons at his waist, peeled back the flap, then straddled the bench.

Before she could think, he reached for her, lifted her easily to him. She grabbed his shoulders; hands about her hips, supporting and directing, he pressed her to him. Her thighs slipped over the outside of his, opening her wider still, then he lowered her; the head of his staff nudged her softness. He adjusted her hips, pressed in, then, hands firming, drew her down. Down, down, until she was impaled.

Breathing was impossible; he was so high inside her, she felt the invasion throughout her body. He reached between them; his hand rose with the orchid in his fingers. He slid the stem into the curls piled atop her head. Then he caught her face, brought his lips to hers, captured her awareness in the kiss. She could taste her essence on his lips and tongue, then he angled his head, drew her deeper and her senses spun. His hands fell away. She felt them slide about her hips, then he wrapped his arms about her, lifted her slightly, and rocked her.

Rocked into her.

It took less than a minute for the frenzy to overwhelm him, for the slick friction of her body sheathing his to cinder the last remnants of control. Martin didn't even register the fact she'd opened his shirt until she wrapped her arms about his torso and pressed her breasts, hot and tight, flush to his bare chest. His arms locked in reaction, crushing her to him, holding her immobile as he drove into her.

He found her lips and took her mouth, found the same driving rhythm and locked onto it, held her tight and drove her wild—as wild as she was driving him.

Until, with a fractured cry, she melted in his arms, a goddess sacrificed in some pagan rite, her body an offering to appease the primitive demands of his.

And every primitive instinct gloried as he filled her, drove deep within her one last time, felt her body clamp tight and hold him as he shattered.

Gasped. Struggled to take in air, fought to clear his wits.

When had lust ever been this all-consuming?

Holding her close, moving his hands slowly up and down her back, feeling satiation and repletion spread through his body and hers, leaving them both heavy-limbed and languorous, he fought to find his mental feet.

Tried to understand why—why it was so different with her. Why it mattered so much more, why it meant more. Tried to understand what he felt, from where the compulsion to have her, possess her completely, sprang. Tried to identify the emotion that spread through him when he had her like this, naked in his arms, completely and utterly sated, completely and utterly his.

Whatever that last was, it scared him. To his bones.

The vise about his chest had eased; he could almost breathe normally. Looking down, he considered all he could see—the jumbled mass of her golden curls, the white orchids still in place, the alabaster satin of her shoulders and back, tinted with the flush of desire.

He hadn't intended to have her again, yet he didn't regret it. Couldn't regret the joy of sinking into her sleek, sumptuous body, feeling her surrender, open to him, take him in. The interlude had only reinforced his considered direction, only etched his course even more deeply in stone.

Bending his head, he nuzzled the side of her face, pressed a soft kiss to her temple. Whispered, "Say you'll marry me."

"Hmm?"

"If you marry me, you'll have all this every morning and every night."

Amanda lifted her head, looked him in the eye—and let her incredulity show. Her temper rose; she pressed her lips tight to stop herself telling him what an idiot he was. "No!"

She scrambled off him, out of his arms, off the bench. On her feet, she grabbed up her chemise; this was becoming a habit. "I'm not going to marry you"—lost for words, she gestured—"for this!" The idea! She was going to have "all this," but she wanted a great deal more besides, and after the last hour, she was certain there was a great deal more to be had.

He gave a disgusted snort, swung his leg over the bench to face her. "This is getting us nowhere. You're *going* to marry me—I'm not going to disappear into the dark while you go swanning off with some eligible gentleman."

She hiked up her gown and looked him in the eye. "Good!" She whirled and presented him with her back. "Now do this up."

He actually growled. Then he stood and jerked her laces together. "If I didn't know better, I'd think you were demented." As he tied off the laces, he asked, "Just tell me—*why* won't you say yes?"

Shoving her feet into her slippers, she faced him. "What is it that you're offering me that I can't get from any other gentleman?"

He stared down at her . . . frowned.

She jabbed a finger, hard, into his astoundingly gorgeous chest. "When you've figured that out, *perhaps* we can negotiate. Until then"—with a swish of her skirts, she turned and headed for the door—"I'll bid you a good night."

As she went through the door, she caught a glimpse of him standing there, the tanned expanse of his chest framed by the white sides of his shirt, his hands on his hips, a black frown on his face, his gaze locked on her.

Chapter 11

The remainder of the ball passed in a blur; Amanda couldn't wait to get home and into bed. Blowing out the candle, she fell back on the pillows—at last she could think.

He loved her—she was *almost* sure of it. Surely it was love that made him treat her like a madonna, as if she held the keys to his soul. Amid all the passion, the fire and the flames, on all three occasions they'd come together, there'd been something else there—something deeper, stronger, hard to define, yet infinitely more powerful than mere lust.

She'd felt it from the first, but she'd never known love before, not this sort of love, a love so enmeshed with sexual need, so disguised by possessiveness. But it had to be love— why else would a gentleman of his ilk, with his background, be so set on a wedding?

For his honor's sake.

She grimaced. That was what he wanted her to believe. Yet if that was so, what had tonight been about? Why bother trying to bribe her with the prospect of physical pleasure? He'd offered his name—she'd rejected it. Honor had already been satisfied, hadn't it?

Muttering imprecations against men's ridiculous obsessions, she thumped the pillow, then snuggled down. Twinges flickered in her thighs, but not as badly as they had four nights before; in contrast, the warm content deep within her had grown. Closing her eyes, she sighed.

At least she knew exactly what she wanted, what she would demand before she agreed to any wedding. She wanted his heart, acknowledged and freely offered, before she agreed, body and soul, to be his.

The library fire was still burning when Martin returned from Richmond. Crossing to the sideboard, he poured brandy into a glass, then sprawled on his favorite couch. The daybed where he'd first had Amanda Cynster.

Deflowered her—that was the correct, socially acceptable term. *Ergo,* he should marry her. That equation seemed perfectly logical to him.

Not, apparently, to her.

Swallowing a growl with a mouthful of brandy, he turned his mind to his next attempt to change her mind. He didn't waste a second on deciding whether or not he would take another tilt at her—that point wasn't in question.

He wanted to marry her. The situation decreed he should. Therefore he would.

As far as he was concerned, that was reason enough. Whatever she'd meant by her nonsensical question could remain veiled in obscurity—it was bound to be some peculiarly feminine, totally impractical ideal.

So what next? A summons to ride this morning?

He glanced at the clock, considered what time she'd get to her bed. Imagined her in her bed . . . then in his.

Shaking aside the distracting vision, he considered waiting until the next morning—thirty hours or so—to see her again. He'd gain nothing from the wait, and very likely nothing from a ride. He needed to meet her in surrounds conducive to his arguments—in other words, conducive to seduction. He was an honorable man; surely in this case honor dictated he use every possible weapon to change her mind, to bring her to accept the socially ordained outcome of their dalliance.

Whether that was rationalization, specious argument or not, he didn't care. The fact was, he'd been spoiled. Spoiled as a wild, rich, handsome and titled youth, equally spoiled as a man. He wasn't—very definitely was not—used to hearing "No" from a lady's lips.

It seemed to be Amanda's favorite word.

He drained his glass, then looked at the pile of invitations his man, Jules, invariably stacked on the mantelpiece as if in so doing he could nudge his noble employer into returning to the sphere in which Jules fondly believed said employer belonged. Jules did not have such influence. However . . .

Martin sighed. Setting his empty glass down on a sidetable, he rose and reached for the stack of white cards.

Not that he intended to formally appear at such functions, but the steady stream of invitations he received made it easy to identify at least one event on any given night at which his prey would be present. Easy enough to pick a house with which, courtesy of the past, he was sufficiently familiar to enter unremarked.

The following evening, he shut the garden gate of the Caldecotts' mansion and calmly strolled to the stairs leading to the ballroom terrace. A waltz was playing as he neared; a couple appeared, whispering as they descended to the gardens, passing him with no more than a glance.

The long windows of the ballroom stood open to the night; he stepped through and surveyed the room, confident that few would recognize him. The majority hadn't seen him for ten long years. Although he would recognize some from the ton's less aristocratic venues, he'd kept a low profile; the few ladies who had reason to remember him well had cause enough to keep their acquaintance secret. While braving the bright light of the chandeliers would be foolhardy, passing briefly through the fringes of social gatherings held minimal risks.

His memory had not failed him; the Caldecotts' ballroom had a gallery circling the room, reached by stairs from each corner. Tacking through the edges of the crowd, he gained the nearest stairs and went up.

The gallery was wide, built for promenading; a number of couples were doing so. With the only light coming from the ballroom's chandeliers, the areas away from the balustrade were wreathed in shadows. The perfect place from which to watch the activity on the dance floor, to track his quarry through the throng of dark coats and bright gowns.

He located Amanda easily—her curls shone like real gold and she was wearing a gown of the same cornflower blue as her eyes.

And arguing with a fair-haired gentleman.

As Martin watched, the gentleman captured Amanda's hand, tried to draw it through his arm. Martin's grip on the balustrade tightened.

Amanda jerked her hand free; furious, she heaped heated epithets on the gentleman's head, then swung on her heel and stormed off through the crowd. While one part of his mind tracked her, Martin watched the gentleman, noted his supercilious shrug, the way he resettled his sleeves, to all appearances not greatly put out by the nature of his dismissal.

Frowning, Martin turned to watch Amanda, saw her reach the foot of one of the gallery staircases.

A minute later, she stepped into the gallery; from behind a large column, he watched her scan the area, then she drifted to the alcove at the end, where wide windows overlooked the gardens. Less than six feet from her, he stood utterly still in the deep shadow of the column. She searched the lawns, then pressed close to the glass, squinting down at the terrace.

Where was he? If he didn't catch up with her here, Amanda didn't think he'd be able to gain access—not without coming through the main door—at the other ball she was to attend that night. She no longer worried that he might give up, leave her and return to his prior existence; she did, however, wonder what tack he'd take next, what argument he'd offer to convince her she should marry him—

She sensed his presence in the instant before his fingertips traced the curve of her hip. Down, around.

Her senses leapt; her lungs seized—then she drew in a quick breath. Remaining, quivering, where she was, she inclined her head. "Good evening, my lord."

The artful fingers stilled. "What—no curtsy?"

Curtsying would shift her silk-clad bottom against those

bold fingers. He was standing directly behind her; anyone glancing their way now would see only her skirts, nothing that could identify her. Glancing back, she murmured, "I believe we've gone beyond such formalities." She'd softened her tone to a sultry purr; she saw his lips twitch before she faced the gardens again.

"Indeed." His fingers stroked sensuously—lightly, tantalizingly—impossible to ignore. Illicit, sexually explicit, yet difficult to take umbrage at. Streaks of sensation slithered down her spine, spread beneath her skin.

With his other hand, he brushed her curls from her nape; bending his head, he touched his lips to the sensitive spot, lingered for an instant, breathing in her perfume, then licked.

Straightening, he let his fingers firm on her bottom, then ease, deliberately shifting the silk of chemise and gown against her skin. His words caressed her ear. "Do you know what I want . . . what I'd like to do to you now, this very minute?"

She suspected that if she leaned back against him, he'd be rigid as a rod. "No. What?"

A rumble of laughter greeted her studiously innocent reply. "Just imagine, if you can . . ."

Her mind streaked in a dozen directions, then he spoke again, his voice deeper, lower, "Imagine we're here but no one else is—that the ballroom behind us is empty, silent. The chandeliers are unlit. There's no music except for the wind sighing outside. It's night—dark—just as it is now. The only light comes from the moon, shining down."

"As it is now."

"Exactly." His voice breathed past her ear, sank into her senses. The hand cupping her bottom remained where it was; his other hand lightly brushed her bare shoulder. "You wait here, for me, knowing I'll come to you. That I'll come in the dark of the night to have you."

"Will you come?"

"I'm here now."

It was impossible to draw breath. "And then?"

"And then . . . I'll raise your skirts, only at the back. If there's anyone watching from the garden, they'll see nothing amiss." The fingers on her bottom shifted as if inching up the silk; he didn't actually raise it, just led her senses to imagine he had. "Then I'll touch you, caress you, raise the back of your chemise to your waist." He paused, then whispered, "You don't wear pantaloons."

"Within the ton, pantaloons are still considered *unquestionably* fast."

"Ah." Humor warmed his voice, then he continued in the same mesmerizing tone, "So I'll then have you naked, exposed, and I'll caress you, arouse you." His hand at her back mimicked the motions; his hand at her nape closed gently, as if holding her steady. Even though her skirts still covered her completely, her body reacted to the suggestive touch. "And then . . ."

She wasn't sure her legs would hold her. "Then?"

His hand at her nape eased; slowly, he ran his index finger down her spine, all the way down to her bottom. "Then I'll bend you forward, have you hold onto the sill—"

He broke off. She sensed his head rise, felt the immediate change in the large body behind hers. A heartbeat later, his hands left her—and he was gone; the sudden loss of his heat at her back was startling.

Giddy, she turned, heard footsteps approaching, caught the shift in the shadows as Martin slid behind the nearby column. She completed her turn.

Edward Ashford was ambling along, looking down at the ballroom, a scowl marring his handsome face. He looked up and saw her, nodded and strolled into the alcove. "You haven't seen Luc, have you?"

"Luc?" Dragging in a breath, she grabbed hold of her wits. Tried to steady them. "No. Are you looking for him?"

Edward's expression turned sour. "Futile, of course. I'll wager he's entertaining some opera dancer. More to his liking than doing his duty by Mama and the girls."

Amanda ignored the clear invitation to join him in blackening Luc's character. She'd remembered the relationship between the Fulbridges and the Ashfords; Edward would recognize Martin. And Martin was trapped behind the column. "Why are you looking for Luc? Does Emily or Anne need him?" Linking her arm in Edward's, she turned him toward the stairs.

"Not at present, but you would think . . ."

Letting Edward ramble, she steered him down to the ballroom.

"You're looking a trifle peaked, Amanda."

Looking up from her plate, Amanda blinked down the breakfast table at her mother. "Ah . . . I didn't sleep well."

The unvarnished truth. Louise seemed to see as much; she nodded. "Very well. But all your gadding before the Season commenced has drained your reserves—you'll need to pace yourself better."

Amanda sighed and looked down at her plate. "You're right—as usual." She flashed a smile at Louise. "I'll rest this afternoon. We've the Cottlesloes' ball tonight, haven't we?"

"Yes, and dinner at the Wrexhams' before it." Laying aside her napkin, Louise rose, shrewd eyes assessing her eldest daughters. Amelia was quiet, as she often was, but a frown inhabited her eyes and her mind was clearly elsewhere as she sipped her tea. Amanda . . . quite aside from her tiredness, she seemed unnaturally abstracted. Rising, Louise passed them both, trailing one hand on one youthful shoulder, then the other. "Don't forget to rest."

At the scratch on her bedchamber door, Amanda turned, unsurprised to see Amelia slip in. Her twin took in her stance by the curtained window, then quietly shut the door.

"You're supposed to be resting."

"I will in a minute. I think I've finally worked out what he's up to."

"Dexter?"

"Hmm. I think he's trying to make me *want*. Make me physically yearn so I'll agree to marry him."

Amelia flopped on the bed. "Is he succeeding?"

Frowning, Amanda joined her. "Yes, damn him—that's why I couldn't sleep." Why she'd tossed and turned, restless and unsatisfied. "He's a fiend, but I'm not going to give in."

After a moment, Amelia asked, "How does he do it—make you yearn?"

"Don't ask. But I'm not going to marry him just because he knows how to make me feel very nice."

"So how are you going to stop him"—Amelia gestured—"working his magic and making you yearn?"

"I'm not." Amanda stared at the canopy, reliving the illicit interludes she and her nemesis had shared. "That's what I was just thinking about. This latest tack of his might well work in my favor. In fact, it might work better than anything *I* could instigate."

"How so?"

"Consider this: for every ounce of desire he evokes in me, then . . . I'm not certain of this, but from all that's passed between us it *seems* to be so—for every ounce of desire he makes *me* feel, then *he* feels the same, if not more."

After a moment, Amelia ventured, "Are you saying that your battle, as it were, might come down to who can resist desire best?"

Amanda nodded. "And I think he's miscalculated. He's used to ladies being"—she gestured wildly—"swept away by desire. He's used to doing the sweeping. I don't think it's occurred to him that I might hold firm."

"Hmm. But he's very experienced, I imagine."

"Very, but in this case, experience might be a disadvantage. He's accustomed to having his desires gratified, more or less instantly. He's not used to having to wait, or negotiate. He wants, he takes. But *this* time, he's using desire like a carrot. He wants something else first, before he agrees to satisfy my desire *or his*."

"So he might well end hoist with his own petard?"

"Yes. And given I'm not accustomed to desire and likewise not accustomed to having it fulfilled, then . . ."

"Then it's possible this tack of his might play into your hands."

"Precisely." Amanda considered the prospect, viewed it from every angle she could conjure. "It's definitely a way forward, and as he thinks it's *his* plan, he's less likely to be defensive." She glanced at Amelia, aware her twin's thoughts had wandered. "How's your plan going?"

Amelia met her eyes, then grimaced. "I've a remarkably long list of possibilities which, every day and every night, I'm steadily reducing." Settling her head on the pillow, she closed her eyes. "It is, however, going to be a *slow* business."

Amanda held back the urge to suggest a shortcut—a flurry of crossing off that would leave only one name. Although it wasn't her way, she understood Amelia's need to be certain in her own mind before she committed herself to pursuing that one name. Snaring that particular gentleman was going to be a Herculean task.

The thought brought her mind back to her own task, her own gentleman. Closing her eyes, she let her mind drift to the delightful prospect of having her lion trapped securely in his coils.

She felt sure he'd appear at the Cottesloes' ball. Their ballroom was on the ground floor; the windows at one end opened onto a terrace giving access to a parterre, which happened to abut a formal shrubbery. The evening was mild, perfect for strolling in the moonlight.

The dinner at the Wrexhams dragged on, but once they reached the ball, her greatest obstacle in meeting with Martin proved to be her increasingly attentive would-be suitors. Now that the Season was in full swing, they'd materialized in hordes.

"Like locusts," she muttered, dodging through the crowd. Having to glance every way at once was distracting. Keeping her social smile firmly in place, she doggedly progressed toward the most shadowy corner of the room.

"At last!" Slipping past the last guests, she was disappointed to find no large and handsome male waiting. Beyond the windows lay the terrace; the doors giving onto it lay to her right.

Frowning, wondering if she'd misjudged, either him or his intentions, she turned and rescanned the room, wondering if she'd overlooked some other useful place where he might be lying in wait for her—

Long, cool fingers slid around her wrist, closed over her

leaping pulse. She glanced around, wide-eyed, and met his mossy green eyes.

"Where . . . ?" She looked beyond him, but there was no door or even window he might have come through. He stood half behind her; she could feel the heat of his body down her back, where it hadn't been an instant before. She lifted her gaze to his face. "You move so silently."

He raised her hand, kissed her fingers, then turned her wrist and pressed his lips to where her pulse beat wildly. Lowering her hand, he turned his head so his whisper fluttered the curls by her ear. "I'm a predator—you know that."

She did. Luckily, he expected no answer. Setting her hand on his sleeve, he waved to the terrace door. "Shall we adjourn to quieter surrounds?"

A smile curving her lips, she inclined her head. "If you wish."

They passed through the fringes of the crowd; no one recognized him—none paid them any heed. Stepping onto the terrace, Martin scanned the parterre. Noted six other couples already availing themselves of the amenity. He inwardly smiled and gestured to the steps. "Shall we go down?"

She acquiesced with a confidence he found disarming; the aura of a lady in charge hung about her. Doubtless an intrinsic, inherited quality; the fact that it was he on whose arm she was leaning made him smile.

Seeing it, she raised her brows. He shook his head. "Come—let's stroll."

They did, but not innocently. By unspoken agreement, they walked close, his thigh brushing her hip, his arm again and again brushing the side of her breast. He only had to glance at her face, lit by the moonlight, to know she was neither oblivious nor reluctant. She was enjoying the subtle contact as much as he.

"Enjoying," however, was not the right word.

They reached a spot where a mulberry tree spread its branches over the parterre; he drew her into their shade. Slid one finger beneath her chin, tipped up her face and set his lips to hers.

He kept the kiss light—teasing, tantalizing. Tempting. Lifting his head, he watched her face as he slowly trailed his finger down her throat, barely touching as he traced over the ivory expanse exposed by her neckline. Looking down, he watched as he slid that questing fingertip over her silk bodice to briefly circle a nipple already pebble-tight.

She dragged in a shaky breath as his hand fell, but smiled serenely and turned when he urged her on, out of the shadows. They continued their stroll. As they rounded the far corner of the parterre, he murmured, "I want you."

She threw him a glance, one too shadowed for him to read. Her lips curved as she looked away. "I know."

Not a quiver shook her, yet he knew she was as aware of him as he was of her. A feminine challenge, one he was perfectly ready to answer.

The entrance to the shrubbery, an archway cut through a hedge, lay to their right. Amanda was not surprised when Martin whisked her through into the dark avenue beyond. They continued to stroll, slowing as the tall hedges, black in the night, closed around them.

She was even less surprised when he halted, and drew her into his arms. When his head lowered and he set his lips to hers—kissed her commandingly, letting her feel his desire. She now knew him well enough to know he kept it leashed, that the fire he let her sense remained firmly under his control. But his was a game at which two could play.

Stretching up, she wound her arms about his neck and kissed him back with flagrant abandon. While his control held, she could do as she pleased in perfect safety. Could tease and taunt and drive him . . . just this side of wild.

Her response derailed his attention; for one long minute, he simply savored her, plundered, tasted. Then he took charge again, wrested all control from her—ripped her wits away, set them tumbling as he backed her against the hedge.

His hands rose to close about her breasts, possessive, too knowing, too experienced. She arched against him, sought to appease the ache his touch evoked, then she realized, recalled, that that was precisely what he wanted.

It was an effort, but she managed, even while returning every kiss avidly, to ease back mentally, to pull her mind free of the drugging urgency. And discovered she could enjoy and savor and incite without getting caught, without drowning in desire. As long as he remained mentally aloof, she could, too. If he dropped his guard, desire—his combined with hers, rising in response—would sweep them both away. As it had before.

But he couldn't overwhelm her, not completely, not anymore, not without letting down his own defenses.

And he wasn't about to do that.

Very wisely, as it transpired. They were engrossed, enthralled, absorbed in the challenge of their exchange, when voices reached them, increasing in volume until they penetrated the fog shielding their senses.

They both broke from the kiss, stared through the semi-darkness. Amanda's senses reported that she was stretched against him, her arms about his neck, her breasts crushed to his chest. His arms were wrapped about her, his hands pressed to her hips, molding her to him. The magnitude of his desire, still leashed, still severely controlled, was nevertheless very evident.

Someone was approaching. With a sigh, she drew away, artfully used the movement to slide one silk-clad hip sensuously against that part of his anatomy most susceptible to suggestion.

He caught his breath, looked sharply at her, but his attention was diverted by the figures—two male, two female—approaching along the walk.

"We'd better return to the ballroom." She looked into his eyes. "I've been gone for quite a while."

A moment passed, then he inclined his head. He gave her his arm; she took it. With no further detours, he escorted her back into the ballroom, then very correctly took his leave.

The next evening, they met at Lady Hepplewhite's drum. The Hepplewhites' mansion was a rambling old place affording numerous possibilities for clandestine meetings. Amanda literally ran into Martin in one of the minor salons. She was fleeing from Percival Lytton-Smythe.

"Good!" Linking her arm with Martin's, she tugged him

about. "If we stand still, we're going to be talked at." She glanced up and arched a brow. "Might I suggest we repair to the conservatory?"

Martin studied her eyes, her eager, open expression. Briefly wondered . . . "I have a better idea."

The garden hall: narrow, deserted, it gave onto a small courtyard beyond which the wider gardens lay. It was reached via a series of interconnecting corridors, but the hall ran alongside one of the major salons.

"I've never been in here before." Amanda looked about as she entered.

Martin closed the door, watched as she turned and looked back at him. The room was dim, yet he still saw the unabashed anticipation in her face as she held out her hands to him.

"Come—dance. We can hear the music, even here."

He went to her. Through the thick walls, the muted strains of an air wafted, created by the orchestra in the main salon. Gathering her into his arms, he slowly revolved.

The beat was undemanding, leaving their senses free to roam. To search, to dwell. His dwelled on the enticing feminine curves filling his arms, on the supple sway of her spine under his hand, on the seductive shift of her silk-clad hips against his thighs. Bending his head, he murmured, "There's another dance I'd like to engage in with you."

"Hmm." Amanda smiled, then freed her arms and draped them about his neck. "Unfortunately"—she deliberately pressed closer and felt his arms tighten in response—"it seems we'll have to make do with the waltz."

A calculated challenge. She lifted her face, offered her lips; he took them without hesitation. Yet restraint was still there, even though he teased her lips apart, surged in, took her mouth, tried to steal her wits away.

More or less succeeded.

She felt her need swell, felt his heighten in response, in reaction as her nails scored his nape, as she shifted provocatively against him. The ache within, raised and left unfulfilled for the past two nights, sprang to life at a touch, at the first caress of his thumb across her breast. More intense, more demanding; she longed for his surrender, longed to tender hers.

Yet his had to come first.

She clung to her wits, let him tempt her, ply her with wordless promises of glory. Focused her talents on returning the invitation. On heightening his desire, on feeding the compulsive need she sensed behind his experienced mask.

Trailing her fingertips down his lean cheek, she let her hand fall to his shoulder, then his chest. Continued to stroke downward, trailing to his hip—

He caught her hand, twined his fingers with hers, closed his fist. Held tight.

She shifted under his kiss, drew away, murmured, "Let me touch you." Kissed him again, long, lingeringly.

"No." He drew back, then reconsidered. "Marry me and you can touch whenever you like."

She laughed, seductive, sultry, supremely conscious as she spread her other hand over his chest how very tense he was. Felt emboldened enough to state, "You won't win me like this."

"Regardless, I won't lose." He caught her other hand, raised both to his shoulders. Released them, reached for her, drew her hard, flush against him, crushing her breasts to his chest, blatantly molding her hips so her soft stomach cradled his rigid erection.

Her eyes on his, she tightened her hold about his neck, drew him to her. Let her gaze fall to his lips. Let her lids drift closed.

His lips touched one corner of hers, then the tip of his tongue lingeringly traced the full curve of her lower lip.

"No other man will ever lay hands on your skin, will ever caress your naked breasts." His breath washed over her sensitized lips. "No other man will ever come between your thighs, will ever bury himself in you. Only me."

The last words were harsh; angling his head, he took her lips, took her mouth. And she gloried in the sudden wash of heat, the unmistakable rush of desire. She stretched higher, met him boldly, urged him on. Caught her breath in anticipation when he backed her into the counter that ran along one wall.

The hand splayed about her hips slid lower, cradling her bottom, holding her as he rocked evocatively against her.

Desire swept her—she wanted to climb up, wrap her legs about his waist, impale herself on him. Knew she could. If he would.

He seemed to have the same idea. His hand firmed on her bottom, kneading briefly, then he gripped her waist—

"*Tee-hee!* No—*don't!* Oh, you *naughty* man!"

They broke their kiss; both looked sideways through the glass doors into the courtyard. A giggling young lady was wrestling with an amorous gentleman. The pair sank onto the bench facing the doors; the young lady shrieked as the man fondled her breast.

Amanda gaped. "That's Miss Ellis! She's only just out!"

Martin swore, straightened. Put Amanda from him, held her until she was steady. "Come on." Taking her hand, allowing his disgruntled disgust to show, he headed for the door. "Before they see us."

Too risky to do otherwise. He escorted an equally disenchanted Amanda back to a minor salon.

"I'll leave you here." He caught her gaze, noted the remnants of desire clouding the blue. Raising her hand, he pressed his lips to her fingertips. "Until next time."

Her eyes widened as she took in his meaning. He released her hand; her fingers clutched his. "Tomorrow afternoon. There's a picnic at Osterley. The others will go to the bluebell wood. Do you remember the dell at the end of the lake?"

He thought back. Nodded. "Tomorrow afternoon." He bowed and stepped back into the shadows.

Reluctantly left her to return to her bright world.

If he didn't have her soon, didn't very shortly convince her to be his, he was going to . . . do something rash. What, he wasn't sure.

In the dell at the end of the Osterley House lake, Martin sat on a large log and waited for relief. Reaching the dell undetected had been easy; the woods stretched unbroken from the lake to the road half a mile away. The favored picnic spot lay on the lawns beyond the other end of the lake, close by the walks that led through the bluebell wood. To join him, Amanda would have to walk around the lake. He doubted any other young lady would be so energetically inclined, which should leave them safe from interruptions.

So he fervently hoped.

Weaving a web of desire tight enough to bind Amanda to him was proving unexpectedly demanding. Admittedly, it wasn't an undertaking he'd embarked on before—he'd never previously wanted to tie any woman to him. However, given how attached women—ladies especially—tended to become even when he wasn't trying . . . surely, if he tried, he could tie her up tight.

So she wouldn't even *think* of saying "No" again, no matter what he suggested.

He heard footsteps, then saw her. She walked into the dell, smiled when she saw him, walked to the log and stopped beside him. She looked across the lake, scanned the nearby banks.

He rose. It was that or suffer worse torments; just the sight of her, let alone that confident smile, had aroused him to a painful degree.

She looked into his eyes. They were almost breast to chest as he looked down at her face. He reached for her, setting his arms loosely about her, fought the urge to seize.

"Marry me."

She held his gaze. "Why?"

Why? "Because I want you." The words were out before he'd thought, then he did, but saw no reason to take them back. Or even disguise their meaning. Instead, he drew her closer, so she could feel precisely what he meant.

Her lids lowered, shielding her eyes; a subtle smile flirted at the corner of her lips. "I accept that you desire me." Her body eased in his arms as she sank, a promise of heaven, against him. "But if desire is the *only* reason you 'want' me, that's insufficient reason for me to become your countess."

She was talking in riddles. Again . . .

A sudden suspicion bloomed in his mind. She peeked up at him through her lashes; he caught her gaze, ruthlessly held it. Considered a possibility that until then he hadn't considered possible at all.

He felt his face harden. "You are playing a very dangerous game."

Her lids rose; she met his gaze without guile, without the slightest trepidation. "I know." Reaching up, she trailed a fingertip down his cheek, then met his eyes again. "But I'm serious, and quite willing to call your bet."

The emotion that roared through him, that filled his ears and overwhelmed his mind—if he'd been able to shut his eyes, able to clench his fists, been standing alone in an empty room, he might have been able to let it well and fade without acting. Without reacting.

Instead, his arms tightened, crushing her to him; he bent his head, took her mouth, took her lips. A prelude to taking her. No quarter.

Amanda asked for none. Clenching her fingers in his hair, she drank in the passion he poured into her, then turned it back on him. Sensed the clash, not of their wills, but of their stubborn hearts. She'd taken her stand, knew the ground beneath her feet was rock solid; he'd made his position clear, and would not be easily driven from it. Would not readily accept the necessity of changing his mind.

She was prepared to wait him out. Prepared to wage their war until she won, then he would win, too. Despite his present stance, despite the implacable resistance that met her now, the wall of male dominance that refused to budge.

If he was a rock, she was the tide that was going to wear him down.

If he was a lion, she was the one fate had sent to tame him.

She yielded her mouth gladly, let him take her breath, give it back. Clung as he ravaged her senses, then gathered herself and pressed her own demands. Drove him on.

His hands had fallen to her bottom, closing, kneading, holding her hips hard against him so the rampant ridge of his erection rode against her stomach. His tongue was deep in her mouth, ravishing, probing, hot and insistent, when the first sound reached her ears.

He slowed the tenor of their kiss; she could sense the harsh saw of his breathing, could feel his chest rise and fall against her aching breasts, could sense the thunder of his heart, and her own, as he listened.

Nothing more reached them; he angled his head and

dragged her once more into the whirlpool of their kiss. Into the path of onrushing desire.

"Which way is it? Over there?"

The high-pitched girlish voice pierced their absorption—hauled them to earth with a gut-wrenching jolt.

"What . . . ?" Amanda looked over her shoulder.

Martin looked, too, and cursed.

"I don't believe it!" Amanda hissed. "It's Miss Ellis again! With a different man!"

Hand in hand, the pair were heading for the dell, crashing along by the lake. They hadn't yet seen the present occupants.

Martin cursed again. "I'll have to go."

Amanda looked back at him, swallowed her "No!" Muttered a curse of her own as his hands slid from her.

His gaze flicked between her and the approaching couple as he backed toward the trees. "Where will you be tonight?"

She put a hand to her whirling head. "The Kendricks'. Damn! It's not possible. There's no terrace or gardens, just one big ballroom. They're friends of the family—I can't not be there."

He paused in the shadows of the circling trees. "The house in Albemarle Street?"

She nodded.

"There's a balcony that overhangs the side garden."

"It's on the first floor."

"Be on it at twelve."

She blinked, then nodded. "I'll be there."

His gaze said she'd better be, then he stepped back; before her eyes, he melted into the shadows, fading away.

Totally disgruntled, her senses in disarray, her nerves tight, tense and flickering, and certain to remain so for hours, she turned to greet the reason. Plastering a smile on her lips, she went to meet Miss Ellis and her cavalier.

If her expectations of the afternoon were to remain unfulfilled, she'd be damned if she allowed Miss Ellis to fare better.

Chapter 12

At precisely midnight, Amanda slipped out onto the narrow balcony at the end of the Kendricks' ballroom. Reached through glass doors, the balcony extended around the corner of the building to overlook the side garden.

Shivering, she wrapped her arms about her. The weather had turned unaccommodating; a blustery wind scudded rain clouds across the moon. A downpour threatened. Hugging herself, she hurried to the corner.

The door behind her opened. "Amanda?"

She whirled, blinked at the fair-haired figure silhouetted against the ballroom's brightness.

"What are you doing out here?" Simon's tone, one that could only be managed by a younger brother, suggested he thought she was insane.

"Ah . . . I'm taking the air. It's stuffy in there." She hadn't even known he was watching her. Worse, his narrowing eyes, the very fact he'd followed her . . . her little brother was growing up. And he was a Cynster to his toes.

So was she. She waved dismissively. "I'll come in in a few minutes."

Simon frowned, and stepped onto the balcony. "What are you up to?"

Amanda drew herself up; she would have loved to look down her nose at him, but at nineteen, he towered over her.

"I'm not 'up to' anything." Yet. And if he didn't leave, she wouldn't be. She skewered him with a censorious look. "Just what are you imagining? I step out on a balcony so narrow it should be called a ledge, and you're concerned about what?" She spread her arms wide. "I'm out of reach of the ground, and there's no one here!"

The clouds chose that moment to empty; the wind gusted, flinging fat raindrops against the house. Amanda gasped and shrank against the wall.

Simon grabbed her arm. "It's freezing! You'll catch cold, and Mama will have a fit. Come on!"

He yanked her back toward the door. Amanda hesitated; the rain began to pelt down in earnest. If she didn't go inside, she'd be drenched. Grumbling under her breath, she allowed Simon to bundle her back into the ballroom.

She just hoped Martin knew she'd kept their appointment.

From his position below the balcony, Martin heard their footsteps, heard the door click shut, then he was left listening to the rain pour down all around him. A Romeo in the rain without his Juliet.

That's what happened when plans were made in the heat of desire.

The essential uselessness of this evening's meeting hadn't occurred to him until he'd reached home after leaving Osterley. It had taken that long for his focus to shift from all that hadn't happened in the dell. And all that had. Once he'd been able to think constructively, it had waxed plainfully clear that given the current state of their discussions, there was nothing to be gained from snatching a few illicit moments with Amanda, let alone on a ledge. For the arguments he wished to put to her, allowing for the way in which he wished to put them, he'd need an hour, preferably two. On a bed.

He'd come here tonight purely to arrange such a meeting. Instead . . .

As soon as the rain eased, he ducked out from under the balcony, slipped out of the garden gate and climbed into his carriage, black and anonymous, waiting in the mews. Stretching out his long legs, he wrapped his greatcoat about him. As the carriage rattled back to Park Lane, it was difficult to avoid the observation that the eruption of Amanda into his life had already wrought considerable change.

Two months previously, he would never have been heading home alone at this hour. He would have been out, hunting—for distraction, for dissipation. For entertainment to fill the lonely hours.

Now . . . despite the fact he'd be alone once he reached home, he wouldn't be lonely, wouldn't feel the emptiness of the house closing in on him; he wouldn't have time. His mind would be racing, assessing, planning how to beguile one stubborn lady into accepting him as her lot, even though that would assuredly mean making even more changes in his life.

Taking Amanda Cynster to wife was going to cause nothing short of an upheaval. The wonder was that, despite his inherent laziness, his dislike of being disturbed, that fact didn't deter him in the least.

Kidnapping her seemed the only viable option.

The next morning, seated at his breakfast table slowly sipping coffee, Martin considered the where and how. And discovered that the card sent to him by Lady Montacute for that evening announced a masquerade, albeit one of the tame, watered-down affairs that these days went by that title. Domino, half-mask and the invitation as entrance, so her ladyship had decreed.

All those, he had.

Deciding how to make Amanda, disguised in domino and mask, readily identifiable to him and only him took no more than a minute.

Fourteen hours later, draped in a regulation black domino, her face concealed by a halfmask, she appeared on the threshold of Lady Montacute's ballroom, accompanied by another lady and a gentleman. Judging by height and the golden curls beneath the unknown lady's hood, Martin assumed she was Amanda's sister; he'd take an oath the gentleman was Carmarthen. He waited only until, after exchanging a few words, the three parted before closing in on his prey.

He was the first to her side, but only by a few strides;

other men had noticed her, alone, looking about, and thought to claim her hand. He didn't bother with her hand; he slid his arm about her waist and drew her to him.

"Oh!" She looked up, knowing him in the same way he knew it was indeed her and not some other golden-haired lady who just happened to be wearing three white orchids at her throat. She blinked. "Where are we going?"

He was already steering her through the crowd.

"Somewhere we won't be disturbed."

He said nothing more as he whisked her into a corridor, then through a deserted parlor and out onto a terrace that rejoined the front porch; his hand at her back, he urged her down the steps, around the curved drive and so to the street. His carriage was waiting, horses prancing.

He opened the door. She clutched his sleeve. "Where . . . ?"

He looked down at her. "Does it matter?"

She glared, then turned to the carriage. He helped her in, then followed, shut the door; the carriage jerked, and they were off.

Amanda set back her hood. "That was—"

He moved—gripped her waist, lifted her onto his lap. One hard hand cradled her face and his lips came down on hers.

She lost her wits in that first assault, clutched his arms and let reality slide. Her senses drowned in the sudden rush of desire, of hot, unmistakable, irresistible passion. He took her mouth and she gave it, pushed her arms up to his neck and clung as the carriage rattled on and he continued to evocatively plunder. His arms locked about her, a warm steel cage cradling her, holding her to him, safe and secure.

It wasn't far to his house; she was dazed but unsurprised when the carriage halted and he set her back on the seat, then flung open the door and she saw, beyond him, the dark, unlighted mass of his home.

This time, the carriage had halted before the front door; he descended, turned, swept her into his arms and carried her up the steps. The massive door swung open the instant his bootheels rang on the porch flags; as he strode through, she glimpsed a figure in the door's shadow, one who inclined his head with dignity.

She waited for Martin to stop. He didn't. "Is that your man?" she asked pointedly.

"Jules."

She'd assumed, as far as she'd thought of it, that he'd head for the library. Instead, he took the stairs three at a time.

Her heart started to beat faster. "You can put me down now."

He glanced at her. "Why?"

She couldn't think of an answer, not one he might accept. That he had only one thing on his mind seemed transparently clear, and only compounded her distraction. Increased the dizzying notion that nothing else truly mattered.

The first time he'd carried her to his bedchamber, she hadn't been awake; it seemed wise, this time, to take note of the way. The vast emptiness echoed; she recognized the gallery, then he headed down a familiar corridor.

He stopped, juggled her and threw open a door.

Gloom, coldness and emptiness were dispelled as he carried her over the threshold. He heeled the door shut; eyes opening wide, she sank her fingers into his arm and he paused.

Let her drink in the sheer, sensual splendor.

Some things she remembered—the massive carved stone overmantel shading the hearth in which a fire blazed, the rich brocade curtains swathing the huge carved bedposts, the sumptuous silk of his sheets and pillows. Elsewhere, carved chests and tables in dark mahogany glowed in the soft light from brass lamps stationed about the room. Brass and gold inlays winked in the flickering firelight. Jewel-hued oriental rugs lay spread across the floor; even more gorgeous examples hung on the walls.

As in the library, there were a thousand points of interest, myriad colors, textures, artifacts, ornaments to please the mind and fill the senses.

The oddity stood out by virtue of its absence.

What wasn't evident, not anywhere in this mecca of sensual delight, was any item, any object, anything at all that hinted that this was the bedroom of an English earl, a man born and bred in this country, schooled at Eton, raised to rule his portion of England.

This was the lair of an eastern pasha, a man ruled by the sun, a man to whom sensuality was second nature. For whom sensuality was life and breath, an inherent part of him, strong, vital, inseparable from the rest.

Walking forward, he swung her down to stand before him on the silk rug beside the bed. She looked into his face, tried to reconcile all that was about them with what she could see there.

He tugged his domino's ties loose, flung the voluminous black cloak aside. His gold-flecked gaze remained steady on her face, on her eyes.

Raising a hand, she touched the cheek she'd traced so often in past weeks—a simple fascination with the aggressively angular planes, so reminiscent of her own Norman ancestors. A thoroughly English part of him.

She looked into his eyes, again recognized her own race, her own kind. Felt understanding dawn.

He'd been disowned, or so he believed. So he'd buried his Englishness, let another side of his personality dominate. But the Englishman was still there, the other half of his coin, yet even here, he hid in the shadows.

She wanted them both, the Englishman and the pasha, wanted them both in one. Stretching up, palms flat against his chest, she set her lips to his.

Kissed him. Encouraged him.

Felt him wait, passive, letting her make her wishes clear, then his lips firmed and he took command, surged in and took her mouth, set his mark on her, on her lips, on her tongue, on the softness of her mouth.

She gave them gladly, heart thudding as she felt his hands rise, felt the tug as he unravelled the domino's ties, set them loose, sent the cloak sliding down. Then his palms slid about her waist, the pressure firming as he grasped, and drew her to him.

Flush against the hard length of him.

She pushed her hands up, wound them about his neck, pressed closer—gave herself to him. The only way she knew to tempt him into the open was to offer herself, all she was, all she could be—to love him as she wished him to love her.

Completely. Without reserve.

Martin sensed her decision; he'd had too many women not to recognize when a woman gave herself without restriction, offered herself without demand. On all others he'd lavished attention, sensual pleasures, transitory joys. With her, now, it was different—there was so much more he wished to give. Deeper pleasures. Greater joys.

A lasting commitment.

He didn't have the words, didn't have any intention of finding them, finding a way to admit to a condition the past had taught him was the ultimate vulnerability, the one true chink in the armor his heritage had otherwise bequeathed him. Caring openly was too costly, the one sacrifice he would not again make. Not even for her. All else, he was willing to give her—his body, his name, his protection. His devotion.

Holding her between his hands, fingers flexing, sensing the supple strength of her, the sleek, slender, unutterably feminine length of her pressed against him, he set his mind to the task of laying heaven before her.

Convincing her to be his.

He deliberately let his reins slide. Let go. Let instinct take him, drive him, guide him. With her, he needed no thought, no logic, no considered plan. All he needed was to follow his heart.

She stood, eager and very willing, gathered against him, her tongue tangling with his, while he peeled her gown away. Blindly stepping out of her slippers, she kicked them aside. He couldn't stop his hands from closing about her breasts, still screened by her chemise, from fondling the soft mounds in anticipation, feeling them firm beneath his fingers. He drew his lips from hers, traced kisses down the taut column of her throat as she arched her head back so he could lave the thudding pulse at the base of her throat. Letting his hands slide down, around, he closed them about the globes of her bottom, lifted her against him, evocatively kneaded.

Felt her breath catch, felt desire well.

He set her back on her feet; the instant she was steady, he sank down, kneeling before her. He looked up at her face, caught her gaze as she looked down, blinking, lips swollen and parted.

"Your stockings."

She blinked again, but when he sat back on his heels, she bent one knee and lifted her stockinged foot to balance it on his thigh.

Inwardly smiling, knowing the sentiment would not shift the stony cast of his features, he reached beneath the edge of her chemise and gripped the scrap of ruched silk circling her leg. He removed that stocking, then the other, openly appreciating the silken wonder of her long legs. Tried not to think of them wrapped about him, as they shortly would be.

Tossing aside the second stocking, he returned his attention to her, cupped both hands about her thighs, ran them slowly down, all the way to her ankles, then reversed direction, slowly stroking each curve, caressing each hollow, sliding his hands to the front of her thighs as he leaned into her, felt her fingers slide into his hair as his own flicked up the hem of her chemise.

Closing his hands about the tops of her thighs, he held her still as he nuzzled the hollow between. She gasped, but didn't pull away, didn't resist, curved her hand about his skull and let him part her thighs, let him part her soft flesh and taste her.

The scent of her sank into him, wreathed his senses, an elemental attraction that called to every primitive instinct he possessed. Her willingness, the acquiescence and encouragement in her stance, in her shivering breaths, fed his most primal need.

Drawing back, he rose, hands sliding up over her body, raising the chemise, drawing it up, over her head. She raised her arms, slid them free.

Reached for him—for his coat. Their gazes clashed, and he stilled. Remembered. Tightening his grip on his impulses, he held still and gave her the moment she sought. Watched the play of her thoughts over her face as she undressed him. He moved only when necessary while she stripped his coat, cravat, waistcoat and shirt from him, then she fell to tracing muscle and bone with a touch that left him aching.

His hand went to his waist; he flicked open the buttons—
she pushed his hand aside and parted the flap. He couldn't
see her face, just the top of her head as she looked down,
stilled . . . then he remembered that she hadn't, until then,
seen him—that part of him—naked. Not until after. Later . . .

Before he could wonder what she was thinking, she
wrapped her fingers about him, and her touch told him. Fascination, wonderment, worshipful excitement. Anticipation.

She moved her hand upon him; he bit back a groan—felt
her start, glance up. Then she closed her hand again, caressed him again. And again.

He reached for her, drew her to him, found her lips. Captured her mouth, let both their senses feast . . . for a time.
Then he closed his fingers about her wrist, reluctantly drew
her hand away. Lifted his head, stepped back, stripped off
his trousers, stockings, toed off his shoes.

Her arms were waiting to slide about him when he
straightened. She came into his arms and he closed them
about her; she lifted her face and he bent his head, covered
her lips. Surged into her mouth, traced her tongue, tangled
with it, and felt her sink against him. Press nearer. Hot body
to hot body, naked flesh to naked flesh.

Passion surrounded them, wings of heat beating steadily,
slowly closing in.

He reached out and hauled back the bedcovers, urged her
the last step to the bed. She hitched herself up to sit on the
silk sheet. He followed, one knee on the bed; she let him
tumble her back so she lay with her head on the pillows,
golden curls spilling across his ivory sheets.

He knew just how he wanted her, knew the position that
would most suit their need. Stretching out beside her, the
covers pushed back behind him, he ran his hands over her
arms, her shoulders, down her back, around her hips, down
her legs, settling her half beneath him in the accommodating
comfort of the thick featherbed so its support would cushion
her against his thrusts, so their bodies could entwine and
merge without restraint.

The firelight shed a warm glow over her milk-white skin,
sent flickering fingers to dance across her full breasts, al-

ready peaked and swollen. He savored the contrast as he closed his tanned hand about one firm mound, then traced possessively down, over her sleek curves, over the sumptuous flesh, over the curve of her hip, down the long line of her thigh. To her knee.

Her body was soft, supple, receptive; his was hard, muscle-bound, menacingly strong.

They were both burning, barely holding the urgency at bay, both struggling to harness the driving need just this much—enough to savor the moment, to know it, see it, feel it all.

Closing his hand, he looked into her face, into the blue eyes, brilliant and dark, that watched him from beneath heavy lids. Their faces were close, his above hers as he lay propped half over her. His gaze shifted to her lips, bruised and yearning, waiting; he felt her breasts rise and fall with each shallow breath.

Desire welled like a tide; passion closed in, ever tighter, around them. If he kissed her, they would both be swept away . . .

He locked his gaze with hers, pressed her knee outward, then let his hand slide up the inner face of her thigh. Eyes on hers, he cupped her, waited through her reaction—her quick intake of breath, her instinctive shift against him—then he parted her, touched her. Probed, caressed, until her breath shuddered, until her fingers gripped and tugged.

Still holding her gaze, he drew his fingers from her, lifted against her, set his erection to her entrance, pressed in.

Slowly. Inch by inch, he sank into her softness, steadily merged their bodies until, with a last little thrust, he seated himself fully within her. She shivered, closed her eyes—her body gripped him. With a guttural murmur, he touched his lips to her closed lids, ran his hand down and around her hip, down her thigh, gripping, lifting, wrapping her leg about his hip.

Then he moved—upon her, inside her. She gasped, arched, breasts caressing his chest, fingers gripping. The repetitive, intimate rocking captured her senses; her body softened, accepted, adjusted, tentatively, then with greater assurance, met and joined with his.

Her lashes flickered, parted—she studied his face, then glanced down, watched her body fluidly shift with each rhythmic thrust as he possessed her.

Her gaze lifted again to his face. Her fingers trailed from his shoulder to his cheek, then slid into his hair.

She drew his lips down to hers, opened her mouth beneath his. Drew him deep when he boldly surged in. Drew them both into the fire.

They burned and bathed in the heat, in the passion, in the elemental tide of desire. Amanda knew nothing beyond the moment, nothing beyond the sensations of his body and hers sliding, merging, cocooned in his silk sheets. The pressure of his chest against her breasts, the rasp of crisp hair against her sensitized skin, the wanton arching of her body, the surrender as she took him in—deeper and yet deeper—all these were imprinted on her mind.

Along with the caress of his hands, the reverence with which he soothed her, eased her into the ever deepening intimacy, the warm brush of his breath across her lips when they paused, fighting for breath, for a moment of sanity, before sinking back into the addictive heat.

Even through the flames, even through her own yearning, she was aware of his, of the way he moved upon her, around her, within her, caressing her in every way a man could, lavishing pleasures, taking his own but not seizing. Accepting all she gave, but not demanding, not commanding as he might have done—as he had the ability to do . . .

Worshipful. The word whispered through her mind as he drew back a fraction, lifted slightly from her to drive deeper still into her pliant body.

Supplicant . . . him or her? She couldn't work it out. Couldn't think, could only spread her hands on his back and hold him to her as the fire rose and took them both.

Yet still there was no hint of desperation, of that familiar all-consuming urgency, only the steadily escalating rise, the inexorable build of that indescribable need.

Until, at the last, they crested, thrown high on a wave of heat and mindless pleasure. Ecstasy swept her; delight and so much more rushed through her veins, turned her body incandescent with glory. She heard her own cry; he bent his head and drank it from her. Moments later, his body stiffened; she wrapped her arms about him, held tight as he thrust deep, then the shuddering wave of his release swept through him.

She held him cradled between her thighs; as his locked muscles eased, she drew him down. Felt his hands, gentle, reverent, settling her beneath him. She closed her eyes and drifted with the tide.

It couldn't have been that long before she opened them again, yet so much had changed. Not on the physical plane—he still lay beside her, stretched out alongside, large, warm and naked, his hand drifting lazily over her, his gaze on his fingers, on the skin they caressed.

His touch was the same as before—reverent. She let her gaze dwell on his face, on the hard planes that gave so little away, that shielded his secrets so well.

She was the one who had changed. Physically in that, having tasted such glory, she would forever want it again. He might as well have branded her, so completely physically his did she feel. But those were the more minor revelations, the lesser adjustments. The knowledge she'd gained in the last hour far transcended that.

It was inherent in the golden glory that held her, and him. That stretched between them, lapped about them—linked them. All she'd felt, all she'd sensed—all she could still not see in his face, but could feel in his touch.

She watched him, felt her heart swell, yet she reined her triumph back. Wondered . . . she might have won the last hand, but it was up to him to provide the next lead.

He'd moved lower in the bed when he'd lifted from her; his shoulders level with her chest, one leg bent, anchoring hers, he watched his fingers trace the curve of her stomach. Spread his hand, as if gauging . . .

She suddenly knew what he was thinking. "I'm not pregnant." Suddenly giddy, she pushed up onto her elbows the better to see his face.

The mossy green eyes that rose to meet hers had one word blazoned in them: *mine*.

"How do you know?" His tone was even. His fingers kept tracing; his gaze remained on hers.

She stared at him, at what she could read in his eyes—he looked exactly like a thoroughly satisfied lion, tail twitching as he surveyed his prize . . .

He was watching her carefully. "You may as well agree to marry me."

She *wanted* to marry him—the revelation burned her tongue: I'll marry you *if* . . .

If he told her he loved her?

That wouldn't work, wouldn't convince her heart. There were at least ten gentlemen searching Lady Montacute's ballroom for her, all of whom would be only too willing to go down on their knees and swear to eternal love despite the fact none of them knew what it was.

She needed to know Martin loved her, completely, utterly, beyond all reservation. But that wasn't the principal reason she needed to hear the words, volunteered, freely offered. She needed to know that *he* knew.

The soft thud of her heart still filled her ears, the warm glow of aftermath still held her as she studied his eyes, considered his direction, and what he wanted her to believe. If she asked for a declaration of love, made her acceptance of his suit conditional on hearing one, he might well oblige—without actually meaning it, without truly facing the fact.

"No." She slumped back onto the pillows, stared up at the canopy. Tried to blot out his nakedness, and hers.

Silence, then he stirred, came up on his hands and knees over her—prowled up to look down at her face.

His was a mask of utter implacability. "I won't give up."

A growl—a warning. She glared up at him. "Neither will I."

The comment took him aback—clearly mystified him—which only added to her ire. "Let me up." Twisting, she bent her knees, pushed at his left arm; he let her slide from beneath him, but swung up and followed on her heels.

"This is ridiculous!" When she didn't pause but, spying her chemise, headed for it, Martin reached out, wrapped his hand in the curls at her nape, and drew her back to him. All the way back, finally looping an arm around her and drawing her flush, once more, against him.

Her eyes snapped at him. "I couldn't agree more."

She tried to free her hair, but he declined to unclench his fist. Looking into her face, he tried to ignore the immediate reaction of his body to the silken caress of hers, knew by her breathing that she was perfectly aware of it, too. "We've been intimate on three occasions."

She narrowed her eyes at him. "Four."

He counted. "Four. Which only increases the odds that you're carrying my child."

"Possibly."

"If you are, we're getting married."

Her eyes clouded; he could see thoughts whizzing through her mind, but couldn't define them.

She suddenly pushed back, her palms to his chest. Releasing her hair, he let her go. *"If,"* she stated, "it proves to be so, *then* we can discuss marriage." She turned away, swiped up her chemise. "Now, if you please, you may take me back to the masquerade."

He narrowed his eyes. "Amanda."

He argued, and swore, then argued some more.

It did no good. And by then she was dressed.

Shrugging into his coat, he followed her downstairs. Jules appeared from the kitchen; Martin flung him an order to have the carriage brought around. Jules retreated. Martin stalked down the hall to the front door where his paramour waited, head high, all but tapping her toe.

He stopped directly before her; towering over her, he glared down into her defiant face. "Why?"

She didn't pretend to misunderstand. She met his gaze directly, appeared to consider how best to explain. "I told you before, I want more. There's something only you can give me, but unless and until you agree to do so, I will not agree to marry you."

"What is this thing?" He managed not to roar, but the bellow vibrated in his voice.

"That," she replied, her tone turning glacial, "is what

you"—she jabbed his chest—"have to discover! I'm only *assuming* you have what I need. If you don't . . ."

Her gaze suddenly unfocused, she drew back, turned her head away. "If you don't, then you haven't, and that will be that."

He gritted his teeth, then opened his lips—probably on unwise words—

Hooves clattered outside and she swung to the door, putting up the hood of her domino. "I wish to return to the masquerade, my lord."

He closed his eyes for one instant, reshackled his temper, then reached out and wrenched the door wide. "As you please, my lady."

His. She was, very definitely, that.

If it hadn't been for the hours they'd spent in his bed, he might have wondered if she'd played him for a fool, if she'd been interested only in an illicit interlude, or four, with one whom her circle would dub seriously dangerous. Even now, he wasn't sure his reputation hadn't, in part, contributed to the attraction, at least at first. But now . . . now, there was more to her motives than simple lust.

Returning to his bedchamber an hour later, having seen her back into the chaos of the masquerade, watched until she'd found her sister and Carmarthen and left, he exhaled. He was relaxed but not at peace, tired but not sleepy. Shutting the door, he headed for the huge armchair before the fire. A splotch of white glowing against the rich hues of the rug caught his eye.

The orchids he'd sent her, the orchids she'd worn at her throat so he'd known her instantly; he picked them up.

She'd left the masquerade as soon as she'd rejoined her sister and Carmarthen; at the time, he'd wondered if that was because she'd known he was watching and he wouldn't allow her to flirt with other gentlemen, or because she'd only attended the masquerade to meet with him. Dropping into the armchair, he turned the orchids between his fingers. His frame of mind, then, had not been all that rational.

Looking back on their encounters, studying the orchids, he knew full well it was the latter—she'd come to meet him, as she had so often before.

Aside from anything else, she was not that sort of woman—the sort who went easily, without thought or affection, to a man's bed. She was a Cynster—he understood her type well. She came from the same stock as he, but he'd never known a Cynster female, one born and bred, only Cynster males. His experience of her thus far suggested he'd be wise to extrapolate.

Thus far, he'd underestimated her at every turn.

He'd known from the first that she was playing some game, yet he hadn't been able to perceive her goal—what she'd wanted to win. He'd let himself be cajoled into playing with her, let himself fall under her spell, all the while confident that she—an innocent no matter her years—could not possibly wring from him anything he didn't wish to give.

He considered the orchids, the thick, milky-white petals soft, smooth, like her skin, then curled his fingers, closed his hand about the flowers.

Breathed in their scent.

Closed his eyes, let his head rest against the chair's back.

He knew what she wanted.

He'd hoped to avoid having to play for that stake, having to defend it, yet she'd taken every trick thus far, and left him with little else to toss on the table to avoid having to risk his heart.

A log in the fireplace cracked, broke. Opening his eyes, he watched the flames leap, felt their warmth roll over him.

Considered his last remaining option.

For there was one thing more, one trump he yet held, a penultimate card that just might see him through, might let him turn the tide and seize her hand—and her—without having to risk his heart's defenses.

The question was: was he willing to play it?

Chapter 13

"These arrived for you a few minutes ago, Miss Amanda."

Reaching the front hall, Amanda looked up as Colthorpe offered a tissue-wrapped spray of flowers on his salver. "Thank you, Colthorpe."

Amelia joined her as she picked up the spray. Together with Louise, presently descending the stairs, they were about to leave for Lady Matcham's grand ball. "That ribbon's gold thread," Amelia murmured.

Amanda studied the spray. The tissue protecting the blooms was caught in the ribbon so it could easily be freed. Holding the beribboned stems, she tugged; the tissue came away, revealing three perfect white orchids.

Amelia stared; Amanda did, too.

Louise arrived beside them. "How lovely!" She picked up the spray, examined the blooms. "Incredibly exotic." She returned the spray to Amanda. "Who are they from?"

Amanda glanced at Colthorpe. "There wasn't a note."

Colthorpe shook his head. "Delivered by a groom in dark brown livery, green-and-gold piping. I didn't recognize the house."

"Well." Louise headed for the front door. "You'll just have to carry it and see who comes to claim your hand."

Amanda glanced at Amelia; Amelia stared back.

"Come along now, or we'll be late."

"Yes, Mama." Amelia linked her arm with Amanda's and urged her forward. "Come on—you'll have to go and see."

"Indeed." Amanda fell in beside her, her gaze locked on the three delicate blooms.

She would have to go and face her lion.

Martin waited until the very last minute, until the last stragglers had arrived and Lady Matcham and her spouse were about to abandon their post at the top of their ballroom stairs. When he handed the butler his card, the man nearly dropped it, but he recovered well enough, stepping forward to announce to the assembled company that the Earl of Dexter had arrived.

If he'd announced the plague, the butler couldn't have gained greater notice. Silence spread, rippling out from the foot of the stairs until it engulfed the entire ballroom. Conversation died as every head turned, necks craning to get a better look.

Martin walked forward. Taking her ladyship's instinctively extended hand, he bowed easily. "Ma'am."

For one instant, Lady Matcham simply stared, then triumph wreathed her features. "My lord. Might I say that it's a signal . . ."—she ran an eagle eye over him, from his elegantly cropped locks, over shoulders encased in fashionable evening black, over perfectly tied cravat and impeccable waistcoat—after all, she had been one of his mother's bosom-bows—then she nodded in approval—"pleasure to see you finally out of your lair?"

In the ballroom below, the whispers commenced—ferociously.

Martin nodded to Lord Matcham, who nodded back, clearly intrigued by Martin's unexpected attendance. Martin replied, "It was time and the arrival of your invitation seemed a stroke of fate."

"Indeed?" With a wave, Lady Matcham dismissed her spouse, took Martin's arm and turned to the stairs. "As I recall you always did have a silver tongue—be warned, you're going to need it. I intend to introduce you to every hostess you've spent the last year hiding from."

His lazy, social smile in place, Martin inclined his head. "If you think it necessary."

"Oh, I do," Lady Matcham informed him. "I most certainly do."

He escorted her down the stairs into the large ballroom. For a hostess of her ilk, tonight—his presence—would greatly augment her standing. The round of introductions would set the seal on her success; for him, it was a small price to pay.

Ultimately, being reintroduced to the senior hostess might be to his advantage; as he bowed and exchanged drawled, occasionally barbed comments with the ladies who, all pretense aside, controlled the ton, he put the final touches to his latest plan. His latest ploy to win Amanda's hand.

Most of the hostesses were simply pleased to meet him, to exchange words and extract a promise to have their next invitations given due consideration. Two—Lady Jersey, the younger, and Countess Lieven—one garrulous, the other coldly haughty, attempted in their wildly differing ways to glean the reason behind his unexpected change of heart, his reacknowledgment of the world that had for the past year been existing ignored on his doorstep; he merely smiled and left them wondering, knowing perfectly well that nothing was more certain to keep their attention fixed on him. It was obvious to them that *something* must have brought him here; such avid gossips as they were, they were rabid to learn what.

When, finally, he turned from speaking with old Lady Osbaldestone—he'd been stunned to discover the old tartar still alive, and still so determinedly terrifying—Lady Matcham threw him a considering glance. "Is there anyone—any young lady—to whom you'd like to be introduced?"

He glanced at her. "Yes." Lifting his head, he looked across the room. "There's a young lady in an apricot gown in the center of that group."

"Oh?" Lady Matcham was too short to see over the circle of male shoulders. "Whoever she is, she doesn't appear to need more dance partners."

"Quite." Martin heard the steely note in his voice. He

smiled at Lady Matcham. "She's my partner for the first waltz, but I suspect she hasn't yet realized. I think we should break the news to her, don't you?"

Fascinated, Lady Matcham clearly debated an order to be told all, but recognized it would gain her nought. "Very well." Placing her hand on his sleeve, she allowed him to steer her toward the group in question. "The Season has been rather dull, thus far."

When they neared the group and the gentlemen parted, revealing the lady who was the focus of their collective interest, her ladyship's eyes widened, then she smiled. "Ah . . . Miss Cynster. Permit me to introduce his lordship, the Earl of Dexter."

"Miss Cynster."

Martin bowed, effortlessly elegant—as if he hadn't eschewed ballrooms for the past ten years. Amanda stared, then belatedly remembered and sank into a curtsy of the required degree.

Martin took her hand and raised her. Faintly arched a brow when she remained silent. She lifted her head. "My lord. I'm surprised to see you here—I had heard you found little to interest you in the ton's entertainments."

His lips curved; his moss-agate eyes held hers. "Times change."

Lady Matcham's gaze sharpened; she turned to the gentleman on Amanda's right. "Lord Ventris—there's a young lady I wish to present to you. You may give me your arm." Without waiting to be offered it, Lady Matcham twined her arm with his lordship's and, like a galleon, towed him away.

Leaving the way clear for Martin to fill the gap at Amanda's side, which he did with smooth grace.

"As I daresay you've heard," he murmured, his voice low yet not intimate, "I've been . . . shall we say, out of touch? . . . for some years. Tell me—does this qualify as an average event, or is it quieter than the usual?"

It had been until he'd arrived. Clinging to wits that had not yet steadied—and probably wouldn't with him so close—she managed a serene smile. "This is an average gathering—wouldn't you say so, Lord Foster?"

"Oh, ah—indeed." Lord Foster glanced around as if studying the room for the first time. "Average enough, don't you know."

An uneasy silence fell. Amanda bit her lip—there were six other gentlemen gathered about, but they'd all been struck dumb by the advent of Dexter—the ton's very own untamed lion—into their midst. They were all eyeing him as if he were some exotic beast who might bite if provoked. Inwardly sighing, she opened her lips to comment on the weather—

Lord Elmhurst turned to Martin. "I say, is it true that you acted for the Government in negotiating with the maharajahs?"

Martin hesitated, then inclined his head. "In certain matters."

"Did you travel much on the subcontinent?"

"Did you meet any Pathan warriors? Fearsome fellows, I hear."

So much for the weather. Amanda stood and listened as Martin fended question after query on his activities in India. She tried to turn her mind to the highly pertinent question of what he intended with this latest start, but found it impossible to concentrate. More gentlemen joined the circle, drawn by the male voices and the potent sense of excitement.

"My cousin works for the Company there—he writes that you were an acknowledged hero within the Company's ranks."

"I heard that you singlehandedly convinced the Maharajah of Rantipopo to allow us to trade in his emeralds."

She pricked up her ears at such details, tucked them away for later dissection, to be added to the sum of all she knew of him.

"Did you ever visit one of their harems?" The eager question from young Mr. Wentworth overrode the first notes emanating from the orchestra.

Martin smiled at Mr. Wentworth, then turned that smile, rather more intently, on her. "That's the prelude to the first waltz, I believe." With a nod, he indicated the orchids she carried in her hand.

She looked down, saw them, remembered.

Heard him softly say, "As you've done me the honor of carrying my token, I presume you'll do me the honor of granting me this dance."

It wasn't any kind of question; she *was* carrying the orchids, and he'd just claimed them. Plastering a smile on her lips, she looked up, offered her free hand. "The honor is mine, my lord." Then she opened her eyes wide. "You do waltz, don't you?"

His smile was feral as his fingers closed about hers. "You may judge for yourself."

She knew he waltzed like a god, but she wanted everyone else to think they'd never met before. She had to let him lead her to the floor, let him take her in his arms, in front of the entire ton. In front of a host of extremely interested eyes.

"What are you doing here?" Despite having to speak through her smile, she imbued the words with an angry hiss.

He met her gaze as they started to revolve. His lips kicked up at the ends. "Changing the rules."

"What rules?"

"The rules of our game."

That did not sound promising, not from where she stood, within the circle of his arms in the middle of a tonnish ballroom.

She'd expected him to appear tonight—the orchids had been a clear warning. But she'd assumed he'd materialize as before, on the outskirts of the crowd, and whisk her away to some private place where they could continue their "discussion" of marriage.

Not that she would again allow him to practice any sexual arguments. After he'd let slip his views on paternity, she wasn't about to take further risks on that front. But she'd hoped to dangle the carrot of further intimate moments as an inducement for him to think more deeply about what he felt for her.

The very last thing she'd imagined he'd do was to walk into the light and come straight for her.

Consequently, on gaining the ballroom, she'd drifted

away from her mother, Amelia and Reggie, drifted toward the other end of the room, dodging those intent on paying court to her. Then she'd heard him announced, looked up, seen him stroll in. She hadn't known how to react. In a flurry, she'd gathered gentlemen willy-nilly to protect her; the instant she'd heard the name "Dexter" intoned, she'd known she'd need protection.

Some protection. And once those tidbits of information he'd let fall did the rounds of the clubs, the lion would be lionized and she'd have no chance of securing better—indeed, *any*—effective protection next time.

There would be a next time—she had little doubt of that.

As to his purpose, however . . .

Refocusing on his agatey eyes, she smiled serenely. She, after all, was much more at home in this arena than he.

He searched her eyes, trying to read her mind; she wished she could read his. Failing that, she gave herself up to enjoying the waltz.

A mistake—one she didn't realize until he drew her fractionally closer as they turned at the end of the room. By then, her senses had succumbed to his nearness, had come alive to the compulsive, primitive call of his too-well-remembered body so close to hers, to the effortless strength with which he steered her through the revolutions. Her nerves had tensed in expectation, in educated anticipation; as his thighs brushed hers, desire rose, achingly sweet.

She caught her breath, felt her smile fade as she fought the urge to step closer, to move into his arms, to feel his body against hers. She let her lids veil her eyes, not wanting him to see, then realized that he knew. That he felt the same.

His hand tightened about hers; the hand at the back of her waist hardened, muscles tensing, resisting the impulse to draw her to him.

She did nothing to break his concentration; the idea of either of them succumbing to such impulses in the middle of a ballroom . . . aside from causing a scandal, it would play directly into his hands.

Her relief when the music ended was acute; the knowledge that he almost certainly knew that, and if sufficiently provoked might be willing to risk scandal to gain what he sought, left her dizzy.

Thankfully, he seemed committed to playing the role he'd scripted for himself to the hilt; with unimpeachable correctness, he bowed, then raised her from her curtsy and escorted her back to the circle of waiting gentlemen.

The fact he'd picked her as his partner for his first waltz on returning to the ton caused other gentlemen to reconsider her attractions, a situation she could have done without. Martin remained by her side as she exercised her considerable social skills, keeping the conversation tripping along the usual tonnish paths. She got the impression he was listening, learning. Accepting that she knew more than he in this sphere, she directed the talk into as many areas of current interest as she could.

She felt she'd done her bit for his reeducation when the orchestra struck up for the second dance. Lord Ashcroft solicited the pleasure of her hand; she graciously bestowed it, but was conscious of the sudden tension that coincidentally gripped the large body still planted beside her.

However when, at the end of the cotillion, Lord Ashcroft returned her to her circle, Martin was still there, watching, waiting. The spot beside him seemed to be where she was supposed to stand. Although she accepted her fate without a flicker of consciousness, she was gripped by faint unease.

Which only grew as the evening progressed, and he didn't quit her side. The impression he projected was that he *permitted* her to dance with others; it was only a matter of time before the observation occurred to the gentlemen concerned. And all the others watching. If it hadn't already.

Seizing the moment when all others in their circle were distracted by a discussion between Lord Flint and Mr. Carr, she surreptitiously tugged Martin's sleeve, quietly hissed when he turned to her, "You should circulate."

He looked down at her. "Why?"

"Because it looks extremely particular if you single me out in this fashion."

His lips curved. "But I am extremely particular." He held her gaze. "Especially over the lady I want as my countess."

Her eyes flew wide. "*Sssssshhhhhh!*"

She didn't attempt to warn him off again. Instead, her smile fixed, she continued to chat and dance, ignoring the increasingly pointed stares of other young ladies, and the disapproving glares from their mamas. Not only was she, as far as they could see, monopolizing the ton's latest lion, but she was also attracting far too much notice from other eligible gentlemen.

No avenue of escape presented itself—if it had, he'd doubtless have blocked it—not until the evening drew to a close and her mother, finally quitting the conclave of matrons at the far end of the ballroom, came strolling through the crowd. Amanda nearly groaned when she saw who accompanied Louise—her aunts, the Dowager Duchess of St. Ives and Lady Horatia Cynster. A curious Amelia brought up the rear, her arm in Reggie's.

"Well, my dear." Smiling, Louise joined them. "Have you enjoyed your evening?"

"Indeed." With no alternative offering, she gestured to Martin. "Allow me to present the Earl of Dexter. My mother, Lady Louise Cynster."

Martin's smile was the epitome of charming. He bowed; Louise dipped.

"And my aunts, the Dowager Duchess of St. Ives and Lady Horatia Cynster."

They exchanged greetings; the Dowager made some comment about his reappearance in the ton being long overdue. Whether it was that, or the shrewd, uncannily knowing expression in her aunt's pale green eyes, Martin decided it was time to lift his paw and release her. He gracefully took his leave of them, at the last bowing over her hand.

"Until next we meet."

That could have been merely a polite farewell. The light in his eyes, the subtle undertone in his voice, said otherwise.

It was a challenge—and a warning.

* * *

The following morning, Amanda sat at the breakfast table, sipping her tea and staring at the spray of three delicate ivory orchids that had been delivered an hour before.

Louise walked in. "Well!" She came forward, her gaze on the flowers. "Dexter, I take it?"

Once again, there'd been no note. "I presume so." Cradling her cup, Amanda considered the blooms. She couldn't imagine any other gentleman sending her orchids; aside from the quite hideous expense, the flowers were so exotic. So decadently sensuous. Dexter, yes—others, no.

Louise noted her expression. Brows faintly rising, she passed on to her chair at the end of the table, waited until Colthorpe had poured her tea and stepped back. Amelia sat opposite Amanda, silently tending her own thoughts, letting her twin cogitate undisturbed. Shaking out her napkin, Louise looked at Amanda. "I imagine it'll be the talk of the ton. For a gentleman of Dexter's rank, let alone his peculiar status, to emerge from his seclusion with his eye fixed so definitely from the outset on you . . ."

She didn't complete her thought, but fell to buttering a slice of toast. Crunching a corner, she meditatively chewed, then took a sip of tea. Glanced again at Amanda. "One thing you'd be wise to bear in mind."

Amanda looked up; Louise caught her eye.

"Whatever the emotion that's moved him to forsake his determined isolation, it won't be anything mild."

Louise's words rang in Amanda's ears as she stood on the verge in the park later that morning, and considered the large hand extended toward her.

Arrogant. Commanding. Impatient. Definitely not mild.

Also difficult, not to say dangerous.

Gripping her parasol, she laid her fingers in his, let him pull her up to the phaeton's seat. She settled her skirts. With a brief salute to Amelia and Reggie, left standing on the lawn, Martin clicked the reins and they were off.

"Tell me," she said, having determined to take the lion by the mane, "why have you decided to rejoin the ton?"

He flicked her a glance. "As I told Lady Matcham, it seemed to be decreed."

"Decreed?"

"By some higher authority."

She ruminated on that. "So you intend to reclaim your rightful place?"

The glance that gained her was somewhat harder. "If necessary." They were nearing the most popular section of the route, currently jam-packed with carriages. "Now you may tell me—who the devil are all these women?"

As "these women" were all nodding graciously, eyes avidly alight, and as their number included the majority of the principal hostesses, she considered it wise to oblige. "That's Lady Cowper—you must remember her?"

He nodded. "Is the one in green Lady Walford?"

She glanced at him. "Your memory's quite remarkable, but she's now Lady Merton." The lady had been an acknowledged beauty before her second marriage some years before.

His lips twitched, but he continued peppering her with questions, not all reflecting felicitously on their subjects. His recollections were erratic, sometimes devastatingly detailed; he'd last seen these people ten years before through the eyes of a youthful hellion. Some of his observations made her laugh; she learned a surprising amount she'd never known, yet equally, there was much he didn't know that she dutifully told him.

When they reached the end of the crowded section and he set the horses trotting, she slanted him a considering glance. She'd wanted to bring him back into this world, his world and hers; part of her rejoiced in his presence—her success. Another, more cautious part warned her not to count her chickens yet.

She'd lured him out of his lair, but he'd come for only one thing.

He was focused on getting it. That became clear as the days progressed. Every morning brought three white orchids; everywhere she went, he was there, waiting for her.

To claim her attention, her hand, the first waltz and if

there was one, the supper waltz, too. Regardless of the nature of the entertainment, he would remain by her side, impossible to shift. His attentions, however, were perfectly gauged—socially acceptable, yet what those watching couldn't see was the sensuality behind every look, every touch. They couldn't see the net he wove, link by link about her. She knew, but could do nothing to prevent it, to deny the hold he already had over her senses and her heart.

He had indeed changed the rules of their game. Between them, there was no longer any pretence that desire didn't burn just beneath their skin, waiting to flare into passion. That they wouldn't much rather be alone, by the fire in his library or anywhere else, rather than whirling about countless dance floors. But he was after her submission, after her agreement to marry him as he now was, to accept him as he had thus far revealed himself to be. To place her hand in his, to give herself up to him, without further promises. He'd shifted the field to the ton, changed the rules to those society played by, but what he was after hadn't changed.

Day by day, night by night, he continued to stalk her. Through ballrooms, drawing rooms, at the opera house, in the park. He never, not once, stepped over the line, yet he continued to single her out, not simply as above all others, but to the exclusion of all others. He was uninterested in any other lady; he hadn't shied from making that brutally plain.

To her astonishment, amazement—to her increasing consternation—he proved adept at bending society's dictates to his own advantage. And worse. She hadn't thought it possible that on this field—one where she was so much more experienced than he—he could run her to earth.

Yet he was winning.

The hostesses were starting to come around, to lean his way.

She could barely believe her ears when at the Castlereaghs' ball she overheard Emily Cowper, kindly as ever, murmur to Martin before she moved on, "An excellent choice, my boy—she'll do very well as your countess."

Glancing around, ceasing to hear the story Mr. Cole was

relating, she saw Martin smile, incline his head and reply, "Indeed. So I think."

Lady Cowper smiled sweetly, patted his arm and drifted away.

Martin met her gaze—and smiled, lionishly.

Just how dangerous the shift in sentiment threatened to be was brought home when Countess Lieven tapped her on the wrist with her fan. She nodded regally at Martin, engaged with Lord Woolley. "I am pleased that you have finally settled your interest. Flitting forever through the ton's gentlemen might be acceptable at eighteen, but at twenty-three . . ." She raised her brows haughtily. "Suffice it to say that an alliance with Dexter would find general favor. There is, of course, the old scandal, but . . ." With a shrug, she continued, "One would expect you to see that buried, one way or another."

With a stiff nod, the countess swanned off, leaving Amanda staring in her wake. One way or another?

She knew what that meant—that she should marry Martin, keep her head high and bear him an heir or three, and make sure neither he nor she caused another scandal. Redemption through association; if she remained as pure as the driven snow, his supposed transgressions would be overlooked.

The thought horrified her. She turned back to Martin to find him frowning at her, then he transferred his frown to Countess Lieven's back. "What did that harridan say?"

She could almost see his hackles rising. "Nothing, nothing. There are the violins—come and dance."

She succeeded in dragging him onto the dance floor; he allowed her to distract him but was not deceived. As she whirled in his arms, some part of her whispered that perhaps she should give in. He'd come into the ton after her, braved the bright lights and the hostesses to win her—did she need more declaration than that?

The answer was an unequivocal yes. She wanted a clear acknowledgment that he loved her, and she'd seen nothing resembling that. And there was a bigger hurdle yet—one that wouldn't bend to either her will or his. Not even society's. Her family was not convinced—at least, not convinced enough to agree to her marrying him.

She'd only recently realized, only recently seen the frown in her mother's eyes, noticed the whispered conferences between her mother and her aunts. As the music died, she felt a strong urge to rub her forehead. Her straightforward, easy-to-navigate world had suddenly developed unexpected reefs and shoals.

"Here! Gel!"

Amanda turned. Lady Osbaldestone was sitting on a chaise nearby.

"Yes, you!" Her ladyship beckoned with her cane. "I want to speak with you."

Martin by her side, she crossed to the chaise.

"Sit down." Lady Osbaldestone indicated the chaise beside her. Then she looked at Martin and smiled. Evilly. "*You* can fetch me a glass of orgeat, and a glass of water for Miss Cynster. She'll be grateful for it later."

Impossible to refuse. Martin accepted the commission with good grace, bowed, and headed for the refreshment room.

"So nice to know I guessed right." Facing Amanda, Lady Osbaldestone studied her. "Well? Have you decided yet?"

Meeting those black, bottomless eyes, Amanda sighed. "I've decided—and so has he, obviously—*but* . . ."

"In my experience, there usually is a but. What's it in this case? And for God's sake, cut line—he won't be long."

Amanda dragged in a breath. "There's two buts. The first is, not *if* he loves me—I'm as sure as I can be that he does—but if *he* knows he loves me. The second might be more serious, more insurmountable. The scandal is still there. I know the ton will gloss over it, but I don't think my family will."

Lady Osbaldestone nodded. "You're right. They won't. You may trust me on that. However, you're wrong about what's serious and what's not." She caught Amanda's gaze and leaned nearer. "Listen, and listen well. You're absolutely right in digging in your heels and demanding an acknowledgment, at least between the pair of you, that he loves you. I presume that's what this week's been about? That he's followed you into the ton to force your hand?"

Amanda nodded. "Exactly."

"A good sign, but whatever you do, *don't waver*. Don't let him, or anyone or anything, turn you from your purpose."

Her ladyship glanced up; Amanda followed her gaze and saw Martin wending his way back to them.

Lady Osbaldestone spoke quickly. "As for the scandal, you'll have to trust my reading of him and his family, but the scandal will only be resolved if *he* wishes it, and he'll only wish it for a reason more compelling than all the reasons to let dead scandals lie, and for him there will be a few of those."

Martin was nearing; Lady Osbaldestone's black eyes bored into Amanda's. "Do you follow, gel?" Her clawlike hand tightened on Amanda's wrist. "There's only one reason I can see that will ever be important enough to make him seek to clear his name."

Easing back, Lady Osbaldestone smiled and accepted her glass of orgeat. Martin looked at her, then at Amanda. He offered the glass of water he'd brought.

Amanda accepted it with a vague nod, and drained it.

Chapter 14

In the days and evenings that followed, Amanda increasingly felt like an antelope cut out from the herd by a lion. A lionized lion—even worse. That fact dealt him far too many aces, which he was never slow to use.

She'd taken to urging her mother and sister to arrive early at every major event so she could assemble a useful circle of gentlemen to serve as a screen. She accepted that she had to deal with Martin, that she could do nothing other than to wait him out, holding steadfast in her requirement for "something more."

If he was the rock, she was the tide, and so on.

If she understood Lady Osbaldestone correctly, then the nature of their future hinged on her stubbornness.

Lady Musselford's ball was certain to be a crush. The Mussleford girls were ravishing and both were making their formal bow to the ton that night. Amanda prayed one or other would do something to keep the ton's collective eye on them—away from her and her determined would-be consort.

She was growing rather tired of having her every move remarked.

"Miss Cynster! I had great hopes you would attend tonight."

Amanda started; she blinked as Percival Lytton-Smythe bowed before her. "Ah . . . good evening, sir."

"I daresay"—Percival beamed delightedly at her—"that you've been wondering where I've been these past two weeks."

She hadn't even noticed his absence. "Have you been in the country?" She continued to watch for Martin's arrival.

"I travelled to Shropshire—one of my maternal aunts is aging. She wished to make her will, confirming me as her heir."

Amanda caught a glimpse of burnished locks at the far end of the ballroom. "How fortunate."

"Fortunate, indeed! Miss Cynster—my dear Amanda, if I might make so bold—"

Percival grasped her hand, jerking her attention from approaching danger. "Mr. Lytton-Smythe!" She tried to pull free, but he stubbornly held on.

"No, no—my apologies, dear lady. The violence of my feelings has startled you, but you must make allowances for my natural enthusiasm at the prospect that, courtesy of my aunt's generosity, now lies before us."

"Us?" Aghast, Amanda stared.

Percival patted her hand. "My dearest Amanda, only the disparity of our fortunes, the idea that some might consider our match too uneven in standing, has prevented me from speaking 'ere now, yet you cannot be unaware that a match between us will confer great benefits upon us both."

"Benefits?" Her temper rose; she fought to suppress it. The ballroom was fast filling.

"But of course. Innocent as you are, your parents have doubtless deemed it unnecessary to burden your mind with the more businesslike aspects of matrimony. No need, indeed, for your father and I will ensure that you are well looked after, you may be sure."

That last was delivered with a paternalistic smirk; before she could erupt, Percival released her and continued, "Regardless of the recent deplorable tendency to invest the institution of marriage with heated emotions, it is absurd to base a serious union on any but sound considerations of wealth and consequence. On the furtherance of the age-old ideals."

"Precisely *which* 'age-old ideals' do you imagine a union between us would serve?" The belief that she had to stop Percival in his tracks was the only reason she asked.

"Why, it will be obvious to all that marriage to me will stem your regrettable levity, the same levity that has kept you from marriage for the last several years. It's clear you require a firm hand on your reins, and I am just the man to supply it." Percival beamed at the surrounding crowd. "And, of course, merging your fortune with mine will create a nice estate, one I will manage to our advantage. The connection with St. Ives will benefit my standing, and all that I undertake. Indeed, an alliance between us will be of inestimable value, as I'm sure, even innocent as you are of such matters, you will agree."

Smugly triumphant, he smiled at her.

Eyes narrowed, she trapped his gaze. "You err." His smile faded; he opened his lips—she silenced him with an upraised hand. "You are wrong. First, in imagining I value the 'age-old ideals' you worship—wealth and status are mine regardless of whom I wed. You also insult my family in believing that any consideration beyond my own happiness will weigh with them."

Her gaze was caught by the tall, commanding figure purposefully heading their way. "While my family will discourage any alliance they believe would not be in my best interests, I assure you they will equally discourage any suitor who does not find favor in my eyes."

"Pish-*posh!*"

Percival's contemptuous tone had her returning her gaze to him; she raised her brows haughtily. "I believe our discussion is at an end, sir. I bid you a good evening."

She turned to sweep away, to slip into the crowd and gather a circle of protective admirers before Martin caught up with her—

Percival grabbed her wrist. "Nonsense! It's past time you gave up such flighty, affected behavior. It may pass well enough in the schoolroom—"

"Unhand me!"

Her furious yet glacial tones struck Percival like a whip.

He jerked upright, tried to look down his nose at her, noticed the spray of orchids she held in her trapped hand. She tugged; Percival held on. His face a study in astonishment, he forced her hand up, examining the exotic spray.

In the tone of a schoolmaster discovering a pupil in severe transgression, he asked, "What is this?"

"Sensual beauty personified," came the deep, drawled reply.

Percival started, looked around.

Martin halted beside him; his gaze touched the orchids, then moved on to Amanda. "Don't you agree?"

The question was clearly addressed to Percival, its object equally clearly not the orchids.

Shocked, Percival relaxed his grip. Amanda twisted her wrist free.

And smiled, delightedly, at Martin. "Dexter—how fortunate. Do let me make you known to Mr. Lytton-Smythe."

"Sir." Martin bowed easily.

Percival's eyes widened; after an instant's hesitation, he bowed stiffly. "My lord."

"Why fortunate?" Martin's gaze met Amanda's.

"Because I was just bidding Mr. Lytton-Smythe farewell before continuing around the ballroom. Now I need not do so alone."

She offered her hand.

Percival stuck out his arm, positively huffed, "I will be more than happy to escort you, my dear."

Martin smiled. "Ah, but I'm before you, you see." One long finger pointed to the orchids. There was a fractional pause as his gaze met Percival's, then, with his usual ineffable grace, Martin offered her his arm.

Ruthlessly ignoring the undercurrents—all of them—Amanda laid her fingers on Martin's sleeve. With a regal nod to Percival, she coolly stated, "Good-bye, sir," then let Martin lead her away.

She was unsurprised when, after less than ten feet, Martin murmured, "Who, exactly, is Mr. Lytton-Smythe?"

"Not who—what. He's a pest."

"Ah. In that case, we must trust he's taken the hint."

"Indeed." Which hint—Martin's or hers—she didn't bother to ask; either would do. Unfortunately . . . she inwardly grimaced, and wished she'd been more explicit in refusing what had all but amounted to Percival's declaration.

Martin watched the irritation, the annoyance, fade from Amanda's eyes, and needed no further assurance of what Lytton-Smythe meant to her. But a faint frown remained, clouding the cornflower blue, lightly furrowing her forehead; the sight didn't meet with his approval.

They'd been ambling around the growing crowd filing into her ladyship's rooms. An alcove containing a bust of some long dead general lay just ahead. Closing his fingers about Amanda's hand, Martin slowed.

Pausing by the alcove, he raised her hand, still holding his orchids; he examined not the flowers, but her wrist, fine-boned, veins showing blue beneath her porcelain skin. "He didn't hurt you, did he?"

Possessiveness rippled beneath the drawled words; he made no effort to disguise it. He met her wide eyes, held her gaze as he slid his fingers over her wrist in a featherlight caress to close, gently, over the spot where her pulse beat, then leapt beneath his fingertips.

He sensed the catch in her breathing, saw her pupils dilate, saw her make the decision to boldly continue to meet his eyes, to let desire rise briefly between them—the warm, beckoning promise of passion—before, of necessity, they let it ebb.

Only then, when they could both breathe easily again, did she incline her head and murmur, "Thank you for rescuing me."

His lips lifted briefly; eyes still on hers, he raised her hand. "The pleasure," he murmured, "was all mine." His last words brushed the sensitive skin of her wrist an instant before his lips touched, pressed.

He returned her hand to his sleeve. In perfect accord, they strolled on.

On the other side of the ballroom, Vane Cynster frowned. He watched his golden-haired cousin and her escort until the crowd blocked his view.

"There you are!" Vane's wife, Patience, swept up and linked her arm with his. "Lady Osbadlestone wishes to speak with you."

"Just as long as she keeps her cane to herself." Vane let Patience tug him into motion, then the crowd parted and he saw Amanda and her escort again. Vane stopped; of necessity, Patience stopped, too. She looked inquiringly up at him.

"Who the devil is that?" Vane nodded across the room. "The fellow with Amanda."

Patience looked, then smiled. "Dexter." She tugged Vane on. "I would have thought you'd have heard—his return to the ton has been a major topic in the drawing rooms."

"You know perfectly well that I and all the others avoid drawing rooms wherever possible." Vane studied his wife's expression, the smile that curved her lips. "What's the speculation?"

"Current speculation concerns just *what* has lured Dexter out of that huge house in Park Lane and back into the ton."

Vane halted—swung Patience around to face him. "Not Amanda?"

Horrified comprehension filled his eyes; Patience laughed. Twining her arm through his, she patted it reassuringly and urged him on. "Yes, Amanda, but there's no need to worry. She's managing perfectly well, and although there is that old scandal which will have to be addressed, there's no reason whatever for you or any of the others to interfere."

Vane said nothing; if she'd looked into his face, Patience would have detected a grimness in his grey eyes that boded ill for her last injunction, but distracted by the greetings of another lady, she simply towed him along. "Now come and do the pretty—and *don't growl*."

On the subject of Amanda, Martin's feelings were not that dissimilar from Vane's. As he now considered her indisputably his, the nights spent in the ballrooms watching over her—establishing his right to her by deed rather than decree—were the ultimate in frustration, a token bow to tonnish expectations.

His own expectations were growing more definite by the

day, increasingly more difficult to subdue. He wanted her his, recognized as his. Now. Today. Yesterday.

Watching as she danced a cotillion with Lord Wittingham, Martin ignored the irritation—the abrasion of his temper caused by seeing her in another man's arms—and turned his mind to his most urgent question: when could he end this charade?

His sole purpose in rejoining the ton had been to establish the *bona fides* of his suit—his pursuit—of Amanda. He'd spent nearly two weeks projecting a patience he didn't possess, his well-honed instincts insisting that establishing the link between them as accepted fact in the ton's collective mind was the surest road to victory.

The Season was rushing on, building to its height, to the weeks when there would be three or more major balls to attend every night. The very thought made him weary; balls, even those spent by Amanda's side, did not offer what he needed to engage and soothe his restless senses.

Amanda by herself, alone, preferably naked, did.

Two weeks had passed since he'd seen her like that—his, all his. How much longer would he need to wait? More specifically, did he need to wait any longer?

The incident with Lytton-Smythe nagged. Not that he imagined Amanda being captivated by another and stolen away—more a case of a primitive reaction against any man casting covetous eyes at her.

While she twirled and linked hands in the dance, he scanned the company. The crowd had swelled to a certified crush; everyone was here, even her cousins. He'd glimpsed two, had heard the St. Iveses announced, but he hadn't come up with any male Cynsters in the crowd. Over the last weeks, he'd been introduced to all their wives, who'd conveyed without words just what the score was—what their familial verdict would be.

They approved of him, *but* . . .

He knew the cause of their reservation. He would deal with it once he'd secured Amanda. From her earlier "investigations" on his behalf and all she'd subsequently said, he knew she cared not a jot, but her family would, a stance he understood.

The old scandal would need to be tackled, *but* . . . he couldn't in all conscience lift the lid on that pot, not unless he had to, not until she was willing to marry him and the scandal was the last hurdle in his path.

Countess Lieven glided past; she nodded regally. Lady Esterhazy had earlier smiled her approbation. As for Sally Jersey—every time she saw him, she looked for Amanda.

His gaze returned to Amanda, smiling at Lord Wittingham as the dance ended and she curtsied. Then she rose, looked about—for him.

Martin pushed away from the wall. Everyone was watching, waiting . . . the next move was his.

Amanda saw him approaching through the crowd; confident, assured, she remained where she was, waiting for him to reach her. In this arena, she had nothing to fear; he couldn't pounce in a ballroom.

The worst he could do he'd already done—convinced the entire ton, certainly all those who mattered, that a match between them was appropriate, even desirable. That whatever obstacles remained would be overcome, so fated was their union.

He'd managed that, but social opinion wasn't powerful enough to make her accept the cake he was offering without the icing. Until he offered all she wished, she was perfectly prepared to stroll the ballrooms at his side, to let propinquity abrade his senses as well as hers.

Her senses were more accustomed to frustration than his.

As he neared, she thanked Lord Wittingham and turned, her smile deepening. To do the lion justice, he'd made no attempt to use society's views to pressure her. He was too expert a player to make such a mistake.

She gave him her hand; he took it, fingers caressing hers as he settled them on his sleeve. They strolled, stopping to chat here and there. The music for the first waltz sounded; one shared look, and they headed for the floor. As they revolved, she noticed he was studying her; she raised her brows.

Releasing her hand, he caught a stray curl bobbing by her ear, set it back, lightly stroked her cheek.

She caught his gaze as he retook her hand. *What?* her look asked.

"You've stopped worrying that I'll bite."

She let mock haughtiness infuse her expression; the observation was accurate, but he didn't need to state it.

His moss-agatey eyes remained sober. "Why do you trust me?"

That was not a question she'd expected to be asked. She searched, but could find only one answer: "Because you're you."

His lips quirked, then he looked ahead, negotiating the turn.

Should she be more wary? The only message her senses sent her was one of unequivocal satisfaction; being in his arms felt right, totally safe. Difficult to feel nervous.

The music ended; they resumed their perambulation around the room, spending time with the many who had decided to cultivate the Earl of Dexter. If she'd thought him naive, she'd have worried, but the looks they exchanged left her in no doubt that he knew how to value such acquaintances.

However, quite aside from the shared glances, she was aware of his eyes returning again and again to her face; he was trying to read her thoughts.

Her court had dispersed—his never-failing presence at her side had made his intention clear. No other gentleman could match his attractions; the rest had given up vying for her hand. Unchallenged, he led her in to supper. Seating her at a table by the wall, he fetched two plates piled with delicacies.

They'd barely settled to their feast when another gentleman and lady approached. Amanda glanced up—and blinked.

"Mind if we join you?" Luc Ashford, as ever the epitome of a heartbreaking rake, raised a fashionably weary brow. Balancing two plates, he favored Amanda with an abbreviated bow.

Beside him, Amelia smiled her thanks as Martin rose and drew up a chair for her. "We spotted you from across the room. We've hardly had a chance to exchange two words."

Luc set down their plates, then drew up another chair,

placing it beside Amanda, diagonally opposite Martin. "I had thought the ton held no interest for you, coz."

"So had I." Martin's smile was easy, but his gaze had grown sharp. "There are some parts I could still do without, but"—he shrugged—"needs must."

Amelia laughed. "You've certainly caused a stir. Why—"

Letting her twin's light chatter flow past her, Amanda inwardly frowned. She knew Martin well, but she'd known Luc forever. If she thought of Martin as a lion, Luc had always been a black leopard, sleek and lethal.

Right now, Luc's hackles were up, but he was wary, not aggressive. Yet. Why, she couldn't fathom, but as she contributed her share to keep the conversation rolling, she grew increasingly certain the lion and the leopard were assessing each other, and communicating, too, on some male-cousin animalistic plane. Lady Osbaldestone's recollection that they knew each other well—had grown up together—was patently true. Martin showed no sign of feeling threatened, but he was watching Luc closely, trying to see past Luc's guard.

For his part, Luc was projecting . . . a warning. For the life of her, she couldn't understand why. Luc and she had never got on; he was one of the few males whose tongues she respected. He could use it like a saber, and frequently had—on her. While they appreciated each other's strengths, there was little love lost between them; she couldn't imagine why he would suddenly ride like a knight to her aid, against his own cousin. If that's what he was doing.

Opposite Luc, sprawled in his chair, Martin was wondering the same thing. He and Luc had been closer than brothers, once. Ten years of absolutely no contact had gouged a chasm between them, yet he could still read Luc well. Knew Luc could guess better than most what he was thinking, how he would react. They'd rubbed shoulders on only a few occasions since he'd returned to England, exchanged no more than a few stilted words. Yet . . .

Amelia paused to sip her champagne. Luc seized the moment; he looked at Martin. "Have you decided to open up Fulbridge House?"

Martin met Luc's dark eyes. "That depends." He let his

gaze flick to Amanda, noted the hardness that infused Luc's face, the face of a fallen angel.

There was challenge and warning in the look Luc sent him; Martin was sorely tempted to ask what the devil he meant. There was nothing between Luc and Amanda; he was perfectly sure of that. Yet his well-exercised instincts recognized Luc's motives; he wanted to protect—

Amelia smiled brightly. "Tell me, is it really true—"

Martin saw the light—caught the fractional softening in his cousin's eyes, so dark a blue they were almost black and therefore difficult to read—in the instant before he followed Luc's gaze—to Amelia's delicate face.

Luc was protecting not Amanda, but her twin. Knew anything that harmed Amanda would impinge on Amelia.

The discovery fascinated, but there was little he could do to ease his cousin's suspicions. Close to the Cynsters as the Ashfords were, Luc would hear the latest soon enough, and realize that Amanda, and therefore, Amelia, were safe from him.

With supper disposed of, they rose as a group and strolled back to the ballroom. Amelia fell silent; Amanda glibly took up the conversational reins, questioning Luc about his sisters. He answered with increasing asperity; when the musicians started up, he turned to Amelia and requested the dance.

She gave him her hand; with nods, the four parted. As Amanda turned into his arms, Martin caught the last glimmer of her satisfied smirk.

"I was right." He steered her into the sea of swirling couples. "There's some understanding between Luc and your sister."

Amanda frowned, then admitted, "I don't actually know, but I think they would suit." She looked into his face. "What do you think? You know Luc well."

As they revolved, he considered it. "It might work." He caught her gaze. "Your sister is not entirely like you."

Her lips quirked. "No—she's more stubborn."

Martin wished Luc luck, if that were true. His choice— the current bane of his life—was bad enough.

She was watching those around them with an easy smile,

unperturbed, content in his arms. He wanted her like that, always, yet to secure that . . .

She trusted him completely, without reserve. How would she react when he took the next step, made the move everyone was waiting on, played the card he'd held back, up his sleeve? She hadn't realized; she was so much at ease in this sphere, so confident as she swanned through the ballrooms, so assured at every turn, that she hadn't stepped back and considered, hadn't seen the option he had.

He had to exercise it, take the next step, yet . . .

Lifting his gaze, he looked across the room, and saw a tall, dark-haired gentleman strolling about the floor stop, arrested, his gaze locking on them. St. Ives—Martin recognized the height, the dominant stance, the arrogant features. Their gazes barely touched before the duchess bustled up and distracted her husband.

Martin felt his aggression subside; recognized the fact. Recalled Luc's attitude. He had to act, or risk a clash with her cousins.

As was common with most married gentlemen of their station, the male Cynsters had not appeared at the early balls. Their wives had clearly seen no reason to apprise them of his pursuit of Amanda, else he'd have heard from them— most likely sustained a private visit—long before now.

The Cynster ladies had given him time to draw Amanda as far as he could along the road they'd both chosen. That time had just run out. He had to play his next card.

"What *is* it?"

He glanced down to find Amanda searching his face.

"You've been behaving strangely all night."

He could have smiled charmingly, turned the accusation aside; instead, he held her gaze as the music slowed, then ceased. "I need to talk with you." He glanced around. "Somewhere private."

At the nearby end of the ballroom, a bay window overlooked the gardens. The area before it was empty. Martin led her to it. Reaching the bay, Amanda stepped into its shadows and faced him, brows rising, yet still assured.

Still certain he couldn't take her by surprise.

He stopped before her, screening her from the company. No one could hear them or see their faces, yet they were in full view of half the ton.

"I intend, tomorrow, to ask for your hand."

"You already have . . ." Her words trailed away, her eyes grew round, then flared wide. "You can't . . ."

"Ask for your hand formally? Believe me, I can."

"But . . ." She frowned, then shook her head, as if to shake aside his suggestion. "There's no point. Until I agree, they won't."

She still hadn't seen it.

"That point is understood—your agreement to our wedding has yet to be gained. However, that's not the purpose of a formal request. I'll be applying for your family's permission to address you."

She continued to frown, imagining . . . then horror poured into her eyes. She grabbed his sleeve, looked into his face. "Good God—you *can't!*" She shook his arm. "Promise me you won't—that you absolutely *will not* mention . . ." She gestured wildly.

"I assure you no mention of our recent intimacies will pass my lips."

She drew back, drew her hand from his sleeve, finally took the long step back she should have taken weeks ago. Horrified, she stared at him. "You won't have to say a word! They'll look at you—and *guess!*"

He raised his brows fleetingly. "Be that as it may, it's not possible to continue as we are without some declaration of intent on my part. Your cousins, if not your father, will demand that much."

He'd seen her defiant before, but now militance flamed in her eyes.

"No! Once they guess, once they know, they'll—"

She broke off, following some line of thought he couldn't for the life of him see. Eyes narrowing, she smiled, thin lipped. "It won't work."

Refocusing on him, she nodded. "Very well. You may take that tack if you wish, if you deem it necessary. However"—

head high, she stepped past him, her eyes holding his—"my father has left London. He'll be traveling through the west country on business for the next week."

With a regal nod, she glided out of the bay. Frowning, Martin watched as she disappeared into the at-last-thinning crowd.

Six yards away, one hand resting on the back of the chaise on which his wife, Catriona, sat talking to Lady Forsythe, Richard Cynster, his expression impassive, watched Martin.

"We should string him up by his—"

"I'm not sure that's warranted."

Cut off in mid-tirade, Demon stared at Richard. "Not warranted? You say he was pressuring her—"

"Yes." From the armchair facing Devil's desk, Richard continued, "But not in the way you're imagining."

Demon frowned, then sank into a straightbacked chair facing the large desk. "What the hell's going on?"

All six of them exchanged glances. Sitting behind his desk, Devil sighed. "Knowing Amanda, it won't be straightforward."

"As far as I could see," Richard put in, "it wasn't."

"Their . . ."—shoulders propped against the bookshelves behind Devil, Vane gestured—"*interaction* is apparently the talk of the ton."

From his place on the chaise before the fireplace, Gabriel asked, "Tell us—what exactly did you see?"

"I saw them first," Vane said. "They were strolling, then stopped a little apart from the crowd. They spoke, then he kissed her wrist—not innocently. It looked like he'd have been perfectly happy to devour her on the spot, and she, silly nitwit, would have urged him on. Then they moved on." He shifted. "Patience said Amanda's managing perfectly well, and although that old scandal needs to be addressed, there's no reason for us to interfere."

The others looked at Vane, then, as one, they all turned to Richard.

"I saw them briefly, during the last waltz," Devil said. "I'm fairly certain Dexter saw me."

"But did he recognize you?" Richard raised his brows, then continued, "What I saw occurred shortly after, more or less on the heels of that waltz." He described all he'd seen. "In short, it appeared Dexter was calmly talking—it was Amanda who was more forceful. And given the way she swanned off at the end, nose in the air, and the way he watched her go, as if he was trying to figure it all out . . ." Richard sighed, "Truth to tell, I felt sympathetic."

Demon humphed. "The man's a certified wolf of the worst sort."

"Just as we once were," Devil murmured.

"Which is precisely my point. We *know* what he's thinking . . ." Demon let his words die.

"And that's *my* point," Richard stated. "Do you remember when you stood there, in a ballroom or wherever, and watched her stalk off—and wondered what the hell was going on?"

Devil's lips twitched. "I don't have to exercise my memory for that."

There were smiles and grins all around, then Devil sobered. "All right. Let's accept the fact that Dexter appears, on the face of it, to be wooing Amanda. I can't see any reason he'd go to the lengths he has to seduce her. For whatever reason, he's playing by society's rules. So, what do we know of him? I don't remember him personally." Devil glanced at Vane, who shook his head. "He was much younger than us."

"Younger than me, too," Demon said, "but I remember he was a hellion. But he was only on the town for a brief time."

"Up until the scandal." Briefly, Richard filled in all he knew of that, ending with, "The *grandes dames* and many others felt it was an overreaction on his father's part—basically, few believed Dexter, the present earl, could be guilty, but no one was asked for their opinion. The thing was done, decided by his father up north, and he was hustled out of England before anyone knew."

Devil asked, "What's the current feeling?"

Richard shrugged. "Innocent until known to be guilty, but still in the dock."

"I've dealt with him once." Gabriel leaned forward. "In the City, he's a legend among the nabobs. He led a syndicate we took an interest in, and he knew his business. We made a nice profit from that venture. The areas he deals in are exotic, occasionally esoteric, but always, always highly profitable. His reputation is formidable; he's known as a man of his word, a trader who deals squarely and straightforwardly, and who does not suffer either fools or rogues gladly."

"He's also a legend in collecting circles." Beside his brother on the chaise, Lucifer stretched out his long legs. "I'd *pay* to get into that old tomb on Park Lane. Hardly anyone has, but those who have set eyes on his library have come away with stars in their eyes. Absolutely lost for words. It's not the books alone, although they're apparently amazing, but all the oriental art he's collected over the years. Seems he has a real eye for beauty."

Demon softly snorted.

Devil tapped his blotter with his pen. "So . . . there's no reason to oppose a match, provided that old scandal is laid to rest."

"And provided he's thinking in such terms." Vane pushed away from the bookshelves.

"Indeed." Devil's face hardened. "Regardless of our ladies' fond imaginings, I believe I should demand some straight answers from the earl."

"I'll come with you," came from five other throats.

A tap on the door had them all glancing that way. The door opened; Sligo, Devil's majordomo, slipped in. "The Earl of Dexter has called, Your Grace. He's asked to speak with you privately."

Devil stared. "Dexter?"

Sligo proffered his salver on which a card lay. Devil took it, studied it, then asked, "Where is he?"

"I left him in the drawing room."

"Where's Her Grace?"

"Out."

Devil's lips curved. "Very good. Show his lordship in."

Chapter 15

Martin stepped into His Grace of St. Ives' study—every self-protective instinct he possessed immediately snapped to full alert. Six pairs of eyes had locked on him; no prizes for guessing the most recent topic of conversation.

Strolling into the large room, he seized the moment to study the other occupants—far more than he'd expected, yet he wasn't all that surprised. He'd heard they operated as a pack.

Led by the man who came slowly to his feet behind the desk and nodded. "Dexter." He held out a hand.

Martin returned the nod. "St. Ives." He gripped the proffered hand.

"Do you have any reservations over speaking before my cousins?"

Martin let his gaze briefly touch the stony faces. "None."

"In that case . . ." Devil introduced them, using their nicknames, then waved to a straightbacked chair before the desk. "Sit down."

Martin looked at the chair, then picked it up and set it down to one side of the desk, so he wouldn't be sitting with four Cynsters at his back.

Demon scowled as he sat. Martin looked at Devil, without preamble stated, "I've just come from Upper Brook Street where I learned that your uncle, Lord Arthur Cynster, is presently from home and not expected to return for a week. I'd wished to apply for permission to pay my addresses to his daughter Amanda. In the circumstances, as you're the head of the family and currently in town, I'm here to apply to you in Lord Arthur's stead."

Absolute silence greeted his pronouncement, confirming his supposition of what they'd been discussing before he'd walked in.

His pale green gaze steady on Martin's face, Devil murmured, "A week isn't a long time."

Martin returned that unwavering regard; he was not prepared to endure another week of inaction. "Much could occur in a week, as I'm sure you'll agree."

Two of the others stirred at his deliberate words; Martin didn't shift his gaze from Devil.

Who sat back, eyes narrowing. "Why?"

Martin didn't bother to misunderstand. "Because it's time." He paused, selecting his words, then continued, "In my view, matters have progressed to a point where a wedding is in order. Hence . . . here I am."

There wasn't one of them who didn't immediately comprehend what particular matters had progressed, and to where; muffled oaths and none-too-thinly veiled threats, including one to hang him by a sensitive part of his anatomy, rose around him.

Devil waved the others to silence, his gaze locked on Martin's face. "You've only recently returned to the ton—stalking Amanda. I take it that was after those matters had progressed. Where did you meet her in the first place?"

Martin held Devil's gaze. "At Mellors."

"What?" "That den?" and various other mutterings came from the sidelines.

Martin glanced down, straightened his cuff. "She'd just accepted a wager to play whist. Against Connor. She didn't have a partner."

The silence that greeted that was one of abject—positively scandalized—disbelief.

"The second time I saw her was in Helen Hennessy's salon."

The room erupted. Various epithets were heaped on Amanda's head. Numerous questions were flung at him; recognizing them as rhetorical, Martin kept silent. Eventually, at a sign from Devil, now seriously displeased, the others quieted.

"Very well." Devil's eyes were hard. "What happened then?"

"She had a list of outings she wished to experience, beyond the ton but not of themselves scandalous. A moonlight drive in Richmond Park, boating on the Thames by night, a visit to Vauxhall in non-approved company, and attending a Covent Garden masquerade."

A wave of low growls swept the room.

"You offered to take her on these outings?"

"No." Martin felt his expression harden. "I had little choice—it was either fall in with her plans, or watch her organize with some other who would. She had Lord Cranbourne in her sights for the drive to Richmond."

"Cranbourne! That slug?" Demon's scowl was black.

"There were others she'd met in Gloucester Street. She had real alternatives. I deemed it safer not to call her bluff."

"And during these outings . . ."

"No." Martin met Devil's gaze. "I took her on the outings on condition she return thereafter to the ballrooms—where she belonged. However, as it transpired, the outings weren't her true goal. Once they were over, she rescripted the rules and returned to Gloucester Street and other venues even less appropriate." His gaze steady on Devil's, he stated, "What happened thereafter was entirely at her behest, if not precisely as she'd planned."

There wasn't one of them who didn't sympathize; he was admitting to being stalked, and caught, by their cousin. Knowing the moment was right, he pressed on, "In the circumstances, a wedding is the prescribed outcome. So . . . do I have your permission to address her?"

Devil blinked, frowned. "Wealth, birth, station, estate—all those are in order. But what of the past?"

He inclined his head. "The past will be dealt with."

"Did you do it?"

"No." After a moment he added, "But the inescapable fact is, someone did."

Devil's uncannily penetrating gaze searched his eyes; Martin endured the scrutiny without shifting. Devil nodded. "Very well—I agree. Provided the old scandal is resolved in your favor, a marriage between you and Amanda is clearly appropriate. You have my permission to address her. I'll speak with my uncle on his return."

"Good. And you'll make the family's stance clear?"

Devil shrugged. "To the ton? Of course."

"I meant to Amanda."

That last was met with silence, a different, slightly uneasy one. Devil broke it. "Why?"

"Because, while she's 'agreed' in a manner we'd all accept, on several occasions, she's yet to manage the word 'yes' in the appropriate context."

"Ah." Devil's eyes widened. "You've asked her."

Martin frowned. "Of course. Immediately and several times thereafter. Why else do you imagine I've been chasing her through the ton, not an arena I particularly relish, if not to tighten the noose a few notches before I ask her again?"

"Has she said why she won't agree?" It was Richard who put the question.

Martin hesitated, then replied, his tone hard, "She wants 'something more,' by which I take it she means something that would not feature in any marriage contract."

The look on their faces told him they knew exactly what he meant.

Devil's grimace was heartfelt. "Commiserations." After a moment, he asked, "I take it you're not of a mind simply to give it to her?"

"No." Martin considered, then added, "Not if there's any other way."

"And if I was to tell you there probably won't be any other way?"

Martin met Devil's green gaze. "I won't know until we get to that point."

Devil sighed. Nodded. "I'll do what I can, but, conversely, there's little I can do."

"You could speak with her."

"I could, but all that will yield will be a glare, a pert recommendation to mind my own business and a guaranteed wall of feminine disapprobation mobilized to ensure we can do no more to assist your suit."

Vane nodded. "And within the ton, *they* rule."

"There's a better way." Perched on the arm of the chaise, Demon looked at Martin. "You tell her Devil's given your suit the nod. She'll expect us to hound her. We won't. She'll credit us with better sense than she'd expected, and very likely not mention the matter to our mothers or wives." Demon grinned. "Then we can help you."

Martin considered the committed glint in Demon's eyes, the sense of fellow-feeling now pervading the room. He nodded. "How?"

He told her that evening, on the Fortescues' terrace.

"Devil?"

"He is the head of your house."

Amanda humphed. Resettling her shawl about her elbows, she continued to stroll at his side. "What he or any of them think is beside the point. *I* have to agree—and I haven't."

"I know." His hard tone had her glancing up; he caught her gaze. "What will convince you to say yes?"

She narrowed her eyes. "I told you before—you need to discover that on your own."

He glanced ahead. Although a dozen other couples were strolling the wide terrace, none had ventured in this direction, to where the terrace was overhung by thickly leaved branches creating a grotto of shadows. "In that case, I assume you're not averse to allowing me to . . . explore."

She glanced at him. Other sounds reached them; they both turned. Everyone else was returning to the ballroom, drawn by the strains of a waltz.

Martin smiled. "My dance, I believe."

He reached for her, drew her into his arms; she came, but warily. His smile deepened; he began to revolve in the area lit by the wall flares, until she relaxed, until she let the moment and the music sweep her away, and she followed his steps without thought.

Amanda wasn't surprised when he whirled her into the shadows, wasn't surprised when his steps slowed and he drew her closer still.

His words ruffled the curls about her ear. "I've waltzed with you often, so presumably what you want will not be found in the dance." His lips touched her ear, traced the outer curve, then slid into the sensitive hollow behind. "I wonder . . ."

The hand at her back held her hard against him; his lips caressed so lightly she shuddered. As if that were a signal, he shifted his attentions to her lips, and she suddenly found herself drowning in an inexpressibly sweet kiss.

Not a kiss of claiming, but a kiss that lured, that tempted with promises not just of glory, but . . . her head spun as she tried to adjust to the sudden shift in his attack. Their steps slowed, halted, as their senses sank deeper and deeper into the enthralling exchange.

His hand didn't leave her back, the hollow just beneath her waist where it habitually rode; his other hand curled about her wrist, lightly stroking.

She was trapped, but not physically. The sensual web he wove was insubstantial yet unbreakable—because she couldn't bring herself to break it, to pull away from the landscape that with his tongue, his lips, his mouth, his breath, he created. It was a landscape where she ruled, and he served. Where, empresslike, she could command, demand, then lie back and have her every desire lavished upon her.

She tried to slip her hand free and reach for him, touch his cheek, but his fingers firmed; he held her hand, drew her closer yet so that the heat and hardness of his body wrapped about her. Shielding her from all else but the communion of their mouths, the drugging promise of the kiss.

"You'll feel much more the thing once you've had a breath of air."

The words, uttered in a voice she recognized, broke their

kiss, shattered the magic. Blinking, peering back along the terrace, Amanda saw Edward Ashford escorting Emily, Anne and their friend Miss Ffolliot out from the ballroom from which music still wafted.

Martin swore softly; she felt the same. He set her back on her feet; the loss of his heat only added to her irritation. They were in the shadows, as yet unseen, but they weren't sufficiently screened to ignore the interruption. Setting her hand on his sleeve, Martin turned her; as if they'd been doing nothing else, they strolled out from the branches' shadow.

Having led the way from the ballroom, Edward was standing waiting for the girls to join him. He saw them first; he stiffened, then adopted an even more supercilious expression than usual.

The girls, juggling shawls and reticules, saw them, smiled and came bustling forward. Edward hesitated, then fell in on their heels.

"Hello! It's quite mild out here, isn't it?"

"Edward thought I looked peaked, so he brought us out here."

"Good evening, my lord."

All three girls had met Martin previously; all were in awe of him, but Amanda's presence gave them courage.

After greeting the girls, Amanda looked at Edward. He was observing Martin narrowly, then he noticed her and inclined his head. Somewhat more stiffly, he nodded to Martin. "Dexter."

Martin nodded back.

Amanda felt like throwing her hands in the air. They were first cousins, for heaven's sake! At least Luc had conversed reasonably. Edward's stiffness, his uneasiness, projected the clear impression he'd be happier gathering the girls and her, too, and retreating from Martin's contaminating presence.

Martin's eyes had narrowed; Amanda gave him credit for not reacting further to Edward's irritating attitude.

Taking Martin's arm again, she smiled at the girls. "We'll leave you to your perambulation. But don't remain out too long—people do notice."

* * *

"I can't believe it—they haven't lectured, they haven't growled. Demon even smiled at me!" Amanda stared narrow-eyed at her cousins, currently standing with their wives on the other side of Lady Hamilton's ballroom.

Beside her, Amelia stared, too. "And Devil's given his permission . . . but surely they've guessed? Perhaps the others haven't heard?"

"According to Patience, they were all there when Martin spoke with Devil."

"Well, then, they've all met him, which means you're right—it's not believable. I'm surprised he's unmarked. They must be up to something."

"Maybe . . ." Amanda's gaze grew distant. "Yes, that has to be it. Martin must have convinced them that, as what's done is done and he does wish to marry me, to let him manage me—my resistance—on his own." She refocused on her cousins. "He knows how I feel about them and their interference."

"Maybe they've realized that our lives are none of their business."

Amanda glanced at Amelia; Amelia met her gaze.

Amanda shook her head. Stared again at her cousins. "They're up to something. But what?"

Whatever their plan was, it didn't include discouraging Martin's suit. Giving permission was one thing; in the circumstances, it might have proved difficult not to grant. But actually approving . . .

As she whirled through the first waltz in Martin's arms, Amanda saw both Vane, and then Gabriel, notice them, then turn away, apparently unperturbed. She refocused on Martin's face. "When you spoke with Devil, did you or he touch on the . . . degree of our relationship?"

Martin met her gaze. "If you mean did we discuss the fact of our intimacy, no. However, my interpretation of the discussion was that that aspect was understood."

She stared at him. "Taken for granted?"

"Let's say 'assumed.' "

"Humph!" She wasn't sure how to react—relieved her cousins had apparently accepted her right to manage her own life, or wildly suspicious, certain they never would. She settled for being watchful, wary. Looking before she leapt.

"This is bedlam," Martin muttered as the music ended and they halted. "Let's stroll in the foyer. At least we should be able to breathe out there."

She was willing enough; Lady Hamilton had invited more than double the number of people her rooms could actually hold. Unfortunately, her ladyship's guests were still arriving; the foyer, although less packed, was still crowded.

They wended their way through the guests, then Martin twined his fingers with hers and drew her into the mouth of a corridor. "Let's leave this madness. The library's this way— there won't be anyone there yet."

Feeling a touch giddy, she acquiesced. He led her down the dimly lit corridor, then opened a door, looked in, then waved her in.

The library was a medium-sized room, comfortably furnished with chaises before the fire and a handsome desk at the other end. A lighted candelabra stood on a table between the chaises, its glow illuminating a silver tray set with decanters and glasses waiting for the older gentlemen who would gravitate here as the evening wore on.

At present, however, the library was blissfully empty.

Amanda breathed in, then exhaled on a sigh. She felt Martin's gaze on her, felt her nerves prickle, then tense. Eschewing the chaises as potentially dangerous, she strolled to the desk. She halted before it, her gaze drawn to the bookshelves behind it. "This library is nothing like yours."

"No?" Humor echoed in his voice as he prowled in her wake. "How so?"

"It lacks color." She turned, and found him all but breast to chest with her, a familiar sensual glint in his moss-green eyes, a taunting tilt to his lips.

"Just the color?" he murmured.

She felt all three words. Reaching up, she twined her arms about his neck. "That, and a few other amenities."

She drew his lips to hers, confident—determined. The chaises were too far away; with the desk at her back, indulging in one, albeit lengthy kiss was safe. A kiss to further whet his appetite, to appease hers. She was hungry, hungry for all they were doing without because of his stubbornness, and hers.

He was hungry, too, perfectly ready to sink into her mouth, to take, to claim, at her invitation. His hands fastened about her waist, holding her steady as he angled his head and feasted. As eager as he, she gave herself up to it—reveled in the heated exchange. Urged him on, confident the situation limited the possibilities. If she wanted to tempt him to give her all, she needed to remind him of what he would gain when he did.

When his hands eased their grip, then rose to her breasts, she exulted. Felt the leap of her pulse, the sudden surge of yearning, saw no need to hide it. Let the need pour through her, glorying in the heady tide of desire, pressed her lips to his and let him sense it, then fractionally drew back, taunting him, challenging him.

He kissed her voraciously; his hands closed, kneading, then through the fine silk of her gown, his fingers found her nipples, closed, squeezed. She gasped, drew back from the kiss, arched her head back; she'd forgotten the intensity, the sheer sensual force. His lips traced the line of her throat, then returned to capture hers again. To pull her ruthlessly back into the fire and the rising flames.

Martin had intended to go slowly, to coax her into passion, to guide her along the road to sensual desire, and its ultimate satisfaction. To lay before her all the splendors like the expert he was, a king wooing his queen, to show her the beauties of the landscape that together they could travel.

He hadn't counted on her fire, on the rush of desire and passion that rose at his touch, welled and poured through their kiss. Hadn't calculated on the arousing effect of her fingers sliding through his hair, then gripping, wordlessly evocative. Hadn't anticipated his own response.

She drove him giddy. Drove him wild.

His lungs locked; suddenly, he could think of nothing beyond the moment of having her, the incredible sensation of sinking into her willing body and feeling her clamp, hot and wet, about him.

He wanted—that, her—with a simple, uncomplicated, ravenous hunger utterly unlike his characteristic elan and all the more powerful for that.

Powerful enough to send his hands skating over her, eager to possess. To repossess, to have again. Devastating enough for his lips to devour hers, to claim her mouth in a primitive prelude. Gripping her waist, he lifted her to sit on the desk, pushing back her skirts, pressing her knees apart.

Gentleness had flown; neither he nor she minded.

Quite the opposite.

One hand was beneath her skirts, frothed up between them, fingers sliding, sinking, over and over, repetitively probing the slick heat of her sheath, all to her urgent murmurs, to the thunder in their veins, when the door latch clicked.

Unsurpassed instincts, lightning-fast reflexes had saved him in the past.

By the time the door swung open, he was concealed behind a Chinese screen that stood five feet from the desk. Slumped against the bookshelves, his chest heaving, his pulse pounding in his ears—Amanda clutched against him, one hand clamped over her lips to stifle her indignant protest. One with which he fervently agreed.

From beyond the screen came silence, then: "This *is* the library."

They both recognized the voice, both held their breath.

Footsteps entered the room. After a moment, Lady Jersey inquired, somewhat disgruntled, "Now what?"

Above his hand, Amanda's eyes were huge. She tugged his hand from her face, mouthed, "Who?"

Martin shook his head slightly. Wondered how long they could stand as they were without making the slightest sound. The faintest rustle.

Who the devil was Sally Jersey, the ton's greatest gossip, talking to? And why were they here? More important, when would they leave?

Heels tapped as Sally wandered the room; luckily, she'd headed for the fireplace.

Then a firm footstep sounded in the corridor; an instant later, someone else paused on the threshold.

"Sally? What are you doing here, all by yourself?"

Amanda stiffened. It was Devil's drawl.

"Truth to tell, St. Ives, I really don't know." They heard the crackle of paper. "I received a note asking me to come here—well, to the library. There isn't another in this house, is there?"

"Not that I know of."

"How strange."

"Are you planning to wait, or can I escort you back to the ballroom?"

"You may give me your arm—and the next dance, too, come to that."

Devil chuckled. "If you wish."

An instant later, the door closed—and they were, once more, alone.

"Great heavens!" Amanda wriggled.

Martin winced, and set her back on her feet.

"That was . . ." She blinked at the desk, remembered all that had happened, and what, just, had not. She blushed. "A very near-run thing."

Tight-lipped, she shook out her skirts, rearranging them, the action and her expression stating louder than words that the interlude was over.

Martin dragged in a huge breath, exhaled through his teeth.

When she threw him a suspicious glance, he offered his arm. "We'd better return to the ballroom."

"Heaven knows what would have happened if Silence hadn't walked in!" Amanda halted, frowned. "No—that's not true. I *do* know what would have happened, and it would have worked more to his advantage than mine."

Eschewing her pacing, she climbed onto her bed where Amelia lay listening. "Being alone with him is too dangerous."

"Dangerous?" Amelia looked concerned.

Amanda bit her lip, then went on, "I thought if we loved more, it would prove my point, because *when* we love, the fact he truly loves me is so patently obvious I don't see how he can continue to ignore it! But . . ."

She grimaced and looked down at her stomach, smoothed

her gown over the curve. "If we do, I risk falling pregnant." She frowned at the slight bulge. "Who knows? I might already be carrying his child."

She heard the wistfulness in her voice, wasn't surprised when Amelia softly asked, "Don't you want to have his child?"

"Yes. More than anything." A simple truth; she dragged in a huge breath. "But I don't want him marrying me because of it, and that's how he'll make it seem!"

She thumped the bed, then fell back and stared up at the canopy.

Amelia grimaced. After a moment, she asked, "Does what 'seems' truly matter when weighed against what 'is'?"

That, indeed, was the question. Amanda faced it squarely, yet couldn't formulate a clear answer. Until she did, she decided to play safe—to talk, but not to kiss. To encourage, yes, but to draw a clear line over which she would not be tempted. Again. Not until . . .

"Miss Cynster?"

She turned; a footman bowed and proffered a salver on which lay a note. She took it; stepping away from the chaise on which her mother and aunts sat, she unfolded the note.

> *If you come to the ballroom terrace now, I believe you will be intrigued with what you will discover.*

The note was unsigned. And it wasn't from Martin. His scrawl was bold and lazy; this writing was cramped, each letter squeezed by a tight fist.

It was early and the ballroom was half empty, yet there were sufficient people about should she need to call for assistance. Refolding the note, she stuffed it into her reticule, excused herself to her mother and aunts and glided across the room.

The doors to the terrace were closed; she peered through, but could see no one. Opening one door, she stepped outside, clutching her shawl as the brisk breeze tugged.

She couldn't leave the door open, not with the curtains

billowing. Looking around, she saw only empty flags, but the terrace was a wide one, bordered by thick bushes that cast dense shadows. Reluctantly, she pulled the door shut. Wrapping her shawl about her, she strolled along, going only as far as the ballroom windows, keeping within the light they shed.

No sound reached her ears bar the sibilant hiss of the wind.

Turning, she retraced her steps, eventually reaching the other end of the ballroom. Increasingly cold, she frowned, then, muttering a curse, swung away—

"Miss Cynster . . . Miss Amanda Cynster . . ."

She halted, peered into the dense shadows of what she now saw was the entrance to a shrubbery. The disembodied voice called again.

"Come to me, my dear, and in the moonlight, we'll—"

"Show yourself!" Scowling, she tried to define just which of her acquaintances it was. She recognized the cadence, but the voice was disguised, syrupy and girlish. Yet it was definitely a man. "Who are you? Only a knave would behave in this manner."

"Which manner is that?"

Amanda whirled; relief flooded her as Martin stepped through the ballroom door, tugging it shut. Distant rustling, then retreating footsteps reached them. Martin came toward her, a frown in his eyes. He scanned the terrace; his gaze settled on her face. "Who were you talking to?"

"I don't know!" She gestured to the shrubbery. "Some fool was in there, trying to lure me to join him."

"He was?"

It was his tone that alerted her, irritated her. She jerked her head up, saw him staring menacingly at the shrubbery. Narrowed her own eyes. "Yes. He was. But he didn't succeed, and he wouldn't have, either!"

Swinging around, she headed for the ballroom.

Martin was at her back in two paces. "Why did you come out here?"

"Because he—whoever he is—sent me a note."

"Let me see it."

She halted; he ran into her, steadied her. She hunted in her reticule and dragged out the crumpled note. "There! See— I'm not inventing him."

He studied the note, then, frowning, slipped it into his coat pocket.

Amanda hummed in her throat, then made for the door. She didn't care about the note or its author.

"You shouldn't have come out here alone, not in response to an anonymous note."

She halted before the door; Martin reached around her and opened it. Catching the door's edge, she whirled and, narrow-eyed, looked into his face. "It was *my* note, *my* decision, and I was perfectly safe. Now, if you'll excuse me, I'm going to go in and dance. With whomever I choose!"

She flung the door open and swept through.

She wasn't going to stand for it—allow him to act the possessive male—not unless she'd agreed to be his. And she hadn't. Yet.

The first dance was a country dance; she bullied Reggie into partnering her. Later, they joined a group of young ladies, chattering animatedly; when the introduction to a cotillion filled the room, Demon tapped her on the shoulder.

"Come and dance."

She was suspicious, but there was not the faintest hint of a scowl or any overprotective reaction in his manner. Flick was expecting their third child and wasn't dancing; sitting beside Honoria on a chaise nearby, she smiled and waved, encouraged her to dance with her handsome husband.

So she danced the cotillion with Demon, and had no reason to complain. The next dance, a country dance, followed hard on its heels, and she found Richard soliciting her hand with a smile.

"I have to dance with you once this Season, before we leave."

"You're returning to Scotland?" She let him lead her into the nearest set.

"Catriona doesn't feel comfortable leaving the Vale, and the twins, to their own devices for long."

He said it with a smile, one she returned. Of all her cousins, Richard was the most . . . not gentle, but understanding. And Catriona was a font of feminine wisdom; Amanda made a comment about speaking with her before they left.

"You'd better speak with her tonight, then, for we leave tomorrow morning."

At the end of the dance, she would have gone with Richard, but others gathered about and she stopped to chat. Then she heard the first strains of the waltz.

She turned and found Martin beside her. He raised a brow. "My dance, I believe."

There was a wealth of warning in the deep words, no drawl to soften them. Inclining her head, she gave him her hand, regally let him lead her to the floor. Let him draw her into his arms and start them twirling.

The orchids that continued to be delivered every day—a spray of three pure white blooms—rested on his shoulder, all but glowed against the black of his coat. She considered them, then lifted her gaze to his face.

To his eyes, green as ever but turbulent, harder—more agate than moss.

"I am *not* yours."

His gaze only grew harder. "*That* is a matter of opinion."

"Regardless, even were we wed . . ." She let her gaze drift over those about them, then looked again at his face. "I would always insist on being my own person."

"I wasn't aware the designations were mutually exclusive." He bit the words off, clipped and hard.

She opened her eyes wide. "You mean I could be yours and still act independently? That, for instance, matters such as how to deal with anonymous notes addressed to me would be mine to decide? That you wouldn't simply interfere as your right?"

"It's my right to keep you safe."

She glared. "If I agreed to be yours, possibly."

"There's no 'possibly' about it."

"I do not accept that such a 'right' extends to shielding me from harm as if I were an incapable lackwit."

"The very last thing I consider you is lacking in wit."

Their aggravated gazes locked, then the end of the room arrived; they both looked away as they negotiated the tight turns. Realized they'd been arguing in the middle of a dance floor, and there were interested eyes aplenty. Then they were sweeping back up the long room.

"This is getting us nowhere." Martin's jaw was set; he briefly met her eyes. "Neither this discussion, nor your latest tack."

Her latest tack? "What do you mean?"

The muscles in his jaw tightened. "I mean that you're going to have to exercise your independence and make a decision—soon." He caught her gaze. "You know what I'm offering—I've laid my cards on the table."

She understood—read in his eyes exactly what he meant, that he'd declared his hand, offered all he would, and there was no more to be gained, no more that he would risk in this game.

"It's your call, your lead." His expression, his eyes, were granite hard.

She didn't answer, looked away, let the revolutions of the dance sweep them along, then the measure ended with a flourish. She curtsied, he bowed, and raised her.

She met his eyes. Let him see her resolution, as set in stone as his. "You've forgotten. I have another option."

He frowned. Smiling lightly, she half turned. "I could resign the hand." Her eyes on his, she stated clearly, deliberately, "I could throw my cards on the table, and walk away."

On the words, she turned and walked to the chaise where her Aunt Helena sat, along with Lady Osbaldestone and Honoria, Devil's duchess.

"Well!" Her ladyship shifted her bombazine-covered bulk sideways to create space for Amanda to sit. "What was that about?" She chuckled evilly and gestured with her cane at Martin's departing back. "If looks could kill . . . I take it he isn't getting his way."

"No. He isn't." Amanda struggled to shackle her temper.

"But he's pigheaded, and arrogant, and determined to win—"

Helena laughed and placed her hand over Amanda's, gripped comfortingly. "He's a male, one of our kind—you can expect no less."

"I'll vouch for that." From beyond Helena, Honoria smiled at Amanda. "If it's any consolation, you could try reminding yourself that Dexter's a mere earl. I had to cope with a duke—one who, for good reason, goes by the name of Devil."

Amanda had to smile. "But you eventually persuaded him to see the light."

Honoria raised her brows. "Truth to tell, I think he'd seen it from the first, but . . ." After a moment, she said, "You might be wise to decide just what form capitulation should take. There are other signs, other forms of communication that ultimately are more telling than words."

"Yes." Lady Osbaldestone nodded sagely. "You'd be well advised to consider that fact. However"—she transfixed Amanda with her sharp black gaze—"remember what I said. No matter what he says, no matter what he does, *you* must not weaken. He has to be brought to reopen old wounds and deal with that old scandal."

Amanda glanced at Helena, at Honoria, and saw them both nodding. Her temper had ebbed, the strength behind her resolution had gone with it. Looking across the ballroom, she saw Martin standing with Luc Ashford. She grimaced, inwardly sighed. "I'll try."

She was no longer so sure she would succeed.

His temper—an emotion he usually, with little effort, kept well reined—all but frizzlingly under his skin—Martin stalked from the dance floor. How much longer he could play the role of sophisticated, civilized male while she tweaked his baser instincts at every turn, he didn't know.

Not much longer was his guess.

At the side of the ballroom, he saw Luc and Edward Ashford standing with two of their sisters. His cousins. The girls saw him and beamed, then took in his expression; their smiles faltered.

Wiping the harsh expression from his face and eyes, he smiled back, and their smiles returned. Changing tack, he joined them. Let them curtsy and chatter at him for a few minutes; they were sweet and very young, and he was the head of a closely related house.

Two young gentlemen, the girls' partners for the next dance, approached with care. While Martin engaged the girls and their would-be consorts, Luc stood beside him, tossing barbed comments at the youthful sprigs, yet he was always ready with an encouraging word for his sisters. They clearly adored him.

Edward, however, stood back, features pinched in what appeared to be disapproval. It took Martin a moment to realize that it was *he* Edward most disapproved of.

Then the musicians struck up, and the girls and their cavaliers left for the dance floor. Martin turned to Edward.

Before he could speak, Edward asked, "I understand you have an interest in Amanda Cynster."

Edward had clearly not yet heard of his formal offer. Martin inclined his head. "I do have to marry."

"Ah, yes." Edward's lip all but curled. "The title, the estate."

Those had been the reasons Martin had been spared a trial; he again inclined his head. "As you say."

Edward tugged down his waistcoat; head high, he surveyed the crowd. "You should know that I, at least, have been upholding *our* family's name in the years you've been absent. I flatter myself that all know me as a man of unimpeachable honor and steadfast character. In due course, I will marry well, once I've seen my sisters suitably joined as befits the family."

As if suddenly remembering he was in the presence of both the head of his family and the head of a senior line, he flushed, threw a narrow-eyed glance at Luc, then stiffly nodded to Martin. "Now my watch over my sisters has ended, I believe I will circulate."

The implied message was: he did not wish to be seen with Martin, to give Martin the imprimatur of his presence.

Martin said nothing, merely watched him go, then glanced at Luc.

Who met his gaze. "No, he hasn't improved with the years."

"Obviously. Weren't you tempted to thrash it out of him?"

"Frequently. But he's such a bore, I couldn't stand the whining."

Martin caught a flash of gold—Amanda's curls as she rose from the chaise and took her leave of its occupants. He tensed, aware of a need to follow her, watch over her at the very least.

Luc had tracked his gaze; he murmured, "If you do have your eye on Amanda, I can only wish you luck."

Martin glanced at him, raised a brow.

"She's a harridan," Luc supplied. "And the very opposite of biddable." He paused, then added, his tone softer, "Come to that, they both are."

Martin asked, "She and her sister?"

"Hmm." Luc was absently searching the crowd. "God only knows why any sane man would want to saddle himself with either."

Chapter 16

The arrival of three white orchids every morning had become a regular feature in her life. When they didn't appear the next day, Amanda felt it like a blow. Yet, after their discussion the previous night, shouldn't she have expected something of the sort? He'd told her it was her call, up to her to accept or reject what he offered. The halting of the orchids presumably meant he'd stopped arguing, stopped trying to seduce her.

Then again, perhaps he'd run out of orchids.

Through the long day filled with social engagements—a morning tea, a luncheon, a drive in the park, an at-home—she vacillated between the two explanations. Her mood swung like a pendulum, even-tempered one moment, deadeningly depressed the next.

When she arrived at Lady Arbuthnot's ball and Martin failed to appear, she plastered on a bright smile while her heart sank to her slippers.

Then she got the note. A footman delivered it—an ivory square inscribed in Martin's strong hand.

Look on the terrace.

That was all it said.

Tucking the note into her pocket, she excused herself

from the group with whom she'd been conversing and crossed the crowded ballroom. That took time; when she finally gained the long windows giving onto the terrace, the room behind her was full. The night was mild; the terrace doors stood ajar, but no one was presently availing himself of the moonlight.

The moonlight that glowed on the petals of a white flower lying at the top of the steps leading to the gardens. Amanda picked up the blossom, a single white orchid. If he was adhering to his usual practice, there should be two more. She looked but could see no other white splashes on the terrace. Then she looked down the steps, wondered . . .

She glanced back at the ballroom, then quickly descended. The gravel path bordering the lawn led away to left and right. Glancing left, she saw the second bloom lying in a shaft of moonlight at the intersection of two paths.

Her slippers scrunched on the gravel, then she added the second bloom to the first, and looked around for the third. The path leading further away from the house lay empty and dark, but the path following a hedge angling around the side of the house . . . along that gleamed another splash of white.

The third orchid lay just before an archway in the hedge, the opening to a courtyard. Adding that bloom to the others, Amanda stepped into the archway; pausing, she looked around.

It was a magical scene. The courtyard was filled with box-hedged beds of summer plants and roses, weeping cherries and iris, separated by paved paths all ultimately converging on a semicircular area before the steps of a white summerhouse. The summerhouse acted as a gatehouse linking the courtyard with the shrubbery beyond. It was set into and through the first high hedge of the shrubbery which formed the back wall of the courtyard.

Moonlight shimmered on the summerhouse, the only white object in a sea of black-greens and faded red paving. From where she stood, she couldn't see if there was anyone inside; the shadows within were impenetrable.

Drawing in a breath, grateful for the mild evening that made it possible to wander outside without a shawl, she lifted her head and walked boldly forward. The three orchids bobbed in her hand.

He was there, waiting for her, a denser shadow in the dark, lounging on one of the wide benches that lined the interior walls, interrupted by the twin arches, one looking out on the courtyard, the other into the shrubbery.

She halted at the bottom of the four steps leading up; he rose, but then remained, silent and still in the night.

A predator—that her senses acknowledged, yet they leapt in giddy delight. He said nothing; neither did she. For a long moment, she stood looking up at him—she in the moonlight, he in deep shadow. Then, gathering her skirts, she went up the steps.

To him.

He took her hands, removed the orchids from her fingers, laid them aside. He turned to her, studied her face in the dimness, then reached for her. Drew her into his arms, slowly. Bent his head—gave her plenty of time to draw away if she would.

She lifted her face, invited the kiss, sensed the growl of satisfaction that rumbled through him as he covered her lips with his. Took her mouth as she gave it, pressed on her the promise of joy in return.

I want you.

Whether the words whispered in her head or fell from his lips, she couldn't tell. She flexed her fingers against his chest, then eased her hands up until she could twine her arms about his neck and arch against him. Glory in the shift and lock of his arms about her, hands spreading on her back, across her hips, holding her to him while their mouths feasted, eager and greedy for the taste they'd come to crave, for the passion, the heady rush of desire so potent they reeled. They let it well and flood through them, let it sweep them away on its well-remembered tide.

The kiss ended only when they were both gasping, burning with need, with one simple desire. Without thought, without deliberation, they fell on the padded cushions in a tangle of clothes, a tangle of hands grasping, wanting, a tangle of limbs, some hard and hot, others soft and yielding.

Their clothing was an obstacle; fingers flying, they fought to overcome it. Then her bodice was open and his lips were on her breast.

She cried out, rocked by the sheer intensity of sensation, by the streak of sensual lightning that forked from her breast to her loins. She panted, gasped, tried to stifle her reaction.

"Ssshh," he warned.

She hauled in a breath, managed to whisper, "Here?"

For answer, he shifted his lips, his hot mouth to her other breast; under her skirts, she felt his hands slide up her thighs.

"How?" She'd intended the word to be horrified, to illustrate the impossibility. Instead, it hovered in the air, a flagrant evocation, an acknowledgement of her need as her eyes closed tight, as his wicked fingers found her. Stroked, opened, pressed in.

"Easy." She could hear the satisfaction, the anticipation in his gravelly growl. "You on top."

It sounded intriguing. She knew he knew what he was doing. She reached for him; her questing fingers found and traced the rampant ridge of his erection, then she stroked, fondled . . . he tensed, then cursed and swung back to sprawl on the cushions, his shoulders against the summerhouse's sill, simultaneously pulling her over him so she ended astride him, her knees on either side of his hips, her hands braced on his shoulders.

His fingers pressed deep and she gasped. His other hand gripping one globe of her bottom, he urged her forward so he could continue torturing her swollen breasts.

With wicked lips, wicked tongue—and even wickeder fingers—he seized and captured her senses, blocked out every other reality but the heat that beat in their blood, the urgent need to join, to be whole.

The hot tide welled, rose higher, higher; his hand, his fingers, rhythmically stoked it, ruthlessly drove her on. She gasped, writhed, panted, until she was sure she would melt with the next deliberate penetration, explode with the next excruciating tug at her nipple. Her breasts burned; her skin felt too tight. The flames inside raged, leaving her hot and wet and empty.

Aching. For him.

"Now—*please*." She barely recognized her own voice, but he heard. His hand left her; she felt him wrestling with his waistband.

Then she felt the hot velvet skin, the heavy weight of his erection beneath her; she reached under her skirts, found him, stroked. Closed her hand about him as he groaned. Then he pushed her hand away—gripped her hips and guided her—

"Oh! Isn't it *beautiful!*"

"Utterly magical!"

"That gentleman was right. It's a jolly place, isn't it?"

"And with *such* a pretty summerhouse."

It was just as well she didn't have breath left to groan—to rant, to order the gaggle of young ladies piling into the courtyard back to the ballroom where they belonged. They started up the path, then stopped to admire the flowers.

Martin was rigid beneath her. She looked down, helpless.

Even in the dim light, she could make out his grim expression. "Ssshh."

The whisper barely reached her, then he closed his hands about her waist and lifted her, set her on her feet, grabbed her hand as he stood—and dragged her out of the summerhouse, down the steps into the shrubbery.

"Ooooh! *Look!*"

Martin yanked her sideways, out of the archway; she landed against him as he paused, his back to the hedge. Shrill giggles followed them.

"I say! Who was it? Did you see?"

Luckily, they'd moved so fast, no one had seen enough to recognize—they would have been no more than two silhouettes briefly glimpsed in the frame of the summerhouse, protected by the darkness within, and the shadows of the shrubbery beyond.

Martin looked around, fiddling with the buttons at his waist, then he tugged her hand. "Come on—we're not out of the woods yet."

"I'm nearly out of my gown!" she hissed, struggling to hold the bodice closed with one hand.

He glanced back at her, but continued towing her behind

him. He stopped when they gained the privacy of a more distant hedge—spun her around, backed her into it, bent his head and found her lips, raised his hands and filled them with her breasts.

The heat was still there, simmering, more potent for the wait, like a volcano dammed, pressure building to break free—

"Is it this way, do you think?"

Martin drew his lips from hers, cursed viciously. The sound of feet on the gravel at the end of the path reached them.

Affected them both like a dash of cold water, effectively dousing their fire. Their eyes met; she let her gaze drop to his lips.

He looked at hers, drew a shuddering breath, his chest crushing her breasts, then he straightened, stepped back. Steadied her. Then reached for her bodice, deftly closing it.

"I want you." His hands dropped to his waistband, fully securing the buttons as she quickly tied her side laces. "But not like this. I want you in my house, in my bed. I want you *mine.*"

She met his dark gaze, sensed the frustration in his words, the longing, the yearning—the need. Felt uncertainty well, undermine her resolution . . . then she heard Lady Osbaldestone's voice in her head. Dragging in a breath, she lifted her chin, held his gaze. "How much do you want me?"

Martin didn't answer. The group approaching along the path, searching for some pond, cut short the moment—saved him from saying something he would later regret.

Amanda's hand on his sleeve, they headed back to the house, exchanging nods with the group as they passed. He frowned; he hoped her years would preserve her from any whispers. At least they hadn't been discovered . . .

That would have made life even more complicated than it already was. His understanding with the Bar Cynster would stretch only so far; they fully expected him to use his polished wiles to convince her to accept his suit. They likewise expected him to avoid any scandal.

Seducing a Cynster female, persuading her to yield and accept his offer without the surrender she was determined to wring from him, under the full glare of the ton's chandeliers, all without raising the slightest ripple of scandal . . . it was the definition of challenge.

One part of him relished the game; another part wished it was all over and she was his, declared and accepted as, in truth, he was hers.

As they went up the terrace steps, he glanced at her face. Her chin was high, her jaw stubbornly set in an expression that had fast become familiar. Yet beneath that facade, he sensed a more fragile, wistful state. Perhaps, with just a little more persuasion . . .

He stopped her before the door; fingers twining with hers, he raised her hand and pressed a kiss to her knuckles, his eyes steady on hers. "It's your decision."

She held his gaze, searched his eyes, then turned and entered the ballroom.

They remained together through supper and the last waltz, then Martin very correctly took his leave. Amanda watched him climb the ballroom stairs, watched his broad shoulders and burnished head disappear through the ballroom arch.

She wished she was leaving with him. Wished she dared.

Wished in her heart that she could simply give him what he wanted and end this emotional game. Knowing he loved her was important, yet she already knew he did. Was knowing he knew really so vital?

According to Lady Osbaldestone and all her wise mentors, with him, it was. She understood the reasons they'd advanced and accepted them, yet she was starting to suspect there might be even more to it than that. Some reason Lady Osbaldestone, old and shrewd, knew but wouldn't say. No point trying to wheedle it from her; if she hadn't said, she wouldn't, and the Coldstream Guards wouldn't shift her.

The notion that there was more idled through her mind as she waited for Louise and Amelia to make their adieus. Her absentminded gaze drifted around the room, then halted on Edward Ashford. He was waiting, rigidly correct, features

pinched with supercilious disdain while his sisters exchanged directions with two other young ladies clearly up
from the country.

As she approached, smiling easily, Amanda cast about for
some opening gambit to swing the conversation in the direction she wished.

Edward greeted her with a curt nod and a frown. "I'm
glad to have the chance to drop a warning in your ear."

"A warning?" She opened her eyes encouragingly.

"About Dexter." Facing the emptying ballroom, Edward
raised his quizzing glass and affectedly peered through it.
"Distasteful as it is to speak so of a connection, Dexter is a
thoroughly untrustworthy individual." Lowering his glass,
Edward looked her in the eye. "He killed a man, you know.
Pushed him over a cliff, then beat him to death with a rock.
An old fellow unable to defend himself. Dexter has a temper
and his reputation's scandalous. Indeed, I'm surprised your
family haven't taken steps to end his squiring of you—now
the Season's at its peak and your cousins and uncles are
about, no doubt they'll see and step in."

Amanda wondered what Martin had ever done to deserve
such a worm as Edward for cousin. "Edward, St. Ives has
given his formal permission for Martin to address me."

Edward's face blanked; the hand holding the quizzing
glass fell. "*Formal* permission. You mean . . ."

Amanda smiled tightly. "I mean exactly what I said. Good
evening, Edward." With a cool nod, she left him, rather
proud her temper—her instinct to protect Martin—had not
got the better of her.

Luc was strolling toward his sisters and Edward; doubtless, he'd quit the ball after the second dance and was only
now returning. Impulse prompted her to place herself in his
path. He stopped, looked down at her. Raised a weary
brow.

Brazen—determined—she locked her eyes on his. "Dexter has asked for and received permission to address me."

"So I'd supposed."

"What's your opinion of his suit?"

Luc considered her for so long she started to suspect he might be drunk, then he raised both brows. "My opinion, for what it's worth, is that he's insane. I've told him as much."

"Insane?" Amanda stared. "Why?"

Again Luc considered, his dark blue gaze unnervingly steady, then he lowered his voice. "I know about Mellors and Helen Hennessy's. I know Martin hauled you out of danger not once but on numerous occasions. He's come into the ton, an arena he doesn't like, has no reason to like—indeed, has reasons to avoid—all in pursuit of you. He's openly courted you, kept his temper on a leash and done the pretty, all as society dictates, a capitulation that must have cost him dearly. He's called on your cousin and made God knows what arrangements—all to be allowed to aspire to your dainty hand."

Luc paused, his gaze ruthlessly direct. "Tell me, what is it that makes you deserving of all that? What makes you worthy of the sacrifice? Even more to the point, what gives you the right to keep him dangling, like some minor fish you can't bring yourself to cut free?"

She refused to look away, refused to lower her eyes. "That," she quietly stated, "is between him and me."

Luc inclined his head and stepped around her. "Just as long as you know the answer."

Someone was stalking Amanda, someone other than him. Watching her, watching them. Who? And why?

Over breakfast the next morning, Martin examined those questions from every possible angle, the one topic that could distract him from the frustration simmering just beneath his skin.

While motive was unclear, the evidence was too compelling to ignore. That note that had summoned Amanda to a deserted terrace had been the start. He couldn't remember any earlier suspicious incident, but later had come the unexpected arrival of Edward and company on the Fortescues' terrace at a potentially revealing moment, then the mysterious note that had sent Sally Jersey to the Hamiltons' library, and last night, the arrival of a bevy of young ladies intent on exploring the summerhouse at precisely the worst moment.

The young ladies had been sent by "that gentleman"—Martin remembered the comment.

Some gentleman was trying to bring Amanda undone.

A good scandal would do it, or so someone not in the know would reason. Those of their circle, aware of the caliber of those involved, aware that he'd formally sought permission to address her, would know better; in reality, a scandal involving her and him, while irritating everyone, would only see them married that much sooner.

Indeed, a potential scandal that did not become public—such as her falling pregnant—was still a wild card he might yet be dealt.

So . . . whoever the gentleman was, he had reason to wish Amanda ill, and wasn't well connected with their circle.

The earl of Connor was the only name he had on his list.

An afternoon call on the earl reduced his list to zero. Connor was genuinely gratified to be suspected, but his explanation of his earlier, benignly avuncular interest in Amanda's welfare rang too true to be doubted. He gave his word he harbored no ill-will toward her, and then seized the opportunity to lecture Martin against the evil fate of waiting too long to take a wife and raise a family, of becoming an old man with no real reason for existence.

Connor's parting shot of "Don't risk it" rang in Martin's ears as he returned to his house, his library, to once more ponder what exactly was going on. And who was behind it.

"If not Connor, then who?" Amanda glanced back as Martin followed her into her Aunt Horatia's conservatory. He shut the door, long fingers snibbing the lock apparently absent-mindedly; the sounds of the major ball in progress beyond the doors subsided.

A long-forgotten memory flashed across Amanda's mind—of the time she'd dragged Vane in here to ask him about some gentleman's suggestion. When they'd emerged, they'd surprised Patience at the door; from her expression, she'd been about to fling it open and storm in. Vane had smiled—untrustworthily—and invited Patience inside to admire his mother's palm-filled oasis. As she'd walked off, she remembered hearing the door lock snib.

She could still recall the dreamy expression on Patience's face when she and Vane had emerged, considerably later.

Shaking aside the memory, she refocused on the discussion in progress. "There's no one else who I've crossed."

"Before you appeared at Mellors, or even later, you didn't encourage any gentleman?"

"I never encouraged, not in the way you mean." She glanced up as he took her hand. "That wasn't my aim."

He raised his brows. Met her gaze.

The conservatory was illuminated only by weak moonlight drifting past the fronds of various exotic palms; he couldn't see her blush. "I can't think of any gentleman who would wish me ill, certainly not to the point of . . ."

When she said nothing more, Martin prompted, "Who?"

His tone left her no option but to admit, "Luc." She met Martin's gaze. "He doesn't approve of me, let alone, as he put it, me leaving you dangling."

"He spoke for me?"

"Most effectively." Amanda wiggled her shoulders. "He's always had a nasty tongue."

Martin suppressed a smile. "Never mind—it won't be him. Aside from anything else, it has to be someone who doesn't know the ropes, and Luc knows every last one."

"Indubitably," she agreed. "And it wouldn't be him, anyway—it's not his style."

Martin glanced at her face as she walked along the path just ahead of him. He couldn't see her features, yet her tone had suggested she was no longer so sure of the wisdom of "keeping him dangling." If Luc's strait words had caused her to rethink her position, he was in his cousin's debt.

Apropos of that, it was clearly time for more persuasion. And this time, they wouldn't be interrupted; he'd taken steps to ensure their privacy, to give him time to reestablish the sensual connection between them, and urge her to yield, tonight and forever.

Vane had suggested his mother's conservatory; as he glanced about assessingly, Martin approved. The air was warm, slightly humid; the light was dim but not gloomy. They came to a clearing where a fountain stood, a statue of a woman in roman halfdress endlessly pouring water from an urn. The fountain stood on a raised dais; Martin considered the possibilities, yet . . . fingers about her elbow, he guided Amanda, still sunk in thought, on.

The path wended down the long room; it ended in another clearing, an isolated and enclosed half-circle containing exactly what he sought.

Chapter 17

"A swing!" Amanda stopped before a padded bench, two people wide, suspended from a cast-iron stand set in the midst of a jungle of ferns and palms. "What a lovely idea. It must be new."

"We could christen it." Martin halted beside her.

She turned to sit.

"No." Fingers firming about her elbow he stopped her. He was waiting when she lifted her eyes to his. "Not like that."

His tone alerted her; her gaze lowered to his lips, then rose again to his eyes. "The ball—my cousins. What if we're interrupted? Again." *By them.*

"We won't be. I can assure you your cousins won't be pounding on the door—they're otherwise occupied. The moment's ours to do with as we please." He made the last phrase a challenge, a dare.

She moistened her lips. "How, then?"

He drew her to him and she came, slightly aloof, as if reserving judgment on his expertise. A subtle taunt, an encouragement to impress. Suppressing a smile of anticipation, he lowered his head and covered her lips.

Kissed her until she'd forgotten all notion of aloofness, until she clung, her lips to his, her arms about his shoulders, her hands sunk in his hair.

"We'll need to remove your dress—it'll get too crushed."

He murmured the words against her lips, then took her mouth again, dragged her willing senses down into the heat of the kiss.

Into the fire and flames that so steadily burned between them. In all his experience, exotic and otherwise, it had never been like this—never been such a simple, easy, rapid descent into ravenous desire. Into that primitive place where the need to possess ruled absolutely. With her, it had never been any other way, which was how he'd known, from the first. Known that, ultimately, he would sell his very soul for her, if that's what was asked.

With her in his arms, he didn't care; with her body arching, flagrantly demanding against his, he knew only the need to appease her, to feed and satisfy her hungry senses and, thus, his.

As he tugged her laces free, he knew exactly what he wanted to see, needed to see, from her that night. What he wanted, needed—had to have. They were both breathing rapidly, both dark-eyed, tense with expectation.

"Lift your arms."

He drew the gown off over her head, leaving her curls and the three orchids she'd tonight chosen to wear in her hair bobbing. His gaze locked on her body, concealed only by a diaphanous silk chemise; blindly, he tossed the gown over a nearby palm. And reached for her.

She came eagerly this time, all pretence at aloofness gone, desire for him in its place, shining in her eyes, in the lips she lifted to his.

He closed his hands about her waist, revelled in the supple firmness of her svelte form, then let his hands slide and gathered her to him. Molded her against him so she could feel his desire, rocked her hips against the iron length of his erection. She all but melted in his arms, her body softening, enticing.

Amanda kissed him back, and set aside all reservations. She wanted him; he wanted her—for this precise moment, that was enough. She needed to be with him again, close, intimate, so their hearts beat together and their souls touched, just for that fleeting instant.

She needed to feel it again, experience it again, before she could make up her mind. Before she could decide to surrender, to give herself to him unconditionally, without stipulations. She was beginning to think it might be the only way, for him, for them, that his surrender could only be won with hers. A risk, one she felt compelled to take.

His hands, roving over her, set her skin afire, then slid lower; he flipped up the hem of her chemise, then his palms were on bare skin, fondling, kneading her bottom, then gripping. Long fingers slid down and inward to stroke, caress, then he opened her, tested, pressed in.

Drank her gasp through their kiss, gave her breath as he stroked and probed. Then he drew back from the kiss, drew his hands from her. One remained on her hip, steadying her, the other slipped between them; she felt him fiddling at his waist, looked down, slid her hands down his chest. Brushing his hands away, she dealt with the closures and opened the flap of his trousers; her lips curved as she laid him bare.

Filled her hand with his length and heard the raspy breath he sucked in, felt him tense. Felt him wait as she decided just what she would do, then she closed her hand lovingly. Marveling anew at the contrast of silken softness enclosing such potent, patently masculine strength, she let her nails gently score upward.

She repeated the torture three times before he carefully disengaged; she didn't think he was breathing. Then he stepped back and sat on the swing, urged her to follow.

"Kneel astride."

She put one knee up, then the other, felt the damask cushion under both knees. She wrapped her arms about his neck, tilted her head and set her lips to his, then shifted closer, until her stomach met the wall of his abdomen, then she slid sensuously down. The touch of his clothes, rough against her soft skin, was a reminder of her nakedness, his relatively clothed state. Her vulnerability, his strength; her giving, his need.

He ravaged her mouth and urged her lower. His hand was beneath her, guiding her, guiding the head of his erection into the softness of her swollen flesh. She felt its touch, felt the strength as he pressed in just a little, just past the constriction. Her lungs seized and she stopped, then, slowly,

slowly—as slowly as she could—she eased fraction by fraction down, taking him in, glorying in the pressure, the fullness, the ease with which her body adjusted, then closed lovingly about him.

She didn't stop until she was fully impaled, until it felt like he was nudging her heart. Her skin was alive, heated, nerves flickering.

His tongue thrust deep into her mouth, fracturing her attention. Then she felt his thigh, beneath hers, flex.

The swing started to rock.

Sensation washed through her. Surprised, she clung, pressed nearer, then she felt his hands on her legs, urging her to wrap them around his hips.

She did, and he was even deeper inside her; the sensations intensified, driven by the swing, by the increasing momentum. The swing was well oiled, well balanced; the occasional push from Martin's foot was enough to keep them whooshing gently back and forth.

Which one of them started the dance, she wasn't sure, layering one rhythm atop another, matching an effortless thrust and withdrawl to the swing's motion. Amplifying the effect. She controlled it, using her arms to ease herself up, using her locked legs for leverage. Once she had the rhythm established, once their bodies were merging freely, deeply, in absolute harmony, his hands left her hips, moved over her skin, caressing, knowingly stroking, igniting a million small fires that slowly, gradually, coalesced to a blaze. Then to an inferno.

A vortex of heat and movement that swept them up, then sent them whizzing dizzily down, that snatched their breath, pressed pleasure and yet more pleasure upon them, through them, one to the other, then back again.

The ultimate give-and-take, the epitome of sharing.

As she clung, her lips melded with his, her mouth all his, as was her body, Martin let past and present slide, let the future free, and gave himself up to this, to her, to what he now needed beyond all else.

This was what he had wanted tonight, this complete, unreserved giving. Her legs, naked but for her sheer stockings, wrapped about his hips, his hands on her skin beneath her chemise, able to touch and savor as he chose. Her body, slick, hot, all but molten, enclosing him, clamping down as the swing descended, easing as it swung up again. Open and generous and his.

Again, and again, and again.

The powerful repetition for once beyond his control held him captive, held his senses in unparalled delight. Until they fractured.

She shattered in his arms, her cry muted by their kiss; he followed, unable to break the link that held them, that fused her pleasure with his, that made them one and the same. One whole—with one beat driving their hearts, one passion melding their souls.

One future. If he'd ever had any doubts, as the swing slowed and he caught his breath, held her tight in his arms and felt her heartbeat deep within her, the last moments had eradicated them.

The power that had flowed, briefly but so powerfully, that had so effortlessly fused them not just in this world but beyond it, was undeniable.

He had to accept it, which meant he had to find a way forward, no longer just for him, but for her, too. For them. He hadn't needed Connor's warning—he knew he couldn't risk losing her.

He dragged in a breath; his lungs were still too tight. He nuzzled the curls about her ear, struggled to speak the words he knew she wanted to hear. Couldn't get his tongue to do it.

"Marry me." Those words came a lot easier. "Soon. This game's gone on too long. We have to end it."

Sincerity rang in his voice. Amanda lifted her head from his chest, looked into his face, raised a hand to his cheek. Tried to smile but her muscles were still too lax to do it properly. Her head was reeling—impossible to think. "Yes" hovered on the tip of her tongue . . .

She wasn't sure what stopped her from saying it, from agreeing then and there to marry him regardless. In faint moonlight and shadow, his face was stripped to its essential lines, to the harshly angular planes, an honest reflection of the man he truly was without the softening effect of his gold-tipped hair and the mossy shade of his eyes. He waited, a sense of darkness still inhabiting his face, a shadow of things denied, hidden. Suppressed, but not for his good— they were the burdens of others he yet carried.

Would he accept that he needed to give them up, that he needed to revisit the old scandal, open it up for investigation regardless of what they might find? If he did, then Lady Osbaldestone's caveat was met, and she could safely agree.

"I . . ." She paused to lick her dry lips, shifted in his arms, fixed her eyes on his. "I'm not saying 'No,' but . . ." She frowned; no matter how hard she stared, she could detect no sign of compromise. "I need to think."

His expression was not one of capitulation. "How long?"

She narrowed her eyes, but he was right; they had to bring this to an end. "A day."

He nodded. "Good." And set the swing swinging again.

A shiver of delight spiralled through her. Eyes widening, she stared as his hands rose beneath her chemise to close once again about her breasts. Inside, she felt him stir, strengthen.

Then he pushed harder. His fingers closed tight about her nipples. Her lids fell. "Good God!"

"They were watching the entire time!"

"What?" Amanda glanced at Amelia. They'd parted from Louise at the top of the stairs and were heading down the corridor to their rooms.

Amelia's expression was grim. "You and Martin slipped into the conservatory. Demon immediately started hovering near the doors, as if he was just propping up the wall, looking around—you know how they do."

"So?"

"So when another couple looked as if they'd try the doors, he was there to head them off. I saw him do it. Then he went back to watching. *Then,* when Flick wanted to leave early, Demon caught Vane's eye, and Vane took over. He was there until you came out—you didn't notice because he was standing back by the wall."

They'd reached their rooms; Amanda stared at her sister,

for one of the first times in her life truly speechless. Her head was spinning. She squeezed Amelia's hand. "Change, then come in and we'll talk."

The minutes spent with her maid, climbing out of her gown for the second time that night, donning her nightgown and brushing her hair, did little to improve her state. When the maid left and Amelia popped in and scurried to jump under the covers, her wits were still whirling, as were her emotions, shifting and swirling until she felt almost ill. Worse than giddy. Both head and heart were swinging wildly; both seemed unreliable. The only certainty seemed gut instinct. Gut instinct told her to take a large step back.

"I can't fathom what's going on." She climbed into bed beside Amelia. "I know Devil gave his permission, but . . ." Anger and confusion clashed; she shook her head. "After all these years of getting in our way every time we showed the slightest sign of even smiling at some wolf, they turn around and happily hand me over to a lion!"

Amelia slanted her a glance. "Is he really that lionlike?"

"Yes!" Amanda folded her arms and glared. "If you knew what went on in the conservatory, you wouldn't ask." Amelia looked like she wanted to ask; Amanda hurried on, "I assumed they'd grudgingly agreed—instead . . ." She narrowed her eyes. "I know why. It's because he's just like *them!"*

"Well, yes. We knew our ideal gentlemen *would* be like them."

Amanda stifled a frustrated scream. "But they don't need to help him. He's quite difficult enough on his own!"

After a moment, Amelia asked, "So what's the state of your game?"

"That's just it—I don't know! Every time I try to think it through"—she rubbed a finger between her brows—"my head hurts. Horribly."

Moments passed in silence, then under the covers, Amelia found her hand and squeezed, then sat up. "I'm going back to my bed. Sleep on it—it'll all seem clearer in the morning. That's what Mama always says."

Amanda murmured a good night, then listened as Amelia slipped away. Closing her eyes, she willed herself to follow her sister's advice.

She didn't succeed until dawn. Even then, her rest was disturbed and fretful. She was distantly aware that Louise came in, took one look at her, and declared she should sleep in.

Later, her mother again materialized by her bed. Louise smiled, then sat and gently brushed the curls off her forehead. "It's not easy, is it?"

Amanda frowned. "No. I thought it would be."

Louise's smile turned wry. "It never is. But"—she stood—"it's worth persevering in the end. Now, I want you to sleep for the rest of the morning. Amelia and I will attend Lady Hatcham's morning tea, then we'll look in and see if you're well enough to come to Lady Cardigan's luncheon."

With another fond smile, Louise left; Amanda considered the door as it shut—considered how supportive her mother had been, how much closer she now felt to, not only Louise, but all her aunts, her cousins' wives. As if she'd passed through some coming of age, another rite of passage, as if in facing a hurdle all the women in her family had faced and overcome, she'd gained a deeper insight, a fuller understanding. Of a great many things.

Like life, love and family. Like what it really took to gain a woman's—any woman's—dream. Like the fact their dreams were all the same, even through the ages—different men, different circumstances, the same yearning. The same single emotion at their core.

With a sigh, she rolled onto her back and stared, unseeing, at the canopy. Contrary to Amelia's hopes, matters did not appear any clearer, but at least she no longer felt quite so overwhelmed.

The central question still remained. Assuming Martin loved her, did he know it? If he did, did she need to hear him state it, out aloud in words, or would other forms of communication do?

But what if she got it wrong—accepted him without any

verbal declaration, and later learned he didn't accept that he loved her at all? Would he still feel compelled to clear his name of the old scandal? Or, despite the assurance she felt certain he must have given Devil to secure permission to address her, would he, once she was his, bend the rules and, for instance, acknowledge the scandal openly and retire from public life himself, leaving her and their children to provide the family's social facade?

If he went that road, there was in reality little the Cynsters could do, other than put a good face on it.

That last had to be the reason Lady Osbaldestone was adamant she settle for nothing less than a solid acknowledgment, in words or otherwise, a lever to ensure he would reopen the matter and clear his name. If he loved her and had admitted it, she could insist he did. Yet if he loved her, but didn't know it, refused to acknowledge it, she would have little power to sway him.

Amelia had asked if an acknowledgment truly mattered. Reassessing all she now knew of Dexter and Martin, earl and man, Amanda thought it might. Not just for Lady Osbaldestone's stated reason, but also for that more nebulous, worrisome concern she'd detected behind her ladyship's black eyes.

That amorphous worry was the most irksome, hard-to-get-to-grips-with feeling, but she now felt it, too. Not in her head, not in her heart, but in her stomach. Her head told her that as long as the scandal was resolved, all would be well. Her heart assured her that he loved her, regardless of what he thought. Her gut told her to beware, that there was some other, deeper wound she couldn't see, something hidden that she—they—needed resolved . . .

"Aaarrgh!" Flinging her hands in the air, she sat up. This was getting her nowhere, other than into another headache. Tossing back the covers, she stood, then remembered. She'd told Martin she'd answer him in a day.

Which meant by tonight.

She sank back on the bed. Just the thought of seeing him sent her wits into a slow spin. "I can't do it." If she saw him now, she'd only get more confused. She might even say

"Yes," while all her instincts were urging her to say, "Not yet. Not until."

Wrapping a shawl about her shoulders, she started to pace. She had to think, get her arguments formulated and verbalized so she could hit him with them when he next narrowed his agatey eyes at her and pressured her to agree. As he assuredly would. Now he had her cousins' backing—after the previous night, their true views were crystal clear—there was little doubt he would pursue that tack as far as he possibly could. They'd knowingly handed him a potent weapon none knew better than they would turn her head . . .

She gritted her teeth against a frustrated scream.

Thanks to their unholy alliance, London wasn't safe for her—not until she was fully armed and knew the ground firm beneath her feet. She had to get away, somewhere she could think, free of him, free of them all, preferably with someone who would shield her, help her to see her way . . .

She halted. "How obvious." She considered a moment more, then, jaw firming, nodded. "Perfect."

Invigorated, already feeling less weighed down—almost hopeful—she crossed to the bellpull.

Martin waited and paced and waited. At four o'clock he surrendered, quit his house and strode to Upper Brook Street. His patience was at an end. Surely she wouldn't still be gadding about, or swanning around the park, not when she'd agreed to answer him today.

All day he'd berated himself for not pressing harder last night, when she'd been swept away and vulnerable. When she'd been a soft bundle of warm, sated female in his arms, and her wits had been wandering. If he'd insisted on an answer . . . he hadn't, purely because a deeply ingrained sense of chivalry had intervened, dictating that an answer gained under duress wasn't binding, and that deliberately exploiting such a scenario purely to elicit a favorable response wasn't playing fair.

Fair. He suppressed a snort. The woman had pursued him for weeks; now the shoe was on the other foot, she was tying him in knots—without even knowing. When he was with her, he simply couldn't bring himself to admit to the truth—cutting off his left arm would be easier. Why it was so . . . he knew why, but dwelling on it solved nothing. Yet when they were apart, uttering the words seemed perfectly possible, if that's what it took to make her his. A strategic decision uncomplicated by emotion.

Emotion set in the instant he set eyes on her; the effect she had on him, the emotional turmoil she evoked, was nothing short of frightening. As for what he was doing to himself . . . he'd dreamed of Connor's "evil fate"; the old man's words haunted him, as he'd no doubt intended.

But he wasn't going to lose her.

Today was the day. Once he had her decision, clearly stated between them, he—they—could go on from there. After last night, she had to know that denying she loved him wasn't an option; she did—she had from the first time she'd given herself to him, and he was far too experienced not to know it. Every time she came to him, gave herself to him, she only strengthened the bond between them.

There was no further reason for her to refuse to agree. No logical reason. Her illogical reason remained, but she wasn't an unreasonable woman. She'd been weakening last night—she'd almost said yes. Today, she would.

If her father had been home, he might have asked for advice, but Arthur was not expected back for some days yet. He'd met Louise and Amanda's aunts—he knew better than to look to them for help, especially in this. They might assist if he sued for mercy, but help him avoid Amanda's demand? Not this side of hell. Which left him very much on his own as he climbed the steps of Number 12. The butler answered the door.

"Miss Amanda Cynster." He handed the man his card.

The butler glanced at it. "I'm afraid you've missed her, my lord. But she left a message."

"Missed her?"

"Indeed. She left just after luncheon, quite unexpected." The butler held open the door; Martin stepped into the hall. "Mr. Carmarthen went with her. I'm sure I saw your name on a note here . . ." The man hunted through a stack of invitations. "Ah, yes. I knew I wasn't mistaken, although why her ladyship left it here . . ."

Martin twitched the note from the butler's fingers; *"Dexter"* was inscribed across the front. Refusing to think, to jump to conclusions, he wrestled the neatly folded corners undone, spread out the single sheet.

His eyes scanned. His mind seized.

His blood turned to ice in his veins.

My apologies. I could not give you the answer you expect. I have taken steps to place myself beyond your reach, but I will return to town as soon as I am able, and you will have your answer then.

The missive was signed with a flourishing "A."

Martin crumpled the note in his fist. For a long moment, he stared across the hall, and saw nothing. It was as if the world had stopped, and his heart with it. Then he spoke, his voice flat. "Where did she go?"

"Why to Scotland, my lord. Didn't she say . . . ?"

His jaw set. Stuffing the note in his pocket, he turned on his heel and stalked from the house.

An hour later, he was whipping his horses up the Great North Road, cursing everything and anything that got in his way. Cursing the few minutes he'd wasted writing a short note to Devil, telling him what had occurred.

Telling him he'd bring her back.

Most of all, he cursed himself. For not saying the words she'd wanted to hear, for not having the courage to admit the truth and damn the past to perdition. He'd had the perfect opportunity last night, but had jibbed and taken the easy way out. Insisted she be the one to bend, to adjust to accepting only as much as he was willing to give. He'd had the chance to open his heart to her; instead, he'd chosen to keep it shielded. Even from her. He'd shied away from the risk— they were both close to paying the price.

His curricle flew onward, weaving around slower conveyances, racing along the flats. He changed horses at Barnet and frequently thereafter, cursing the necessity of travelling without a groom. He hadn't wanted any other witness present when he caught up with her carriage. Having to deal with Carmarthen and their coachman would be bad enough.

But she and Carmarthen wouldn't be racing, they wouldn't be constantly changing horses to keep up their pace. He'd wondered about her note, then he'd realized. It had been left to be delivered later that night, once pursuit was an impossibility. Instead, he was less than five hours behind them, and his curricle was much faster than a coach.

Fate—that fickle female—had given him one last chance. If he'd been less restless, more confident of her answer, he wouldn't have gone to Upper Brook Street at the unexpected hour of four o'clock. But he had, so he had one last opportunity to give her the words she wanted—to pay the price for her "yes." One last opportunity to convince her to be his.

And not Carmarthen's.

The light slowly faded as he flicked his whip and sent the horses careening on. He could hear Connor's cynical, mocking laugh on the wind.

Amanda closed her eyes as the lights of Chesterfield faded behind them. She'd dozed for most of the journey; she wasn't sleepy, but Reggie, seated opposite, had shut his eyes the instant they'd left Derby. At least he'd stopped lecturing her.

She'd been waiting with her plan when Louise and Amelia had returned from Lady Hatcham's morning tea. Louise had listened, then agreed, but had stipulated she had to have company on the long trip to the Vale. Louise had glanced at Amelia—who had stared, silently, at Amanda. It was then Reggie was announced; he'd arrived to escort them to Lady Cardigan's luncheon.

The instant she applied to him, he'd stiffened his spine, and like the true friend he was, declared himself willing to journey north with her. He'd visited the Vale with them before and enjoyed it; he'd shot off home to pack his bag. She'd picked him up in the coach, and they'd headed out of town.

Only after Barnet had fallen behind them did it occur to Reggie to ask why, exactly, she was heading north so precipitously. Where was Dexter?

She'd explained—entirely unexpectedly, Reggie had taken Martin's part. He'd been as angry as she'd ever seen him; he'd lectured her for miles on her "unrealistic expectations," on why holding to such an intransigent line when Dexter had shown himself willing to accommodate her in so many ways was exceedingly bad form. He'd gone on and on and on.

Luc she'd expected, not Reggie.

She'd sat there stunned and let his words flow past her. There'd seemed little point trying to argue or defend herself. On this one point, it appeared there was a masculine view, one instantly espoused by each and every male, while the feminine stance was diametrically opposed.

Reggie had finally shut up when they'd reached Derby. They dined in silence at the Red Bells, then set off again. He'd taken his seat, folded his arms, glared coldly at her, then shut his eyes.

He hadn't opened them since; she'd heard a small snore.

The coach rocked along. It was a long, tiring journey to the Vale, but she'd made it many times in the years since Richard and Catriona had married. Then had come the twins, and they now had a second little daughter, Annabelle . . . her mind drifted over the happiness that stood at the heart of the Vale. What she wanted for Martin and herself had never seemed so clear.

"Hold hard!"

The shout from behind jerked her to attention, jerked Reggie from his nap. He frowned. "What the—"

The coachman hauled on the reins; the horses plunged, the coach rocked wildly, then settled. Amanda righted herself, stared, stunned, into the black night, utterly unable to believe her ears.

It couldn't be. It wasn't possible—

The carriage door flew open; a large, familiar shadow filled the gap.

"There you are!" The relief that poured through Martin

nearly brought him to his knees. Evoked, instead, a need to seize. He reached out, locked his hand about Amanda's wrist and hauled her out of the carriage, into his arms.

He stepped back as she wriggled furiously.

"Martin! What the devil are you doing? Put me down!"

He set her on her feet and scowled at her. "What am *I* doing? It wasn't *me* who ran away to Scotland!"

"I wasn't running away!"

"Indeed? Then perhaps you can explain—"

"If you don't mind"—Reggie's cool tones cut across their altercation—"the coachman and I don't need to be regaled with this. We'll drive on around the bend and wait there." He reached out for the carriage door.

Martin glanced up the road to the next bend. The curve would hide the coach from view. He looked at Reggie and nodded curtly; the other man was being remarkably understanding, but then, he'd known Amanda all her life. He pulled Amanda back from the coach. "We'll join you shortly."

"You're going to leave me here, alone with him?" Amanda's astonishment, and her rising temper, rang in her tone.

"Yes." Reggie frowned at her. "With luck, you'll come to your senses." He shut the door; reluctantly, the coachman flicked his reins and the carriage slowly rumbled on.

Amanda stared after it, then turned on Martin, eyes narrowing. With regal disdain, she looked down—to where his fingers encircled her wrist. "Kindly unhand me."

He set his jaw. "No."

She looked him in the eye . . . her eyes narrowed even further . . .

The growl that issued from his throat was entirely instinctive; glowering back at her, he eased his grip, forced his fingers from her skin.

"Thank you." She drew in a quick breath. "And now, if you please, you can explain what you think you're doing, dragging me out of my parents' coach in the middle of nowhere in the depths of the night!"

"What *I'm* doing?" He aimed a finger at her nose. "*You* were supposed to give me an answer tonight!"

"I explained! I left you a note."

He searched in his pocket. "You mean this?" He brandished the crumpled sheet in her face.

She grabbed it, smoothed it out. "Yes. As I'm sure Mama explained when she gave it to you—"

"Your mother didn't give it to me—your butler did."

"Colthorpe?" Amanda stared at him. "*Colthorpe* gave it to you? Oh." Her face blanked. "That's why you caught us—"

"This side of the border. Luckily for us all, because I would have damned well caught up with you at Gretna Green or later, and that wouldn't have been pretty."

Her eyes only got rounder. "Gretna Green?"

Her stunned look had him frowning. "God only knows why you thought tying the knot with dear Reggie was a good idea—"

"We weren't going to Gretna Green—and I would never marry Reggie. Why on earth did you think that?"

She was telling the bald truth—the fact was written all over her face.

His frown turned to a scowl. "The note—what you wrote. What else did you mean if not that?" He was starting to feel as lost as she looked.

She glanced at the note, read the few lines, then grimaced. "Mama asked me to write a note so she had something from me to give you—it was supposed to be read once she'd explained. It wasn't supposed to be a communication in itself."

Disgruntlement swept over him. "Well, what the hell was I supposed to think?" He ran his fingers through his hair, drew in a huge breath for what felt like the first time in hours. She hadn't been about to marry Reggie. He blinked, then scowled at her again. "Where the devil are you heading then, if not to Gretna Green?"

Her pert nose rose. "There *is* more to Scotland beyond Gretna Green."

"But not much is habitable. Why the devil do you need to travel all the way up there?"

She narrowed her eyes at him. "I'm going to visit Richard and Catriona. They live in the Vale of Casphairn, north of Carlisle." She swung on her heel and stalked toward his curricle.

He fell in beside her; his mind supplied a picture of an exquisite, flame-haired young matron—Richard's wife. Supplied all he'd heard of her . . . eyes narrowing to shards, he glanced at the woman walking by his side. "Catriona . . . isn't she a witch?"

She nodded. "A wise woman—a *very* wise woman."

"One who works with herbs, and other medicinal plants?"

She went to nod, then halted, looked at him. Astonished anew. Then her lips thinned. "I am not going to Catriona for any . . . herbal remedy! As if I would! *Oh!*" Hands flying as if to push him away, she turned and stalked on. Shaking her head furiously. "You are *impossible!*"

"*I'm* impossible! You haven't yet told me why—"

"All *right!*" She swung to face him, jabbed a finger into his chest. "I needed time to think *away from you!* I was trying to make the decision you wanted me to make, but . . . I needed time, and calm, and a little peace, for goodness sake!" She waved her hands, blinked rapidly. "I can't afford to make the wrong decision. And Catriona is very good at listening . . ." She turned to the curricle. "Anyway, that's where I'm going."

He handed her up to the seat, then hestitated, his head for once level with hers. Then he blew out a breath. "I'll come with you."

She fixed him with a strait look. "That would defeat the purpose."

"No. It won't." He returned her gaze steadily. "If this Vale and Catriona are as good as you say . . . perhaps she can help me, too."

She stilled; he remained were he was, their gazes locked, her eyes searching his, verifying his meaning . . . hesitantly, she reached out one hand.

He did the same.

Their fingers touched, slid, twined.

A detonation ripped through the night.

Chapter 18

Amanda's fingers clutched Martin's; his hand locked over hers. They stared up the road to the bend around which the coach had gone. Another shot rang out, hard on the echos of the first, shredding the silence.

Martin cursed and clambered into the curricle.

"Reggie!" Amanda's eyes were wide.

"Hold on!" He glanced to make sure she had before slapping the reins to the leader's rump.

The team bolted, but he held them, steered the curricle at top speed toward the bend, checked only at the last minute to trot smartly around it.

Pandemonium lay ahead. The coach lay slewed across the road, the horses screaming, kicking, half out of the traces. The coachman, one arm tucked to his body, was hanging onto the harness with his good arm.

He saw them; face pinched with pain, he nodded at the coach. "The gen'leman . . ."

Martin halted his horses, swiftly tied the reins, then leapt down and raced to the carriage. Amanda all but fell out of the curricle, then she was on his heels. *"Reggie!"*

Moonlight played on one white hand, palm up, fingers gently curled, resting, lifeless, on the edge of the open window set in the carriage door.

Martin reached the coach. He lifted the hand, opened the door.

"My God!" Amanda stared past him at a scene beyond a nightmare. Eyes shut, Reggie lay slumped back, half on and half off the seat. All around him, black pools gleamed dully in the poor light. Blood. Everywhere.

"Watch out." Martin hauled himself up by the doorframe; he stepped over Reggie, then bent over him, pushing aside Reggie's cravat.

"He's alive."

Amanda's breath left her in a rush; she felt giddy but fought off her faintness. Frothing up her skirt, she grabbed her petticoats and started ripping. Martin grabbed the first long strip she pulled off. He'd untied his cravat, folded it into a pad; he bound it into place with Amanda's strip.

"It's a head wound. Looks like the ball hit him above the temple—high enough, thank God. It's ripped a groove along his skull but didn't lodge."

"But the blood." Amanda kept ripping and handing strips up; Martin used them to secure his makeshift bandage.

"That's the danger. Head wounds always bleed profusely." He tied a knot, waved aside her next strip. "We may need it later."

He straightened as far as he could in the confines of the coach. Amanda crowded the door; reaching in, she took Reggie's hand. Closed both her hands around it. "He's so cold."

"Shock combined with blood loss." Martin pulled down folded blankets from the rack above the seat. "Thankfully, you came prepared for Scotland."

He shook out one blanket and laid it over the other seat. From the door, Amanda helped straighten it, fighting to keep her lip from trembling.

Martin shot her a glance. "I'm going to lift him across, then we'll wrap him in the blankets. You stay with him while I help the coachman, all right?"

She nodded.

"You won't faint because of the blood?"

The look she threw him told him not to be daft. Martin read it with relief. He was going to need her help; hysterics, Reggie couldn't afford. He lifted Reggie, angling his body, an awkward manuever in the limited space. The instant he laid him down, Amanda was up in the carriage beside him, shaking the second blanket out and tucking it about Reggie's still form.

He glanced at her face, saw grim resolution. Squeezing her shoulder, he edged past her and jumped down.

The horses were quiet, but the coachman was sagging. He hadn't been able to free the beasts, just calm them. "Mr. Carmarthen?" he asked.

"He's alive. Here—sit down." Martin caught the man, helping him to the rising bank, keeping one eye on the restive horses. "How's your arm?"

"Shot went right through. Missed the bone, thank God. I tied my kerchief 'round the hole. Painful, but I'll live."

Martin checked the wound; satisfied, he asked, "What happened?"

"Highwayman."

Straightening, Martin returned to the horses, crooning, soothing; he set to work disentangling their harness. He glanced back at the coachman. "Think back—describe what happened, step by step."

The coachman sighed. "He must'a been waiting for us—can't see how it could'a been otherwise. We came round the bend, and I saw him there—"

The man nodded; Martin glanced over the horses' backs to the entrance of a lane leading east. A bigger lane lay to the west; he didn't look that way.

"He was sitting his horse, calm an' patient. Couldn't tell he was a highwayman. He just looked like a gen'leman waiting for someone. Mr. Carmarthen had told me to stop there, so I slowed. The bugger waited 'til we was almost level, then he reached under his greatcoat, came out with a pistol and shot me. No warning, nothing. Cool as you please."

Frowning, Martin unravelled a tangled rein. "What happened next?"

"I yelled, grabbed my arm and fell off the box. Then I heard the second shot." The coachman paused, then added, "After that, all I heard was the horses' screaming, and the horseman galloping away."

"He didn't come up to the carriage?"

"Nope. I'd have seen if he had."

"So he just turned and rode . . . which way? He didn't pass us."

"He went that way." The coachman again nodded to the lane east. "Just turned his horse and galloped off."

Martin considered the lane as he checked the realigned harness. "There's a shortcut to Nottingham that way." And from Nottingham, a good road that dropped back to the Great North Road, and thence south to London.

He returned to the coachman. "You're in no condition to drive, but we'll need you to keep Mr. Carmarthen from rolling around in the carriage."

The man let Martin help him up. "Sheffield's the next town."

"Unfortunately, it's too far for Mr. Carmarthen, and it'll be so late by the time we reach there, getting anyone to open up for us would be a feat."

The man grimaced. "Aye." He nodded to the carriage. "Will he be all right?"

"With luck, but we need to clean the wound and get him warm quickly." Martin glanced at the surrounding country-side, silent and empty. "The temperature here will plummet in the next few hours."

Having ascertained that the coachman's name was On-slow, Martin beckoned Amanda out of the carriage. "Onslow will watch Reggie while I drive."

Puzzled, Amanda scrambled out, frowning when he closed the carriage door on Onslow. "What about me?"

Martin led her to his curricle. "They aren't my horses and I've driven them hard. They're tired and reasonably bidda-ble. Can you manage them?"

She stared at him. "You want me to drive them?"

"No. But it's the only way not to leave them out all night. It'll freeze before dawn and they've run for hours and haven't been rubbed down."

It was only then that Amanda noticed the temperature. She glanced around and shivered. "Where are we? Where are we going?"

Martin's already grim expression turned grimmer. "We're in the Peak district—it's high, so it's cold, and will get a lot colder through what's left of the night." He drew in a breath, his eyes meeting hers. "Reggie's not out of the woods. If we can tend the wound, keep him warm—with luck, he'll pull through. But shock combined with blood loss compounded by serious cold . . . we have to get him to shelter soon."

She got the distinct impression he was convincing himself, not her. "So where . . . ?"

It suddenly occurred to her that he knew where they were. He confirmed it by nodding to the lane leading west. "We go that way." He grasped her waist, lifted her to the curricle's seat. She settled her skirts; he untied the reins and handed them to her. "You can drive a team, can't you?"

"Of course!" She took the reins.

"Follow a good ten yards back, just in case I have to stop suddenly."

As he turned away, she asked, "What lies that way?"

He didn't look back as he strode to the coach. "Hathersage." He took another two strides before adding, "My home."

In daylight, it would have been an easy drive; in fitful moonlight, every nerve was taut as she urged the tired horses along in the coach's wake. At least the lane was wide. It led due west, dipping, then rising, winding onward and upward between wood-covered hills.

They reached a river; the coach trundled slowly, carefully, across a stone bridge, then turned north. She followed, easing the horses along. Hired nags, they were not as responsive as she would have liked, but she managed to keep them plodding.

A village lay sleeping, scattered cottages standing back from the lane. A church stood at the end; as they passed it, she felt a rising breeze. Looked up, sensing a change in the landscape—and discovered the countryside open and spread before her. Rising up all around her. Twisting on the curricle's seat, she marveled at the towering cliffs hovering darkly over the valley, over the patchwork of fields and coppices, at the river tinkling softly beside the lane, moonlight reflecting in silver ripples.

Stark and dramatic in the moonlight, the scene would be even more impressive by day when it would be possible to appreciate the colors and the sheer magnitude of the wild expanse encircled by the massive bluffs.

The coach rumbled on. The lane dipped, wound around. Some sixth sense had her looking up, searching ahead . . . then she saw it. A house—a large, long mansion—stood halfway up the slope directly ahead, veiled in the shadows cast by the cliff behind it. The river curved westward; the road followed it, but she felt sure their destination lay directly ahead.

So it proved. Martin turned the coach up an overgrown drive; a little way on they passed through a pair of heavy gates left wide. The trees closed in, monstrous oaks and elms and others she couldn't be sure of in the night, a silent corps of guards watching their arrival. Leaves shifted; a soft soughing filled the trees, not frightening but gently mournful.

Otherwise, all was deathly silent.

She was accustomed to country estates at night, to private parks that extended for miles, yet the sense of emptiness here was profound. It touched her with a wraith's fingers, again not to frighten but to plead . . .

The drive ended and the house appeared before them, silent and shuttered—deserted. She could feel it. A short lawn lay before the house, rudely tended; a fountain and shrubs stood further down the slope, the remnants of a parterre to one side. The view back down the river valley was breathtaking even now. Wild, rugged, heartbreakingly beautiful.

Martin didn't stop before the front steps but followed the drive around the side of the house, into a large courtyard behind it. Reluctantly turning from the view, she kept the curricle rolling in the coach's wake, drawing rein so the horses finally stopped, hung their heads, a yard from the back of the coach.

She applied the brake, wound the reins around it, dragged in a relieved breath, and only then noticed how chilled she was. Her breath misted before her face; her gloved fingers felt frozen. She flexed them, then climbed down and hurried to the coach.

Martin had already checked the occupants; he was striding to the back of the house. She looked into the coach, received a nod from Onslow, then followed Martin.

He pounded on the back door as she neared the covered porch. There was no lamp burning anywhere. Stepping aside, she peered through one window, and glimpsed a spark of light.

"Someone's coming." She joined Martin in the porch.

"Aye?" came from the other side of the door. "Who is it?"

Martin opened his mouth, hesitated, then stated, "Dexter."

"Dex . . ." The sounds of bolts being drawn back reached them, then the door was hauled open. A wispy-haired old man stood holding a candle high, peering, wide eyed at Martin. "Praise be! Is it really you, Master Martin?"

"Yes, Colly, it's me." Stepping forward, Martin turned Colly and guided him back inside. "We've two injured men to tend. Are you the only one here?"

"Aye—just me. It's been that way since . . . well, Martha Miggs went back to her brother's farm, and I stayed on to keep the place tight."

A few steps had taken them through a small hall into a cavernous kitchen. Martin stopped; on his heels, Amanda stared. Cobwebs hung in the corners; only the area before the main hearth looked lived in. She blinked, then stepped forward. "We'll need the fire built up, first. Then we'll have to see about a bed."

Martin glanced at her. "This is Miss Amanda, Colly—I want you to do whatever she asks." Briefly, he surveyed the room.

Colly watched him, worried, fretting the knitted shawl he'd thrown over his nightshirt. "We don't have much to do much with, m'lord."

Martin nodded, his expression grim. "We'll have to make do with whatever we have." He turned back to the door. "Get the fire going—I'll bring in the wounded."

He left; Amanda went straight to the huge cast-iron oven. "How do you open it?"

Colly hurried after her. "Here—I'll show you, miss."

They got the fire in the stove blazing; at Amanda's suggestion, Colly set a second fire in the open section of the hearth as well. He was dazed, but readily followed her instructions. But if she didn't order, he dithered. Grabbing a cloth, she wiped down the deal table, the only place she could see to lay Reggie. She was arranging on its surface the cushions she'd taken from an old chair when Martin ducked through the door, Reggie in his arms.

"Good." Easing Reggie down, he nodded toward the hall. Onslow stood braced against the archway. "Close the back door—slide the bolts."

Feeling the icy draft, Amanda dashed to the heavy door, swung it closed and bolted it. Returning to the kitchen, she urged Onslow into a dusty chair. Colly was setting two kettles to boil. "We'll need more bandages." She looked at Colly. "Old sheets? And old towels, too."

He nodded and hurried off. Martin was inspecting Reggie's bandage. She checked Onslow's arm, then the first of the kettles hissed.

The next half hour went in tending their patients. Amanda washed Reggie's bloodied face and head, then Martin took over, gently probing the wound while she watched, hands clenched, knuckles white. Then he washed away the fresh blood.

"As I thought." He reached for the towels she'd stacked ready. "The bullet didn't lodge, but it was a near-run thing." They rebandaged the wound, then Martin went out and brought in their bags. He rummaged in Reggie's and drew out a nightshirt. Between them, they stripped him of his blood-stained coat and shirt and eased the nightshirt over his head.

Onslow, weak but still awake, was easier to deal with. Then Martin looked around. "I'll have to stable the nags. Can you see what you and Colly can do about beds?"

Amanda nodded. Martin left; she turned to Colly. "The first thing we need is light. Lanterns would be best."

He found two, but they were empty. Armed with a huge, seven-armed candelabra, with Colly on her heels supporting its five-armed cousin, Amanda started into the house. Both candelabras had been fully set with fresh candles; given the likelihood of those being the only candles available, she'd lit only two in each holder. So the light was soft and wavering as she ventured into the long corridor beyond the kitchen; it led to a front hall so huge the candlelight didn't reach the corners. An equally impressive staircase led upward, then divided into two. She started up. "Which rooms were last used here?"

"Family rooms—family wing's to the right."

She took the right fork in the stairs; the gallery above was deeply shadowed. The candlelight played over gilt frames as she headed in the direction Colly pointed, toward a corridor that appeared to run half the length of the long house.

The mansion was silent and still, like Martin's London residence but with one vital difference. This house seemed to breathe, alive but dormant, quietly waiting tucked up in holland covers. Although the temperature was lower here, the coldness in London had been more profound. This place had been a home, once; it was waiting to be a home again. There was a sense of whispers in the shadows, as if, if she strained, she would hear the echo of laughter and flying feet, of children's shrieks and men's rumbling chuckles.

There was warmth here, albeit in abeyance; the promise of life still lay richly upon this house. The fable of Sleeping Beauty occurred to her—the house was waiting for her prince to return and reawaken her. Lips lifting wryly at her fancy, she let Colly ease ahead and open a door.

"This room was always kept ready for the master."

Holding the candelabra high, she surveyed the chamber. "The earl?" It didn't seem large enough.

"Nay, the young master. Lord Martin. They was expecting him back anytime."

She crossed to the curtained bed. "They?"

"The old earl and Lady Rachel. Looked for him for years they did, but he never did come back." Colly rattled back the curtains, ignoring the cloud of dust. "Gave me a right turn, seeing him standing there, large as life. Too late for his lordship—his father, I mean—and her ladyship, more's the pity."

Colly fell to shaking the pillows and the covers. Setting aside her confusion, Amanda placed her candelabra on the bedside table and helped. The room and this bed would do for Reggie. Leaving Colly with instructions to get the fire going, she headed back to the kitchen.

Back to Reggie. She'd never seen him so pale, so lifeless, stretched out on the table before the fire. Their last words rang in her head; she swallowed and chafed his hands, but her own hands were icy. Gently, she brushed back a tuft of hair that had fallen across his bandage; her heart constricted—she forced herself to look around. To do something to hold the unbearable at bay.

Shock, loss of blood—how did one treat that? She'd never felt so helpless in her life. Tea—people always prescribed tea for everything. She rummaged through the few canisters standing on a sideboard, Colly's meagre provisions. She found the tea.

Martin walked in as she stood hovering over a steaming kettle, a spoon in one hand, the open canister in the other. She glanced at him, gestured helplessly. "I've no idea how much to put in."

He heard the wavering in her voice, saw the rising panic in her eyes. He crossed to her. "I'll do it." He took the canister and spoon from her, deftly measured tea into the kettle. "How is he?"

"Icy." She dragged in a tight breath.

"Did you find a decent bed?"

"Yes, but it's in the room Colly said had been yours."

Martin set the canister aside and dropped the lid back on the kettle. "That doesn't matter—it's a good choice. It's smaller than some of the other rooms. Easier to heat."

Amanda shivered. He glanced at her. It was no longer that cold in the kitchen. "Why don't you find some cups? We can all do with something hot."

She nodded, and went to the cupboards.

Colly returned with a pile of blankets. "Here you go." He handed one to Onslow, nodding in the chair he'd pulled closer to the fire.

Amanda set down the mugs she'd found and hurried to take a blanket and spread it over Reggie. Martin watched, then glanced at Colly. "Why don't you make up a bed in the

room next to yours for Onslow? He can have some tea, then
he should sleep."

"Aye. I'll do that." Colly left by a narrow stair that led to
the rooms directly above the kitchen.

Martin poured the brewed tea into four mugs. "Here." He
handed one to Onslow, who cradled it in his hands. "How's
the arm?"

"Throbbing, but I'm thinking that's a good sign." Onslow
sipped. "I've been hit before, years ago. I'll live."

Martin offered one of the mugs to Amanda. Eyes on Reggie, she shook her head. "No—it's for him."

"I seriously doubt he'll wake tonight—he's lost too much
blood."

Her expression turned stricken; he drew her to him,
hugged her within one arm. "He'll most likely awaken all
right in the end, just not yet. Now—you need this." He
curled her fingers about the mug; she shivered and took it,
wrapped both hands about it and sipped, but her eyes never
left Reggie.

Colly returned; Martin handed him the fourth mug, and
they all sipped, standing before the hearth.

"The horses all right?" Colly asked.

"As well as can be." Martin looked down at his mug,
swirled the tea. "Where are the other horses—my father's
hunters, the carriage horses? What happened to them?"

"Sold. Years ago."

Martin frowned. His father had died only a year ago, yet
the stables had been deserted for much longer.

Colly set down his empty mug and took Onslow's. "Come
on, let's get you settled, then."

The pair headed up the narrow stair. Martin tugged the
chair Onslow had vacated nearer the ebbing blaze, and drew
Amanda to it. She sank down, but her worried gaze remained on the silent figure on the table.

When Colly returned, Martin nodded to Reggie. "It
should be warm enough upstairs—let's move him."

Not an easy task. Reggie was slight, but he was no light-
weight, and Martin didn't want to ask Colly to help; the old
man was too frail. Balancing Reggie, Martin had to stop in

the front hall, then again at the top of the stairs to catch his breath, but they reached his old room without catastrophe. Amanda rushed in and drew down the covers, pulling out the warming pan Colly had set in place.

Martin laid Reggie down; Amanda covered him, straightening his arms, brushing back his hair. Martin turned to Colly. "We'll need some bricks."

"I set some warming downstairs. I'll bring 'em up."

Crouching before the hearth, Martin built up the fire, noting the coal shuttle and woodbox were both full. The chill had left the room. Standing, he stared down at the fire, trying not to look around, see and remember.

He didn't begrudge Reggie the room; he doubted he could ever sleep here again. Besides, he was no longer the heir, but the earl—his room lay at the end of the corridor.

Colly returned with the heated bricks wrapped in blankets; they slid them between the covers, creating a cocoon of warmth around Reggie's inanimate form. Glancing at Amanda, tight-lipped, wide-eyed, nearly as pale as Reggie, Martin wished Reggie would stir, show some sign of life. But Reggie was still unconscious; the longer he remained so, the less good his chances. Martin saw no reason to voice that fact.

He dismissed Colly with a nod. "Get some sleep. We'll see where we are come morning."

Colly bowed and left. Martin glanced at Amanda. She'd sunk down on the bed beside Reggie, staring at his white face. It was long past midnight; they both needed rest, but he knew better than to suggest she leave her vigil.

"I'll hunt up some quilts and pillows." He picked up the smaller candelabra. Amanda didn't look up as he left the room.

In the corridor, he hesitated, then walked further into the family's private wing. Toward the double doors at the end, oak carved with the family crest. He stopped before them, seeing not them but visions from the past. Turning his head, he considered the door to his left; after a long moment, he stirred and opened it.

It was well over ten years since he'd last entered his

mother's boudoir. All through his childhood, it had been a place of irresistible delight, a cornucopia of stimuli to his imagination and his senses.

The room was exactly as he remembered it, draped in satins and silks, in rich brocades and laces. No sultan's harem had ever been so blatantly lush. It was from his beautiful mother he'd inherited his wild and sensual nature, his tactile sensitivity, his love of color and texture. Closing the door, he raised the candelabra, looked at her escritoire sitting between the windows. He could almost see her there, writing some note, turning to greet him with that laughing smile that had been her hallmark, and her greatest gift.

She hadn't smiled at him that day; she hadn't believed him, either, or rather, hadn't known what to believe. She'd hesitated, hadn't immediately thrown her loyalty and support behind him, and that had been enough. Enough to bring life as she and he had known it to an end.

Slowly, he moved into the room, recognizing figurines, a clock, a letter opener. Breathing in, he could almost believe he could smell her perfume, weak and stale beneath the weight of the years, but still there.

Still evoking her presence, her smile.

He'd stopped blaming her long ago. He halted by the bed. The counterpane was of padded silk; there were silk shawls and wraps of the finest wool draped about the room. Cushions with silk tassels, pillows edged with lace; he gathered them all in the middle of the bed, then wrapped them in the counterpane. Picking up the candelabra, he headed back to Amanda. Reaching the door of his old room, he paused. All inside was quiet. Setting down the silken bundle by the door, he continued on, back to the gallery.

He knew the house intimately, like a second skin. He walked through the downstairs rooms and checked every window, every door, every place someone could effect an entry. His great-grandfather had built the house—he'd built it to last; a year of neglect hadn't harmed the fabric, had barely left a mark beyond the dust and cobwebs. Confident no "highwayman" could surprise them in the night, he returned upstairs. Opening the door to his old room, he heard Reggie blathering.

"You know, you look just like a young lady I used to know. You can confide in me, I'm quite safe. Do we—I suppose I mean *I*—have to actually have an interview with the Great Man? With St. Peter, I mean. Or is it the done thing to just swan in, assuming no stain on one's conscience? I don't believe I have one on mine . . . not really. Nothing too damning, y'know."

Reggie was twisting restlessly on the bed; as Martin closed the door and set aside his bundle, Martin saw him stiffen, straighten, then tug at the bedclothes Amanda was struggling to keep over him. Martin had seen Reggie make the same gesture many times, tugging his waistcoat into place.

"Truth is," Reggie went on, his voice lowering, "I always imagined he'd look like my old headmaster, old Pettigrew. I'm quite keen to see the old fellow." He paused, frowned, then amended, "St. Peter, that is. Not Pettigrew. I know what old Pettigrew looked like—well, he looked like Pettigrew, don't you know?" Reggie continued, but his words became harder and harder to make out, degenerating into a delirious mumble.

Amanda was silently crying, tears rolling down her cheeks as she struggled to keep Reggie from thrashing about, from disturbing his bandages. The mumbling continued, rising, then falling; Reggie continued to twist and turn.

Martin nudged Amanda aside. "Sit by the headboard and hold his head. I'll deal with the rest of him."

She nodded, sniffed, scrubbed at her cheeks as she scrambled up on the bed. Together, they made a better job of letting the delirium run its course while limiting the damage Reggie did to his head. And them; Martin had to lunge across the bed and catch Reggie's arm before he hit Amanda. As far as Martin could judge, he'd been demonstrating cracking a whip.

How long the attack lasted he had no idea, but it eventually subsided, and Reggie slipped once more into deeper unconsciousness. Martin gradually straightened, stretched his aching back. Amanda slumped back against the headboard, her hands reluctantly unbracketing Reggie's bound head.

"He thinks he's dead."

Martin looked at her stricken face, reached out, drew her off the bed into his arms. He hugged her, cradling her head against his chest. "He's not dead, and there's no reason to suppose he will be anytime soon. We just have to wait and he'll wake up." He prayed that was true.

She sniffed, then lifted her head and turned to the bed—as if she intended kneeling by it until Reggie regained his wits.

He held onto her. "No—you have to rest."

She turned huge eyes on him. "I can't leave him."

"We can make up a bed by the fire, and be close enough to hear if he starts rattling on again." He drew her with him, picking up the bundle he'd collected. "You'll be no good to him later if you're worn to a frazzle."

Amanda allowed him to bully her into helping him lay out the beautiful counterpane and build a bed of the puffy cushions and pillows, the shawls and wraps. She knew he was right. But when he tried to make her lie on the side closer to the fire, she put her foot down. "No. I can't see him from there."

He narrowed his eyes at her; the suspicion he'd intended just that, so if Reggie stirred, she might not hear and he could deal with it and leave her asleep, blazed in her mind. She set her chin. "I'm sleeping on this side."

She lay down on the side closer to the bed, settled her curls on the pillow and fixed her eyes on the bed. Hands on his hips, lips thin, Martin glared down at her, then, with one of his low growls, capitulated. Stepping over her, he lay down between her and the fire.

With his body screening her from the hearth, she should have remained cold, iced to the bone by shock and concern. There wasn't any warmth left in her. But Martin settled his chest to her back, curved his body around hers, slid his arms about her—and his heat enveloped her. Sank into her, gradually permeated her bones . . . until her muscles relaxed, until her lids grew heavy . . .

A strange noise woke her. A cross between a snort and a choke, a snuffling . . .

Then she remembered. Eyes flying wide, she looked at the bed. And realized what she was hearing. Snoring. Not from Martin, but from Reggie.

She eased from Martin's arms, stood and hurried to the bed. They'd left one window uncurtained; faint light seeped into the room. Reggie lay on his back—the snorting, choking noise was definitely coming from him, but he didn't seem distressed. The sound seemed too regular for a death rattle.

The lines of his face seemed relaxed, not slack in the utter blankness of unconsciousness. Daring to hope, to believe in the relief welling inside her, she put a hand to his cheek.

He snuffled more definitely, raised a hand, caught her fingers, patted them with his, then pushed her hand away. "Not now, Daisy. Later."

Turning away from her, he drew up the coverlet and snuggled down, frowning as he shifted his head. "You really need to get better pillows, dear."

Amanda stared. A softer, muffled snore emanated from under the humped covers. Another sound reached her; she turned to see Martin come up on one elbow. He raised a brow.

She gestured at the bed. "He's sleeping." Then it hit her; she smiled gloriously. "That means he'll be all right, doesn't it?"

"Yes, but it's barely dawn. Leave him to sleep." Martin slumped back down. "Come here." He beckoned sleepily.

After one last look at Reggie, she returned to their makeshift bed. Wriggling back under the covers, facing Reggie, she whispered, "I touched his face and he thought I was someone named Daisy. He said 'Later.' "

"I daresay."

After a moment, she asked, "Do you think he's still delirious?"

"It sounds like he's in his right mind, if a little weak."

She frowned, then Martin turned, and curved his body once more around hers. And she felt . . .

Her eyes widened.

"Now go back to sleep."

He sounded more disgruntled than Reggie. Amanda wondered . . . then smiled, closed her eyes and obeyed.

Chapter 19

They were still snuggled in the warmth of his mother's counterpane when Martin heard Colly's footsteps plodding up the stairs. He kept his eyes closed, for one last moment let his senses bask in the simple peace, the simple joy that held them. Cradled in his arms, Amanda was no more asleep than he, equally reluctant to move—her body remained quiescent in his arms, relaxed against his. Savoring what would very likely be their last instant of quiet togetherness for the day.

But the morning beckoned; there was much to do. He stirred, then rose. Helped Amanda to her feet. When Colly arrived at the door, he opened it. The old man had brought a small ewer and basin. Martin dallied long enough to suggest they leave Reggie sleeping until he awoke on his own, then followed Colly back to the kitchen.

On the way, he took stock; when he reached the kitchen he was frowning. "We'll be staying for a few days at least. We need to open up some rooms—brush down the cobwebs, get rid of the dust—enough to be comfortable."

Colly looked at him in dismay. "The drawing room?"

The drawing room was monstrous. "No. The small parlor will do."

"I'll get onto it after breakfast . . ." Colly glanced at the stove. "I'm not much of one for cooking."

Martin sighed. "What have you got?"

His years of traveling had given him skills not generally taught an earl's son; when Amanda joined them, he was stirring a pot of porridge on the stove. "Colly unearthed some honey, which should make it more palatable."

Amanda looked. "Hmm."

But she ate it; Martin suspected she was as famished as he. At his insistence, Colly and Onslow ate with them. Onslow was quiet; Colly had already washed and redressed his wound. Martin used the time to get an idea of the state of the larder.

"We've tatters in the cellar, and some cabbage. There's a bit of game pie left over from last week." Colly thought, then grimaced. "Not much else."

The nearest market town was Buxton; Martin didn't want to waste the entire day it would take to go there and back. Let alone so widely advertise his return. The truth was, he hadn't meant to return; stirring his porridge, he wasn't sure he'd yet digested the fact he was here.

Focusing on the necessities, he nodded. "I'll take a gun out and see what I can find, then I'll saddle one of the horses and visit the bakery."

"Aye." Colly rose and gathered their empty plates. "The game's been running wild hereabouts, and the bakery always has pasties and pies."

Amanda stood. "I'll dust and air rooms and make up some beds. I'll need to watch Reggie."

Martin glanced at her. "Colly will show you where everything is."

Two hours with a shotgun, tramping over rugged hillsides he knew like the palm of his hand, produced three hares. And a mindful of memories. He handed the hares to Colly to dress, cleaned the gun, then headed for the stables. It took half an hour to find and check sufficient tack to saddle one of the carriage horses; after that, there was no further reason to put off the inevitable.

The sun was high by the time he trotted into the village of Grindleford. Trotted past the church, presently empty, standing like a benevolent guardian keeping watch over its small congregation. The cottages of the flock were scattered about the nearby fields; only the bakery and the forge stood on the lane itself, one directly opposite the other. The forge was open but there was no one in sight, either there or in the fields.

Martin dismounted before the bakery and tied the horse's reins to a nearby tree. A bell attached to the door tinkled as he opened it; girding his loins, he ducked beneath the lintel and entered the bright little shop. Savory aromas from the bakery behind filled the enclosed space. A girl wrapped in a white apron bustled through from the back, her face alight with query.

She didn't recognize him; she was either too young or had arrived in the last ten years. Knowing how little the population hereabouts varied, he assumed it was the former.

"Can I help you, sir?"

Martin smiled and had her show him the latest offerings. He chose two loaves of bread, unable to resist the lure of the cob loaf he hadn't tasted since boyhood, and a variety of pies and pasties, a selection large enough to have the girl eyeing him curiously.

Inwardly congratulating himself on having accomplished his task without encountering anyone who knew him, he paid and received his change. He was turning away when an older woman, wiping her hands on her apron, appeared in the archway connecting the bakery with the shop. "Heather—"

The woman stopped the instant she set eyes on him, as if she'd run into an invisible wall. She stared as if she couldn't believe her eyes.

Martin could understand. His smile faded; the only thought in his brain was that she hadn't previously been a baker. His expression impassive, he inclined his head. "Mrs. Crockett."

Belatedly, she bobbed. "Sir—I mean . . . my lord."

With a curt nod for both her and the now wide-eyed girl, Martin turned and left the shop.

If Mrs. Crockett had said "Good Lord!" he'd have agreed. Of all the people to meet! She'd been old Buxton's housekeeper and Sarah's nurse; she more than most had reason to remember why he'd left—why he'd been banished.

Despite the fact Grindleford was so tiny and the population so widely scattered, the news he was back would be all over the county within hours. That, he could count on. He was still grim when he reached the empty kitchen and laid his purchases on the table. Colly wasn't in evidence, but there were vegetables laid out, and the dressed hares were hanging over the sink. At least they would eat.

He headed for the front hall, wondering where the others were; a feminine huff made him look up. Amanda was teetering on the landing, struggling to balance a large ewer and basin. He took the steps two at a time, lifted the heavy weight from her hands.

"Thank you." Her beaming smile erased his scowl before it had even begun. "Reggie's awake! And he's lucid."

"Good." Side by side, they continued up the stairs.

"Colly's helping him get undressed. Onslow's asleep." As they reached the gallery, Amanda's smile faded. "Reggie's still very weak."

"That's to be expected. He'll take a few days to recover."

She seemed to accept that. Martin didn't add that infection of the wound was the next battle they might face; he was hoping they could avoid it.

She knocked, and Colly bade them enter. Reggie was lying propped up in bed, resplendent in a paisley silk robe that only threw his pallor into sharper contrast. Delighted, Amanda bustled forward.

"Now we need to change your bandage, and wash the wound."

Reggie looked startled. "You?" Then he looked at Martin. "I don't—"

There followed an argument of the sort that could only occur between two childhood friends. Martin listened, inwardly smiling, refusing to agree with either, unsurprised when Amanda had her way and, despite Reggie's dire grumblings, unwound the bandage and laid bare his wound.

Angry, red and raw, it was not a pretty sight. Martin glanced at Amanda's face but she chattered on, brightly, incessantly, while she gently sponged it and patted it dry. Not even when Reggie tensed and winced did her patter falter. Then he saw the glance she threw Reggie and realized her brightness was all for show, so Reggie wouldn't realize how worried and upset she was by the wound. As soon as she'd finished, he replaced her by Reggie's side and deftly rebandaged, tightening the pad against the wound, winding the long bandage round and round to secure it.

The ordeal had drained Reggie's strength; he was paler than ever as they eased him down to the pillows to rest.

Martin hesitated, seeing the fight Reggie waged to keep his eyes from closing, then asked, "Do you remember what happened?"

A frown formed on Reggie's face, quite comical because of the bandage. "We rolled around the corner and Onslow slowed—I'd told him to stop and wait. Then there was a shot. I heard Onslow yell, then a thump—I leaned forward to look out. Saw this fellow on a horse. Next thing I knew there was this searing pain across my skull—then I heard the crack." He frowned harder. "Can't remember more than that."

"There isn't much more. We heard and came running, but the horseman was gone. Did you get a decent look at him?"

Reggie looked up, studied his face, then shook his head. "That's the strangest thing about it. Don't know if my mind's playing tricks on me or what."

"Why?" Amanda asked.

"It was cloudy, remember, but just then, the moon came out and shone right on him—the fellow on the horse—and he wasn't that far away. I *did* see him clearly. I think. Only it might have been a trick of the moonlight."

"Why so unsure?"

Reggie looked at Martin. "Because the devilish thing is, he looked just like you."

Silence, then Amanda stated, "But that's impossible. It couldn't have been Martin—he was with me when we heard the shots."

"I know *that's* impossible!" Fretfully, Reggie plucked at the coverlet. "But he asked what I saw—that's what I saw. I know it wasn't *him*. It's just what I said—the man *looked* like him."

Amanda sat back, as if marshaling her arguments. Martin tweaked her sleeve. "We'll leave you to rest. Just sleep and recover. We'll leave the door ajar—if you want anything, ring the bell."

Still frowning, but with his eyes now shut, Reggie nodded.

Martin indicated the door with his head; Amanda hesitated, then leaned down and kissed Reggie's cheek. "Just get well."

Reggie's frown eased. The line of his lips did, too.

They left him.

"I don't understand." Frowning, Amanda carried the empty ewer into the kitchen. Martin followed, carrying the discarded bandages in the basin. They headed for the scullery. Amanda was still frowning when they returned to the kitchen.

Onslow was coming down the stairs.

They both saw him; Amanda opened her mouth—Martin grabbed her arm, squeezed in warning. She looked at him in surprise.

"Onslow—you must have got a glimpse of the highwayman." The coachman wavered on his feet; Martin waved him to the armchair. "Sit down, and tell us what you saw. Don't worry about how it sounds. Just describe the man as best you can."

Onslow sighed as he settled into the chair. "I'm right glad you said that, m'lord, 'cause truth to tell, I thought I must've been seeing double. The geezer looked a lot like yourself." As Reggie had, Onslow studied Martin anew. "Wasn't you, I know, and not just because I'd left you down the road having an argy-bargy with Miss Amanda, who I know wouldn't've shut up quick."

Martin glanced at Amanda; she didn't know whether to smile or frown.

"Thing is, I can't put my finger on just why I knew 'twasn't you. You don't have a brother, do you?"

"No." Martin frowned. "But—" He cut off the revelation; when Amanda raised her brows at him, he shook his head. Asked Onslow, "How's the wound?"

"Aching, but not as bad as it was. I reckon I'll rest and gather my strength, then I'll see to the horses after lunch."

There was at least an hour remaining before luncheon. Amanda headed back into the house. "I still have to air rooms for us and make up the beds. I'd only just started when Reggie woke."

Martin followed her into the front hall. "Wait." From the foot of the stairs, she looked at him, arching a brow. Beneath her animation, she was weary. "Come out to the garden for a few minutes—you need some air yourself."

She glanced up the stairs. "But the rooms—"

"Will still be there after lunch. Don't forget the light fades earlier here—you won't be able to stroll in the garden of an evening."

Amanda smiled, but left the stairs and joined him. "I came prepared for Scotland, remember?"

He took her hand, then turned, not for the front door, but down a side corridor.

"Where are we going?"

"A special place."

She could see that for herself when he guided her through the French doors at the end of the wing into a protected court leading to a garden that must, once, have been a fantasy of scent and color. Although overgrown, remnants of graceful beauty remained, colorful blooms splashing against verdant growth hinting at what, with a little taming, could still be.

"It's beautiful." Walking by his side, she swung about and looked back. The garden was protected from the north and east by the rising cliffs, from the west by the house. To the south, the river valley spread before them, basking in mild sunshine. Looking ahead again, she spied a seat at the end of the garden. "Was this your mother's garden?"

He nodded. "She loved roses especially. Roses and iris, and lavender, too."

The roses were everywhere, massed and rambling. Spears

of iris leaves showed here and there; the lavender needed clipping.

Reaching the bench, Amanda sat. She waited until he sat beside her—they both looked up at the house. "What happened?"

His hesitation suggested he hadn't expected any question quite so bold. Then, leaning forward, resting his forearms on his thighs, he linked his fingers, and told her. Related how, when the villagers had come storming up to the house, herding him with them, to tell their story and demand justice be done, his father had accepted their tale without question. "The only thing he said to me was: 'How could you?' "

His gaze remained on his interlaced fingers. "It never entered his head that I might not have committed the deed. In exculpation, I have to admit I was known to have an ungovernable temper."

"You don't seem to have one now."

"No. That's one thing dealing with the Indians teaches you—there's no point having a temper.

"The whole family was here—uncles, aunts, cousins. It was the usual Easter gathering my father loved to preside over. I think it was the ultimate sin in his eyes that I should do such a thing at such a time, in front of the entire family. Few of them approved of me either, so . . . for the good of the family, they decided to bundle me off that very night."

Amanda quelled a shiver. Being disowned by one's family, thrown out and cut off—banished. Without justice, without recourse. For herself, she couldn't even conceive of it; the very thought made her heart ache for him.

She asked the question she most wanted to know, "Your mother?"

"Ah—Mama. She of them all understood my temper—temperament, nature, what would you. It was the same as hers." Raising his head, he looked across the garden, his eyes narrowed, seeing the past. "She wasn't sure. She knew I *could* have done it, but . . . she, like the others, didn't believe me when I swore I hadn't. If she had believed . . ."

When he continued, his voice had hardened, "What's done is done and the past is behind us."

The change threw his earlier tone into contrast, revealing the underlying truth. "You loved them, didn't you?"

He didn't look at her but at the house. "Yes." After a moment, he added, "Both of them."

He said nothing more but she could now see the whole clearly. Earlier, she'd returned their purloined bedding to the countess's boudoir. That room had been an education into his background, yet the earl's room, beyond it, also held echoes of the character traits that lived in him.

His gaze on the house, he stirred. "When we're married, we won't live here."

No if, but or maybe. Qualification rose intinctively to her tongue, yet she left it unsaid. Fate had taken a hand; they were here, in a deserted house without even a housekeeper to lend them countenance. The time for games was past. The time for decisions was nigh. Although uncertainty lingered, she drew an even breath. "Whyever not?"

He glanced at her.

She studied the house. "It needs refurbishing—well, perhaps more than that, and I haven't seen all of it yet, still . . ." Tilting her head, she considered the mellow stone, the steeply pitched roof. "It has potential—all the right bits and pieces—it just needs people to bring it alive. The structure's impressive—stately on the one hand, charming on the other. I like the windows and the layout of the rooms, and . . ." She hesitated, then impulsively gestured, arms wide. "It simply fits. This is a magnificent area, and the house is somehow set in, an integral part of the whole. It belongs."

His gaze on her face, Martin leaned against the seat's iron back. "I thought you were a Londoner, born and bred?"

"I've lived most of my life there—my parents' house is there—but my uncles and aunts and cousins have houses all over the country. I've spent years in the countryside, in various places, but . . ." Rising, she walked a few steps and stopped, looking south over the vista of the valley. "I've never seen a place as fabulously beautiful—no, that's not the right word—*dramatic* as this. I could stand here and stare for hours, and never grow bored."

Her voice faded as the view drew her in. Martin knew how mesmerizing the play of cloud shadows over nature's patchwork could be. It hadn't occurred to him that it would speak to her, too, or that her affinity for the dramatic would extend to this wild and rugged landscape.

The landscape of his birth. The wild, wide spaces were as much a part of him as his sensual nature—this, as nowhere else in his travels had ever been, was his home.

Home.

He'd turned his back on it, thought he'd shut it out from his life and would never return—never again fall prey to the siren-song of the wind whistling over the crags, to the wrenchingly majestic beauty of the peaks.

Home.

Rising, he stood beside Amanda, thrust his hands in his pockets, felt the wind ruffle his hair. As if in gentle benediction, as if welcoming a prodigal son, hopefully wiser and more experienced, back to the hearth.

Home.

As he stood beside her, its aura rolled over him, the memories of the good times that he'd pushed out of his mind along with the bad. The sounds of his childhood—the bright laughter, the chatter, running footsteps, shrill voices—the neverending happiness. Childhood giving way to the awkwardness of youth, a time that had been so rich with experience, with the thrill of discovery, the deepening of knowledge.

Then had come the break; it had shattered his world and sent all the good spiralling away like autumn leaves. Leaves he hadn't known how to catch.

Perhaps catching was not the way. Perhaps what was needed was simply to return, to let the tree bud and bloom again. To start anew.

He glanced at Amanda; simple delight still played over her features. He looked past her to the house. Considered what could be. And how much it might cost.

She looked up, joy and sunlight in her face. "Thank you

for bringing me here." She linked her arm in his. "But now we'd better lunch, then knuckle down to our chores."

He let her lead him back into the house.

Colly had been slaving in the small parlor all morning; he insisted on serving them their lunch—pasties and bread—in there, as befitted their station. Realizing it made both Colly and Onslow uncomfortable to be sharing a table with their masters, they accepted their banishment from the warm homeliness of the kitchen with good grace.

At the end of the meal, however, they forbore to tug the bellpull, but piled the empty dishes and carried them to the kitchen, and thence, despite Colly's protests, into the scullery. They returned to the kitchen just as the back door was forcibly thrust open.

"Humph!" A large country woman stumped in.

Amanda's eyes widened. The woman wore a hat perched atop a bonnet, a muffler wound around her throat, and a shawl tied about the shoulders of her serviceable black wool coat. Beneath the gaping coat, she was wearing a quantity of wraps and blouses, and a veritable mountain of skirts. Her feet were encased in large boots.

In each hand, she carried multiple string bags bulging with produce, from turnips and leeks to pigeons and pullets.

Head down, the woman barrelled straight for the table; with an "Oomph" of relief, she dumped the string bags on its surface.

Only then did she look up. She was tall and heavy-boned, with a round, ruddy face and straight grey hair pulled into a tight bun. She noted Onslow, Colly and Amanda, then her gaze locked on Martin. She nodded. " 'Bout time you got here."

Amanda glanced at Martin; a smile was flirting about his lips.

"Good afternoon, Allie."

"Aye—it's that an' all to see you back where you belong." With a nod for Colly, the woman started to unpack her bags. "I'll tell you straight I never believed you'd done it—what they said—and now you're back, I'll expect you to set to and get the matter sorted. It ain't the thing for a belted earl to have hanging over his head."

In between thumping packages on the table—packages Colly was quickly unwrapping and putting away—Allie had been shooting narrow-eyed glances at Amanda. "Now, who's this?"

"This," Martin responded with unimparied calm, "is Miss Amanda Cynster." To Amanda, he said, "Allow me to present Allie Bolton. Originally my nurse, Allie continued to hold that title long after I'd left the nursery. We had a cook-housekeeper but in reality, it was Allie who ran this house."

Walking forward, he continued, "As you'll quickly learn, she's distressingly tyrannical, but has a heart of gold and always has the family's best interests at heart." Reaching Allie, he hugged her and kissed her cheek.

"Get away with you!" She batted him back, flustered, pleased as punch and trying to hide it. "That's not the way I taught him to behave," she humphed to Amanda, "you may be sure."

"I'm quite sure he was a handful." Amanda tried to interpret the shooing-like gestures Martin, now behind Allie, was making. Colly, too, was nodding encouragingly. She glanced at the last of the packages being unwrapped—a pat of butter. The penny dropped; she stepped closer. "Of course, we don't know what your present arrangements are, but we'd be very grateful if you could see your way to returning to your position here."

"Humph! Aye—with only him"—Allie nodded at Colly—"to look after the house, I imagine the place is in a right state."

"We've started opening up rooms, but . . . well, as I don't know how things used to be . . ."

"Leave it to me." Packages stowed, Allie untied her bonnet, set bonnet and hat on the dresser, then started to unbutton her coat. "I sent word to Martha Miggs—she'll be here tomorrow and we'll have the place to rights in no time."

The determination behind the words made it clear nothing

would be permitted to stand in Allie's way; Amanda felt a
weight lift from her shoulders, felt relief slide through her
veins. "We have an injured gentleman upstairs—he was shot
by a highwayman, and my coachman was, too." She waved
at Onslow, who was edging toward the door.

"Gracious heavens!" From under her voluminous skirts,
Allie pulled out an apron and tied it about her ample waist.
"I'd best take a look at their wounds, then."

"Mine's healed well enough—I've got to see to my
horses." With a nod to Martin and Amanda, Onslow escaped
through the back door.

"I'll see to you later!" Allie called after him. She turned to
Amanda. "Right, then! You'd best take me up to this gentleman, and then we'll see about opening more rooms. Colly,
you'll be needed—don't disappear."

Martin watched Allie hustle Amanda before her on into
the house. Colly sighed, but he was smiling as he bent to
stoke the fire. Martin felt his own lips curve, felt the gesture
warm a place deep inside him that had been cold for a long,
long time. He hesitated, then, smile deepening, turned and
went to help Onslow.

Household activity the next morning approached the recog-
nizably normal. Reggie was still weak; he'd boggled when
Allie had descended on him, making eyes at Amanda, pleading for rescue, but Allie had quickly subdued him. He ate the
breakfast she presented him without a murmur, then let her
bully him downstairs to doze in a chair in the sunshine.

After a good night's sleep in the room next to Reggie's,
aired and dusted to Allie's high standards, then breakfasting
with Martin in the sunny small parlor, Amanda, restored to
her usual, stubborn and determined self, went looking for
Allie to thank her and put herself at the older woman's dis-
posal. There was a great deal to do; helping seemed a quick
way to learn the ins and outs of the household.

She found Allie in Martin's room, shaking out the bedclothes that draped the huge bed. Yesterday, after finishing
with Reggie and completing the room Amanda now used,

Allie had stridden straight down the corridor and flung the double doors at the end wide. The windows had been next, then she'd swept, dusted and polished with a passion, stripping the bed and remaking it, chattering all the while. Amanda had helped, listened and learned.

When she and Martin had retired the previous evening, in response to his question over which room Allie had readied for him, she'd indicated this room. She'd seen his hesitation, but had given no sign, merely smiling wearily and bidding him good night. She'd closed her door and listened; after a minute, he'd walked down the corridor, then she'd heard the door open.

A long pause had ensued, then the door had shut.

She'd peeked out; he'd gone in. She'd retreated to her bed, speculating on what he might be feeling, what might be going through his mind. She'd been tempted to go and find out, but she'd known in her heart it wasn't yet time. And she'd been too physically weary to do much beyond sleep, which she had, deeply.

Now . . . while she felt she understood Martin's relationship with his mother, his relationship with his father remained veiled. Yet last night, Martin had slept in this room, previously his father's. That much—that he was his father's son—he'd accepted.

Walking into the room, she looked for any evidence that he'd changed things, any little sign he'd made the room his. His brushes had been moved, the mirror atop the tallboy shifted.

Puffing the pillows, Allie saw her noting the changes. "Aye—he'll come around." She eyed Amanda, then asked, "Am I right in thinking you didn't expect to land here?"

"Yes—it was pure chance the highwayman struck so near here. I was heading for Scotland, to my cousin and his wife. Martin . . . followed me."

"Aye." There was a wealth of understanding in Allie's tone. It had taken her a mere few minutes to guess how matters lay between Amanda and her erstwhile charge. While she'd said nothing directly, Amanda was aware she'd been vetted and examined during the previous day, and Allie had approved.

Allie turned from the bed, then stopped, staring out of the window. "Now I wonder what . . . ?"

Amanda walked to the window and saw Martin setting off on one of the horses. "He must be going to the village . . ." Allie hadn't asked him to fetch anything.

Allie came up beside her, a frown in her old eyes as she watched Martin disappear down the drive. Then she nodded brusquely. "Ah—of course. He'll be going to the cemetery."

"The cemetery? I thought I saw a mausoleum in the woods."

"Oh, aye—his parents are buried here." Allie shook out her duster, and attacked the tallboy. "But it's Sarah he'll want to see first. That's where it all began." Allie glanced at Amanda. "He has told you, hasn't he?"

"Yes."

"Well, then." Allie nodded at the window. "You'll know what to do."

The rock-solid confidence in Allie's tone overrode the doubts rising in Amanda's mind. Leaving Allie, she headed for the stable.

Onslow helped her saddle the other bay, then mount. They hadn't been able to find a sidesaddle and she hadn't had time to change into her habit; with her skirts rucked up to her knees, she felt utterly hoydenish as she cantered down the drive.

Keeping the house at her back, she took the lane south and followed the river. The morning was bright and fresh; spring was in the air, the buds plump on the branches, just waiting to burst. A haze of green had already replaced the dull brown of winter. Beside the lane, the river ran strongly along its rocky bed, fracturing the sunlight, its murmuring a paean to the morning.

She reached the church and saw the other horse tied to a tree. Reining in, she dismounted, an ungainly exercise she was thankful no one was around to see. The bakery stood just a little way along, a blacksmith's opposite, the forge glowing inside the shadowy workshop. Tying her mount alongside Martin's, she headed for the lychgate.

It stood open; she climbed the steps to a narrow path that led to the church's front door. Glancing about, she followed the path; before the door, it bisected, circling the small building. She turned to the right and walked on, scanning the graves. None of the stones were big enough to hide Martin, yet she arrived back at the church door without sighting him.

Frowning, she looked across the road at the bakery, then peered at the forge. Searched the surrounding fields. No Martin. Puzzled, she walked back to the gate, then around to the horses—they were both still there.

Then she remembered. Sarah had taken her own life.

Amanda looked to either side, then headed left around the outside of the cemetery wall, seeking the small plot that often existed outside hallowed ground. It lay along the stone wall toward the back of the cemetery. The grass grew longer there, the graves bare mound only just detectable.

Martin stood before one, distinguished only by a rock placed at its head, the letters SB crudely carved into one face.

He must have heard her approaching, but he gave no sign. What she could see of his expression was bleak, intimidating. Stepping between two graves, she slipped her hand into his, and looked down at the grave of the girl he'd been accused of dishonoring.

After a moment, his hand closed, tight, around hers.

"I never had a chance to say good-bye. When they bundled me off that night, they wouldn't let me stop here."

She said nothing, just returned the pressure of his clasp. Eventually, he drew a huge breath and looked up. Then he glanced at her. She met his gaze. He studied her eyes, then nodded ahead.

He led her out of the small plot to a jumble of boulders at the corner of the cemetery. He lifted her up to sit on one, then hoisted himself up alongside.

They looked up the sunlit valley to where the house stood high on the rise with the cliff at its back. The sun struck the windows, made them wink and gleam.

She didn't need words to know they were thinking the same thing.

"Which cliff was it?" Swivelling, she studied the ragged cliffs that formed a backdrop to the village.

He pointed to a towering escarpment. "That one. Froggatt Edge."

She considered it, considered the distance from the village, the sheer drop to the broken ground below. "Tell me again—what happened that morning when you set out to find Sarah's father?"

He hesitated for only an instant, then turned and pointed to a cottage down a narrow lane. "I went to Buxton's house first. When the housekeeper told me he'd gone walking, I thought for a minute, then took that path." Pointing, he traced a well-worn path that led from the lane across the fields to the escarpment. "It climbs around the side of the Edge, and comes out some way back from the lip."

He paused, then went on, "I didn't see or hear anyone or anything, but the path goes up that cleft and needs concentration—it's not an easy stroll. On top of that, I was in a rage—a gunshot I might have heard, but anything less might well not have penetrated.

"When I got to the top, it was deserted, as I'd expected it to be. I'd gone up because from there I would have been able to see Buxton if he was anywhere around. I walked to the lip and looked. All around, everywhere. I didn't see anyone. I remember suddenly feeling cold, deathly cold. Then I noticed the buzzards. They were circling below the lip. I went right to the edge and looked down."

He stopped; after a moment, she prompted, "Where was it that he'd fallen?"

Martin pointed to the base of the escarpment, to where the ground was broken by upthrusting rock and scattered boulders. "There's a gap between the rocks. You can't see in until you actually reach it—or unless you look down from the top. I remember . . . it looked like Buxton, and the first thought I had was that I was glad he was dead. I thought he must have thrown himself off in remorse and guilt."

"You came down to check."

"I wasn't sure it was him. He was lying facedown, and besides, what if he wasn't dead? I couldn't just leave him there."

"How did you get down?"

"The same way I got up."

She considered the distances. "Is there another way down from the top to where he fell?"

Martin pointed to the other side of Froggatt Edge. "There's a much steeper path down that side. It's shorter, but I didn't take it because it's more dangerous, and usually that means slower."

"So you got to the bottom, to where the man was, and . . . ?"

"He'd been turned over and his skull had been bashed in with a rock."

Amanda stared. "Between the time you saw him from the top and reaching him at the bottom?"

Martin nodded. "Someone had been there in between and whoever it was had made sure he was dead. The rock was covering his face. I still wasn't sure . . . so I picked up the rock."

"And that's when the villagers found you."

He nodded. "I lifted the rock and saw . . . then I heard them coming and looked up, and there they were, crowding in . . ." He refocused and shook his head. "I must have been in shock. I know that now, but then . . . nothing like that had ever happened in my life. I'd just learned Sarah had died, that people assumed I'd . . . and then that. I don't know what I said, truth to tell, although I do know that later I insisted I hadn't done it."

Amanda frowned. "You said the villagers had seen a gentleman they thought was you throw the old man over the edge."

Martin waved at the forge. "The blacksmith was working—the back of the forge was open. He happened to glance up and see two men—old Buxton and a young gentleman he mistook for me—struggling on the Edge. He saw the man push Buxton over. He downed tools, doused what he was working on, then rounded up some others and raced for the spot."

Amanda fitted the information together like a jigsaw in her mind. "So . . . Buxton goes out walking—he goes up to Froggatt Edge. Is that likely?"

"Many walk up there. It's a popular spot."

"Very well—he goes up and walks. You come to his house, then set off for the Edge, quite coincidentally, to locate him. But someone else who also wanted to find Buxton is before you. While you're climbing up, he struggles with Buxton and pushes him off. The blacksmith sees, douses his work and rushes off to get help. Then, not sure Buxton is dead, the murderer pelts down by the other path to finish him off. Meanwhile, you reach the top, look around, and see Buxton, lying facedown. You couldn't see that other path from the top, could you?"

His face impassive, Martin shook his head.

"You decide to go back down and check for life. You go down by the first path. Could you see the spot where Buxton fell from that path?"

"No."

"While you're on the way down, the murderer reaches Buxton, turns him over and bashes him dead. Then he runs away. Could he have done that without being seen by you or the villagers?"

Martin hesitated. "It would have been dicey, but yes. The ground's so uneven near the base of the cliffs, he could have got out of sight of both me and the villagers without having to go far. Later . . . once the villagers found me, no one was watching for anyone else."

Amanda nodded. "So then you get to the body, and the villagers find you there. That's how it happened."

Martin eyed her calm, determined—stubborn—expresssion. "You seem remarkably sanguine about murder."

She met his eyes. "I'm remarkably *unsanguine* about you being wrongfully accused of murder." She held his gaze, then continued, "But you worked all that out years ago."

He didn't deny it. She let the moment stretch, then asked, "So . . . how do we go about proving the truth?"

"I don't know that it's possible. There wasn't a shred of evidence at the time. If there had been, even in shock, I would have waved it."

Amanda remembered Lady Osbaldestone's words. "Things happened very quickly. It's possible something was overlooked, or only came to light later." When he said nothing, she urged, "It can't hurt to ask."

It could, but it wouldn't be him, or her, who might be hurt. Martin didn't say the words; he knew the time had come. He had to choose—her, or that other he was protecting. She hadn't begged, but if he resisted, she would do even that; she was committed to his resurrection because the future she envisioned for them hinged on that.

It was a future he now coveted more than anything else in life. He looked into her cornflower blue eyes, then lifted his gaze, looking up the valley to Hathersage. His father's and grandfather's and great-grandfather's house. Now his.

Now theirs. If he would . . .

He drew in a breath, exhaled, and reached for her hand. "Let's see if we can find Conlan."

She jumped off the rock, looked her query.

"The blacksmith who thought he saw me pitch old Buxton over Froggatt Edge."

Chapter 20

"Da's in the cottage out back, m'lord." The blacksmith set aside his bellows; his demeanor was eager as he waved them in. "He'll be right pleased to see you. That old matter's weighed heavy on his mind these last years. If you don't mind going through? He's not too steady on his pins, these days."

"We'll do that, Dan. I remember the way. You won't want to leave that." With a nod, Martin indicated the glowing shoe Dan had been working.

"Aye—well, you've the right of it, there."

As they crossed the yard behind the forge, Martin looked up, slowed. Amanda followed his gaze to the escarpment. Froggatt Edge was clearly visible, yet could anyone be sure who it was they saw at such a distance?

"Country eyes are notoriously sharp," Martin murmured.

"Hmm." Amanda matched his stride as they headed for the cottage flanking the cobbled yard.

Martin knocked on the door. A buxom young woman opened it. When he gave his name and asked to see Conlan, the woman's eyes grew round.

"Oh, heavens!" She bobbed a curtsy. "My lord, I—" She glanced back into the room behind her.

"Who is it, Betsy?"

Martin raised his brows. Flustered, wiping her hands on her apron, Betsy backed and waved them in.

"It's Dexter, Conlan."

An old man in the armchair by the hearth squinted, blinked, then his face cleared. "Yer lordship? Be it really you?"

"Indeed. It's me."

"Praise be!" Conlan struggled to his feet and bowed. "Welcome home, m'lord—and I thank the Lord I can finally tell you. It wasn't you I saw."

"How can you be so certain?" Martin asked, once they'd all sat and Betsy had closed the door. "I can understand you being unsure if it was me or not, but how can you be certain it *wasn't* me? There's no way even you could have distinguished features at that distance."

"Aye, you're right there, but it wasn't features that told me." Conlan sat back in his chair, gathered his resources. "Let me tell it like it was, then you'll see how it happened."

Martin nodded the permission Conlan waited for.

"I saw the figures on the Edge, wrestling, fighting, then I saw the young gen'leman shove old Buxton over. I knew it was Buxton 'cause of that yellow-striped waistcoat of his. I ran and fetched Simmons and Tucker, and Morrissey, too. Others joined us as we ran to the cliff. Tucker asked who'd thrown Buxton over. I said 'twas a young gen'leman looked like you. Well—you were the only young gen'leman we had round about, and we all knew what you looked like, even from a distance. And I'll still take my oath on it—the gen'leman who threw Buxton over looked just like you. At the time, that's all I said—all I really knew, clear in my mind. And then we found you, and it fitted. You'd done it. Even though you said otherwise, what was we to think with you standing there with the rock in your hand and Buxton dead at your feet?

"So we hiked you to your Da, and he acted swift—that was a shock, I can tell you. We never expected he'd up and send you away like that. But it was done . . . we all went home." He nodded to the window. "I sat right here, and heard the carriage rumble past as they took you south."

Conlan sighed. "I tried to sleep but there was something nagging at me. Wouldn't let me go, kept forcing me to see it all again and again in my mind, see the gen'leman force Buxton to the lip and over. Buxton was no fool—he hadn't been walking close to the lip. The other had to force him back, and o' course he didn't go easily . . . *that's* when it all came clear and I knew we'd got it wrong."

Martin frowned. "How? What did you remember?"

"It was the quirt the gen'leman was carrying. He used it on Buxton. I saw it clearly—saw the gen'leman's arm rise and fall, saw Buxton put up his arms to shield his head. That's how the gen'leman forced him to the lip, then he pushed him over. I saw the gen'leman standing there, looking down at Buxton *with the quirt still clutched in his hand*."

Conlan sighed. "So you see, I knew 'twasn't you. Couldn't've been."

Amanda glanced at Martin's face, saw a lightening of the darkness that had always—as long as she'd known him—been there. She turned to Conlan. "Why did that convince you it wasn't his lordship you saw?"

Conlan blinked at her. "The quirt. He never used one. Not ever. Not even when he was first on a pony. We'd all known him since he was a babe—we'd seen him riding for years. No quirt. According to Smithers, used to be head groom at the big house, he never even owned one."

Conlan turned to Martin. "So I knew then, and you may be sure I told everyone who'd listen. In the morning, I went up to the big house, but they wouldn't let me see your Da. I tried to tell them, but there was a great to-do going on. I spoke with old Canter—he tried to speak with your Da but seems they'd been forbidden to say your name. Canter tried, but his lordship wouldn't listen.

"I told myself I'd done my best, but I couldn't let it go. I went into Buxton village and spoke with Sir Francis, but he said as how your Da was the magistrate for this district, and he couldn't see his way to interfere. He told me your Da no doubt had his reasons and I should leave it be."

Conlan paused, then said, "And that's where it's laid. I've

been waiting ten year to tell you to your face. I thought you'd be back—that your Da would change his mind, 'specially when your Ma died. But you never did return." He lifted wondering eyes to Martin's face.

"They didn't know where I was—they couldn't have called me back." Martin patted Conlan's shoulder. "Thank you for telling me."

He rose; he had to get out of the small cottage. Out where he could breathe. Think. Try to comprehend. His smile felt strained as he took his leave of Conlan and Betsy. Amanda sensed his tension; she chatted brightly, easing their way out of the door.

Martin waved to Dan but kept walking, striding. Amanda's skirts shushed as she hurried to keep up, then her hand clamped on his arm and she yanked. Hauled.

He halted, swung to face her.

"Slow down!" She frowned at him. "You heard—you're not guilty!

He looked down at her. "I always knew that."

"But you never *were* guilty as far as these people are concerned." She searched his face. "Doesn't that mean anything to you?"

"Yes. It does." He spoke through his teeth, then exhaled, looked over her head. "Only . . . I don't know *what* it means." He passed his hands over his face, then cursed and swung away.

Amanda was right beside him. "What do you mean?" Hustling along, she peered at his face. "What do you mean you don't know?"

"I mean—" His whole world was disintegrating before his very eyes. "I—" He couldn't find words to describe the tectonic shift in his thinking. With an oath, he grabbed her arm and towed her past the horses. Stopped by the stone wall of the cemetery. Turned her to the cliffs.

"Look at Froggart Edge. It's much the same time it was that day, the same season. The light's the same. Imagine me standing up there. Now imagine Luc there. Would you— could *anyone* possibly confuse us?"

Amanda stared. Then she looked at Martin. "You thought it was Luc?"

"I couldn't think of anyone else Sarah would have given herself to, but Luc never carried a quirt, anymore than I did."

They sat on the stone wall, side by side, and he explained.

"Luc knew her, too, not as well as I did, but . . . well enough. He was always startlingly handsome—I could imagine it happening. And Luc had been at Hathersage for Christmas, and he'd driven up from London ahead of me that day. I knew he was at the house before me—he would have heard of Sarah's death as I did, as soon as he arrived. He had the opportunity to do what had been done, and I thought he had the motive they gave me." His lips twisted. "And as much as they called me wild, Luc was wilder."

Amanda nodded. "I know. You forget. I've known him since birth. But why didn't you realize, if Conlan said the murderer looked like you—"

"I thought he'd made a mistake, one others had made often enough."

"Confusing you and Luc?"

He nodded. "We're alike enough now, but then . . . it was easy at a glance to confuse us. Only . . . it wasn't until I heard Conlan describe the scene just now that I realized about the light."

Amanda looked up at the escarpment. "It was as it now is on that day?"

"Yes. A clear sky with weak sunshine bathing the entire Edge. Quite aside from the quirt, I can't believe Conlan would have missed the difference in coloring—not in that light."

"Which means it isn't Luc." Amanda turned to Martin. "So who . . . ?" Her voice trailed away; she felt her eyes grow round. *"A gentleman who looks like you."* She grabbed Martin's arm. "The highwayman!"

The frown in his eyes told her he'd already made the connection, and would have preferred that she wasn't so perceptive; she ignored that. Her mind was racing. "That's why he was waiting at the crossroads—he was waiting, not for Reggie, but . . ." She frowned. "How could he have known you were on the road north?"

"I don't know, but I seriously doubt Reggie was his target."

"Reggie said the shot came immediately he leaned forward."

"And the 'highwayman' didn't check his victim, so we don't know whether he realized he shot the wrong man."

"But why does he want to shoot you?"

"To stop me from investigating the events surrounding Buxton's death—and Sarah's." Martin was silent for a moment, then, jaw firming, he jumped down from the wall. "Come on—there's someone else we need to speak with."

Mrs. Crockett stared at him for a long moment, then stood aside. "Come in. Can't say as I'm surprised to see you."

Amanda glanced at Martin; unperturbed, he ushered her past him, then followed her into the cottage's small parlor. Mrs. Crockett waved them to a sofa; she returned to a rocker that was gently rocking.

"Well." She faced them across the hearth. "I have to say I thought it was you who'd done the old man to death, given they'd found you with the rock in your hand. You could of done it easy with that temper of yours—damned righteous, just like your Da. And it'd be just like you to fly to Sarah's defense. But then Conlan said otherwise, and there's no one hereabouts had sharper eyes than he, not then."

She started rocking, her gaze drifting from them. "Truth was, I wasn't agin seeing old Buxton dead, not after what he did. The sins of the fathers was all on his head, and rightly so. But"—she paused in her rocking, refocusing on Martin—"there was one thing I knew you didn't do, and that was take advantage of my Sarah."

Her voice had grown fierce. "I tried to tell them it wasn't you, but they saw it as all of a piece. Everyone knew she was yours if you wanted, anytime you'd thought to crook your finger." She shook her head. "But you never saw her that

way, not that I ever saw. You never had brother nor sister—
she was a little sister to you."

"Yes."

"Aye." Mrs. Crockett drew her shawl tighter. "Nitwits, the
lot of them, thinking it was you. I knew. I saw the bruises."

Amanda felt the room—felt Martin—grow still. Then he
asked, softly, "Bruises?"

Mrs. Crockett's lips worked, then she blurted out, "Whoever he was, he forced her. I saw the marks—aye, and the
change in her. All laughter and smiles, then the next day it
was all I could do to get her to look at me. Cried all night,
she had. I didn't know, not then. But she was never one to
make a fuss, my Sarah, and with a father like she had, well,
no wonder, was it?"

She rocked faster, shot a fiery glance at Martin. "If you'd
been here, like as not I'd've sent word—seen if you could
talk her round, but she wouldn't say naught to me, no matter
what I knew."

"She was forced." Martin's voice was even. "You're
sure?"

Mrs. Crockett nodded. "As I'm sitting here. On the second
of the year, it was, two days after the ball at the big house."

When both Martin and Mrs. Crockett remained silent,
Amanda prompted, "You said you knew it wasn't Martin."

Mrs. Crockett looked directly at her. "Stands to reason,
don't it? If he"—she nodded at Martin—"had wanted her,
all he had to do was say. He wouldn't have needed to hold
her down." She sent another glance at Martin; her lip trem-
bled, her voice softened as she added, "He wouldn't have
hurt her, either—there were enough lasses round here, even
then, would have sworn to that. But my Sarah had bruises,
big black bruises, all the way down her back. The blackguard had thrown her down on rocks to have his way with
her." Mrs. Crockett jerked her head at Martin. "Wasn't him."

Martin stirred. Amanda could feel his suppressed rage vi-
brating through him; he was tense as a coiled spring. But his
voice remained even when he asked, "Did she say anything,
drop any hint over who it was?"

Mrs. Crockett shook her head. "*Never*. You may be sure I'd have remembered if she had." After a moment, she continued, staring at the fire, "I still remember how she gathered her courage and faced her father when it had to be done. She tried to make him see reason, but him?" She snorted. "Locked her in her room, he did, then the beatings and the preachings began."

Amanda broke the ensuing silence. "Did he truly force her to take her life?"

"He *took* her life—he might not have tied the knot, but he made damned sure she did! He left her no choice—none." Mrs. Crockett hugged herself, and rocked back and forth, back and forth. "If only she'd kept a diary . . . but she never did."

They left the old woman rocking in her chair, and stepped back into the present, into the sunshine and light.

Amanda held her tongue on the ride back to the house. Allie took one look at Martin's face, then instructed them to ready themselves for luncheon; she served them in the parlor, now spick and span. Her eyes met Amanda's frequently, but she forbore to voice her questions.

She did, however, inform them that Reggie had eaten earlier and was now napping in his room. "Looks a lot improved, and no sign of any fever."

Relieved on that score, at the end of the meal, Amanda pushed back her chair. "Come, my lord earl, and conduct me around your family portraits." Rising, he raised a cynical brow at her; she opened her eyes wide. "Isn't that what gentleman do to impress potential brides?"

He studied her as he neared. "You're as transparent as glass."

She smiled and linked her arm in his. "Humor me."

The portraits hung all around the gallery at the top of the main stairs; as they went up, she glanced at his face. "Am I right in thinking that on your return to England, you didn't pursue the matter of who had committed the crime because you thought it was Luc?"

He didn't immediately reply. Reaching the landing, he

stopped, then turned left. "I didn't know what to think—not to begin with, not later. Luc and I . . . until that time, we'd been closer than brothers. We grew up together, our mothers were sisters, we went to Eton, then on the town together . . ." He shrugged. "I honestly never came to any conclusion—it was possible, and that's as far as my thinking ever got."

"But you don't suspect Luc now?"

"No—triply no. Conlan's eyesight's too good, and as for using force . . ." His lips twisted; he glanced at her. "You know Luc—when it comes to women, the only force he's ever employed is to hold them off."

Amanda humphed. "Indeed. So it's not him. Who else could it be?" They stepped into the gallery.

"The answer is not what you think—but you'll see." Martin led her to the portraits.

Allie had been busy; the curtains had been drawn back and secured with their cords. Light flooded in, reflecting off dust motes still swirling in the air, washing over the portaits hanging in regimented rows along the walls.

"We may as well start with old Henry, the very first earl." Martin led her to a portrait of a crusty-looking gentleman, posed with a bevy of spaniels gazing adoringly up at him. "The story goes he was more fond of his dogs than he was of his countess. That's her."

Amanda looked at the neighboring portrait—a severe-looking woman with pinched features and iron-grey hair. "Hmm."

They progressed along the portraits until they came to one a little more recent. "My grandfather, the third earl."

A study done in the subject's prime; Amanda studied it, glanced frowningly at Martin, then at the picture. "He doesn't look much like you."

"I don't look much like him." Martin met her gaze. "In features, I take after my mother."

He nodded ahead and they continued, strolling past various Fulbridges, every portrait, especially those of the males, confirming his words. The Fulbridges had a different shaped head, a heavier brow, a less clear-cut jaw. An altogether different cast of features, and even more important, a heavier, more sloping-shouldered frame. They bred true, from the first earl all the way to the last, Martin's father.

Amanda stopped before that portrait, not needing to be told, aware of the quietness that stole over Martin, the hooding of his eyes. She studied the man who had banished his own son—as it now seemed, without cause. The portrait showed a stern face and, yes, a righteous stance, but there was no hint of cruelty, no sign of distemper.

Frowning, she looked ahead—the next painting captured her attention. Focused it dramatically. "Your mother?" She stopped directly in front, gaze shifting avidly from one to the other of the three faces shown.

"And her sister."

"Luc's mother—I know. She looks so much younger here."

"They were in their twenties at the time."

He'd said he took after his mother, and to some extent that was true; the resemblance was clear, but muted by the difference between feminine and masculine forms. But Amanda could now see what he'd actually meant by the comment. She pointed to the man standing between the two sisters, behind the table at which they sat, one on either side. "Who's he?"

"My uncle, their older brother."

The man was, if not the exact image of Martin, then a very close replica. Such a good match that it took no imagination at all to see how one could be mistaken for the other, even at relatively close quarters.

Amanda stared at the painting, drank in all it told her, all Martin had wanted her to see with her own eyes. Then she turned and met his agatey gaze. "The murderer's a relative of yours, but not a Fulbridge. Someone from your mother's family."

When he said nothing, she continued, "And that someone is still alive, and doesn't want you looking into the old murder, because if you do . . ."

After a moment, Martin spoke, his eyes on hers. "That someone was hoping, because I'd let the matter rest for so long, when I returned to London and made no move to immediately proclaim my innocence and search for the real murderer, that the matter was closed and they were safe. Now, however, my interest in you has become public, and the murderer has learned I've formally offered for you, and no one who knew the Cynsters would imagine I could have gained the family's approval without giving an undertaking to resolve the old scandal, so, suddenly, unexpectedly, the murderer finds himself under threat."

She nodded, her eyes locked on his. "And so he struck back—it was you he was trying to kill when he shot Reggie."

"Yes."

"Do you think he's realized? That it was Reggie and not you he shot?"

"Possibly. But even if he had, he had to leave, let us go, and he can't risk coming after me here."

Amanda frowned. "Why not? He presumably knows the place—"

"And, very likely, everyone here knows him." When she didn't look convinced, Martin continued, "If he was seen and recognized . . . killing me would accomplish nothing if he was caught. If he could kill me and get away with it—it was worth a try. Now, however, he'll most likely reason that there's still a good chance I won't be able to clear my name, or even if I do, that, after all these years, there'll be no evidence to link him with Buxton's death."

Martin grimaced. "As, indeed, will very likely be the case." He took her arm, twined it with his and turned her along the gallery.

She let him steer her while she juggled facts, slotted more pieces into her mental jigsaw. "But," she eventually stated, "the best and surest way to clear your name socially, especially after all this time, will be to prove that someone else was the murderer."

He hesitated, then nodded. "The most effective way but not, perhaps, the only way."

She looked into his face. "Did you give any undertaking? About resolving the scandal?"

"Not in words, but it was understood."

"Well, then!" She closed her fingers on his arm, let her determination ring clearly; she wasn't about to let anyone or anything come between them now, certainly not a murderer. "I suggest we start looking for one of your maternal relatives who fits the bill—one who was here, who knew Sarah, and so on."

He halted in a wide swath of sunshine. "There might be other options."

She studied his face, then raised both brows. "You aren't, by any chance, imagining I'll agree to you letting the matter rest, opting instead to live your life in the shadows?"

His gaze remained somber. "Whoever it is, they've a family depending on them—innocent people will be harmed by their fall." He held her silent with his gaze, drew breath, then went on, "Sarah's dead—nothing can bring her back. As for Buxton, righting the injustice there worries me less, but—"

"Wait!" She waved her hands. "Go back. You're worried about harming the murderer's family by exposing him?"

When he merely raised a brow—a sign she could interpret perfectly well—she suddenly saw the problem Lady Osbaldestone in her wisdom had foreseen. Saw the hole—the pit a surfeit of protective commitment could bury a man in—and knew she had to address it, overcome it, here and now.

She locked her gaze with his. "Your family disowned you wrongfully. I know you will not, could not bring yourself to ever turn your back on any other as they did you. You'll make whatever sacrifice is asked to protect your family, all of its members. Am I right?"

He frowned, shifted.

"However," she pressed on, "no matter the situation, no matter what arguments you propound, nothing can ever change the fact that your principal goal must be to protect the future of your house. You've been reared and trained to put that above all else"—she dragged in a breath—"and the future of your house lies with you"—she jabbed his chest—"and me, and our children."

His eyes abruptly narrowed; she blushed, waved dismissively. "That's not the issue here."

The hardening of his expression suggested that their potential offspring was very much an issue with him; she realized, changed tack. Gestured. "Just think—this murderer has already shot Reggie mistakenly. What if he decides he needs the certainty of your death and again tries to kill you, but kills me, or one of our children—or both!—instead?"

His expression told her she'd overplayed her hand, that he knew precisely which string she was pulling. She kept her eyes wide, hands splayed, palms up, and held his gaze; whatever else, that string was an extremely strong one.

He exhaled. Glanced away.

She caught his hands, twined their fingers, felt his tighten, lock. Held his gaze when he looked back, her expression open, without guile. "The future of your house is you and me and our children. Sacrificing your own future to protect others of your family is one thing. Sacrificing *us* is another.

"No one would ever expect it of you. It's not something anyone can ask. Some may be hurt, but we'll be there—you and me and the others who'll help us—we can help them through whatever comes. But you can no longer shield the murderer." She looked into his eyes, then quietly added, "Aside from all else, he isn't worthy of your care."

They stood there, handfasted, gazes locked. The sun washed over them, warming, bringing the promise of growth and abundance, of future happiness. About them, the house seemed to stretch, as if waking from a long sleep. From somewhere downstairs came Allie's voice and a clattering jangle of cutlery.

Martin drew in a long breath, briefly squeezed her fingers. Glanced away through the window.

She waited, praying. What more she could say?

"He's a member of the family who was here over Christmas and New Year that year, then returned for the Easter gathering." Martin looked down at her.

She smiled brilliantly, joyously. "Can you remember . . . ?"

He shook his head. "There are more candidates than you suppose. That side of the family's extensive, and many visited frequently. Every Christmas and New Year, every Easter, and at least twice every summer, there were huge house parties held here. We regularly slept more than seventy."

"So who would know? Allie?"

"No." After a moment, he said, "I'll need to check in my father's study."

She knew he hadn't been in there yet, knew he would want to check alone. She smiled. "I need to look in on Reggie, then talk to Allie."

Slipping her fingers from his, she stretched up and kissed his cheek. He accepted the caress but immediately turned his head. Met her eyes, then bent his head and touched his lips to hers.

In a simple, achingly sweet kiss.

"Join me when you finish with Allie."

Martin opened the door of his father's study, a square room with windows looking west along the cliffs. Allie had yet to penetrate this far; the room was dim and dark. Crossing to the windows, he pulled aside the curtains, stood looking down, watching the river glint as it wended eastward.

All about him was quiet . . . watchful. Was it fancy that made him feel his father so close, as if his presence still permeated this room a full year after his death? Drawing breath, mentally girding his loins, he turned.

Took in the mahogany desk, the admiral's chair behind it, the leather worn to a smooth shine. The blotter, a few marks upon it, the pen sitting in an inkstand long dry. There were no papers left lying on the desk. Everything had been tidied away. Not by him, by the solicitor.

He didn't even know where his father had died, or how, only that he had. Martin recalled the date, realized it had been exactly a year later that he'd first set eyes on Amanda.

The thought of her, of all she'd said, melted his inertia. Sent the past retreating to a manageable distance. Put the present into perspective.

Walking to the desk, he drew out the chair and sat. Scanned the account books and ledgers lining the room, noted new volumes, none unexpected, none out of place. His lips twisted—naturally not. Looking down at the desk, he ignored the dust and reached for the first drawer on the left.

Pens, pencils, various odds and ends—and a piece of scrimshaw he'd given his father as a gift years ago. Martin considered it—knowing his father's propensity for rigidity it seemed odd he'd kept it there, where he would have seen it every day . . . frowning, he slid the drawer closed and opened the next.

Letters, old ones, yellowing with age—quite a pile. Curious, he lifted them out, shuffled through them . . .

They were all addressed to him. In his father's hand.

He stared. Couldn't imagine what . . . wondered when they'd been written.

There was only one way to find out. Reopening the top drawer, he found a letter opener and slit the first packet. He glanced only at the date, then opened the others, placing them in chronological order. The missives spanned nine years; the first had been written four days after he'd left— been banished.

Drawing a breath, he steeled himself, and picked up the first sheet.

> *Martin, my son—I was wrong. So wrong. In my arro-gance and . . .*

He had to stop, look up, force himself to breathe. His hand was shaking; he put the letter down—rose, paced to the window, wrestled with the latch and threw the sash up. Leaned out, welcomed the rush of cool valley air. Breathed deeply. Steadied his whirling wits.

Then, returning to the desk, he sat, picked up the letter and read every word.

Reaching the end, he stared at the door as the past as he'd known it disintegrated, then re-formed. He closed his eyes, for long moments sat absolutely still, imagining . . .

What the break must have meant to his mother.

What that, and the guilt and anguish poured out in the letter, must have done to his father. His righteous, always so concerned over doing the correct thing—being seen to have done the correct thing—father.

Eventually, he opened his eyes and read the rest of the letters. The last included an enclosure from his mother, written just before her death. In it, she pleaded with him to forgive them both and return so his father could right the wrong he'd done. Her words, more than any, left him shattered.

He was still sitting in the chair behind the desk, those letters and others before him, the shadows lengthening on the floor, when the door opened.

Amanda looked in, hesitated. Emotion hung heavy in the room, not threatening, yet . . . closing the door quietly, she crossed to Martin's side.

He heard her, glanced up, blinked—he hesitated, then put out one arm and drew her near. Leaned his head against her side. The arm around her tightened.

"They knew."

She couldn't see his face. "That you weren't the murderer?"

He nodded. "They realized within a few days, and sent off posthaste after me. But . . ."

"But what? If they knew, why were you banished all these years?"

He dragged in a shaky breath. "They'd arranged for me to go to the Continent, where all wealthy, titled scoundrels go when England gets too dangerous. But I decided if my father was effectively disowning me, then I didn't need to follow his instructions. Instead of going to Dover and then to Ostend, I went to Southhampton. The first boat to sail went to Bombay. I didn't care where I went as long as it was far from England. From here."

"They couldn't find you?"

He flicked the pile of letters. "They sent couriers and others to search, but they never caught up with me because they were looking on the wrong continent. If they'd tried India, they'd have found me—I wasn't incognito."

With one hand, she smoothed his hair. "But surely someone in London who'd visited or had dealings with India—"

He shook his head violently. "No—that's the worst part." His voice sounded raw. She felt him draw breath. "They waited here—for me. It was like a form of penance—instead of living their lives as usual, going down for the Season, visiting friends, the shooting and hunting, they stayed here, in this house. From the day I left to the day they died, as far as I can tell they were here, waiting for me to come back and forgive them."

And I never did.

He didn't need to say the words; Amanda could hear them in his mind. His arm tightened about her; he turned his face to her side, for one moment blindly clung.

She stroked his head, tried but couldn't cope with the feelings—the empathy, the sympathy, the sheer frustration that all this—so much sadness—had come to pass. All because of one cowardly man. Whoever he was.

That last occurred to Martin. He disengaged, drawing Amanda down to sit on the padded chair arm. Lifting the stacked letters, he returned them to the drawer, then slid it shut.

What's done is done—the past is dead and buried.

He couldn't go back and make his peace with his parents, but he could avenge them—and Sarah, even Buxton—see that whoever had destroyed their lives was brought to justice, then go on as his parents would have wanted and hoped he would.

He refocused. "I came here to find my father's entertaining ledger. He was a regimented man, exact, precise. He kept a book with all those invited for each family gathering, and marked down who turned up and when. He used to keep it in this desk . . ."

It was in the bottom drawer. He lifted it out, blew off the dust, then flicked through the pages.

"One thing I don't understand—if they knew, why didn't your parents clear your name?"

He glanced up, saw her concern for him in her eyes, managed a fleeting halfsmile. "It's in the letters. My father imagined making a formal declaration—a grand gesture before all the ton. It was the sort of thing he would do, in expiation.

But he wanted me there, by his side, when he did it." He looked back at the ledger. "He died unexpectedly."

The matter had been too painful a subject, a guilt so deep his father had not been able to face it, not without the promise of absolution his presence would have given.

"How did you hear that he'd died, that you could return?"

"After a few years away, I engaged a London solicitor to watch over my interests here. It was from him I learned of my mother's death, and more recently of . . . my father's."

His tone alerted her; she glanced at the ledger. "What?"

It took a moment before he could say, "I told you my father loved family gatherings. After that Easter, there are no further entries."

No further gatherings. They'd lived here, all alone, completely cut off from family and friends, as he had been. He sighed, felt the blame and the bitterness, his companions for years, dissipate, flow away; his parents had suffered far more than he.

Jaw setting, he placed the ledger open on the table. "This is the list of all those who attended that Easter."

They pored over it, then turned back to the list for the previous New Year. Notations against the names indicated when various guests had arrived. Amanda hunted out a fresh sheet of paper and a pencil.

"Give me the name of every male of your mother's line who was here that New Year, on the second, then again at Easter, on the right date. Don't judge, don't exclude—we'll do that later."

He picked up the ledger, sat back and obliged. Then they culled the list of those who, due to age or some other reason, could not have been the murderer.

"Twelve." Amanda considered the list. "So he's one of these men. Now, what else do we know of him?"

Martin took the list, ran his eye down it. "You can cross off Luc and Edward."

She took the list back, obliterated Luc's name, then hesitated. "How old was Edward at the time?"

"He's almost two years younger than Luc . . . he would have been sixteen, almost seventeen."

"Hmm."

"You can't seriously imagine he did it." Martin reached for the list.

Amanda whisked it out of reach. "We have to be logical about this. I agree about Luc, but only because in full daylight no one could possibly confuse you. But Edward?" She raised a brow. "Think back—what was Edward like at sixteen?"

Martin looked at her, eyes narrowing, then waved. "Have it your way—leave Edward on the list for the moment."

Amanda humphed. Edward had the same coloring as Martin, and while she wouldn't have said they were that similar now, then . . . ? If he'd been anything like the males in her family, by sixteen, Edward would have been nearly full grown. Easy enough to mistake at a distance.

Not that she seriously believed he'd done anything so horrible, but keeping stuffily righteous Edward's name on their list, having eliminated Luc's, seemed—however childishly—satisfying. "Very well. Now we need to check with the others who were here that Easter, and eliminate those gentlemen others can remember being with at the time of the murder."

Martin looked at her. "How's Reggie?"

She grinned. "Much better, and quite ready to travel back to London."

Martin rose. He rounded the desk to join her. "That's one other thing we know about our man. He was on the Great North Road two nights ago."

She let him turn her to the door. "Actually, that's several things."

He raised a brow at her.

"Our man was someone who knew *you* were headed up the Great North Road two nights ago—but not why, and not in what carriage."

Chapter 21

After making arrangements to leave the next morning, they retired early to their beds. Arms crossed, coatless, cravatless, shoulder propped against the frame, Martin stood at the bay window of the earl of Dexter's bedchamber and watched moonlight and shadows drift over the valley. Let the sight sink into him, along with an acceptance that the title, the room, the house, the fields he could see spread out before him, were now his.

His responsibility, his to care for.

Acceptance brought the first hint of peace—a peace he hadn't believed would ever again be his, that hadn't touched his soul for the past ten years.

It was within his grasp once more, all because he'd chased a golden-haired houri up the Great North Road. She'd been his beacon, the light that had drawn him first from the shadows, and now further, back into the life he'd been reared to consider his destiny.

Without her, he wouldn't be here. She'd given his future back to him. Intended to be an integral part of it.

His lips quirked. He thought back over the past weeks, over the vacillations, the qualifications. None seemed important anymore; they both knew where they were headed.

Thinking of her had the inevitable effect, knowing he

could go to her, now, tonight, and she would open her arms to him, welcome him . . .

But she hadn't yet given him her answer. The fact she'd felt it necessary to put miles between them just to think clearly . . . he couldn't, in all conscience—in all wisdom—act as if he took her decision for granted, even if he knew very well what it would be. Regardless of how hard she thought.

It wasn't logic that bound them, and logic couldn't tear them apart.

The latch clicked; he glanced back at the door, expecting Colly on some errand. Instead, his houri, dressed in a soft robe, slipped in. She looked around and saw him, closed the door, then headed toward him.

He turned, beyond surprise. He'd blown out the candles so he could see outside; the room was awash in moonbeams and shadows, elusive, mysterious, enticing.

She came to him with a soft smile on her lips, a gentle, questioning light in her eyes. She said nothing as she walked into his arms, reached up to lay a hand against his cheek. As she had so often before.

Their eyes met in the dimness—no demand, no command, nothing beyond the moment and them—the here and now of their reality.

She tilted her face, lifted her lips, drew his lips to hers. He bent his head—their lips melded, then, with the familiarity of practice, their mouths fused. Tongues tangled as the world fell away. Reality shrank—to this room, then further, until their senses knew no more than each other, nothing beyond the inch of air that caressed their heating skins.

Wrapped in the wonder she so effortlessly conjured, the promise of sensual delight, he sank his fingers into her curls, spread them wide—stood still as she unbuttoned his shirt, dragged it from his breeches, pushed it back over his shoulders. He shrugged, stripped the shirt off, flung it aside—reached for her. Captured her mouth again, drew her to him, molded her against him, then sent his hands skating, searching for the tie of her robe, easing the garment over her shoulders while she dealt with the buttons at his waist.

It was cool in the room but when they broke apart, she reached for the hem of her ivory nightgown, bunching the long skirt, then lifting it up, wriggling it over her head. He sat on the window seat, stripped off boots and stockings, watching her, then stood and dispensed with his breeches.

Naked, he reached for her as she emerged, tossing her curls free of the voluminous gown. She let it fall, drifting from her fingers to pool in the moonlight behind her as his hands closed about her waist and he drew her up on her toes against him. Skin to burning skin—need to aching need.

Amanda wound her arms about his neck and gave him her mouth, took his, urged him on. Tonight was theirs—whatever else happened, nothing could change this. Their oneness was absolute, unshakable—on that she harbored no doubts. Being in his arms, feeling the abrasion of raspy male hair against her sensitized skin, sensing the strength in the muscles that flexed and locked about her, most of all sensing the blessing of the place—of the room, of the house, the estate, the cliffs and the valley and the moon beyond his window—it all came together, coalesced and sent her heart soaring on a wave of emotion too deep, too powerful to be mere delight.

She was where she was meant to be—here, now, in his arms. She'd searched for so long to find her place—now she'd found it, found her future, found her life.

She was his—her decision was behind her, commitment was upon her. That was why she'd come to him tonight, to make it plain her acceptance was unconditional—no if, no but, no maybe.

He understood. She could feel it in the tide of possessiveness that rose through him and surrounded her. In the strength in his splayed hands as they held her to him, molded her provocatively to his aroused body—a promise, both of what he would give, and what he would take.

That was echoed in his kiss, bold and commanding, an intent so blatant, so primal, it made her knees weak.

Hands spread on his back, she clung, glorying in the powerful muscles flexing beneath her fingers, in the masculine power that, regardless of all appearances, existed, first and last, to please her. To take pleasure in her delight, to let her pleasure him in return.

She set her mind to that, eased back so she could run her hands over his bare chest. It had been too long since she'd had him like this, naked in her arms, hot skin beneath her palms. He let her have her way, slid his hands down to her bottom and cupped, kneaded, held her up, her hips against his thighs while his tongue and lips teased, tantalized, made all manner of explicit promises. She let her hands roam, filling her senses with the curves of muscle and bone, with the weight of him, with the heat, the solidity—with his maleness.

He let her explore as she would, let her reach down and close her hand about his erection, rigid and burning, pressed against her soft belly. As before, the contrast of steel encased in peach silk fascinated; she stroked, circled with her fingers, slid them down, marveling, then closed her hand again.

Kissed him more urgently—and was swept away by his reaction, by the surging, rolling tide of possessive need. It crashed over them, pushed aside all restraint, drove them before it.

Not, to her surprise, to the bed, but to the bay window.

He lifted her to the window seat. "Kneel facing the window."

She did, recalling another time, another place, when she'd faced a window and he'd appeared behind her. He urged her feet and calves apart, then stepped between; his hands closed about her hips as she shifted her knees to accommodate him. Then he pressed close.

His hands rose, closed about her breasts, possessively kneading, then his fingers found her nipples, artfully teased, caressed . . . then delivered on the promise, fingers squeezing tight, tight—until she arched, her head falling back against his shoulder as she shifted restlessly before him.

At her back, he was hard, ready, an eloquent assurance of all that was to come, but he didn't immediately join with her. Instead, his hands roved her body, flagrantly possessive, stamping his brand on every inch of her skin until she writhed, on fire, hips pressed against him as she rocked, evocatively pleading.

One hard hand splayed over her stomach, anchoring her as the other slid between her thighs. He stroked, caressed, opened her—exposed the entrance to her body—then probed. He filled her with his long fingers, worked them until she sobbed and sank her nails into his thighs.

He drew his hand from her. She lifted her head, gasped, struggled to fill her lungs. Stared, dazed, at the moonlit beauty beyond the window as she felt him slide slowly, possessively, into her body. Felt every inch as he filled her, let her lids fall, felt her body ease and joyously accept him.

And then he was there, sunk in her softness, his stomach flush against her bottom. She exhaled, one long sigh of contented expectation. His arms wrapped around her, one crossing her chest, hand closing about one swollen breast, fingers stroking the aching nipple; his other arm wrapped about her hips, hand splayed across her lower stomach. Holding her trapped, captive.

Then he flexed his spine and sent pure delight rolling through her. Withdrew and thrust again. Sent a slow, repetitive undulation of hot pleasure coursing under her skin, spreading to every corner of her being, focusing every last fragment of her awareness on him, on them, on their joining.

In the last lucid corner of his mind, Martin gave thanks to the carpenter who had created the window seat—it was at precisely the right height. So he could hold her like this, her bottom flush to his groin, only slightly bent forward, his chest to her silken back, his hands full of her bounty, and effortlessly love her.

Effortlessly take her, all of her, slide so deeply into her and possess her so thoroughly that there would never again be any sense of separateness. Her body, hot, wet, yielding, closed lovingly about him; she rode his thrusts, each deep penetration, welcoming him in, encouraging him to linger, reluctantly letting him go—so he could return again, press deeper still, make her breath seize. Fill her deeply, give himself to her and claim all she was, take and give again.

It was elementally primitive, joining naked and free in the

night. Feeling the burning heat of their bodies contrast with the cool night air. Feeling the mystery of the night enclose them, the caress of the moonlight on their merging bodies a gentle benediction.

Feeling the hunger grow and swell and stretch, feeling it roar and race through their veins. Feeling desire explode and drive them, turning their bodies slick and hard and tight.

They were both gasping, valiantly clinging to the last shreds of sanity, wanting, desperately, to prolong the moment, so intense, so intimate, so compelling, when he lowered his head, ran his teeth along the taut curve of her neck, exposed as she arched her head back. And thrust deeper still.

"I'll never let you go." The words were gravelly and harsh. "You know that, don't you?"

Her "Yes" was a whisper, a silver surrender wafting on the moonlight.

She lifted one hand from his thigh, reached up, back, touched his cheek. Lovingly traced as she had so often before, the simplest communion.

He turned his head, pressed his lips to her palm, then bent, pressed his lips to the base of her throat, tightened his hold on her.

Slipped the reins and let them free.

Let the power flow through him into her, felt it reflect back, thrust it back, felt the inexorable rise, the overwhelming rush, the irresistible escalation that caught them up, fused their souls, sent them soaring into bright ecstasy. Until they shattered.

The power gently ebbed, leaving them floating on a golden sea.

Martin woke before dawn as he had once before with Amanda's soft weight snuggled against him. This time, he closed his eyes and let contentment wash over him.

After wallowing for some moments, he sighed, turned on his side, and ran his hands slowly down her body. She murmured sleepily, arched, turned to him and wound her arms about his neck. He kissed her lingeringly, then murmured, "We'll have to separate when we get back to town."

"Hmm . . . but not for long . . . and . . . not yet."

Eyes still closed, she drew him to her.

He closed his arms about her, rolled her beneath him, and left tomorrow to take care of itself.

It took them most of the day to drive back to London. Onslow's arm wasn't healed sufficiently for him to drive; they left him recuperating under Allie's eagle eye, and drove down in Martin's curricle. Martin handled the reins with Amanda beside him; Reggie sat behind in the tiger's seat.

As the curricle sped south, Martin and Amanda outlined all they'd learned, all they'd concluded—all they suspected. Reggie listened, then soberly said, "He won't stop, y'know. If he was prepared to kill to see the matter left alone, when you appear again, he won't just let be."

Expression grim, Martin nodded. "The question now is, should we let him know who he shot—or should we let him worry about that, too?"

Reggie voted to increase the pressure. "In that case"—Martin flicked his whip and urged the horses on—"we'll have to hide you."

They accomplished that by taking a roundabout route once they reached London's outskirts; they approached the fashionable district along the south side of the park as the last of the daylight faded, slipped into the drive of Fulbridge House, and quickly rattled around into the coach-yard behind it.

"No one saw us." Amanda scrambled down.

"Not a soul who would recognize us, anyway." Reggie climbed down from his perch more slowly.

Martin handed the reins to a groom, then turned to Reggie. "How's your head?"

Straightening from stretching his back, Reggie thought, then replied, "Not as bad as it was—the fresh air seems to have helped."

"Good. We'll have Jules, my henchman, take a look at the wound. He has tried-and-true remedies for all injuries."

Amanda slipped her arm supportively through Reggie's

and turned him to the house. "Presumably Jules knows how to make tea."

Later, when Jules had redressed Reggie's wound after announcing it was healing well, then supplied them with a sustaining if somewhat exotic dinner, they took refuge in the library and settled to plan.

On the drive down they'd agreed that the one other person they needed to involve was Luc Ashford. Martin wrote a note and sent it off to Ashford House, then they turned their minds to more immediate concerns.

"Reggie can stay here, which will keep him out of sight and also mean there's always one of us here—at the center of operations, so to speak."

Reggie had been wandering the room, looking at this and that; he considered, then nodded. "Everyone will know I left with Amanda." He looked at her, curled up in one corner of the fantastically draped daybed. "If you say I went to visit friends in the north, no one will expect to see me."

"Except your mother," Amanda reminded him, "who won't believe me. And I don't think you'll want me to tell her you've a hole in your head."

Reggie blanched. "Good God, no! I'll write a note. Tell her I'm going to see those friends. She'll accept that."

Martin looked at Amanda. "I'll take you home later tonight. Will your father have returned from his trip?"

She counted, then nodded. "But why do you want him?"

"Because he needs to know the truth." When she frowned, he raised his brows. "I'm going to marry you, and I haven't even spoken to him yet."

She knew better than to argue, but made a mental note to be present at any discussion between her sire—a Cynster born and bred—and her soon-to-be husband, another rigidly protective male. She had no wish to find herself somehow excluded from the pending excitement.

Martin made three copies of their list of suspects. He was blotting the last when the front doorbell pealed. Picking up the lists, he rose, crossed to the daybed and handed a copy to Amanda; Reggie came up and took another.

The door opened; Jules stepped in. "Viscount Calverton," he intoned in his heavily accented English.

Luc walked in, his gaze swiftly roving the room before coming to rest on them, gathered before the hearth. Jules stepped back and quietly shut the door. Luc blinked, surprised to see Amanda and Reggie—even more surprised as he took in the bandage swathing Reggie's head.

"Good God! What happened to you?"

Reggie frowned. "Some relative of yours shot me."

"*What?*" Luc glanced at Martin; reserve infused his expression. "I received your . . . summons, Dexter." He gestured. "So here I am."

Martin grimaced, and waved him to the chaise. "My apologies for the phrasing—I needed you here."

Luc's brows rose. When Martin said no more, he came forward and sat, effortlessly graceful as ever, opposite Amanda. He shot her a hard, considering glance, then looked at Martin. "Why?"

Martin met his gaze. "I've just returned from Hathersage."

Concisely, Martin related all they'd learned. Luc listened, his concentration absolute. He didn't interrupt; Martin seemed to anticipate his questions, digressing here and there to fill in details. He ended his recitation at the point where he'd discovered his parents had realized the truth, and tried without success to find him. He concluded with his resolution to discover which of their joint relatives had committed the dastardly deed.

Martin fell silent, waited. Luc dragged in a huge breath. "My apologies. I should have known better, but . . . at the time, I honestly didn't know what to think."

Martin's lips lifted wrily. "As it happens, I can say the same to you."

Luc thought, then stared. "You thought *I* did it?"

"Well, I knew I hadn't. And I didn't know until yesterday that Sarah had been forced. If not me, then the most likely to have swept her off her feet was you."

Luc pulled a face. "I thought of her as you did—like a younger sister. To do that . . . it would be like casting covetous eyes on Emily or Anne." He shuddered.

"Quite." Martin sat on the daybed, stretching one arm along its back so his fingertips touched Amanda's frothing curls. He set the remaining two copies of their list on his knee, gestured to them. "We've made a start at defining the field—the murderer, presumably also Sarah's defiler and Reggie's attacker, must be one of these men."

He explained about his father's ledger; Luc remembered it. Taking one list, Luc scanned the names. "It can't be Giles or Cameron." He glanced at Martin. "I'd stopped at the Millikens' near Derby, so I reached Hathersage mid-morning. I didn't make it to the house. As I was crossing the yard, Giles and Cameron came out carting guns and a hamper; they challenged me to join them and I did. I was with them all day. We didn't get back until dusk." He grimaced. "When the commotion was over and the decisions made. We were told not to attempt to speak with you. They took you away an hour later."

His face impassive, Martin nodded, and considered the list. "That leaves nine."

Luc rescanned the list. "All were at the house when we got back that day." He glanced at Martin. "It's not going to be easy checking where people were, who remembers what, ten years after the fact."

"True, but we have something more recent to check. Who was on the Great North Road three nights ago?"

Luc looked at Reggie, perched on an ottoman. "They actually shot you?"

Reggie looked at him. "Would you like to see the furrow in my skull?"

Luc winced. "I'll take your word for it." He looked at Martin. "But why?"

"My guess is that he assumed *I* would be the man in the coach. Amanda and I were back down the road, before the curve before the turn-off, discussing matters. Reggie took the coach around the bend, intending to halt and wait for us. When the coach slowed, the murderer no doubt assumed it was turning for Hathersage. You know the place—it's an ideal ambush."

Luc nodded. He looked down at the list.

Amanda steeled herself to insist that Edward's name remain on the list, but instead of arguing that point, Luc nodded again. "Right. I can check these names more easily than you. I'll have to ask Mama"—he held up his hand to stay their protests—"*without* telling her, to get the directions of Oliver and Bruce, who I haven't seen in years. I should be able to run most of them to earth at their clubs."

Martin nodded. "If we can place people at a ball or any public function three nights ago, we can cross them off the list."

"You're sure it's the same man—the murderer and the man who shot Reggie?"

"For the sake of the family, I sincerely hope so." When Luc looked his question, Martin explained, "We have witnesses who'll swear they both 'looked just like me.' "

Luc eyed Martin's face, then grimaced. "I'll start tonight." He rose.

Martin rose, too. "Reggie's staying here, out of sight. Whoever he is, if the murderer isn't already wondering if it really was me he shot, he'll certainly be wondering who he hit once I reappear."

"And when will that be?" Luc asked.

"At the Duchess of St. Ives' ball." Amanda smiled as Martin turned to her. "Tomorrow night."

"Well, my dear." Her father shut the drawing room door having seen Martin out. "I thoroughly approve of your choice."

He smiled as he crossed to stand before the fire, his eyes touching Louise's as he passed her, reclining on the chaise a book forgotten on her lap.

"There is the scandal to be dealt with but, overall, my verdict concurs with Devil's." Taking up his stance, Arthur smiled fondly down at Amanda. "It'll be an excellent match, and Dexter's precisely the sort of gentleman we would have hoped to be welcoming into the family."

Amanda exchanged a glance with her mother. Louise smiled, and rescued her book. "Amanda has suggested Honoria's dinner and ball tomorrow night as the most suitable time to declare the family's stance—by demonstration rather than proclamation, in the circumstances—and with that, I concur. And so will Honoria and Helena, I'm sure."

"I feel confident I can leave Dexter's social ressurrection safely in your delicate hands." The twinkle in Arthur's eye was for them both. He continued to hold Amanda's gaze, his own rich with affection, but also, she realized, with shrewd assessment.

"I'm convinced, from all Devil and your cousins have reported, that the old scandal will prove to have been a dreadful mistake, and Dexter will emerge blameless. His character from the time he left England to the present . . . impossible to hide such a flaw for so long, especially under such challenging circumstances as those he has faced. From all you and he have now told me, it seems his plans to resolve the issue are well advanced."

Arthur paused; she found herself trapped in his blue gaze. "Which brings us to the matter of the real culprit, who, judging by poor Reggie's head, remains dangerous. While I have no qualms whatever for your safety while in Dexter's company, you will please me, for the time you still remain in my charge, by taking all due care when you are not under his protection."

There'd been a subtle change in her father's tone; he rarely laid down the law, but when he did speak in such fashion, Amanda knew better than to argue. "I will—I promise." She glanced at Louise, who, one brow arched, was looking at her spouse.

"Is there truly any danger?"

Arthur met her gaze. "Dexter believes the potential exists, and he isn't the sort to jump at shadows."

It was the perfect setting in which to effect a grand entrance—a grandiloquent gesture to capture the attention of the frenetic ton. The details were discussed and debated over the dinner that preceded Honoria's ball; the support of the ton's most influential hostesses—all of whom were present—was therefore engaged and assured from the start.

All agreed that Martin should make his bow with Amanda on his arm only once most of the ball guests had arrived.

When the moment came, Webster announced, first, Mr. Spencer Cynster and his wife Patience, escorting Lady Osbaldestone—who'd insisted on being part of the fun—and the Dowager Duchess of St. Ives.

That was enough to have people glancing toward the entrance, primed to hear the announcement of the next arrivals—Lord Martin Fulbridge, Earl of Dexter, accompanied by Miss Amanda Cynster.

Eyes widened, lips parted in momentary surprise, superseded by rabid speculation as the assembled host watched Martin, tall, starkly handsome, leonine mane winking golden in the chandeliers' light, bow before Honoria, then shake hands with Devil, all with Amanda at his side. The whispers had started even before they'd turned, side by side, Amanda's hand on Martin's sleeve, to descend the stairs in the Dowager's and Lady Osbaldestone's wake.

The ton was wide awake to the implications; everyone watching read the message with ease. When the next guests announced proved to be Lord Arthur and Lady Louise Cynster, there was no doubt in anyone's mind that an alliance had been sealed between two major aristocratic houses, and a formal announcement would be made in due course.

Formal announcements were never so much fun as being privy to such news ahead of others.

"I should think"—Lady Osbaldestone directed an evil grin at Martin as he and Amanda joined them in the ballroom—"that your impending nuptials will be the principal item of interest at every gathering tomorrow."

Martin raised a nonchalant brow.

"Tomorrow?" Arthur, with Louise, joined the group, his gaze raking the frantically chattering hordes. "I'll wager the news will reach half the ton before they find their beds tonight."

"No point wagering," Vane replied. "You'll never get anyone to take you on."

The three men exchanged long-suffering glances; their ladies had already turned to greet others, all dying to learn details of this most intriguing affair.

Amanda chatted, smiled, played her role of serenely con-

fident countess-to-be to the hilt, all the while guarding
against those sly, probing questions that sought to define just
where she and Martin had first met, just how she had come
to know him, when he had proposed. With her mother on
one side and her aunt Helena on the other, she encountered
little difficulty maintaining the facade necessary to achieve
tonnish acceptance.

Sharp-eyed matrons and shrewd observers departed, if not
deceived, then satisfied that the proposed union was secure,
stamped with the Cynsters' and others' unconditional approval, and all was as it should be.

A "suitable and felicitous match" was the ton's overwhelming verdict.

As the notes of the first waltz floated over the crowd,
Amanda turned. Surrounded by their ladies chatting animatedly, Martin, her father, Devil and Vane stood in a group,
tall, broad shouldered, arrogantly handsome, exchanging
cynical comments—and keeping watch. Devil's gaze rested
on Honoria; Vane's gaze flicked again and again to Patience.
In her father, it was the habit of a lifetime. As for Martin, he
caught her gaze, then took the step that closed the distance
between them.

He smiled charmingly at the ladies with whom she'd been
chatting, then his gaze returned to her face, "My dance, I
believe."

"Indeed, my lord."

He took her hand and led her to the dance floor; she went
into his arms and he whirled her away. Into the dance. Into
their future.

Others held back, watching, then Louise and Arthur
joined them, then Devil and Honoria, and Vane and Patience, then other couples stepped in and swelled the ranks.

"So far, so good." Martin looked down into her smiling
face and felt equally smug. "I'd forgotten how such things
were done."

"We're not finished yet—one appearance does not a solid
facade create."

His smugness faded. "You mean I have to attend more
functions like this?"

Amanda's dimple winked. "Perhaps not quite as intense as this. But you needn't think you can slink back into that great house in Park Lane, deeming your duty done."

He read the determination behind her smile. He glanced around, caught the odd disgruntled eye. "At least I no longer have to pretend to approve of those man-milliners you had in your train."

"They weren't man-milliners!"

They spent the rest of the dance in a bantering discussion of those gentleman who'd previously vied for her attention. When the music ended, they were beseiged by those wanting to be able to claim acquaintance with the latest news. When the orchestra struck up again, numerous gentleman offered to partner Amanda; she smiled and declined, turned her smile on Martin and gave him her hand. "Perhaps we could stroll?"

With an easy nod, he excused them; covering her hand where it rested on his sleeve, he led her down the room.

They were stopped constantly; it was some time before Amanda could ask, "Have you heard from Luc?"

"He's somewhere here." Martin scanned the crowd. "He must have learned something . . . there he is."

They changed tack and came up with Luc, standing a few feet from a group that included his sisters and Amelia, surrounded by a court of earnest young gentlemen and some less young, focused on Amelia.

Luc nodded. "I can eliminate some names . . ." The introduction to a cotillion rang out; his gaze returned to the group. His attention didn't shift when his sisters accepted partners and headed for the floor; only when Amelia brightly gave her hand to Lord Polworth did Luc look back at them.

"Is there somewhere we can talk without being overheard?"

Martin nodded. "Devil said to use his study." He glanced at Amanda.

"We can go out through the side door."

She led them into the main house. The sounds of the ball faded. Reaching Devil's study, they walked in. A desk lamp was alight, turned low. Amanda adjusted the wick. "What have you found?"

Luc searched, patting his pockets. "Damn! I've forgotten the list."

He glanced at Martin, who went through the same pantomine with no better result.

Amanda sighed, lifted her reticule, opened it, hunted, and pulled out her copy of the list. Luc held out his hand; she pretended not to see. Spreading the sheet, she held it so the light fell on it. "Now—who have you checked?"

Luc walked to her side; Martin came up on the other.

They all studied the list.

"Moreton." Luc tapped the list, glanced at Martin. "I was standing beside him when you made your entrance in there—he was genuinely delighted at the sight. He's no more capable of dissembling now than he was ten years ago. If he was the murderer, he would have been reeling. Instead, he was thrilled."

Martin nodded. "Cross off Moreton."

"And George and Bruce and Melville, too. They haven't set foot in London this Season, and from what you told me, the time between either of you deciding to go north and Reggie being shot leaves no leeway for anyone out of town to have been alerted in time to act."

"That hadn't occurred to me," Martin murmured, "but you're right. Not only did the murderer have to learn of my departure, there was only an hour in which he could have heard."

"Actually"—Luc glanced at Amanda—"it probably wasn't *your* departure he heard of, but Amanda's."

"Mine?"

"Your recent entrance notwithstanding, your relationship hasn't been any sort of secret. If the murderer heard that you"—Luc nodded at Amanda—"were going to Scotland for a visit, he might well have assumed Martin would accompany you, and that you would stop at Hathersage."

"That makes more sense. There was very little time between me deciding and leaving." Martin looked at the list. "We have five names left."

"And I doubt we'll do better." Luc leaned against the desk. "I've checked four of those five, and none of them can offer verifiable evidence of where they were five nights ago."

Amanda blinked. "How can four gentlemen not be *somewhere* someone saw them?"

"Easily." Luc glanced at Martin. "Radley's the one I haven't had a word with yet, but you can bet he'll be the same as the others."

Martin grimaced. "I see."

"See what?" Amanda looked from one to the other.

Luc looked at Martin, then said, "Radley and the others are cousins, much the same age as us."

When he said no more, Amanda stared at him, then looked at Martin. "You can't mean . . ." She looked again at Luc. "*All* of them?"

He gave her a helpless "what-would-you" look.

"Humph!" She looked at the list. One name leaped out at her. "What about Edward? You're not going to tell me he wasn't doing his duty accompanying your sisters and mama to some ball."

The cynical look Luc bent on her was answer enough. "According to Cottsloe, our butler, Edward came home early, told Cottsloe to tell Mama he was in bed with a migraine and didn't wish to be disturbed, and left. He returned sometime during the night, but no one was awake to know when."

Her racing thoughts must have shown in her face, for Luc added, "I wouldn't read too much into the timing—he's done much the same before. Unfortunately, the . . . establishment he favors is usually afloat on gin. I wouldn't trust the word of anyone there. The same goes for the others—not the gin, but that they can't produce a reliable witness, which means we can't cross them off our list, but their movements don't necessarily make them guilty."

Amanda wrinkled her nose; she studied the list while Martin and Luc made arrangements to meet at Martin's house the next day.

She stared at one name, continued to frown. She was acquainted with the five men still on the list, although other than Edward, she knew them only distantly. The other four were as Luc had said, very like him and Martin; she had no difficulty imagining that they might have been visiting some lady whose name they wouldn't divulge. That was one thing, but to frequent an establishment that "floated on gin"?

She knew Luc too well to think he was exaggerating; if anything, he would have—and had—glossed over his brother's less-admirable predilections.

Which left her feeling decidedly equivocal about Edward. What sort of man actively posed as a long-suffering, righteous puritan to society, but secretly visited dens of iniquity?

"Come on." Martin took her elbow. "We'd better get back to the ballroom before imaginations become overheated."

Amanda stuffed the list back into her reticule and let him lead her to the door.

Chapter 22

Under orders from his prospective bride and mother-in-law, Martin called in Upper Brook Street the next morning, took Amanda up beside him in his curricle, then drove across Park Lane and into the park.

Tooling down the Avenue, he glanced at Amanda, noted her bright eyes, sensed the sheer triumph that gripped her— decided it made the sacrifice worthwhile. She'd assured him he only had to do this once; he'd deduced it was some strange rite understood only by the female half of the ton.

That deduction gained credence as the matrons and senior hostesses, sitting regally in their carriages drawn up along the verge, preceptibly brightened at the sight of them, then smiled graciously and nodded; Amanda smiled radiantly and nodded back. Martin contented himself with the occasional impassive nod to the more influential ladies and those he recognized as his parents' friends, and concentrated on guiding his high-bred bays through the obstacle course of the fashionable area.

They drew up to chat with the Dowager Duchess of St. Ives, and later exchanged pleasantries with Emily Cowper. Then they were through the gauntlet, past the last carriage; Martin let the bays trot. He was congratulating himself on having survived the ordeal, when Amanda tugged his sleeve and pointed to where carriages were queueing to turn.

"Now we go back again."

He glanced at her—she wasn't joking. He grumbled, but complied. He'd agreed to perform as requested until she and her female relatives—a pack of assertive and willful ladies—decreed his resurrection within the ton accomplished. Thereafter, he'd gathered, he could retire from the fray, returning for command performances, much as their husbands and sons.

He'd deemed it prudent not to mention he intended retiring for most of the year to Hathersage. As they drove once more between the lines of carriages, his home had never seemed more attractive.

They were back in the thick of things when Amanda grabbed his arm, squeezed so hard he felt her nails through his sleeve. *"Look!"* She pointed with her parasol.

He followed the line to two young ladies strolling in the sunshine, a gentleman following a few paces behind. "Edward, Emily and Anne."

"It's Edward." Amanda's tone was shocked.

He glanced at her; the color had drained from her cheeks. She looked at him, eyes wide. "I never realized . . . at a distance, he looks *just like you.*"

Martin swallowed a dismissive snort. "Don't get carried away—all five on our list look like me at a distance." He glanced again at Edward, but the press of traffic forced him to drive on. "He doesn't look *that* much like me."

"I know—that's my point. He's shorter and slighter and his hair isn't as bright. And his features aren't as strong. I didn't truly think he was that likely . . ." She swivelled to look back again. "But just now . . . it's the distance. It reduces everything to just proportions."

She faced forward again; a quick glance showed her face had taken on that stubborn cast he knew well. "If it *is* Edward—"

"Amanda—"

"No." She held up her hand. "I'm not saying it's proven, but just suppose it was him. How did he find out about us—you or me—going north . . ."

Her voice trailed away; he glanced at her again. Her face

had blanked, then she looked at him and excitement rushed in. "Amelia! We have to find her."

She looked around, scanning the lawns. "I haven't seen her . . . she wasn't with Mama, which means she's strolling, but she wasn't with Emily and Anne, and Reggie isn't about . . . *there* she is!" She grabbed his arm again. "Pull over. Quickly."

He squeezed the curricle between an ancient landau occupied by a bedizened old harridan with a yapping pug and a cabriolet overflowing with giggling girls. Who took one look at him and giggled all the more.

Amanda was all but jigging in her seat. Amelia had seen her waving madly; escorted by Lord Canthorp, she came strolling up.

Amelia touched fingers with her sister, smiled at him, then introduced his lordship. While he and Canthorp exchanged a few drawling words, Amanda and Amelia exchanged meaningful glances.

As a result, Canthorp received a pretty dismissal and was sent on his way. As soon as he was out of earshot, Amelia looked at Amanda. "What?"

Amanda drew breath, opened her lips, paused, then carefully asked, "The day I left for Scotland, did you tell anyone where I'd gone?"

Cornflower blue eyes reflecting her curiosity, Amelia nodded. "At Lady Cardigan's luncheon, Lady Bain and Mrs. Carr asked where you were."

Amanda's excitement faded. "No one else?"

"Well, no one else *asked*, but we stopped in the park on the way to the luncheon and met the Ashfords. It came out in conversation with them."

"It did?" Amanda gripped Amelia's hand. "Who was there—of the Ashfords, I mean?"

"The usual four—Emily, Anne, their mama and Edward."

Martin closed his hand over Amanda's, squeezing to silence her. "Amelia, think back. What exactly did you tell them?"

Amelia smiled. "That's easy. Mama and I discussed what we should say before we left home. We decided we should

be deliberately vague. We agreed to say Amanda had gone
north for a few days, nothing more."

They drove around the streets for an hour, debating the possibility that Edward—*Edward!*—was the villain they
sought.

"You cannot—simply *cannot*—argue that it isn't possible," Amanda declared.

They'd parted from Amelia, both so subdued, so shocked,
that Amelia had been openly concerned. Amanda had
calmed her twin with a reassurance and a promise to tell all
later, then they'd driven on, quickly leaving the noisy Avenue behind.

"I'll allow that it's possible." The deadened tone of Martin's voice told her he was, in truth, more convinced than
that, but . . .

She glanced at him, at his stony expression. "If you're
thinking that exposing him will cause Luc, Lady Calverton
and his sisters pain, don't forget all the pain he's already
caused people no longer able to seek justice."

The frowning glance he threw her told her she'd hit a
nerve; she hurried on, "And we can't forget that, if he thinks
he's got away with it, he might do something like it again.
You cannot expect me to believe that half the men in your
family frequent the stews. And, you see, Edward has built a
reputation as steadfastly righteous, stuffy and pompous but
always rigidly correct—you haven't been here to see it, but
he has. Melly and I always thought it was his way of puffing
himself up, especially because, although he's handsome
enough, he could never hold a candle to Luc. Or you."

Martin grimaced. After a moment, he said, "When we
were younger, he was always in our shadow."

Amanda kept silent; if she was struggling to reconcile the
possibility, then how much harder would it be for him?

Two minutes later, she closed her hand over one of Martin's, twined her fingers with his, felt him glance at her. "I
just remembered something Lady Osbaldestone said. I'm
not sure what she was alluding to, but it wasn't just your situation. She said that in even the best of families, there's of-

ten a bad apple in an otherwise sound crop. She said that in your case, no one believed *you* were a bad apple. She didn't say it in so many words, but I gathered she considered it a family's duty to weed out the bad apple."

She met his gaze. "I was just thinking—wasn't that what your father thought he was doing? What he felt, for the family's sake, he had to do? Only he picked the wrong apple."

He held her gaze for a moment, then his grew distant; he looked back at his horses. A minute passed, then he stirred, glanced around. "Luc will be God knows where at this hour."

"But he'll meet us at Fulbridge House at four."

When Martin nodded, his expression grim, she quietly added, "And between then and now, we have Lady Hetherington's *al fresco* luncheon and Lady Montague's at-home."

He looked at her, then swore.

They attended both events. Although Martin cloaked his impatience in effortless charm, his temper had never been so close to his surface; Amanda could feel it, a thrumming tension just beneath his skin. It grated on her nerves. When, ten minutes after they'd arrived at Lady Montague's, Martin grumbled in her ear, "Can we go now?" she obligingly developed a headache, and excused them both.

Martin helped her into his curricle, then whipped up his horses for Park Lane.

"Edward?" Reggie stared. "The blackguard! Yes, I can just imagine it, the way he proses on and on—"

"Wait!" Martin cut him off.

Together with Reggie, Amanda looked at Martin, standing before the library windows, staring at the courtyard filled with greenery.

"We shouldn't condemn him without proof. As yet, we have none."

She conceded, "All we know is that it *might* be him."

Martin sighed. "In all cases—Sarah, Buxton and Reggie—Edward had both knowledge and opportunity, something we've yet to establish for anyone else. However, until we have unequivocal proof, I suggest we temper our stand."

From the chaise on which he was reclining, Reggie grimaced at Amanda, perched in her favorite spot on the daybed. She leaned forward and whispered, "Could it have been Edward you saw?"

"Yes, damn it!" Reggie whispered back. "I said it looked like Dexter because I'd just seen him, and it was him who was asking—I was facing him then and there. I know it wasn't Luc because his hair is pitch in the night, but if Dexter hadn't been there to compare with, I'd have said the blackguard looked just like Edward." Reggie glanced at Martin's back. "Not that that will wash as proof, unfortunately."

Luc arrived as the clocks struck four. He took one look at Martin's face, and asked, "What?"

Martin told him, repeating Amelia's unprompted words.

When Martin fell silent, Amanda spoke, pointing out the discrepancy in Edward's known behaviors. "The image he consistently paints of himself is a fabrication. He's not a kind and caring brother, not truly, and he's not an upstanding, righteously moral gentleman, either."

Slumped in an armchair, Luc stared at her; his face was pale, but his expression wasn't disbelieving. After a moment, he looked at Martin, then heaved a heavy sigh. "I still remember Sarah." He closed his eyes briefly, then opened them and fixed his gaze on Martin's face. "And yes, I can believe it of Edward."

It was the last thing Martin had expected to hear—his shock, his quick frown said as much. "How . . . ?" He came closer. "Are you sure?"

"Sure he did it? No. Sure he could have done it—yes." Luc glanced at Amanda and Reggie, then looked at Martin again. "I know him—the real Edward—a lot better than any of you. What Amanda said is right—the image Edward projects to the ton is quite different to the man he really is. And no, it isn't something that's happened recently."

Luc looked down, straightened his sleeve. "I used to wonder if it was just jealousy, a reaction to the fact that you and I were always . . . just more—better, stronger, whatever. Edward could never measure up, even if no one used that particular yardstick but him. But when he was seven, I caught him torturing the household cat. I rescued her, took her away—I didn't tell Papa, but I tried to explain to Edward that what he'd done was wrong. He didn't understand, not then, not later."

He glanced at Martin. "You probably never heard, but Edward was frequently in trouble at school—for bullying. Since he came on the town, I've had little real contact with him; he knows I don't approve, so takes care I don't hear. Nevertheless, his attitude for years has been that we—the wealthy, the titled, the chosen few—matter, while all those of lesser degree are merely here for our convenience." After a moment, he added, "The servants hate him. If it wasn't for Mama and the girls, they wouldn't bear with him.

"So could he have forced Sarah, killed Buxton, said nothing when you, who he always resented, were accused? Could he have shot Reggie thinking he was you? Yes." Luc looked at Martin. "If he let you take the blame for him once, I doubt he'd hesitate to make that permanent."

Martin held Luc's gaze, then stepped around and dropped onto the daybed. He shook his head, and slumped back, staring at the ceiling. After a time, he glanced at Luc. "We still need evidence."

"Short of wringing a confession from Edward—and you won't—I can't see where you'll get it. He's clever, calculating and there's not an ounce of warmth to what runs in his veins. Appealing to his sense of honor would be a waste of time—he doesn't recognize the concept."

The bitterness behind Luc's words, the set of his long lips, spoke eloquently of his feelings—he'd tried and knew he'd failed to reform his brother. Amanda watched him, wondering if he would accept the need to bring Edward to justice.

His next words answered that.

Luc glanced at Martin, his dark blue gaze sharpening. "We need to think of this as a challenge, coz—we rarely failed, not when we put our minds to something."

Martin looked at him, met his gaze, then his lips twisted wrily. "You're right—a challenge, then: how to prove Edward's guilt. There must be a way—there *is* a way. So what is it?"

Luc looked at Reggie. "How did he get up north?"

"It sounds like he went via Nottingham."

They tossed questions back and forth, defining how Edward must have acted, trying to see where evidence—something they could prove—might lie. Amanda and Reggie joined in; Jules brought in platters and decanters. They drank and ate, and racked their brains.

After an hour, Martin sat back. "This is getting us nowhere. Even if we prove he was up there, it's another thing to prove he pulled the trigger. And even if we did, there's nothing to connect that with Sarah and Buxton."

Luc grimaced, but his eyes were hard. "It's Sarah I'd like to see him pay for. That's where it all started." He sighed. "If only she'd said *something*—chattered to her nurse . . . ?"

Martin shook his head. "Mrs. Crockett was adamant, and she wouldn't have forgotten—"

"Wait!" Amanda grabbed Martin's arm. "That's *it!*"

"What? Sarah left no clue—"

"No. But only the four of us and Mrs. Crockett know that."

Luc's eyes narrowed. "We fabricate something—"

"Not exactly." Amanda waved for silence. "Listen. This is what—as far as anyone beyond this room knows—is going on." She drew breath, her mind whizzing from point to point as the details fell into place. "Martin has offered for my hand, and that means he has to resolve the old scandal. So for the first time, he's revisted the scene and asked questions of the people involved. The murderer knows Martin's been back home, so all that fits.

"One of the people he'd naturally have spoken with is Mrs. Crockett. While she didn't know anything, *after* we'd left, she rummaged through the trunk where Sarah's father had put Sarah's belongings. She hadn't previously looked because she'd assumed Martin was guilty."

Amanda glanced at Martin. "I know that's not the case, but it's better for my story if she thought all these years it was you. That explains why she didn't until now look in Sarah's diary. You were hauled away, essentially convicted of the crime—no proof was needed years ago. Now . . . after we left, Mrs. Crockett remembered the diary, but wasn't sure it still existed. But when she looked in the trunk, she found it, and in it, of course, Sarah doesn't name but describes enough to identify the man who forced her, the one who's babe she was carrying."

She glanced at her audience. "All men think young girls write everything in their diaries, don't they?"

Luc shrugged. "If one was dealing with innocents, it would be a concern."

Amanda nodded. "Just so. Mrs. Crockett sent word to Martin, asking what you wanted her to do with the diary. You wrote back to send it to London." She looked at Martin, Luc, Reggie. "The diary will be delivered here, on a certain day at a certain hour, because it'll come down with the coach, so *when* it arrives will be fixed. And we'll be here, waiting for it to be delivered, to open it and read what's written there—"

"And Edward will move heaven and earth to stop that happening." Luc sat forward, his expression intent. "It might work."

"And," Martin said, "the scheme will work even if it isn't Edward." When the other three looked at him, he went on, "Other than circumstantial evidence, we have no proof it *is* Edward. We'd be foolish to assume it's definitely him." He glanced at Amanda. "Which is why your plan is so sound— it'll work no matter which of the five on our list is the one. Whoever he is, he'll try to stop us reading the diary."

"But we haven't got a diary," Reggie said.

"Any book will do." Martin glanced at the shelves all around them.

"No, it won't," Amanda countered. "It should at least look the part. I've an old schoolroom diary with ribbons and roses on the front. It hasn't got my name on the cover—I'll write Sarah on it. That will look convincing."

Luc frowned. "If it was me, I'd try to get the diary back from Mrs. Crockett. I'd turn up at her cottage and say Martin sent me to fetch it."

"You won't have time," Martin told him. "We're going to settle this quickly." He glanced at them all. "The diary will arrive tomorrow evening—the coach from the north arrives at St. Pancras at five o'clock. To make it more realistic, and to make sure the diary arrives here and no attempt is made to waylay it en route, I'll send Jules up north to fetch it. In reality, we'll wrap the diary, give it to Jules, and one of my grooms will drive him to Barnet at dawn tomorrow. He'll be there to catch the coach when it stops on its way south later in the day."

"But what about Jules?" Amanda turned to Martin. "We know the murderer's dangerous. We don't want Jules harmed."

"You needn't worry about Jules—he can take care of himself." When Amanda didn't look convinced, Martin's grin turned wry. "Jules is an ex-Corsican bandit, an assassin, among other things. He was once sent to kill me."

Luc considered Martin. "He obviously wasn't much good at his job."

Martin raised his brows. "Actually, he was very good— I'm just better."

The cousins exchanged cousinly glances, then turned back to the business at hand.

"However, just to make sure, and lend further verisimilitude to our tale, I'll send two grooms to meet the coach at St. Pancras and escort Jules and the precious diary back here."

Luc nodded. "Yes. That will do it. Setting guards about the diary is a masterstroke—you wouldn't bother unless you were convinced the evidence it contains is crucial."

"As it would be in more ways than one. It would prove I was falsely accused, clear me of the old scandal, restore my standing within the family, pave the way for me to marry Amanda—connecting me with the Cynsters—and ensure I'm the darling of the ton for the foreseeable future." Martin glanced at Luc. "If it is Edward and he craves social standing and also resents me as you say, then the combination of all that good to come my way, all hingeing on the information in the diary, will make it utterly impossible for him not to react."

* * *

The next day dawned, and everything was in place. Amanda had unearthed her old diary, written "Sarah's" on the cover; wrapped in brown paper, it was now in Jules's possession. Together with one of Martin's grooms, he'd left for Barnet at dawn.

All of them had their alloted tasks. Reggie remained at Fulbridge House in charge of the command post. The others reported to him throughout the day, confirming their tasks completed, checking that all was on track.

After intense discussion, they'd agreed on how to get their story to all five gentlemen still on their list. They needed to be sure that all five received the message—the warning of impending exposure—before five o'clock that afternoon. It took the combined arguments of Amanda, Luc and Reggie to convince Martin that it was impossible to keep the matter private.

"However," Amanda had pointed out, "the best way to make sure the story is repeated enough to be believed, quickly, is to tell it to selected people 'in confidence.' "

Luc had studied Martin's stony countenance, then sighed. "You can't have it both ways—it's either going to be quick and public, or drawn out and potentially more dangerous if we try for secrecy."

Martin had finally capitulated and they'd settled on their approach. Even though it had been by then very late, Luc had left to do the rounds of the clubs to seed the story into the right circles. After that, he would stop by the ball his mother, sisters and brother were attending, but let Edward sense no more than that there was something in the wind. Something to do with Martin.

This morning, Luc would visit Limmers; later, he'd swan through the clubs, idly coming upon the other four on their list, checking they'd heard without asking. They would assuredly ask *him* for the latest news, which, of course, he'd give.

As for Edward, they'd agreed he should hear the news from a source he'd never suspect—his sisters, Emily and Anne. Amanda was delegated to tell them the tale; with

Amelia beside her, primed to lend assistance, she set out with Louise in the carriage that morning for their usual drive in the park.

Meeting the Ashfords, deciding to join the girls strolling on the lawns, was normal practice. As usual, Edward remained close but did not walk with them. Amelia and Amanda artfully turned the conversation to Amanda's upcoming wedding. Emily and Anne peppered her with questions, innocently enthusiastic about what would be their first haut ton wedding.

It was easy for Amanda to confide, breathless with relief, that the cloud over Martin's name would soon be lifted. When the girls, who'd heard whispers of the old scandal, eagerly looked for an explanation, she divulged all they needed to know, skating over the details of the old crimes but ensuring they had a firm grasp of what was to occur later that afternoon and, even more importantly, the expected outcome and all that would ensue.

Delighted, Emily and Anne declared it seemed just like a fairy tale. Exchanging glances, Amanda and Amelia encouraged them further, confident that both girls would sit in their carriage and happily chatter to their mother all the way home, with Edward sitting by listening in.

There was no safe way to confirm that Edward had heard all the necessary details. Martin, on horseback, screened by low-hanging branches, watched the unfolding scene, watched Emily and Anne part from Amanda and Amelia and return to their mother's open landau. Edward climbed in and sat beside his mother. The landau rumbled off along the Avenue.

It passed Martin, concealed beneath the tree; he heard Anne relate: "It—the diary—is to arrive at five today!" Shaking the reins, he ambled out, following the carriage, not close enough to be sighted amid the other traffic but close enough to keep the Ashfords in view.

The girls talked non-stop. His aunt smiled, nodded and questioned. Edward sat next to her, po-faced, utterly still. When the carriage reached Ashford House, Edward descended, handed his mother down, then his sisters. Lady Calverton swept up the steps; Emily followed. Anne stepped out in her sister's wake—Edward stopped her.

From the corner of the street, Martin watched as Edward interrogated Anne. In sisterly fashion, Anne heaved a sigh and recited answers. Eventually satisfied, Edward let her go; she climbed the steps and went in. Edward remained on the pavement, his expression unreadable, then he whirled and strode quickly inside.

Martin watched him go, then returned to Park Lane to make his report.

After that . . . throughout the day, he and Amanda had to play the part of ecstatic lovers, projecting the image of a couple for whom the last hurdle to wedded bliss was teetering, about to fall. As indeed it was, but they were so keyed up, so focused on what would occur later, that billing and cooing was an unexpected strain. In large part, he left it up to her. Plastering a smile on his face, he aimed it at anyone who came up, stayed planted by her side, and thought of other things.

Until she jabbed him in the ribs. Turned a sweet smile on him. Her eyes sparked. "Your face keeps changing. It starts pleasantly besotted, then gradually gets harder until you look positively grim! Lady Moffat just asked if you're feeling quite the thing."

"Well . . ." He stopped himself from frowning at her. "I'm distracted."

"So think of something else—*distract* yourself with something else. Something pleasant."

There was only one thing he could think of that might work.

It did. The discovery that, despite all, she was still so deliciously flusterable, focused his predatory senses, and after that, an interlude in Lady Carlisle's music room while all her ladyship's other guests were indulging in post-prandial discourse on the lawns, seemed the perfect opportunity to distract them both.

Her shivering sigh as he slid into her was the sweetest music he had ever heard, her soft, smothered, keening cry as he drove her to ecstasy and she shattered in his arms the ultimate benediction.

When they drifted back to earth, finally caught their breath, she lifted her head, studied his eyes, then her lips, swollen from his kisses, curved in a smug smile. She scored her nails lightly up his nape, an evocative caress that made him shiver. She touched her lips to his. "You're mine," she whispered.

"Always."

He kissed her back. Realized they were both still too tense, too wound tight with expectation. Realized her ladyship's guests had much yet to discuss.

Decided to give them something more.

They gathered at five in Martin's library. Reggie and Jules's nephew, Joseph, currently acting in Jules's stead, had rearranged the furniture, swapping the daybed with a chaise from further down the long room.

"It was too distracting," Reggie declared when Amanda stood staring at the replacement chaise.

She had to admit that was true. Noting the daybed, still intact but at the other end of the room, she nodded. "It does make this area more formal."

"Precisely."

Luc joined them, nodding briskly. "The other four all know, but I saw no sign that any of them might interfere. Quite the opposite—they seemed delighted you were so close to clearing your name."

Martin's lips twisted. "Edward knows at least the vital details."

Luc met his gaze. "So the trap is set."

They settled to wait.

The library shared a wall with the front hall; when the front doorbell pealed, they all tensed. Listened to Joseph's footsteps cross the hall. Listened as he spoke to the caller.

It quickly became apparent that whoever the caller was, it wasn't anyone they'd expected; they listened as Joseph strove to get rid of the gentleman. But the voices behind the wall only rose higher; Amanda frowned. The tone seemed familiar . . .

Then she heard her name. Realized who it was.

"Good God!" Reggie glanced at her. "Isn't that—?"

She snapped her mouth shut, surged to her feet. "I'll deal with this."

By the time she reached the front hall, her temper was on a seriously strained leash. Joseph heard her coming, glanced around, then stepped back and left the field to her. Left her facing the gentleman who had forced his way into the front hall.

"Mr. Lytton-Smythe!" Eyes narrow, she drew herself up. "I believe you were asking for me?"

Any wise man hearing her tones would have turned tail and run. Percival tugged down his waistcoat and frowned at her. "Indeed." He locked a hand about her wrist. "You will please me by leaving this house this instant!"

"*What?*" Amanda recoiled. Percival was gentleman enough not to drag on her arm, but neither did he release her; he stepped further into the hall as she stepped back.

Amanda halted and glared at him. "Mr. Lytton-Symthe, you appear to have taken leave of your senses! What has got into you?"

"Nothing at all—I have merely reached the limit of my patience. I have been—I am sure anyone would agree—*extremely* forbearing. I have watched you play games with others"—he wagged a finger at her—"and not sought to curtail such lighthearted pastimes. A last fling before taking on the sober mantle of marriage was reasonable enough, and while I can excuse your motives in assisting the rehabilitation of a relative of close friends, I of course did my duty to ensure that no interaction of a scandalous nature could ensue."

Amanda had been following his diatribe, absolutely astounded, but she fastened on that confession like a terrier. "Are you saying that *you* were the one who sent those girls out to Lady Arbuthnot's courtyard? And the other times—on the terrace at the Fortescues', and the Hamiltons' library? You thought to *avoid* scandal?"

Nose in the air, he nodded. She stared at him. "Why?"

"That ought to be obvious. I could not marry a lady whose reputation had been besmirched, however innocently. Now, given our agreement, I insist that you leave this house immediately. I'd heard you'd gone north, I assumed to visit relatives and so went to visit my aunt, only to learn on my return that you've been spending your time even more openly in Dexter's pocket. I will not stand for it. Now—"

"To which agreement are you referring, sir?"

Her tone finally penetrated; Percival stiffened. "To your agreement to marry me, of course."

"Mr. Lytton-Symthe, I can with a clear conscience swear that I have *never,* not *ever,* given you the *slightest* encouragement to believe I would welcome your suit."

Percival frowned at her as if she were splitting hairs. "Well, of course you haven't! Not the sort of thing a well-bred young lady would speak of—quite rightly, too. But I've made my position plain, and as there's no impediment to our marriage, there's no reason for you to say anything."

Her eyes narrowed to slits. "Oh, yes, there is. If I intend to marry a man, I will tell him—you may be absolutely sure of that. I will tell him out loud, in plain words and without the slightest blush! I will make up my *own* mind who I will marry, and I will definitely voice my decision. If you'd done me the courtesy of asking, I would have told you that in your case, my answer was and will always remain: No."

Percival continued to frown. "No? What do you mean: No?"

Amanda drew a long-suffering breath. "No, I will not marry you. No, I will not leave this house with you. No, I have not been playing games. How many more nos would you like?"

Percival's frown turned black. "You have had your head turned. Dexter is a regrettable influence. I insist you leave with me at once."

"Aaaah!" Amanda muted her scream through her teeth.

"It is clearly my duty to save you from yourself." Percival started to tow her to the door. Despite his soft head, he was stronger than she; she jerked back, looking for a weapon—

her eye fell on a pewter jug standing on the table in the center of the hall.

With her free hand, she grabbed it, hefted it—realized it held liquid. Gave Percival, eyes fixed on the door, one last chance. "Let me go."

"No."

She flung the water at him—right at his head. It splashed, then cascaded down.

Percival stopped, shook his head, but his grip on her wrist only tightened. He turned to her.

She set her chin stubbornly. "Let me go."

"No."

Her temper erupted. She hit him on the side of the head with the jug—it gave a hugely satisfying clang. He staggered; his grip eased and she twisted her wrist free.

"You foolish woman! You have to come with me—" Percival lunged for her.

She hit him again. "No!" She waited until his eyes focused. "Get this through your thick skull: I do not want to marry you. I never did. I am not going to marry you. I've chosen a far better man. Now, *go!*" She pointed to the door.

He stepped toward her.

She clobbered him again. *"Out!"*

He reeled in that direction; she helped him along with a thud on his shoulder.

"Go *away!*" She kept swinging the jug and he was forced to retreat. Joseph, eyes shining with admiration, held the door wide. Percival tried to make a stand on the threshold. Amanda thumped him again, then shoved him out. He stumbled down the steps.

She stood in the doorway and glared. "I would never marry a dolt who even *imagined* I didn't know my own mind!"

Slamming the door, she turned, nodded regally to Joseph and handed him the jug. "Mop up the water before someone slips." She stalked toward the corridor to the library, and realized Martin had been standing in the shadows.

She narrowed her eyes at him. "Why didn't you help?"

He opened his eyes wide as he moved to let her pass. "I would have if you'd needed it, but you seemed to be managing perfectly well on your own."

Inwardly astounded, she merely humphed and swept on. The man had actually learned that lesson? Gracious Heaven! Would wonders never cease.

She walked into the library to find Reggie and Luc doubled over with laughter. Her lips twitched, but she maintained her dignity.

Luc lifted his head and looked at her with more approval than he usually showed. "What the devil did you hit him with?"

"The jug on the hall table."

That set them both off again. Resuming her position on the chaise, she glanced at the clock. Twenty minutes past the hour; the diary would have reached London and be on its way to them in Jules' care.

Luc considered her, then asked Martin what had happened in Lady Arbuthnot's courtyard. Martin suggested he mind his own business.

The diary would arrive before six. Sometime between then and now—

Voices reached them, muffled, but from inside the house. Mystified, they exchanged glances, then heard a barked order, and footsteps, bootsteps—more than one set—striding down the corridor—

Joseph was first through the door. "My lord—" He gestured helplessly and held open the door.

Martin and Luc were on their feet.

Lady Osbaldestone swept in.

"Aha!" Her black gaze swept them. "As I thought. Well enough, but you haven't adequately covered your rear."

Martin stared, then lifted his gaze to the two gentlemen who entered in her wake—Devil and Vane Cynster.

Devil nodded, his gaze also taking in those present. "Much as it pains me to concur, I believe her ladyship's right." He met Martin's gaze. "You need disinterested witnesses unconnected with your family."

"We have Reggie," Amanda pointed out.

Devil glanced at Reggie. "Judging by that bandage about his head, he can hardly be disinterested in bringing the man who wounded him to justice."

Martin dismissed Joseph, then turned to the others. "What do you have in mind?" He glanced at the clock. "We have very little time, and if the villain is who we believe, he'll know this for a trap the instant he sets eyes on any of you."

"Which is why we came via the back door." Lady Osbaldestone had been examining the furnishings. "What a treasure trove you have here. However"—she looked down the room—"*that* is precisely what we need."

With her cane, she pointed to a carved wooden screen of four hinged panels. Then she waved the cane at Devil and Vane, who promptly stepped back out of range. "You two—fetch it and set it just there." The cane indicated a line angled away from the library windows. "The fool won't be coming via the courtyard, so he won't see us behind it. You may set that armchair behind the screen for me, and both of you may stand on either side."

They all leapt to do her bidding—there was no time left to argue.

Luc set the chair in place, Martin helped her into it. Devil and Vane wrestled the heavy screen into place, then took up their positions behind it.

"Perfect!" Lady Osbaldestone's disembodied voice rose from behind the screen. "We can see the whole area before the fireplace through these tiny holes. Wonderfully sensible, those oriental pashas."

Turning away, Martin and Luc exchanged glances. They returned to their positions and sat.

The front door bell pealed again.

Chapter 23

The sound jangled through the house, jangled over their nerves. They didn't look at each other but listened intently, straining to hear.

A man spoke, his voice reduced to a rumble by the walls. Joseph answered, then, faintly at first, growing more definite, they heard footsteps approaching down the long corridor. Joseph, and one other.

Like a troupe of actors with the curtain swishing up, they masked their tension, relaxing against the chaise, in the chair, assuming expressions of calm anticipation.

The door opened; Joseph appeared. Amanda held her breath.

"Mr. Edward Ashford, my lord."

Martin's expression showed nothing more than mild surprise as he rose from the chaise beside her. "Edward?" Martin extended a hand as Edward came forward, grasped Edward's without a glimmer of revulsion. "What can I do for you?"

Edward had noted them—Luc sprawled in the chair facing the hearth, Reggie on the chaise opposite Amanda. He looked at Martin. "Actually, I thought to be of some assistance here. Am I too late, then?"

It was Luc who answered, swivelling to look up at his brother. "Too late for what, Edward?"

Edward looked down at Luc; Amanda prayed Luc's dark eyes would conceal his true feelings.

Edward's expression remained supercilious. "I came to bear witness, of course." His glance swept them again. "I would have thought it obvious, in light of the gravity of the crimes in question, old though they may be, that there ought to be . . . disinterested spectators here when Martin receives this diary."

His tone carried his implication, the insinuation that the diary was a hoax, that Martin's innocence was a joke. Neither Martin nor Luc reacted; their faces remained impassive. Amanda bit her cheek against the urge to defend Martin; she forced herself to remain still.

It was Reggie who stiffened in outrage; she glanced at him as he shifted, disguising the reaction in a querulous movement.

Edward's gaze had gone to him; it lingered on his bandage. "You've met with an accident, Carmarthen."

Stiffly, Reggie inclined his head.

"Sit down." Resuming his position beside her, Martin waved Edward to the chaise next to Reggie—the only available seat, facing Martin, next to Luc.

"If you don't mind, I'll warm myself by the fire for a moment." Edward stepped past Reggie to stand before the hearth. "It's deuced chilly outside."

On the words, the doorbell rang. Voices sounded in the hall, then footsteps neared. A knock fell on the door. When Martin called, "Enter," Jules came in, carrying a brown-paper-wrapped package done up with string.

Martin rose; Jules presented the package to him. "The old lady wished you well."

Jules bowed, then withdrew.

Martin looked at the package, then tugged at the string. His face unreadable, he spread opened the paper, revealing the girlish diary with its fraying ribbons and faded roses. He let the paper fall, in so doing turning the book so the word "Sarah's" on the cover was visible to Edward.

Amanda glanced fleetingly at Edward; he was putting on a convincing performance of being merely—distantly—interested.

Facing the group before the hearth, Martin opened the diary, read the first page, then started turning pages, flicking to the later entries—

Edward stepped forward, wrenched the diary from Martin's grasp, and flung it facedown on the fire.

The flames flared. Amanda leapt up with a cry. Luc was on his feet, as was Reggie. Martin hadn't moved.

Amanda sank back, half kneeling on the chaise, her gaze on Edward's face. One thing to imagine, another to know. She glanced at the diary; the fire was greedily consuming the old, dry pages, turning them brown, then black.

"Edward?" Martin's voice was level, calm but cold. "Why did you do that?"

"It's obvious." Facing them, standing squarely across the hearth, Edward lifted his chin haughtily; Amanda all but gaped at his dismissive, contemptuous stance. "You two— you never think of anyone but yourselves. Have you considered what pain you'll cause others by raking up this old matter—a crime that's been judged, paid for, the case long closed? The families—the Fulbridges, Ashfords and all our connections—finished with the scandal years ago. There's no purpose in pursuing the matter now. What can you hope to gain?"

His lip curled. "You"—with his chin he indicated Martin— "were judged and found wanting ten years ago. Regardless of whether you'd committed the crime, they all believed you had, so you paid, then, for your wildness. It was your own doing." Edward shrugged. "You were deemed the right one to carry the burden of guilt." His gaze raked their surrounds, the sumptuous, expensive decor. "You've managed. No reason you can't continue to bear the load. It'll be the best thing for the family." Edward glanced at Amanda. "Even if it means you won't be able to have everything you want."

Amanda knew just how a rabbit felt when facing a snake. She'd known Edward all her life; she could barely credit the coldness in his eyes.

"So," Martin said. Edward looked back at him and Amanda breathed again. "You burned the diary because you believe *I* should continue to bear the odium for a crime I didn't commit to spare the family further scandal."

Edward's expression hardened. He nodded. "It's for the best."

"Whose best, brother dear?" Luc ranged alongside Martin, blocking access to the door. "Are you sure you don't want the old scandal left alone because any thorough investigation will implicate you?"

Edward sneered. "Of course not. Everyone knows—"

"That when riding you invariably carry a crop." Luc nodded. "Indeed. Just as we now know it was you who murdered Buxton—you who found him up on Froggatt Edge, who struggled with him and drove him to the lip, wielding your *crop*."

For a moment, Edward's face blanked.

Luc's lips curved but his blue eyes were cold as the grave. "That's right, brother dear. The crop. Martin never had one, never needed one. You couldn't manage a horse without one. And that, all the family knows."

Edward jerked as if Luc had struck him. His lips twisted oddly, then he refocused. "Nonsense! Anyone could have picked up a crop." He glanced back at the diary, nearly reduced to ashes.

"Sarah never kept a diary, Edward."

"Heh?" Edward jerked upright, blinked at Martin, then glanced back at the burnt book.

Amanda seized the moment to edge around the chaise.

Edward saw her, but looked at Martin. "What are you saying?"

"That there never was any real diary. We let it be known there was one, and that it identified the man who raped Sarah, the same man who killed Buxton to ensure he was never brought to answer for it—"

"To ensure his reputation, which even then was all he had, wasn't harmed," Luc put in.

Martin waited, then said, "It was you, Edward, wasn't it? You who hurt Sarah . . ." For the first time, emotion glimmered in Martin's voice; rage glowed in his eyes. He stepped forward. Edward backed away—his boot hit the hearth.

"Can you even begin to imagine how she died?" Martin's voice steadily gained strength. "Or the pain Buxton must have suffered—before you finished him off." He stepped closer. "Let alone the anguish you caused my mother, and my father, before they, too, died?" His tone lashed as he asked, "How many lives were ruined, Edward—all by you?"

Edward gasped, looked down. Amanda saw his chest swell.

Then he vaulted the chaise, landing beside her—he shoved the chaise into Martin and Luc. She screamed and turned to flee.

Edward grabbed a hank of her hair, cruelly yanked her back, twisted his hand until she whimpered in pain. He hauled her up to her toes against him.

Click! From the corner of her eye, she glimpsed a sliver flash, then felt cold steel against her throat.

"Stand back!" Edward yelled as Martin and Luc surged to their feet. They teetered on the brink of lunging across the chaise, but stopped. Their faces, and that of Reggie behind them, registered their shock.

"That's right."

She felt Edward nod.

"Stay where you are. You don't want your latest love to die, too, do you?"

Crash!

The sound was so startling it made them all jump—the boom echoed around the room.

"You dreadful boy! Your mother wouldn't believe her eyes could she see you now. How dare you, sirrah!" Lady Osbaldestone surged forward, the tap-tap of her cane loud on the boards. The screen behind which she'd been sitting lay rocking to one side; Devil and Vane were close on her heels.

Edward gaped, frozen, as she stormed toward him.

"You're a *worm*, same as your sire! Should have culled you at birth. You're a blot on your household escutcheon." She halted a yard away. "Take *that!*"

Before anyone could blink, her cane sliced through the air and came down with a *thwack* on Edward's wrist.

"*Yahhhh!*" He dropped the knife.

Martin and Luc launched themselves over the chaise.

Lady Osbaldestone got in one good lick with her cane as she closed a claw about Amanda's arm and yanked her free, dragging her to safety—helped on by a shove from Martin—as he and Luc wrestled Edward to the floor.

Reggie watched from the chaise, egging them on.

"Hah!" Sighting one of Edward's hands groping on the floor, Lady Osbaldestone stamped on it. "Sniveling coward!"

Devil forcibly drew them aside.

The door burst open. Jules, a scimitar gleaming in his hand, his expression ferocious, rushed in, followed by Joseph. Vane quickly crossed the room to reassure them.

It was over quickly; neither Martin nor Luc were in any mood to pull their punches. Battered and bloody, Edward lay snivelling on the floor as his brother and his cousin slowly rose to their feet.

Martin turned to Amanda; Lady Osbaldestone released her with a surreptitious push. Not that any push was necessary to send her into Martin's arms. He hugged her hard, then tipped her face up and examined her throat. "The bastard nicked you."

Fury vibrated in his voice. "I can't feel a thing," she lied. The cut was stinging, but stinging was a lot better than what might have been.

The reality suddenly hit her; she sagged against Martin, glad of his strength, his solidity. He looked across the room, nodding an affirmation to Jules that all was well. He and Joseph departed. Vane closed the door.

On the instant, a furious knocking, followed by the bell pealing incessantly, heralded what sounded like an invasion. Everyone in the library froze, listening, hoping Jules and Joseph could hold the line . . .

That hope proved futile.

Feminine tones, decidedly autocratic, penetrated the room. Amanda knew them well. She glanced at Devil, saw his jaw harden. He looked, pointedly, at Lady Osbaldestone. Who narrowed her eyes back.

"Wasn't me," her ladyship declared. "Must be one of you two"—she waved her cane at Devil and Vane—"who can't keep his secrets."

"We haven't even seen them since you grabbed us," Vane growled.

The door opened; Honoria, Patience and Amelia swept in. Honoria's gaze swept the room. "Now *this* is more like it! Amanda, you are going to have an enormous job decorating all this before the wedding."

Descending on her, Honoria hugged her without removing her from Martin's embrace. "Patience—here. She's been cut and it's bleeding."

Honoria turned to Lady Osbaldestone, who, Martin now noticed, had paled; the old harridan allowed herself to be guided to a chair. Patience took over with Amanda, taking her to sit on a chair near the window so she could tend her wound. "We don't want any unslightly scars."

Martin let Amanda go, and watched, amazed. They were only three women, yet . . . within seconds, they'd seized the whiphand.

Amelia had settled Reggie, also rather pale, back on the chaise. She inquired after the bellpull, then crossed to tug it; when Jules appeared she ordered warm water in a basin and cloth to tend her sister's cut. After glancing at Luc, she also ordered an ice pack.

Martin looked at his cousin. A large bruise was spreading over Luc's chiseled jaw. It was from a blow Edward had aimed at Martin; Luc had intercepted it.

After one pointed look at her spouse, Honoria had dispatched him to get a glass of something for Lady Osbaldestone. Vane had been similarly dealt with, and ordered to supply drinks to all others in need. From what Martin overheard, Honoria, Patience and Amelia had worked out their plan for themselves; they'd kept watch from a carriage in the lane beyond the courtyard wall. They'd heard Amanda's scream and come running.

Having had all his hostly duties usurped, Martin crossed to Luc, still standing over Edward, prone and moaning on the floor.

"Leave him." Martin looked down at Edward. "If he moves, Lady Osbaldestone will just hammer him again."

Luc laughed shakily. "I still can't believe she did that."

"She's a terror with that cane." Vane handed them glasses, then nodded toward the fireplace. "Let's go over there— there are things we need to discuss."

Devil brought a glass of wine for Reggie. "No spirits for you, so I was instructed." Reggie humphed but accepted the wine.

Jules returned with a basin and cloths; Amelia hurried to take them, then went to help tend her sister. The men gathered before the hearth, Reggie beside them on the chaise, and got down to business: how to deal adequately with Edward, and how to minimize the social damage his perfidy would inevitably cause. The first was easy enough, the second anything but.

Then the ladies joined them, disposing themselves on the chaises. Honoria looked at her husband. "What have you decided?"

Devil glanced at Martin, then stated, "Neither the law nor society will accept anything less than banishment for life." He looked at Edward who'd dragged himself up to slump against a bureau. "He can choose where, but we'll need to see him off English soil, and that as soon as maybe. Too many people knew the revelation was to occur this afternoon. A result will be expected."

Honoria looked at Luc. "You agree?"

"Yes." Luc glanced at Edward. "I'll see him on the packet myself."

"Very well." Honoria's gaze rested on them all. "Now, what about the rest?"

"That," Devil admitted, "was as far as we'd got. We need to do something to protect the Ashfords, but what . . . ?"

Honoria humphed. "Indeed."

"Quite ridiculous," Lady Osbaldestone opined. "This business of the sins of the brothers being visited on their sisters and all others in sight, no matter how undeserved. In this case, it's quite clear the felon"—she bent a vengeful glance on Edward—"was in no way insane or unstable. He was simply rotten to the core, and that's all there is to it. An unfortunate throwback to the less admirable side of the paternal line, but you"—she pointed at Luc—"will clearly relieve future Ashfords of the taint."

Luc blinked, looked nonplussed.

Lady Osbaldestone ignored him. She looked at Honoria. "Well, my dear? You're a duchess, Amanda here is an almost-countess, and I'm not entirely without influence myself. I suggest we get busy." She glanced at the clock, sent a sly glance Martin's way. "Unfortunate timing, but I daresay you and I alone can reach enough ears to ensure that the important dinner tables hear of the wonderful relief."

The men exchanged glances; it was Devil who asked, "Relief?"

"Good gracious, man! Of course *relief!* Just think how unhappy the situation would have been if the Ashford girls had received offers before this dreadful business had been resolved! A positive *morass* of potential uncertainty has been avoided! Now those girls can come out and gentlemen can marry them with confidence that there's no rotten apple left in the family's basket, that all has been settled and everything's as it should be." Her ladyship surged to her feet. "You just have to think of these things from the right angle."

Leaning on her cane, she looked at Patience. "You know Minerva Ashford well enough, I believe?"

Patience nodded. "I'll go there immediately and explain it all."

"She's a level-headed woman for all her once-wild ways. She'll see quick enough how we mean to go about it and know just how to have her girls behave." Lady Osbaldestone nodded. "Right, then! We'd best set to."

She stumped toward the door. Everyone else sprang into action.

Martin rang for Jules; Jules summoned Joseph who with Devil helped Lady Osbaldestone out to her carriage, left waiting in the mews.

A quick discussion decided that Luc and Jules would escort Edward to Dover and put him on the packet. Vane, parting from Patience, who left with Honoria to spread the social word, returned as Edward started a moaning, carping monologue; Vane leaned down and said something—Edward shut up.

Straightening, Vane regarded Edward through narrowed eyes. "I'll come with you. You might just need an extra—totally disinterested—hand."

With that settled, Jules and Luc hauled Edward, growing more vocal by the minute, to his feet. One look from Vane and he shut up again.

Joseph arrived somewhat belatedly with an icepack. Amelia grabbed it and raced after Luc.

"Here." She caught him at the door and hauled him back. Vane took his place and bundled Edward on. Amelia framed Luc's face with one hand; with the other, she molded the icepack to his injured jaw. He winced, but she held him still. "There! Now hold it in place until the ice melts. The others can manage Edward until then."

Luc took the icepack, held it in place. His eyes touched hers.

Amelia smiled, turned him to the door and pushed. He went, pausing in the corridor to glance back at her, nod his thanks, before following the others away.

Amelia sighed, then returned to the chaise as Amanda reappeared after seeing Honoria and Patience out. Amelia glanced at her, then slipped her arm under Reggie's and helped him to his feet. "Come on. I'll have them find a hackney and you can tell me all about your head on the way home."

"Like how much it hurts?" Reggie managed a weak smile for Amanda and Martin, then let Amelia lead him away.

"You haven't even told me how you got hurt. I haven't heard all the details."

Their voices faded as they headed down the corridor. Joseph looked in and raised a brow. Martin waved him away; Joseph closed the door after him.

Martin looked at Amanda, then opened his arms. She walked into them; he closed them about her and buried his face in her hair.

* * *

Later, when night had claimed the courtyard beyond the library windows, they lay on the daybed, skin to naked skin, the fire roaring in the hearth, the platters of delicacies Joseph had brought hours before on a low table before them.

Replete, at peace, sated to their bones, they simply lay and savoured the sweet taste of happiness.

Dreamed of the future.

Martin glanced down at Amanda. She was lying on her side, facing the fire, her back to his chest, her bottom fitted snugly to his loins. He'd draped a translucent silk shawl over her naked limbs, not to conceal them but to shield her from drafts. She shifted, reaching for a canape; the silk shimmered over milk-white skin, fine-textured, sheening like satin. He'd spent the last hours gorging his rapacious senses, filling his mind with the wondrous sensation of touching her—all of her, every last inch.

Filling his soul with the bone-deep knowledge that she was his, now and forever. Filling his heart with the wonder of it all.

Bending his head, he pressed a kiss to the sensitive spot behind her ear. "Never, ever, did I believe I would have all this."

Not even prior to that day ten years ago. *This,* this wondrous emotion that had somehow taken over his life, had never been a part of his dreams, his expectations. Now he couldn't imagine life without it.

Her lips curved, her smile serene, mysterious, elementally feminine, but she only leaned back against him, letting her body sink against his—a wordless acceptance of what was.

He knew it, but yet . . . it was now he who needed more.

He nuzzled her ear. "You haven't given me your answer."

She glanced at him, met his gaze. Smiled. Lifted a hand and lovingly traced his cheek. "Do you really need to hear it in words?"

"Just once."

"Then yes—I'll be yours. I'll marry you and be your countess, and bear your children and redecorate your house. Although apparently Honoria thinks the order should be reversed."

She turned onto her back, wound her arms about his neck and drew him down for a kiss—a kiss that lengthened, deepened, opened the door to desire again, but Martin held it back, kept the fires at bay.

Eventually he lifted his head. There was one more question unresolved between them.

He looked down into her eyes, as blue as cornflowers under the sun. "You asked me before why I wanted to marry you. I gave you an answer, a truthful answer, but it wasn't the whole truth."

She stilled; he closed his hand around hers, and could have sworn he felt her heart quiver.

"I want to marry you because . . ."—his eyes on hers, he raised her hand to his lips, pressed a kiss to her fingers—"it's my duty to marry some lady like you, because I feel honor-bound to marry only you, because our marriage is dictated by society, and not least because of the child you may very well be carrying."

He held her silent with his eyes, pressed another lingering kiss to the fingers he held trapped. "But most of all, I want to marry you for a very simple reason—because I cannot imagine living without you."

He looked down at their hands, shifted his grip, twining their fingers. "And if that's what the poets call love, then yes, I love you. Not in myriad ways, but in one all-consuming overwhelming way. In a way that has come to define who and what I am—in a way that now forms the very core of me."

Lifting his eyes, he met her gaze. "That's why I want to marry you."

Amanda smiled mistily, freed her hand, traced his cheek. Then she drew his lips to hers and kissed him—gently, delicately, a caress as fragilely beautiful as the moment.

Then she let her lips firm, taunt—parted them when he reacted, urged him to plunder, to ravenously claim.

Gave herself up to the lion she'd snared.

And knew she'd never need more.

* * *

The marriage of Martin Gordon Fulbridge, fifth earl of Dexter, and Miss Amanda Maria Cynster, took place at a private ceremony in St. George's Church in Hanover Square four days later.

Despite the fact the ceremony was private, it was not small. All the Fulbridges, celebrating not only the resurrection of the head of their house but his nuptials as well, plus many of their connections, joined with all the Cynsters and their myriad connections, to provide a host of witnesses that overflowed the church.

Because the ceremony was "private," the Ashfords could attend without society deeming their presence in some obscure way ineligible. For her part, Amanda had insisted that Emily and Anne be present—knowing their enthusiastic anticipation had been squashed would have dimmed the happiness of her day—and Martin had had only one choice as his best man—Luc.

So the ceremony was decreed to be "private," and everyone was happy.

Giddily so—a sense of euphoria took hold in the instant Amanda walked down the aisle, beaming with exuberant joy. The light that shone in the groom's eyes was no less uplifting—the entire congregation was utterly convinced they were witnessing a marriage made in heaven.

Joy burgeoned and spread through the day, through the wedding breakfast and beyond, unmarred by any adverse occurrence. And then it was time for the bride and groom to commence the long journey to their home in the north.

As was customary, all the unmarried young ladies gathered before the coach, drawn up by the pavement in Upper Brook Street. Others filled the space around and behind them, crowding the house steps, pressing close for their last sight of the radiant bride.

A cheer rose inside, then rolled out of the front door as Amanda and Martin left the ballroom and progressed through the corridors, farewelling first family, then guests as they went, finally bursting through the front doors to a rousing hurrah, and a not inconsiderable number of helpful suggestions, mostly aimed at the groom.

Luc and Amelia, Amanda's principal bridesmaid, had escorted the happy couple to the door. They paused on the porch. Viewing the press of bodies on the steps, jostling in a seething mass now Martin and Amanda had reached the carriage, Luc touched Amelia's arm and nodded to the side of the porch, to where, beside a column, they could stand and see the departing couple clearly.

They took up their positions as Martin lifted Amanda to the top step of the coach. Clutching the frame, she laughed and turned, brandishing her bouquet. She looked up, then flung it—

Straight at Luc.

He swore and went to step back, but the column was behind him. Reflexively, he caught the bouquet. Shot a scowl at Amanda and saw her grin delightedly.

Turning the bouquet in his hands, he presented it to Amelia with a bow. "Your sister's aim is atrocious. I believe this is for you."

"Thank you." Amelia took it, looking down to hide her grin, to suppress the wicked impulse to inform him he was wrong on both counts. Then she glanced at the coach, saw Amanda blow a kiss, then wave as Martin urged her in.

Amelia smiled, saluted her twin with the bouquet—knew she understood. Knew she approved.

Amanda was married, and her own decision was made. It was her turn to snare her mate.

Luc inwardly frowned as the carriage door shut and the coachman flicked his whip. Just before he'd disappeared into the coach, Martin had looked directly at him, then smiled—an expression Luc couldn't interpret.

Then he felt Amelia's hand on his arm, instantly suppressed his habitual reaction.

"We'd better go in."

He nodded and turned to follow her, grateful when she removed her hand and led the way. She glanced over her shoulder and smiled lightly.

The sort of smile he'd seen a million times before.

He stepped into the house, and wondered why the hairs at his nape had lifted.